The Sins of Jesus

a novel

Richard A. Muller

Auravision Publishing
Berkeley, California

Acknowledgements

I thank Flossie Lewis for her gentle criticism and patient tutoring, Suzanne Lipsett for her detailed help, Fred Hill for his valiant work as my agent, Pandora Nash-Karner for her graphic design, Shawn Carlson for teaching me true secrets of magic, and many others whose insights and comments were invaluable, especially my family Rosemary, Elizabeth, and Melinda.

Auravision Publishing
Berkeley California

ISBN: 0-9672765-1-9

Part of this novel is available on the internet, at:

www.richardmuller.com

The author encourages free distribution of the internet file, provided that it is kept unchanged.

Cover Art: *Christ Goes to the Mountain to Pray*
James Jacques Joseph Tissot, 1895

The Sins of Jesus ...

A compelling novel of Jesus as a man—not as God—who learns the art of magic and illusion from the Magi, and uses it to establish his authority as a Prophet. This book will forever change your beliefs about what really did happen two thousand years ago.

"Two means of proof—miracles and the accomplishment of prophecies—could alone in the opinion of the contemporaries of Jesus establish a supernatural mission. . . .

"If ever the worship of Jesus loses its hold upon mankind, it will be precisely on account of those acts which originally inspired belief in him."

—Ernest Renan
The Life of Jesus (1863)

The Sins of Jesus

Prologue

I have sinned.

    I promised truth but practiced deception.

    I professed miracles but performed magic.

    I permitted my disciples to worship a false god.

    Have mercy on me, O Lord!

Thomas, I also beg your forgiveness, for I sinned against you too. You devoted three years of your life to my ministry. How could you have had such faith in me? Did you truly believe that God intended his kingdom to be delivered to Jews and gentiles by a sinner?

I was taken from the cross alive, but I am mortally wounded. Yet death will not be my greatest punishment—no, that will be the loss of my teachings. The Scriptures say, "Accursed by God is any man hung from wood." To the Jews I am now but another false Messiah. Whatever good my revelations may have done is now undone. Whatever suffering I might have eased will now endure.

I ask you to record these words, Thomas, and to deliver them to the other apostles, to my disciples, to those who have accepted my teachings and to those who have rejected them, to the Pharisees and Sadducees, to the am ha'arez and to the Herodians, to Jews and to gentiles alike, to all who will listen. Stay with me until I finish. Do not let me rest, Thomas, even as I grow weak.

I thank you, O Lord, for this your last blessing: that you allowed me to survive the crucifixion, so that I can confess and repent and do penance. I must undo the misunderstandings and misconceptions. I must expose the lies and deceptions. I must put my faith, finally, in the power of truth. This history, in which I shall relate the events of my life and ministry with honesty and candor, will be my last confession.

1. Nazareth

WE LIVED IN THE VILLAGE OF NAZARETH, AN INSIGNIFICANT hillside town in Galilee, nowhere mentioned in the Scriptures—you probably haven't heard of it even if you come from northern Israel yourself. Nazareth is located just four miles from the famous city of Augustus, formerly called Sepphoris, and I was born nine years before the great catastrophe that befell that city and its residents. Near the upper reaches of the Nazareth hill, below the woods but far above the single well, is the mud and brick house where I spent the first fourteen years of my life. Regardless of the mockery of our adversaries, I am proud of this humble origin.

We had but a single room, just large enough to sleep the family. Inside was dark and cool even during the hot and dry summer months; outside was whitewashed and cheerful. Around the corner to the rear was my father's carpentry shop, with a workbench, table, two stools, and shed. A ladder led to the roof, which was my mother's favorite work area and my favorite play spot.

My first revelation—and the beginning of my tragedy—began that day, one spring, when my father and I went down to the valley to search for fresh shallots.

No, we didn't go just for the shallots. We went to listen to the happy gurgle of the runoff from the recent rains, and to smell the fragrance of the yellow blossoms bursting from the jasmine vines. "These are the Lord's gifts to us," my father said, and he pushed aside the flowers and led me to the edge of the brook. "They're little gifts, but they're given with love. You show the Lord your gratitude by enjoying them." The cool water trickled between my toes and I thought I saw a tadpole. Yes, those were my happy days.

A willow blocked our route along the edge of the stream, and my father climbed the bank to get around. I threw a flat stone over the water and watched it skip two, three, four times! "Father!" I shouted out, but he was gone. I waded into the deeper water, hoping to see fish, while groping with my feet for balance on the larger stones. The water rose to chill my thighs. It was quieter here—until the silence was broken by the trill of a mockingbird. I searched for the bird and finally spotted it nodding its head on the top of a nearby cedar. What, I wondered, is it impersonating? My mother would know, but she wasn't here, so I listened as it repeated its song. A mountain sparrow!—That's what it was. The song had been transformed into a delightful lilting warble, lacking the delicacy of the original, and yet beautiful in its own way.

Shouting up ahead broke my reverie. My father appeared by my side, took my hand and led me back to the shallow water. We followed the yelling around a bend towards the main crossing. On a small knoll I could see a group of a half dozen boys, older than me but still not adults, throwing stones down at the stream. I followed the flight of one rock as it splashed next to an old man, whom I hadn't previously noticed. He was standing at the edge of the water and was trying to fill a goat-hide water skin. A puff of dust kicked up on the shore next to him as another rock landed. The boys were trying to hit the old man! I was suddenly afraid, and I clutched my father's leg.

Farther up stream was a small bridge, and three men stood on it. They wore blue cloaks with tassels, the clothing of Pharisees. They were watching the boys, but they just stood there. They did nothing to help the old man.

My father put his large hands under my arms, lifted me as if I weighed nothing, and gently placed me on the top of a moss-covered boulder. "Wait here," he said, and he ran through the shallows towards the old man and the boys.

One tall boy held a small sling. He whirled it above his head and lofted another rock. I watched it arc down towards the stream—but to my horror it struck my father on the head, and he stumbled and fell. In terror, I dug my fingers through the moss into the hardness of the boulder. I couldn't move. Bright red blood streamed down my father's face as he knelt in the water. He slowly staggered to his feet.

"Move away!" the tall boy jeered as he spun the sling again. "The rock was for the Samaritan, not you!"

My father moved closer to the old man. The boys held their stones. The tall one shouted, "Why do you stand with a sinner?"

My father's response was so soft as to be almost inaudible: "Let he who is without sin throw the next stone."

The boys stood still for a few moments, just staring at the two men. I was sick with anxiety. Why didn't those men on the bridge help?

Then the tall boy let the rock drop out of his sling. He turned to the others and said something that I couldn't hear. They laughed and walked away together, vanishing behind the knoll.

It was a miracle. My father had stopped them—with nothing but words, and with courage.

He talked for a few moments with the old man, rinsed the blood off his own forehead, and then worked his way back along the bank to me. He picked me off the boulder and hugged me. In one burst I let loose a stream of tears. Tears came to his eyes too, but then he laughed. "You needn't have worried, Jesus," he said. "The Lord was protecting me." He carried me to where the old man was standing, put me down, and talked with the stranger for a while. I picked up the man's goatskin and filled it with water. "Come with us to our home," my father told him. "We would be honored." I looked down the stream towards the bridge, and noticed that the Pharisees had disappeared.

As we approached our house, I saw Mother washing clothes on the roof. She saw us, smiled, and then, when she noticed the stranger with us, scowled. She raised her hands and eyes towards heaven, as if to ask the Lord, "Why does my husband make so much trouble?" But as we got close she gasped, perhaps from noticing the blood on my father's face and clothes. She rushed down the ladder, examined my father's forehead, went inside and brought out a bowl of rainwater. She sat him on a bench and gently washed his forehead. Then she wrapped it with linen. "Joseph, you are so foolish," she chided. "You never worry about yourself!"

The old man did stay for dinner. At my father's insistence, my mother added a piece of meat to the stew, to let the stranger know that he was an honored guest. I still remember his odd, darkly colored clothes, his strange accent, and the peculiar little cap he wore on the back of his head. Despite my mother's obvious discomfort, my father invited him to stay overnight. But he refused. "I know your neighbors consider Nazareth a clean village," he said. "You've been kind and generous. I don't want to cause you more trouble."

The next day my mother collected all the rainwater from our cisterns and borrowed more from our neighbor Esreth. Such water is prescribed by the Torah as the only kind suitable for ritual cleaning. She muttered quietly to herself as she scrubbed the floor of the house and all the walls she had seen the old man touch. Submerging our dishes and plates in a large bowl and letting them soak, as she repeated the rote prayer, "Blessed be you, the Lord our God, who has made us holy with his Law and has commanded us about the immersion of vessels." Only after the sun set did she deem that our house was once again clean. My father didn't interfere with this ritual, although he clearly wasn't pleased.

As usual, Mother cooked dinner in front of our house that evening, and we ate on the roof. As it grew dark, we watched the stars appear. A cool breeze came from the north, carrying with it the fragrance of the green hills. "That's the breath of the Lord," my father said. As he looked up, he didn't seem to notice that I was staring at him, the hero. His lean face was softened by a gentle smile. Suspended behind his ear, as a symbol of his trade, was a chip of oak, the best and most durable wood. I had tried to put a chip behind my ear, but it wouldn't stay—because I wasn't yet a good enough carpenter, I assumed. He had removed the linen bandage, and a scab sat like a badge of honor on the large bluish bump that had grown on his forehead.

I was still consumed with the events by the stream. Why had the boys attacked the old man? Why had the Pharisees stood passively by? Why had my mother scrubbed the house afterwards? Suddenly I spoke aloud: "Why did they call him a Samaritan?" I asked. "He wasn't ugly or dirty."

My father smiled as he briefly continued to examine the stars, but then his face turned serious, and he looked right towards me. "I know," he said, "that your friends use the word *Samaritan* as an insult. But really all it means is that the man comes from the west bank of the Jordan, the region called Samaria. Many Jews hate the people of the west bank. And many of the west bank people hate Jews. Guess what Samaritan children call someone they want to insult?" I shook my head. "A Jew!"

I was astounded—and momentarily speechless—as I pondered the incredible idea that anyone could consider the word *Jew* to be an insult.

"Why do we hate them? I mean, why do our neighbors hate them?" I asked.

"Probably because they are so similar to us, but different. They worship the same God as we do, but they interpret the Scriptures differently. A hundred years ago—not very long ago—they were considered Jews. But then the disagreements started, and they grew like an avalanche. First, the Samaritans began to marry gentiles. The gentiles converted—but our pious Hasidim called the families mongrels and half-breeds. Next the Hasidim excluded them from the Temple in Jerusalem. So the Samaritans built their own temple, on Mount Gerizim, which outraged the Hasidim even more. Our king, John Hyrcanus, interpreted the Scriptures to prove that all Palestine belonged to him. So he attacked the Samaritan's temple and destroyed it, and built a special canal to flood their city and wipe clean all signs of their existence. A ritual washing—that's what he called it."

"I can see why they hate us."

"Yes, Jesus, as most Jews hate them in return. Those boys yesterday were only doing what they had seen their parents do. The Scriptures say that punishment is passed on from sinners to their children, on to the third and fourth generation, but I believe it's not the Lord who does this, but parents, when they pass on their hatred, like a disease. Love is contagious too," he said, "and it too can be passed on from parent to child." He drew me to him, and embraced me. "Do you know what is the greatest blessing that comes directly from the Lord?" he asked with a smile.

Of course I knew the answer, because he had asked this so many times before. "Children," I replied.

"Yes, children. Now, go to bed."

❖ ❖ ❖

My mother spoke in Hebrew, the language she used when she didn't want me to understand: "You are paid by the piece, Joseph, not by the hour." But she didn't realize that after two years of lessons with Rabbi Shuwal, I could now understand virtually everything she said. Needless to say, every time my parents switched from Aramaic, the common language of Israel, to Hebrew, I paid much closer attention.

I peeked out from the corner of the house. My mother stood with her arms folded across her chest, watching my father work in the carpentry area. I couldn't see what he was doing, but I could hear the tap of his chisel. He had been repairing an oxen yoke, and I guessed that he was carving the little decoration he called his signature.

"I earn a denarius a day, Mary, and that's good pay for a carpenter," he said, in controlled tones.

"Even a farmer earns that much," she said sarcastically. "Carpentry is cleaner, so you should earn more. And you would if you didn't waste your time on those little carvings."

"Those little carvings show I am proud of my work," he said. "Besides, I wouldn't get more work if I finished sooner. Nazareth is a small town."

"Nazareth is the stinkhole of Galilee," she snapped. She had good reason behind her complaint. In Nazareth the tanners' shops were right in town, not on the outskirts as in other villages. A west wind could fill our house with their fumes.

"So maybe you would like us to move to Sepphoris," my father retorted.

"Keep us from the abyss!" She glowered at him, turned around, and walked away. I ducked behind a low wall and watched her pass, fuming with anger.

Sepphoris, the *abyss*, was one of the most important cities in Galilee. It was only four miles away by dirt trail over the hills, but it was close to the Via Maris, a major route that led to the coast and Egypt. So unlike Nazareth, Sepphoris was visited by traders, pilgrims, caravans, gentiles, and Jews of every profession from miles around. It was diverse, colorful, noisy, exciting, and pagan—all the elements that added up to sin. In my mother's opinion, no righteous Jew would want to live in Sepphoris.

There was only one water spring in all of Nazareth, and the shortage of water (my father said) would always keep our village small and unimportant. Most of our water came from rain collected from the rooftops by cisterns. But when the weather was dry, my mother sent me to the spring. After one of these trips, I came back with many questions.

I found my father working beside the house, building a cradle for a wealthy family in Sepphoris. It was an important commission, and it meant that we might be able to afford lamb for the coming Passover. My father was humming as he carved an intricate pattern of flowers, gourds, and palm trees on the tiny headpiece made of expensive acacia.

"Father," I asked, "who is Judah of Gamala?"

"Ah—you were at the spring today." He put aside the cradle and turned to me, as if I had raised an important issue.

"Everybody was talking about him. They say he may be the Messiah."

"No, Jesus. The Messiah will not be a man of violence. Judah is a Zealot."

"They say the Romans killed his family."

"That is true, Jesus. He preached that the Lord, not the Emperor, is our only true ruler, and to the Romans, that is treason. And they reacted predictably, with cruelty and violence. They slaughtered his wife, his children, and even his cousins. But Judah escaped, and now has become as dangerous as a wounded hyena. He is crafty, but he can't elude the Romans for long."

"But isn't he right, that the Lord is our only true ruler?"

"He's partially right. The Lord will always be the king of our spirits. But Augustus Caesar rules our land and our bodies. He can do with these whatever he wishes, as he has demonstrated many times."

"Rabbi Shuwal says the Romans bleed us with their taxes and they insult the Lord with their paganism," I said

"Their taxes are a burden," my father responded. "But at least we live in peace. No, the Romans don't insult the Lord—he is too great to be insulted. They insult only the Jews, and they do this to anger us. But insults don't hurt if they are ignored. The Romans do let us worship as we please. There was far more violence when we ruled ourselves, under the Maccabees."

"What if Judah wins?"

"He isn't going to win, Jesus. The Romans will capture him, and crucify him, to prove to us that he was a fraud. *He who is hung from wood is accursed in the eyes of God.* No, he cannot win through violence. The few Roman soldiers we see in Galilee may look vulnerable, but Caesar can send as many legions as necessary, enough to obliterate any rebellion. That's how he controls the world."

"I hate Caesar!"

My father's reaction was subtle, but I thought I detected a sigh. He said, quietly, "Don't hate Caesar, Jesus. To hate is to be poisoned by spiritual illness. Don't hate, not even the Romans. Not even Caesar. He is already the most hated man in the world. And hatred is the most contagious disease."

"No, father," I said with a smile. He gave me a quizzical look. "Love is even more contagious," I said. "You taught me that."

He chuckled, and turned back to his work.

But I kept thinking. I had a new image of Caesar—*the most hated man in the world.* Our neighbors hated the Samaritans. The Samaritans hated us—a thought that still made me uncomfortable. And thousands, *millions,* of people hated Caesar. What was it like to be so hated? I felt a strange compassion for the most hated man in the world.

"Maybe we should love Caesar," I said.

My father suddenly turned and looked at me. "What did you say?" he asked.

"I just thought that maybe it isn't enough to get rid of our hatred. Maybe we have to learn to love the Romans, to love Caesar. To love our enemies."

His brows folded, as he seemed to ponder my thought. "That is an extraordinary thing you just said, Jesus." But then he turned back towards his carving. He tapped the chisel gently. "No," he said. "Let the Romans love each other. There are plenty of citizens who glorify Caesar. It is enough to rid ourselves of hatred. We can show kindness to our enemies. But it does not make sense,"—he paused for a few seconds, as if reconsidering, but then he when back to chipping—"to *love* them."

I sat there quietly with him, not so much thinking, as feeling. I watched my father work. How much I loved him! How much I had learned from him! But this was perhaps the first time in my life that I considered the possibility that maybe, just maybe, he was wrong.

Several minutes passed. Tap, tap went his chisel. Suddenly I asked, "Father, when will the *real* Messiah come?"

"Maybe not for many generations," he said, as he worked. "Although it's possible that the Messiah is alive today."

"Then why doesn't he say so? What is he waiting for? Why doesn't he announce himself?"

"If he did, the Romans would kill him." He held up the cradle and looked at it with pride. He turned it so I could see his little carving—his signature. It was a delicate image of a dove in flight. "Of course," he added, "it's also possible that he's silent because he doesn't yet know that he is the Messiah."

2. Sepphoris

I ALWAYS FELT A THRILL OF ANTICIPATION WHEN APPROACHING the walls of Sepphoris on market day. We entered through the South Gate, and were immediately hit by the din. In front of us the narrow, meandering streets were filled with pilgrims, merchants, beggars, soldiers, mules, and camels. Next to the shops the traders shouted at each other, over each other, and through the braying of the donkeys, arguing and haggling and trying to gain the attention of potential patrons. The smell of freshly baked bread vied with that of aging meat, day-old fish from the Sea of Galilee, and the strong odor of dung, to inundate and saturate my sense of smell. What a strange, alien, yet exhilarating world!

My mother had sent me to buy sea salt and seeds for her garden. My cousin John came along, and my best friend Lazarus, as well as my little brother Thomas. My other brother James was still a baby. My mother had given us a few lepta to pay for the goods, and to buy sweets if there was any change. John's favorite treats were fried locusts dipped in honey.

Along the edges of the street, the houses pushed up against each other like trees clustered near a stream. The noontime sun beat down on the cobblestones, and we sought relief in the shade of many-colored fabrics that had been strung from roof to roof. Exciting as the city was, I found it hard to understand how anyone could actually *live* in the midst of such crowded squalor, but freshly-washed swaddling clothes drying on a cord above the street clearly showed that they did.

"Stay close to me," I cautioned Thomas. "Sepphoris is an easy place to get lost in."

"Or to get crushed in," Lazarus said with a laugh.

I held Thomas's hand as we worked our way through the seven markets, which sold everything from necessities like sandals and cloth, useful items such as bronze basins and iron tools, to luxuries like perfume, jewelry, gold, and glass. An entire block was devoted to selling honey. The hot streets were made hotter still by the kilns of the potters and the ovens of the glassblowers—a new art that had recently been brought to Israel from Syria.

Lazarus liked to spend his time with the metalwork, John preferred the food market, but I was drawn to watch the magic of the glassblowers. I couldn't stop looking at the wondrously hot fluid, with its aura of red heat, suspended mysteriously at the end of the rotating pipe as the craftsman gradually pulled the glass from the glowing oven. I felt its heat on my face even though I stood several feet away. The glassblower put the pipe to his mouth and inflated his cheeks to the size of small melons, but then gradually the melon shape seemed to flow through the pipe to the glass. There was a quiet hiss as he flattened the glass bulb gently against a damp wooden board. He cut the glowing stem with a knife, sliced neatly around its waist to liberate the bowl, and placed it on a bench for us to admire. The limpid green glass glittered like the surface of a stream. Glass was not only beautiful, but it was easy to clean. I vowed that someday, somehow, I would surprise my mother with a beautiful gift of glass.

As we were leaving Sepphoris, a Persian rose above the crowd on a stool and cried, "Magus! Magus! At the Via Maris gate. Magus! Magus! Come and hear the words and wisdom of the Magus! Magus! Come and see the power of Zarathustra! At the Via Maris gate! Magus! Magus!" He stepped down from his stool and disappeared into the crowd, presumably on his way to make the announcement in a different part of town.

Thomas fervently tugged at my arm. "Please, Jesus! Oh, please, can we go? Maybe he'll do a miracle!"

"Those 'miracles' are just tricks," I said. Even though many Jews took their magic, as their wizardry was called, to be true miracles, I felt Thomas should know better. "Besides, we're going the other way, and Mother will worry if we are late."

"The Magi are unclean," John added, as he popped a locust into his mouth. "They aren't Jews, and they worship a false god."

"I won't touch the Magi," Thomas said. I could see the fear of disappointment growing in his face. "I only want to watch," he pleaded.

"They are charlatans, liars, and perverters," John continued, clearly borrowing his fancy rhetoric from things he had heard my father say. "They are parasites who deceive in the name of righteousness, while seeking only to engorge themselves on the flesh of others." The Magi were the only group towards which my father directed such contemptuous words.

Yet he had once allowed me to watch a Magus perform. He seemed to enjoy figuring out how they did their tricks, and when he succeeded, his contempt grew further. Their fundamental secret, he told me, was *misdirection*, getting the observer to look at the wrong thing when the deception, the *sleight*, was performed. He had even shown me how to do some of their simple tricks.

I looked at Lazarus, and he shrugged his shoulders. We both knew we couldn't take Thomas to see a Magus, not on a day when John was along. John hoped to be a priest some day, and was very careful about rules.

But Thomas kept on pleading. What would my father do? No sooner had I asked myself that question than I knew the answer.

"Here, I'll perform a miracle for you," I said to Thomas. His eyes widened expectantly, although John frowned. I put my hand in my pocket, and with exaggerated importance I pulled out a large brass four-lepta coin, tossed it from one hand to the other, and held it out into the air. It appeared to vanish in front of Thomas's eyes. A moment later I produced it from behind his ear.

Thomas grabbed the coin from my hand and turned it over, examining it for signs of the magic he was certain must still be in it. He thrust his hand up in the air, closed his fist, opened it, and the coin fell to the cobblestones with a jingle. He picked it up, and looked at me. "Show me how you did that!" he insisted.

"It's just a miracle," I said diffidently. "If you've obeyed all the rules in the Torah for a week, then the Lord lets you do little miracles. If you obey for a whole year, he lets you do big ones." John glowered.

"No. Show me how you did it really!" Thomas insisted.

"If I show you, then you won't believe in miracles anymore."

"Yes I will. Please!"

I knew Thomas would have kept after me all the way home, so I gave in. I showed him how I let the coin drop into my palm just as I pretended to toss it into my other hand. "But the important thing, Thomas, is to really believe *yourself* that you're putting it into the other hand, even though you aren't. Look at the empty hand as if you are absolutely convinced the coin is there. That is the misdirection. Meanwhile the hand that really holds the coin must be completely relaxed, as if it couldn't possibly be holding a coin. If you believe the coin is in the other hand, so will everybody else."

"If you believe it yourself, then it really is a miracle!" Thomas laughed.

❖ ❖ ❖

Every morning the children in our neighborhood went to a class taught by Rabbi Shuwal in a house that served as our synagogue, part way down the hill from our home, next to the potters quarter. We entered through a curtain into a small room. In the center was a raised mound of dirt, and on this was a stool that we secretly called "the Rabbi's throne." We took mats from a corner of the room, spread them in a semi-circle around the stool, and waited.

After a long wait, Rabbi Shuwal finally appeared. He was short and gaunt, with features that appeared sculpted from clay: deeply set but bulging eyes, a long gray beard, and a long nose, the focus of jokes when he was absent. As a child I imagined that the Lord must look just like him. I suspect Rabbi Shuwal thought that too. Although I didn't particularly like him, the stories he read from the Scriptures riveted my attention, and he seemed to have an enormous knowledge of facts about them that were not in the Scriptures themselves.

One day the rabbi had been teaching the history of circumcision, how the custom had been given to us by the Lord as part of the covenant. The Maccabees had forcibly circumcised the gentiles they conquered, even those who would not convert, the rabbi said with a smile, "to please the Lord."

"Rabbi," I interrupted. "If a man is scarred, then he is not allowed to become a priest. Isn't that right?"

"Of course, Jesus." He talked slowly and cautiously, as if expecting a trap. "Just as we discussed last week. If a man isn't perfect, then he's not worthy of the station. It's in the Torah, dictated to Moses by the Lord himself. Just as on Passover we sacrifice an unblemished lamb to the Lord. . . ."

"But circumcision leaves a scar. So *all* male Jews are blemished!"

He was momentarily speechless. Then he scowled. "Do you do this to your parents?" he said with mock sincerity. "Do they send you to do this to me, so that I will share their suffering? Why are you always the only one here who is confused, Jesus? Is it because you don't want to learn? You will never be a Pharisee! You are doomed forever to the am ha'arez!" This was his ultimate insult. The am ha'arez were the "people of the land," the vast majority of Jews who called themselves Jews but were careless about the Law—the people who were more concerned with survival than in following the detailed commandments of the Torah.

Finally he returned to the question I had asked. "Circumcision is in the covenant," he said. "So it leaves no blemish. It makes you more perfect. It is one of the reasons you should be grateful you weren't born female, for it gives you another way to please the Lord. That's all there is to it. Now, please don't interrupt again, Jesus. Some of your classmates are serious about learning."

That evening on the roof of our home, I told my father what had happened.

"Don't let him upset you, Jesus," he said. "Rabbi Shuwal is like the shittah tree: his bark is full of tannin, but there's good wood underneath. But it goes against his nature even to question the Law. Sometimes I think he loves the Torah more than he loves the Lord." He looked thoughtfully down towards the valley, which was illuminated only by the stars.

"What about my question?" I asked. "How can circumcision perfect the body if it leaves a scar?"

"Circumcision isn't done to make us perfect, Jesus. It is done to set us apart, to make us different from the gentiles."

"Is that why the Lord wants us circumcised?"

"Perhaps. Circumcision is a very old rite, once practiced by the Egyptians, Ammonites, Arabs, by virtually all except Philistines and Greeks. I don't know why they did it, unless the Lord spoke to them too, and I don't know anyone who does know, not even Rabbi Hillel." My father quoted Rabbi Hillel the Babylonian almost as much as he quoted the Scriptures. In his youth my father had once heard Hillel teach, and he seemed to remember every word he had said. "But only the Jews still practice it."

"That makes it sound like it's just custom. But it's in the Covenant," I said.

"Understanding the wishes of the Lord is not always as easy as the Rabbi would have you believe. Do you know how many rules there are in the Torah?" he asked.

"Six hundred and thirteen," I said.

"Yes—good—but that is only the beginning. The Rabbis keep elaborating them. They love rules, because then we need the Rabbis to guide us. They can turn each rule into ten others. For example, you know the Pharisees say we should use separate dishes for meat and milk. Do you know why?"

"Exodus," I said. "And also Deuteronomy. The Lord commanded that we not 'cook a young sheep or goat in its mother's milk.'"

"Yet the Pharisees declare that everyone should use separate pots, plates and utensils for milk and meat, to avoid the remote danger that meat will accidentally touch a tiny spot of its mother's milk. As if the Lord would care! And it is the poor who most can't afford to do this. Rabbi Hillel said the Pharisees invent these rules only to make themselves appear more righteous. The Pharisees are all hypocrites."

"But I thought you *wanted* me to be a Pharisee."

"Heavens no, Jesus, I just want you to be a good Jew."

"Then why do you send me to the synagogue every morning?"

"Because you learn so much there."

I frowned. Slowly and sarcastically I repeated Rabbi Shuwal's maxim in a monotone: "Because a child ought to be fattened by the Torah as an ox is fattened at the stall."

My father smiled. "You've learned the Scriptures—I see that every time I ask you a question—but more importantly you've learned to see through nonsense." I laughed. "And that's a skill that will serve you well. A blade can only be kept sharp with a whetting stone." So the Rabbi was my whetting stone? As I was visualizing this, my father continued, "Rabbi Hillel said that the detailed rules were really the creation of scholars and scribes, not of the Lord himself. I heard him say, 'What is hateful to you, do not unto your neighbor; this is the entire Torah; the rest is just commentary.' So perhaps circumcision isn't as important to the Lord as it is to the priests and rabbis."

I was struck by the enormity of what my father had just said. He was questioning the Covenant—the contract that defined our lives—that defined what it meant to be a Jew. "But then . . . could there be an uncircumcised Jew?" I asked incredulously.

My father looked up to the night sky. "What is it that makes a Jew?" he seemed to ask the heavens. He turned towards me. "When a gentile is converted, he is circumcised, but he also takes a ceremonial bath, a *Mikvah*. Hillel said that this ritual cleansing, this *baptism* as they call it in Greek, is what turns him into a Jew. But to me even the concept of clean and unclean is repugnant. We can't touch a gentile without having to wash ourselves afterwards. We can't eat in his home for fear unclean food will be served on unclean plates. So we never get to know gentiles as people, and they are always strangers, disliked and distrusted. We need less ritual, and more kindness, charity, and love."

"Even love of the Romans?" I asked.

"Maybe, Jesus, maybe. Maybe we even have to love the Romans."

The moon had just come over the horizon, and Father seemed to glow in its delicate light. I sat there looking at him, his large powerful hands resting on his knees, his strong but gentle face, his kind eyes sparkling like stars. That was what the Lord looked like, I decided, not like Rabbi Shuwal. This rooftop was my true synagogue and my father was my true rabbi.

✧ ✧ ✧

At the Nazareth spring one day I came upon a great commotion. A man who had just been in Sepphoris was telling a crowd of an incredible event: Judah of Gamala, the Zealot rebel, the crafty hyena, had attacked the city and captured the arsenal.

"He is surely the Messiah!" the man proclaimed.

Another shouted back, "A star has come forth, and a scepter has risen out of Israel! He shall crush the forehead of our oppressors, and break down all the sons of Satan!" It was a slight misquote from the book of Numbers. "And he shall stand and feed his flock in the strength of the Lord, and they shall dwell secure, for now he shall be great to the ends of the earth."

Others shouted their own modified quotes from the Scriptures. Still others disagreed and debated, but I couldn't wait—I ran breathlessly up the hill to tell my parents the news. I could see my mother on the roof our home.

"Judah of Gamala has defeated the Romans!" I shouted. "He's taken Sepphoris!"

My mother had been kneading bread in a pine trough. With my words she stopped, and frowned. Then she continued and punched the bread even harder. She was clearly upset. I didn't understand why she was unhappy.

"He's pushing the Romans out of Galilee. Maybe he'll come to Nazareth next!" I said, beside myself with excitement.

"Gamala won't bother with Nazareth." She continued to knead.

"Yes he will!'He must! This is the most wonderful thing that has ever happened in my whole life!" I was sure she was wrong about him ignoring Nazareth. We would soon be free of Roman rule and Roman taxes and all the other bad Roman things I had heard about. I desperately wanted to go to Sepphoris, to see the liberated city myself, to feel the joy that must be on every street, in every home, in every shop!

"You will not go," she said, without looking up. How had she read my mind?

"Please, Mother! I can find out what is really happening! I'll come back and tell you and father."

"You will not go. Suppress your joy, Jesus. Rebellion, war—it is the most terrible thing that could happen. You have no idea. You will go nowhere near Sepphoris."

I was dejected. I would miss it all. I looked at my mother, and could see that there was little hope in talking to her. I walked around the house to the carpentry shop, where my father was repairing an oxen yoke. He picked it up gently, as if it were weightless, and placed in on a special stand he had built. He chose a bow drill from his tool rack and began to cut a dowel hole.

"Father, I—Mother said I can't go to Sepphoris, but . . ."

"No, Jesus," he said firmly. "No. She is right." It seemed as if he knew everything already.

"But Gamala has taken the city. He's defeated the Romans!"

"What happened to your love for the Romans?" he asked with a gentle smile. I blushed with mild embarrassment. My father stopped his work, put the drill away, walked over to me, and held me gently by the shoulders. "Come, sit with me for a moment," he said. We walked over to an old pine bench and sat down facing each other.

"Jesus," he said, "we've had a good life in Nazareth. We have many friends. We've been poor, but we've rarely known hunger. We've been ill at times, but we've recovered. You may hear complaints from your mother and me, but the Lord has been kind to us and to our neighbors. The Romans have ruled over us, but they've allowed us to worship the Lord in our own way. They've taken our money in taxes, but they've also assured peace.

"As you grow older, you'll cherish your memories of this childhood. You'll learn, I regret to say, that the happiness you've experienced is far from common. To you the suffering of Job is just a story, but before you grow much older you'll understand why it's the favorite book of so many people. The world is filled with pain and sorrow. You'll see misery among your loved ones and friends, and you will likely have to endure great suffering yourself. Most people do.

"Those who take the sword will perish by the sword. There's soon to be dreadful evil in Sepphoris. This is not a time to satisfy your curiosity, but a time to pray. It's not safe to go to there now. Terrible things will happen, Jesus. Learn from them, but don't let them change your spirit. Remember that the Lord loves us."

But I could not stop wondering what was happening. Two days passed, and no news came. My father kept me busy with tedious and time-consuming wood finishing jobs. Lazarus was kept equally busy by his parents, and we hardly had a chance to share what little gossip we overheard. My mother took over from me the daily trips to the spring, but if she learned any news, she didn't pass it on to me. There seemed to be no joy in our home.

On the third day I heard my mother shout, "Sepphoris is burning!" She was holding her dress and running up the hill towards our home. "Sepphoris is burning!" she sobbed. She pointed behind the hill. Hanging low behind the hill we saw what looked like a large dark pillar of smoke rising slowly into the sky. We moved away from the house to see better.

Grass fires give white smoke, almost indistinguishable from clouds. But this smoke was black, convoluted, ugly. We watched the pillar of smoke build all afternoon as it grew in size, eventually blocking our sun— I could not imagine a fire so great that it could do that. But the black column writhed above us like the body of a horrid serpent, its head hidden behind the hills, its jaws consuming the city.

Late in the day the smoke finally faded. In the evening all of Nazareth was unusually quiet. The sky turned a vivid red at sunset. We went to bed early, but I couldn't sleep. What had been destroyed? Who had survived? What was left?

"I can smell the smoke," I said from my mat.

"Be quiet, Jesus, or you'll wake baby James," my mother whispered from the darkness. "Go to sleep. The smoke has been gone for hours now. That's just the tanners' fumes."

I knew better. It was smoke. My thoughts grew turbulent. Several hours passed, and I twisted and turned on my mat. I could hear my father snoring. I didn't want to sleep. I couldn't stop thinking, imagining, wondering what was left of Sepphoris. What had happened to the people? Had Judah of Gamala escaped?

Very quietly I pushed aside my goat-hair blanket, picked myself up on my arms and legs, and maneuvered myself like a spider off the mat and onto the floor. I waited for a reaction from my parents; there was none. Thomas and James were motionless on the other side of my mat. A loud snore from my father encouraged me on. Using my fingertips and toes only, I crept towards the door, gently pushed aside the curtain, and slipped outside. The evening was warm and still. Even the crickets were quiet. The smell of burnt wood was stronger out here. I glanced up at the stars and saw it was near midnight. I would have several hours to make it there and back before my parents arose. I continued to crawl until I was well away from the house, out of view of the windows, and then I stood up and started at a quick pace down to the spring, and along the path to Sepphoris.

It was a moonless night, but the stars painted the path as a colorless ribbon winding in front of me. Where it entered the woods, nothing was visible, and I had to slow my pace while following the trail by feeling for the wagon ruts with my bare feet. After I had gone about three miles, I thought I heard a breeze stirring the trees, coming from up ahead, but as I continued along I realized that I was hearing the sound of high-pitched human voices, women wailing. When I entered the clearing I couldn't yet see Sepphoris, but in the distance there were torches along the road where it widened. Structures that looked like tall posts lined the road; they hadn't been there before. As I got closer I could see that they were crosses. Women and old men were at the bases of the crosses, weeping and ululating. One woman was ripping her clothing and pulling her hair. I saw something move on one cross, and I walked closer to see what it was.

It is impossible to describe the dread and horror felt by a child looking upon a crucifixion. Even now I shudder to remember the experience, the man roped to the cross, nails through his wrists and ankles, his eyes screaming in pain, screaming with an anguish his exhausted body could express in no other way. My eyes froze as it all came into sharp focus in the dim light, the blood dripping from his mouth, the quivering of his muscles, the lacerations of his flesh, the shame of his nakedness, and the filth of defecation on his legs. I forced myself to look away.

Suddenly I found myself running in terror back towards Nazareth, in the midst of a nightmare from which I couldn't wake up. I had looked only at the first cross, but as I ran I remembered that there had been many, perhaps more than a hundred, all along the path. In my mind I saw on each one a pulsating body with screaming eyes. My throat tightened and I had trouble breathing. As I entered the darkness of the woods, every vague shape brought new frightful images to my mind. The route seemed infinitely longer than before. Despite my terror, my legs grew heavy and I could no longer run. It took forever to reach the crest of the hill and to descend the slope to Nazareth, but finally I reached the end of the dirt path and plodded up the cobblestone street that led to our house. I had hoped that my parents were still asleep, but when I saw them standing outside the door I was thankful. I ran sobbing to my mother, threw my arms around her, and almost knocked her down. As she tightly hugged me, I could feel that she was crying too.

✧ ✧ ✧

A light drizzle settled quietly on the debris of the houses, driving a dank odor out of the burnt wood. A slight hiss attracted my attention to a place where a rivulet of water had just reached a hot spot. A puff of white steam rose from the spot and faded into the air.

It was devastation so great that my imagination could only say to me, *this is not possible.* As I looked to the distance, the landscape was punctuated by the remains of chimneys and ovens, standing there like tombstones in a pagan graveyard. They were the only parts of the homes built from stone. Even the walls, made of a mixture of straw and mud, had disintegrated in the fury of the fire. I stood in the middle of the city square. How strange, to be able to see the hills from here, covered with spring wildflowers, blooming. The dense buildings of Sepphoris had previously hidden the view.

It was the wealthy part of town that was most devastated. Those houses must have contained more furniture, I guessed, and that served as fuel for the flames. The elaborate iron gate of a large house stood undamaged, guarding the rubble behind it. I walked around the gate into the steaming debris. With irony I thought, this is my first time in a rich man's house. Enough of the layout was discernible that I could count four separate rooms. I wondered, how could they have used so much space? I pushed aside some ashes with my sandals, and scratched my toe on something hard. I picked up a small piece of green glass. I expected it to be hot from the fire, but it was cool to my touch. It looked like it had partially melted. I wiped it with my wet shirt, and it shone unlike anything I had ever seen. As I turned it over in my hand the reflections changed its appearance, almost as if it were alive. What a lovely amulet it would make for my mother! That would be looting, I realized. I threw the glass back down on the ground, and looked around to see if anybody had seen me. Roman soldiers, who had purposely set the city ablaze, were now notably absent. They would stay away, my father had predicted, to encourage looting. But there was little left to take; the fire had been thorough. I had been afraid to come, lest someone think that I too was looking for something to steal, and now I almost had done so.

The ugly black smoke of three days ago was gone. The bodies had been removed from the crosses, wrapped in cloth, and buried. Everything now was white. This wasn't death, I thought. It was a ritual sacrifice, an offering, through fire, to the Lord. This was holocaust.

3. Bat qol

THE ROMANS HAD BEEN SYSTEMATIC IN THEIR VICIOUSNESS.
They had evacuated the city before they burned it, lined up the men, and
sent every tenth to crucifixion or slavery, an official procedure called dec-
imation which they used in rebel cities. Varus, Governor of Syria, had been
Caesar's surrogate in the destruction, my father explained, to help fester
local hatred. The city was to be rebuilt, in a pagan style, and renamed
Augustus, in honor of Caesar. With its important location and with all possibility of Jewish rebellion wiped out, the new city would become the capital of Galilee. Soon there was an influx of Greeks and Romans, and construction began. Several of our neighbors in Nazareth moved to the city.
This angered my mother, even though the shortage of workers in Nazareth
kept us busy.

Despite the enormous tragedy, our life was remarkably unchanged.
The Roman forces were temporarily concentrated in Sepphoris, but no
Roman soldier "bothered," as my mother would say, to come to Nazareth.
The mundane tasks of working, eating, and sleeping consumed the days
and distracted my thoughts. During the day I even found it possible to forget the horror that had taken place four miles away. But I still woke at
night, gasping in terror at the dreadful images of eyes spouting blood and
entrails dangling from eviscerated bodies, scenes even more hideous than
my actual memories.

❖ ❖ ❖

I pulled my chin to the top of the wall, and peeked over into the small
yard of Lazarus's home. His sister Mary was alone, playing with sticks.

This was the moment I had waited for. Doing my best not to make a sound, I struggled up onto my arms, rested my stomach on the top momentarily, spun my legs around, and landed like a cat on the other side, just behind her. Mary was startled and emitted a slight gasp, but I covered her mouth gently with my hand. I looked around, and nobody else was within sight. "Quick!" I whispered to her, "Let's make a run for it! If we're gone by the time they come out, they'll never be able to find us!" I took her hand and tugged her towards the gate. As soon as she started to run with me, I stopped, crouched, and put my finger to her lips. "No! Don't giggle," I said solemnly, "whatever you do, don't giggle! If they hear us now, all my plans will go awry!" She put her own hand to her face to hide her smile.

We went out the gate, tiptoed over the cobblestones, and moved onto the grass. It was only a few hundred feet up the hill to the woods. Once we entered the trees, I looked back. I could see most of the village, and had a clear view of the roof of our house. "Come this way," I said. "It's not a trail, so we'll be safe. But be careful not to step on mushrooms, or you'll anger the Witch of Endor." According to the Book of Samuel, the Witch of Endor lived only a few miles away on Mt. Tabor, so she was a favorite bogey for the children of Nazareth. "Follow these marks," I said, pointing to some almost invisible cuts I had made in the bark of the sycamore trees. We soon arrived at a small clearing with an ancient oak in the middle. Nazareth was completely out of sight, hidden behind the forest. I took her around to the side of the tree, and showed her that the base was hollow and large enough to crawl in. As she started to go in, I warned solemnly, "That's the wolf's house."

Mary pulled back, and said, "Is it really?" She moved herself closer to me and took my arm, feigning fear.

"No, not really," I replied truthfully. Her gentle touch on my arm made me feel manly. "But I think it is what a wolf's house should look like. What it really is—is the house of the hermit."

Mary smiled. "Is it a good hermit or an evil hermit?"

"Oh, a good hermit. One who will protect us from the witch. But he's only a baby. He must be nurtured and raised to be a man, so that when he is strong he can protect the entire town of Nazareth from all evil spirits."

"I don't see a baby. Where is it?"

"Right here!" I reached into a pile of dry leaves in the hollow, pulled out a small cloth-wrapped object that I had hidden, and handed it to her. Her bright cinnamon-colored eyes shone over her high cheekbones with a smile that I'll never forget. "Go ahead, unwrap... take off the swaddling clothes." As the face was uncovered, Mary let out an audible gasp. Her eyes filled with tears. "Don't you like him?" I asked rhetorically. I had carved the face from acacia wood, painted a gentle smile on it, and made the body from several small pieces of white linen stuffed with straw and tied with cord. As I sensed her joy, my eyes too began to fill.

She blinked, and the tears ran down her cheek. She wiped it with her arm. "It's the most beautiful doll I've ever seen!" she said.

"But remember, Mary, he's a hermit. This is his home, here in the wolf's house. He can visit you, of course, but only in secret. You must never let anyone else know you are caring for him, or the witch of Endor will come to kill him."

"I'll care for the child in secret until it's fully grown," she said as she pressed the doll against her chest. "But how did you know?"

"That you wanted a doll? I heard you crying when your parents refused you," I said. Rabbi Shuwal said children shouldn't be allowed to own dolls—they are graven images, forbidden by the second commandment. But Mary had just been visited by her cousin Martha, who had brought her own doll, and Mary coveted one for herself.

"Why can Martha have a doll but not Mary?" I had asked my father.

"Her rabbi in Bethany is more lenient," he answered. "He considers the doll just a toy, not an image."

"That's unfair!" I said. "We're supposed to please the Lord, not rabbis!" My father didn't counter me. I was, after all, using words I had heard him say. And now Mary had her doll.

"But you don't own him," I reminded her. "You're only taking care of him, until he grows up. And since you don't own him, you're not disobeying your parents," I added. I had carefully thought through the logic.

"I don't care if I am disobeying my parents!" she said, to my surprise. "Jesus, you are the most wonderful boy in the whole world!" For a moment I thought she was going to kiss me, and my heart seemed to stop. But she showed restraint. She just hugged the doll and looked at me, and I grew self-conscious.

"You have to give him a name," I said.

"I've already picked one. Deborah."

"That's a girl's name."

"Of course. Deborah is a girl."

"How can a girl defend Nazareth from the witch?"

"Just as the prophetess Deborah inspired her people to fight the Canaanites. She'll lead the people of Nazareth up the mountain of Tabor to kill the witch!"

If Mary really wanted a girl, I guessed it was all right with me.

✧ ✧ ✧

I sat on the roof, trying to enjoy the coolness of the early evening. My mother was weaving black sackcloth with her loom; Thomas and James had already gone to bed. My father was sitting beside me, counting the stars as they appeared, one by one. He was up to fourteen when a shooting star suddenly streaked in front of us, right through the Goat Herd, the group of stars that the Greeks call the "Pleiades." For some reason that event triggered my question.

"Father, why are there no miracles anymore?" I asked.

He looked at me as if I had just asked the silliest question he had ever heard. Then he covered his smile with his hand and said with mock seriousness, "The Magi can turn water into wine." My mother pointedly stopped throwing the shuttle for a moment, turned around on her stool, and looked at him with a scowl.

"But that's just trickery, magic, not a true miracle," I said

"Many of their followers seem to think their magic is real," he said.

"I don't. People are just easily fooled."

"A man is wise, not when he's no longer fooled, but when he knows how easily he is fooled." From the sound of the loom I could tell that my mother had resumed her weaving.

"But why aren't there any *real* miracles any more, like there were in the Scriptures?" I persisted.

"Suppose I walked on water," my father said. "Would that be a suitable miracle?"

"Yes. If you weren't using some trick." Rabbi Shuwal said the Messiah would walk on water when he came. It was a miracle that even the Magi couldn't perform.

"Suppose I walked on water every day, and so did everyone else, and we didn't use any tricks. Would you consider that a miracle?"

"Yes, of course."

"No, I don't think you would. When you see the same miracle every day, you lose the sense of awe. You just think that that's the way the world is. You don't call it a miracle."

"Maybe," I answered. That was a favorite word of mine when I suspected that my father was right, but I didn't want to admit it.

"Jesus, we're surrounded by miracles, true miracles. If only we would notice them, we would always be filled with awe at the Lord's power." He placed his hand gently on my shoulder. "A shooting star is a miracle. A lightning bolt is a miracle, more of a miracle than splitting the Red Sea, but we take it for granted because we see it so often. The more common the miracle, the less awe most people feel. A butterfly is more of a miracle than a lightning bolt, and far more of a miracle than walking on water! Water itself is a miracle. It comes from heaven and nurtures life. Life is a miracle, the greatest miracle of all. Children are miracles. It was a miracle that you were given to me, to raise and to love."

"No, you just don't understand." I pushed his hand off my shoulder. I wanted real answers, not just philosophy. But he didn't say anything more. He just quietly smiled, as if he knew that I would think about what he said, regardless of how I seemed to dismiss it. I hated it when he did that.

I sat there in the darkness, unsatisfied. I looked away from my father and towards the fading orange glow behind the hill where the sun had set. Up above me there were too many stars to count. Some of them sparkled with brilliant colors, like the sapphires and rubies worn by the high priest. I caught myself starting to enjoy them and then pulled back. My father would probably consider those stars to be miracles.

I would not give up. "Then why doesn't the Lord speak to us anymore, as he did to Moses?" I asked.

"He does, every day."

I groaned inwardly. It was the answer I should have expected. "He never talks to me," I retorted.

"Not in a thunderous voice pealing from the heavens, but I believe he does in a gentler way. He doesn't shout at us, but he speaks in whispers, through a holy spirit, usually only when we need him. In Hebrew we call it *bat qol*, or *the daughter of the voice*. He puts good thoughts in our heads when we're tempted to sin. He gives us courage when we're afraid. Tell me, Jesus, did you ever have doubts about something that you were going to do, not knowing whether it was the right thing or not?"

"I don't know what you're talking about," I said somewhat ruefully.

"Well, let's take an example. What about that doll that you made for Amos's daughter? When you were thinking about doing that . . ."

I froze. That doll had been my dark secret, the one deception for which I was fearful the Lord would one day hold me accountable. And my father knew about it! But how? Mary's parents didn't know, or they would have severely punished her. Even her brother Lazarus didn't know about it.

". . . How did you know that you were doing the right thing?" my father continued. "You probably had some feelings of guilt, after all, since you were disobeying not only the will of her parents but also of Rabbi Shuwal."

He hadn't included himself in the list. Did *he* feel I had done the right thing? I finally found the courage to look him in the face. He was just looking at me, as if we were discussing some interesting matter of religion, as if he still trusted me despite his discovery of my deception.

"So how did you decide to go ahead and give her the doll?" he asked.

"I don't know," I answered, truthfully. I felt myself blushing, and was grateful for the darkness. I recalled my confused feelings while making the doll, the thought that I was breaking the covenant. I remembered arguing to myself that I was doing the right thing, but for every reason I gave myself, I could hear the counter. Yet my confusion and my guilt hadn't stopped me.

"Did you hear any whispers while you were pondering your actions? Was something inside you encouraging you on?" he asked.

"I don't think so."

My father said nothing more. He turned towards the hills and watched them, as if expecting to see them do something.

My guilt had caused me great pain, up to the moment when I gave the doll to Mary and saw her smile. Then I felt that I had acted righteously. But why had I gone ahead, despite my misgivings? That's really what my father was asking. Because I had to do it—it was as simple as that—because despite my guilt, I had some inner sense that I was doing the right thing. Is that what he meant by *bat qol*? We had both been silent for a few minutes. I sensed that he was awaiting a reconsideration of my previous answer.

"Well, maybe," I finally said.

He turned to me again. "Pay attention to that spirit in the future," he said, "and you'll learn to recognize the Lord's voice. When you recognize it, it will be easier for you to pay attention to it. If you learn to pay attention to it, it will give you enormous power and joy."

"Power over Caesar?" I asked. I immediately regretted my question.

"It will give you power over those things that really matter," he said ambiguously. I grew to learn that ambiguous answers often are less misleading than direct ones.

4. Tragedy

IT WAS A QUIET AFTERNOON. THOMAS HAD TAKEN JAMES, WHO was now six, to Sepphoris to buy salt. I had finished cleaning the tools, and was alone with my father, who was carving. A light wind blew towards the tannery, rather than from it, and the sweet smell of myrtle blossoms was drifting down from the hills. Puffs of clouds wandered past like sheep grazing on the sky. Tap, tap, tap—my father gently hit the chisel with his palm. I didn't want to work; I didn't want to move; I didn't want to think. Tap, tap, tap. I just wanted to feel, and I felt wonderful. I thanked the Lord for the joy he gave me. Tap. My father leaned over, and reached out into the empty space beside his bench. He had his chisel in his outstretched hand and was pushing it against the air. He leaned further on his seat, almost falling off, stretching towards space.

"Father, what are you doing?" I was puzzled, perhaps somewhat amused. "What are you doing?" I asked again, a little louder.

"Putting the chisel back," he said, his voice strangely slurred.

"But the cabinet is over there, next to the table . . ." He waved the chisel in mid air. Something was dreadfully wrong. "What are you doing?" I demanded.

"Putting the chisel back," he said again, as he stretched into space and started to fall from his bench. I caught him and looked in his face. One side of his face drooped badly, as if all of the muscles had been removed. His eyes were open, but motionless. They looked flat, with none of their usual brightness.

"Father!"

No response.

"Father! Can you hear me?"

His dull eyes weighed heavily in their sockets. His mouth was open, and fluid dribbled down his chin. His skin was pale gray. He slumped into my arms. "Father! Can you hear me?" I repeated. I struggled unsuccessfully with his weight, and he fell to the ground. I couldn't lift him. His face was on the dirt. I pulled off my linen shirt and put it under his head, turning him over in the process. As his face came upwards and I saw his lifeless eyes, a cold dread flooded my body. I put my ear to his chest and listened for his heartbeat. There was none. This can't be happening, I thought. I turned him slightly, adjusted his arms gently, and listened at his chest again. Nothing.

No!

I sat on the floor, and adjusted his head onto my lap. I felt utterly helpless. Should I run for help? Should I scream? Should I cry? I looked down at his lifeless eyes. The Torah says that they should be closed. I moved my fingers towards them—and hesitated. How could I touch the eyes of my father? My whole existence seemed to focus on those eyes. I turned away from them. They aren't his eyes, I thought. His eyes always sparkled with intelligence, with affection, with—life. These eyes were the dead eyes of a corpse. I shuddered slightly as I thought those words and forced my fingers to gently close one eye, then the other. My fingers are now unclean, I thought. And now I shall make my lips unclean. I leaned over and kissed him gently on the forehead. I pressed my face against his, and my tears fell onto his face and ran down his cheek.

I don't know how long I sat there, but eventually I placed his head back on the linen, got up, covered his body with a cloth, and forced myself to walk around the corner, into our home, where I knew my mother was working. I couldn't say any words when I got to her—I tried, but nothing came out. But she seemed to read my face, to see something she had never seen before, for she left me and ran to the shop. A moment later, I said to myself that I must follow her. She needs me. I went quickly to the shop and found her crying and sobbing on the corpse. She wailed, and soon Esreth, Amos, and all of our neighbors knew of our tragedy, and several of them came to sit with us. I tried to comfort my mother, but I had no comfort to share. Amos sat next to me but said nothing. I was grateful for both his presence and his silence. His wife Esreth put her arm around my mother, who continued to sob over the body.

I moved off the bench and sat on the ground, feeling numb. I looked at my mother and watched her mourning. Her wailing had grown more intense. She pulled at her hair and scratched at her face and arms, just as

I had seen many other women in mourning for their husbands in Nazareth. It suddenly occurred to me, however, that she wasn't tearing her clothes, as was the custom. We were very poor, and without my father's income, she knew that clothes would not easily be replaced.

We buried my father that same day, with no coffin, wearing his carpenter's clothes. I removed the oak chip from behind his ear, so that it wouldn't be there on the Sabbath. Our neighbors joined us in mourning for a week. Amos and Lazarus helped Thomas and me scrub the carpentry area, the place of my father's death, to make it clean again.

✧ ✧ ✧

My mother had always worked hard, but now she seemed to take no rest. Even before the first glow of daylight, I was often awakened by the sound of her grinding coarse barley meal between stones. She mixed it with water and salt to make a dough, and then added leaven, and shaped it into several loaves, which she set aside to let sit for a few hours. She then took the loaves to a baker, who baked them for the price of keeping one loaf. Thomas then carried the other loaves around the village, selling them to our more fortunate neighbors.

My mother spent the evenings weaving. She couldn't compete with the professional weavers who made fine linens, but she could make a little money by purchasing black goat hair from the goatherds and weaving it into sack cloth. I often went to sleep to the sound of her working her loom.

Lazarus's father Amos hired me as an assistant, but the only work he could give me was hauling, wood cutting, and the laying of roofs. He paid me a denarius each week, although even that was charity on his part.

One night, as I lay on my mat exhausted from a day repairing roof beams and laying clay, I listened to the rhythmic *schlump, schlump* as my mother tossed the shuttle back and forth. We couldn't afford oil for a lamp, so she was working by the open window using moonlight.

"Mother?"

"Go to sleep, Jesus. You need rest."

"Mother, how will we live? We have no money left. We earn barely enough for food. Without your garden, we would go hungry. When winter comes, things will just get worse."

"Have faith in the Lord," she said quietly. "This too shall pass." The words sounded vaguely familiar, but I didn't recognize them from Scripture.

"I think the Lord has abandoned us," I said.

"Shame, Jesus! Never say that again! You are always questioning, just like your father. It was his weakness, not his strength, as you seem to think. He always wanted to figure out for himself what was right and what was wrong. Maybe that's why the Lord is punishing us. Now we need faith more than ever."

"How long will we have to suffer?"

"This too shall pass."

"Where does that come from, Mother? It's not from the Scriptures, is it?"

"No. It's what my mother Anna said when there was hardship. And she was right; the hardship did pass. Don't worry, Jesus. The death of your father is a great tragedy, but we'll survive. Someday we may even be happy again. I have lived through worse. So I know, this too shall pass."

Worse? How could she suggest that she had been through worse? That was unimaginable. She must have sensed my disbelief, for she continued.

"I was fourteen, Jesus, just a little older than you. I visited cousin Elizabeth, here in Nazareth, who was pregnant with your cousin John, and he had moved inside her, and she and her husband Zacharias were very happy. But she didn't let her joy blind her. She could tell that something was wrong with me, even before I knew, and she discovered that I was pregnant, with you Jesus. You know, of course, that Joseph wasn't your real father."

Yes, I knew. My father had told me when I was very little. But he said he loved me more than he would his own son, and so it didn't matter.

"My father, Joachim, wanted to compel marriage, but I wouldn't tell him who the father was. I was so young—I think that at the time I didn't even understand what had happened to me. Then he took me to Magdala and showed me the prostitutes, and told me that that was what I would become. I came home in terror. I'll never forget those oiled women with their heavy perfume and blond wigs. I was to be driven out, away from everything I loved, into an alien, horrid, squalid world. That was worse, my son, worse than now.

"It was my mother who restored my faith in the Lord. She told me, 'This too shall pass.' I decided to have faith, to believe her, not my father. And a miracle happened, Jesus. Joseph was a friend of Zacharias, and he learned of my condition. He visited our house and asked to wed me. My father thought Joseph acted from poverty—to marry a pregnant girl he wouldn't have to pay the *mohar* to my father. My mother thought he was acting from charity. But I came to understand that Joseph was just picking the woman who most needed him. It was his way of doing things. I was blessed with him, and with you, and with Thomas and James. The Lord rewards faith. That's why I named you 'Jesus,' because it means 'God saves.' We'll survive now too. This too shall pass. Let us thank the Lord for our blessings."

My mother stopped talking, and I said nothing. I still couldn't sleep. The moon gradually set and I could no longer see her. In the darkness of the room the loom became silent. But after a while, coming from the corner where she was sitting I thought I heard quiet, suppressed sobs.

Despite my mother's courage, we sank slowly but surely into deep poverty. I soon learned that except for our closest friends, my father's premature death was looked upon with suspicion. Many Jews believed that death before old age was a judgment for sin, and that the calamity was meant to extend to the wife and family. So to them we were disgraced by our tragedy.

Our hopes were at their lowest level when I noticed that some of our neighbors had begun to refer to me as "Jesus, son of Mary" rather than as "Jesus, son of Joseph." It was the traditional way to disparage a bastard. The secret of my birth had apparently worked its way into the gossip. But I considered it a slight against my father, and I resented that. He was the most sin-free man I have ever known.

✧ ✧ ✧

I could no longer be spared for shopping, so my mother began walking the four miles to Sepphoris, now officially renamed Augustus, to search for bargains. The first part of the city that came back to life had been the market place. One day she came back with a sack of moldy nuts. "But the mold just washes off," she said proudly. I knew better than to ask her if she had asked the rabbi whether this was adequate "ritual washing."

On another occasion she surprised me with a pair of sandals. "How can we afford these?" I asked. I rubbed the thick leather between my fingers in admiration. "They must be worth two denari."

"You've been going barefoot, Jesus. You need them."

"But where did you get the money?"

"Just be grateful. The Lord provides, just as the prophets say."

"But I'd like to know *how* he provides. Where did the money come from?"

"Don't worry! Some of our problems have passed. A good man named Pantera has taken pity on us. He's a Roman merchant who was brought in to help rebuild Sepphoris. He's married to a Jewish woman, so he knows our customs. He even follows the dietary laws."

"Mother, we shouldn't be taking charity from a Roman."

"Pantera isn't a typical Roman. He's kind. Besides, it's not charity. He just sells me things at cost, things we couldn't afford to buy otherwise, so he isn't losing money. He's talked to other merchants, and they save defective items for me, things that they otherwise would throw away."

The sandals were finely made. They didn't look like rejects.

One day as my mother was grinding barley flour, I could just see the back of a delicate brass chain that she was wearing under her smock. It seemed too fine to be something she had purchased.

"Mother, what's that around your neck?"

"What? Oh—that. It's—a miracle," she replied with a smile.

"Mother! Don't tease. Where did that come from?" My tone was intended to be innocent, but she may have sensed the concern in my voice.

"Don't worry, Jesus," she replied. "I didn't spend our money on this. It's a gift from Pantera." She pulled the chain out. There was a little amulet on it, a beautiful clear piece of glass that sparkled in the light of the doorway with the aquamarine color of the Sea of Galilee. The green glass I had found in the ashes of Sepphoris flashed into my memory.

"This came all the way from Rome," she said proudly. I must have been looking at her in an accusatory way, for she swallowed, glanced at the floor briefly, and then seemed to force herself to look me directly in the eyes. "There was a Roman holiday last week," she said, "called 'The Birthday of the Unconquered Sun.' They celebrate it every year on the 25th day of December, the tenth month of the Roman calendar, at the end of the Saturnalia, when the days start to get longer. It's a traditional day to exchange presents." I didn't say anything, but I looked hard at her. She seemed nervous, and chattered on. "It's just tradition. It's a seasonal holiday, not a religious one. It wasn't a religious gift."

I wondered what gift she had given Pantera in exchange.

"There's nothing wrong with it," she continued to protest. "It's just a pretty piece of glass. It made him feel good to give it, and it made me feel good to take it. Do not judge me, Jesus," she snapped angrily. "Show respect for your mother."

I lied to Amos, saying I had an urgent errand to run for my mother, and he allowed me to take the morning off from work. It took me half an hour to run the four miles to Sepphoris. I stopped at a glass shop and asked if the merchant knew a man named Pantera. He directed me down the cobbled streets to the main square, near the synagogue. I asked a rabbi, and he pointed to a centurion who was watching over construction being done by Roman soldiers and slaves. "Can you direct me to Pantera?" I asked the centurion, in the best Latin I could manage.

He looked right at me, and I was startled by his penetrating green eyes, eyes that matched the color of my mother's amulet. "I am he," he said, in Aramaic. "What do you want?"

I was paralyzed. I stared at him, noticing his battle-hardened features, his evident strength, his roughness, the dagger he wore at his side. I felt a surge of hatred towards my mother. Pantera turned away from me, and issued an order to several of his men.

Then I was overcome by shame. I kept looking at Pantera, at the same harsh features, but now they made me feel sad for my mother. She was supporting us in the only way she could. It was my fault, for not being a good carpenter, for having indulged myself thinking about religion rather than concentrating on work and sharpening my practical skills. Now my mother was paying the price for my laziness. I flushed with guilt and I turned away from Pantera, who was no longer aware of my existence.

I was to blame. It was up to me to find the solution, even if it meant sacrificing myself. I was the oldest male in the household, and I had to support the family. There was only one plausible way that I could get money.

5. Sin

MUCH TO MY SURPRISE, A FEELING OF LIBERATION, ALMOST OF elation, accompanied my decision to sin. To most Jews, righteousness means following the strict rules of the Torah, and although my father had been lenient, I often felt guilt at my frequent failures at perfect compliance. But now my mother was sacrificing herself for the family, for me, and if I had to disobey God to save her, then I would do so willingly—with no qualms, no second thoughts. It was evident that I loved her more than I loved God. So be it.

Rather than money, I thought, it will be safer to steal something valuable and sell it. But not too valuable. No more than I need. Items displayed in the market stalls are handled by many people. Taking something from a stall shouldn't be much harder than vanishing a coin. I never consciously decided what to steal, but I somehow knew it would be glass.

I walked to the potters' street, and lingered at a place where I could see the glass merchants' stalls. I picked my target, a small but elegant decanter, the type the glassblowers call a "baqbuq," after the gurgling sound that wine makes pouring out its narrow neck. How would I misdirect the watchful merchants? I was pleased with myself when I realized the obvious answer: the sound of breaking glass.

However breaking pottery would have to do—it was cheaper. I bought a crude earthenware water jug for a half denarius, and a piece of hard wax from a honey dealer for two lepta. I filled the jug with water at the well, and placed it on a corner of a sun-lit wall, within earshot of the glassblowers. I balanced it with the wax so it would fall onto the cobblestone street when the wax softened. I took a short piece of cord that I had brought from home, looped it around my neck, tied a wooden hook on the end, and put it under my tunic.

I returned to the corner near the glass stall and waited. I looked not at the wares, nor at the shopkeeper, but at the water jug sitting in the hot sun. Ten minutes passed, and I worried that the wax wasn't softening. But suddenly the jug began to tip. I forced my eyes away from it and planted them firmly on the eyes of the glass merchant. Crash! He jerked his head towards the accident, as did everyone on the street—everyone except me. I walked quickly past the stall, my eyes glued to his, picked up the baqbuq and slipped it onto the hook under my tunic.

I turned a corner, and went directly to the main square to the tables of the moneychangers. One was carefully arranging Hebrew coins along-side pagan ones, to show exchange rates even to the illiterate. From the looks of his fat belly I guessed that he had cheated many people. He looked up at me suddenly, and his thick nose and narrow eyes flashed hostility.

"Sir, my father died, and my family is poor and in need of money," I said.

"Go away! No begging allowed in this square! I'll call the soldiers!"

"No, no! I'm not begging!" His mention of soldiers frightened me. "My mother sent me here to sell our baqbuq." I pulled it from my tunic and held it out for him to see. He eyed it suspiciously. "It was a wedding gift," I said.

He took it and ran his fingers over the smooth glass. Then he seemed to examine me with equal care. "Why don't you sell it at the glass shops?"

I had anticipated that question. "They'll only give me a shekel for it, yet I know it's worth more. My mother says the moneychangers are more honest." I hoped my flattery wasn't too blatant.

"I'll show it to my partner. Wait here." He disappeared through the crowd. If it weren't for his coins arrayed on the table, I wouldn't have trusted him to return.

So far, everything was going as planned. I anticipated my triumphant return home. What will I tell Mother when I hand her the money? I'll have to lie, as she lied to me. It was a reward, I'll say, for returning a lost purse. She'll want to know the details, how I had found the purse, to whom I took it. What did he look like? How much did he—?

Suddenly I felt a wrenching pain in my right shoulder, as if it were being crushed in a wood vise, but when I looked I saw only a leathery hand covered with mail armor. An instant later my left arm was jerked vio-lently behind me, almost pulled out of its socket. I turned my head and saw the glassy green eyes and rough face of Pantera scowling at me. "Is this the thief?" he demanded.

"Yes, that's him." The answer came from the moneychanger who had returned and was standing behind me. Next to him was the glass merchant, holding his baqbuq.

There was no hope of escaping the strong hold of Pantera. As he pushed me through the street, he twisted my arms and grinned. My attention alternated between the pain in my shoulder and the shame I felt as everyone watched me being arrested. My eyes watered with tears, as if I were still a child. I thought, I must not allow myself to be taken to the judge, or all will be lost. I'll tell Pantera who I am—then he'll release me, or at least allow me to escape. I looked at him and tried to speak. My pride made it difficult to ask a favor of this man who had exploited my mother, but my impending doom won out. I shouted his name, "Pantera!"

"How do you know my name?" he demanded, without stopping as he pushed me down the street. He seemed to have no memory of our earlier meeting, that meeting that stuck so firmly in my mind.

"I am Jesus, son of Mary."

"A bastard, eh? I'm not surprised."

"I'm the son of Mary of Nazareth," I said through my tears.

"I don't care if you are the son of Jupiter himself. You'll soon regret your crimes."

"But you know Mary! Her name in Hebrew is Mirriam—Maria in Latin and Greek. You gave her a necklace—for the Feast of the Unconquered Sun!"

"I've known many Marys, and I've given gifts to many of them, but never just to celebrate a holiday!" He laughed loudly, and crudely.

I have never felt such hatred in myself, before or since. If I had not been totally overpowered, at that moment, regardless of all the teachings of my father, I would have tried to kill him.

Pantera shoved me to a side door of the magistrate's palace, which contained both the jail and the courthouse. Inside he spoke briefly with a man dressed in an elegant tunic. "This is the hazzan," Pantera said to me as he left. "Do as he says, for he won't be as gentle as I was."

The hazzan was the utility man of the court, a man of poor family who had worked his way into a role of power (and fine clothes) by performing menial jobs—jailer, clerk, scourger. He looked me over, as if trying to determine whether I had the resources to bribe him, decided I didn't, and then took me to a small empty room in the cellar of the stone building. Without saying a word, he chained me to a column and left.

As I sat on that cold dirt floor, the reality of my situation finally hit me.

I had never seriously imagined getting caught, nor considered the possible consequences. But now I feared that I would be punished with the scourge, the triple whip with thirty-nine barbs of bone and metal. The bloody image of the crucifixion flashed into my mind and I felt sick. But even that fear faded when I realized that, following the Law of Moses, I would have to pay back twice the value of the stolen object. Our family had been poor, but now, because of my reckless scheme, we would be deeply in debt.

It grew dark, and I was exhausted. Chained to the pillar, I lay down, put the back of my head against the hard dirt, and slept.

A brutal thump to my ribs, and I awoke with a start. The hazzan stood above me. Without speaking, looking slightly bored, he motioned me up and removed my chains. He led me to a large room and stood me in front of a bench. "Don't move from this spot," he ordered, and he went to stand by the door.

In a few minutes a man entered, the judge, I presumed, elegantly dressed in a blue silver-embroidered cloak and a fine leather belt with a large brass buckle. From his rich clothes and air of authority, I assumed he was a Sadducee, a member of the ruling party of Jews whose loose interpretation of the Law allowed them to work comfortably with the occupying Romans. Following the judge came the moneychanger and the glass merchant, also dressed resplendently. I felt their clothes alone passed judgment on me, as I stood there in my dusty tunic.

I must have looked frightened. The moneychanger walked around beside me, leaned over and whispered in my ear, "My name is Manasas. Yesterday you did something that you now regret. I know that. I also know you're a not a common criminal, but a fine, strong young man, who wishes to do the righteous thing. So don't worry. I'll see to it that they don't hurt you."

The judge began to speak solemnly. "Listen, Israel! There is no Lord but the Lord our God, and you shall love the Lord your God with the love of your whole heart, and your whole soul, and your whole strength!" He looked around the room. "A criminal court must have three judges," he said, "for it is taught that no one alone may judge except the Almighty. Yet in exceptional cases, a single man may decide without colleagues or assessors, if the parties declare that they will accept the decision. Is there any objection?" There was none. "Then we may proceed. Hazzan, has the inquiry been completed?"

"It has, my Lord."

"Will the accuser please step forward?"

The hazzan walked over to the merchant and whispered something. The merchant took a single step towards the judge and said, "I, Bezalel the glass maker, am the accuser. This boy of the am ha'arez stole a fine glass baqbuq from my stall yesterday, worth four shekels, and then attempted to sell it in the marketplace."

He's lying, I thought. The baqbuq was worth no more than two shekels.

"If a second witness is present," the judge said, "will he please make his presence known."

"I, Manasas of Sepphoris, am the second witness. The thief attempted to sell the stolen merchandise to me."

The judge turned to me and asked, "What is your name, boy?"

"I am Jesus of . . . ," I began to say. I had almost said Nazareth. I paused, and pretended to cough. Perhaps I could save my family. "I am Jesus," I said, using the Greek form of my name. "Jesus, the carpenter."

"You are too young to be a carpenter."

"I am an apprentice, your honor."

"Who is your master?"

"He died a few months ago. I have had no teacher since. And no home."

"Indigent, as I suspected. Too bad." He looked down at several sheets of parchment that he had carried in with him. "Yesterday you were caught with a stolen decanter worth four shekels. We have learned that you have a long history of thievery." What was he talking about? "We know of nine other crimes you have committed. I will now read the indictment. Two days ago you stole three jars of honey from the stall of Gershon, worth eighty lepta. A week earlier you cut the purse of the merchant Zemach, which contained three shekels, four denari, and thirty lepta. On the seventeenth day of Shebat you stole six loaves of bread from the bakery of Abiram, worth thirty-six lepta . . ."

Lies! Lies! With each word my outrage grew. I shouted out, "I stole the decanter! Nothing more!"

"We'll take your confession later!" he barked back, his large eyebrows bristling in anger. "Do not speak until I have finished the indictment!" He sighed, looked at me sternly, as if I were an ungracious child, brushed his long hair out of his face, and then turned back to his papers. "On the fourteenth of Shebat you toppled and broke six bowls of pottery at the stand of Emach, worth three denari, and ran away before you could be identified. . . ."

"How could you know it was me if the thief couldn't be identified?"

I was incensed.

"Hazzan, silence the prisoner," he said in a calm voice.

Before I knew what was happening, my arm was wrenched behind my body and I was jerked around by the hazzan to stare into his grinning face. "Be silent, as the judge requests," he said quietly, emphasizing his will not with words, but with a slow cruel twist of my arm.

The judge went on with his list. "On the twenty fourth day of Tebeth you stole eight pairs of sandals from the shop of Lemeul the cobbler, . . ."

I stood there bewildered as the judge went on with his list. He finished, and then said, "You have been charged with the theft of goods valued at a total of fifteen shekels of silver. You were caught in the act of theft, and the evidence is overwhelming. Do you admit your guilt?"

"I stole only the baqbuq!"

The judge sighed. He looked plaintively to Manasas, who walked over to him. They exchanged a few whispers. Manasas walked back to me, took my arm away from the hazzan, gently brought it to my side, and then escorted me to the side of the room. "I strongly advise that you plead guilty," Manasas said to me.

"Only the baqbuq!" I sobbed. "It was the first—the only crime I ever committed. Never anything else. And it is worth only one shekel."

Manasas stroked his chin thoughtfully, frowned, and looked me in the eyes. I averted mine to the floor, as I still felt shame at being a criminal. "Son," he said, "I believe that you are a good Jew, but you are hopelessly naive. Let me explain to you how this works. Many petty crimes have been reported in Sepphoris in the last two months, for which the soldiers failed to apprehend the criminals. If you plead guilty to these acts, then the crimes are 'solved,' and the Roman governor will be pleased. You can help us with this, and in exchange, we'll help you. If you plead guilty, then I guarantee that your family will not have to pay a widow's mite in fine." He had correctly deduced my true fear.

I shuddered at his words. Although a scourging terrified me, I knew it would not last. But a fine would be disastrous. I didn't dare to think what my mother would do—or become, if she had to pay. Manasas had a kindly manner, and I decided to trust him. So I nodded. He took my arm again, and we walked together back to the judge.

"How do you plead?" asked the judge.

"I am guilty," I stammered.

"Good!" The judge sighed. "You are a smart fellow. You will wait in the prison while we determine your punishment."

It was over. The hazzan led me out of the room and put me in a small bare chamber with a heavy oak door. After just a few minutes, the door opened and I was brought back to the judge. The moneychanger and merchant were gone.

"Jesus, the carpenter's assistant, you have pleaded guilty to thefts totaling fifteen shekels of silver," the judge said sternly. It was an enormous sum, more than two months' wages for a skilled carpenter, more than a year of wages for me. "The Torah prescribes that the fine for this crime is twice the amount of the theft. Therefore, you are required to pay this court thirty shekels of silver. Half will be used to reimburse the merchants and other victims of your crimes, and the remainder shall go to this court, for our expenses."

These events crashed down on me so swiftly that I could not believe them. None of this could be happening. My head swam. I grew dizzy and I fainted.

My father was down by the stream. I cried out, "I thought you died!"

He looked at me and smiled. "No, Jesus, I was only ill. I'm well now." He was talking quietly, but I could hear him clearly. "Everything is well now. Your mother is back home. She's never going to leave again, and neither shall I." He bent down to collect water into a small wineskin.

Suddenly he looked old and frail. One side of his face was slack. No water flowed but he kept on trying. He scratched at the dirt in the streambed.

Several Roman soldiers appeared on the hillside. They started throwing rocks at him. One hit him on the head. He staggered, but kept on trying to gather water. Another stone hit him on his temple, and he started bleeding badly. His face, his clothing, all was soaked in bright red blood.

He called to me, "Jesus, stop them! Stop them!" I tried to run to him, but my feet were too heavy; they wouldn't budge. The soldiers were throwing more rocks, and laughing. I couldn't move anything but my eyes. More stones hit my father, and he collapsed. He was dying. The stream was flowing now, with his blood. The soldiers laughed louder. I frantically tried to move, but my legs were frozen in place. One soldier went down to my father, and lifted him up by his tunic. My father looked toward me with frightened and protruding eyes. His body was pulsating. "Jesus! Help me!" he cried. "Help me!" The soldier looked at me and laughed. It was Pantera. I was overwhelmed with helplessness and terror.

They were all gone, my father and the soldiers. I could move again. I walked down to the stream, which once again had water in it. The wineskin had been left behind. I picked it up, and dipped it in the stream. The water receded, sank away. From nowhere a soldier appeared at the hilltop and threw a rock at me. More soldiers came, and they too threw rocks. One hit me on the head and blood poured out. I wiped my head, and blood dripped from my hand. But then I realized that my wound didn't hurt. Another rock hit me on the face, but it didn't hurt either. The water in the stream was flowing more strongly through my feet. It felt cool between my toes. I dipped the wineskin, and it began to fill. The soldiers threw more rocks, and they hit me but I laughed.

When I woke I was back in the cell, once again chained to the column. I sat on the hard dirt floor in despair, fiddling with the iron manacle on my wrist. Gradually a little light entered the room from a small window near the ceiling. Soon I could hear the sounds of the awakening city. A wagon. People shouting. A donkey brayed. Several horses passed by. I almost imagined I could count them by the sounds of their hoofs. Close to the window I heard laughter. Laughter! Will I ever laugh again? Do those people outside realize the joy they have? Do they know how quickly it can be shattered? I listened to the people laughing, the happy people of Sepphoris. Happy? This was the city destroyed by the Romans. How could they be laughing?

The gay sounds of the outside world made stark the misery of my plight. I was cut off, adrift from my family, with no hope that I would ever see them again. Indeed, I prayed that I would never see them again, and that they would never learn of my fate. I felt as if a tide were sucking me into an alien and hostile sea, and I couldn't call for help. Nobody could help. I was overwhelmed by despair and loneliness.

A few hours later I was taken back to the judge. "Please tell this court how you plan to pay the fine," he demanded. I felt that I was being led along a prescribed path, and everyone seemed to know where it led except me.

"I am destitute," I said. "That was why I stole."

He went on, as if reading from a script. "Since you cannot pay, you will be sold as a slave, and the payment will used as restitution to those who have suffered from your crime. But the Lord our God is a merciful God. He has prescribed in the Torah that you must be released in your sabbatical year. You will be sold for six years of servitude," the judge said.

A violent shudder shook my body. I fell to the floor sobbing. I was trapped by my own evil, and I deserved no mercy, not even from the Lord.

6. Slavery

RUFUS WAS NAKED, EXCEPT FOR THE IRON WRIST SHACKLES. A crowd had gathered to watch, and he stood close to the post to hide himself as best he could. How pitiful, I thought, that in a few minutes he will likely be dead, and yet he worries now about his nakedness.

I had been forced to watch three scourgings before this one, but this was the first of someone I had worked with, someone I had grown close to. I knew what would happen, all too well. With the first lash would come that hideous scream. By the second or third stroke Rufus would be hanging helplessly from his shackles like a lamb being butchered. After the fifth stroke he would no longer be capable of screaming. And by the tenth his blood would splatter on any spectator who foolishly stood too close.

As noon approached the crowd grew larger, mostly local Jews of Sepphoris who came to help inflame their own hatred of the Romans. They brought their children, and whispered to them, *See the gentiles beat the Jews! Never forget what you witness here. If I do not see justice in my life, then you must see it in yours, and if you do not, then you must teach your children that they must, and they must teach theirs.* And so on, to the third and fourth generation, I thought.

Unlike the families, I was not there out of choice, but because my master wanted me to witness again the punishment for attempted escape. Well, he could force me to attend, and force me to face the scourging, but he couldn't control my eyes. I averted my gaze from Rufus and focused instead on the Roman soldier. To inspire terror in the victim, and anticipation in the crowd, he had begun orbiting the scourge over his head, trying to make the leather thongs whistle. My father had said that the cruel suffer more than their victims, and that I could see this if I looked hard enough.

Rufus's scream came tearing through the air as the thirty-nine barbs of brass and bone ripped across his back. The soldier smiled, then paused, as if to give Rufus a chance to recover, in order to keep him conscious for as long as possible. Again the scourge whistled in the air. The second scream wasn't the same, for Rufus's energy had already been spent. It came out more as a howl or wail. The lashes continued, the screams died completely, and the only sound was the sickening one of shredding flesh. With his victim now quiet, the soldier worked faster to finish, one stroke after another, as if he were chopping a tree. I looked hard but I could see no pain in the soldier's eyes as he completed his deadly work. Had my father been wrong? Or had I failed to look deeply enough?

Rufus was removed from the post and then dumped in the slave quarters for us to tend. I stood over his shredded back, anxious to do something to help him, to stop the pain, to stop the bleeding, to do anything, but Rufus had become conscious, and at my slightest touch he gasped in agony. There must be something I could do, but what? None of the other slaves knew either. Never before had I felt so powerless, so desperately helpless. I promised myself, someday, somehow, I must learn how to heal.

Our master knew we could do nothing other than watch Rufus slowly die. Better for the final agony to be witnessed up close by the slaves, he reasoned, for it to serve its purpose.

My religion offered me no comfort. Why had the Lord allowed Rufus to suffer so? His crimes—a petty theft like mine, followed by attempted escape—had these so offended the Lord that this savage punishment was just? And if it was not retribution from the Lord, then why did he permit it?

As a child, my only experience with true evil had been the destruction of Sepphoris, and Rabbi Shuwal had called it an evil city. But I had known Rufus. He had been a good man.

❖ ❖ ❖

I was now fifteen years old, nearly a year older than my mother had been at my birth. I had been purchased by Manasas, the moneychanger, who traded in slaves as well as money. To him I was a commodity, to be exchanged for profit. While Manasas waited for a wealthy buyer, he put me to work under Roman supervision in the continuing reconstruction of Sepphoris. Out of the rubble and ashes were arising alien structures, columns, and buildings in the pagan style to obliterate all evidence of the old Jewish city. And I was to help.

I was set to work hauling stones to the cutters, loading and unloading them from carts and sledges. The sharp edges of the stone cut my hands; the gritty dust choked my eyes; the constant *ping ping ping* of the chisels hurt my ears. Stone has none of the gentleness of wood. My back ached with the weight, and by afternoon my arm muscles quivered with exhaustion. I sought relief in fantasizing that I was dragging stones not in Sepphoris, but in Egypt under Rameses.

But my physical distress was nothing to my fear that Thomas or James or my mother would come to the city and see me, or that someone else from Nazareth would learn of my fate and tell them. And every thought of my family brought back the almost unbearable anguish of loneliness.

It was then that my father would return to me. Not physically, but in my thoughts. Yet the image was so clear that it could have been real. My memories surprised me. Surrounded by the grit of stone, I thought of wood.

"Feel this backrest," my father said to me. He was repairing a chair made from hillside oak, a far fancier piece of furniture than we ourselves would ever own. He had just spent half an hour polishing it with pumice cloth. I gently rubbed my fingertips over it. "How does it feel?" he asked.

"Soft," I said.

"And yet isn't it also hard?"

I rapped my fingertips against it. "Yes, it is," I said, with a degree of wonder, and I smiled at the paradox. "How did you do that?"

"I didn't do it. It's in the wood itself. The wood is naturally hard, full of roughness and splinters, like many people, but if you show enough care, you can entice out the softness. That's part of our job, as carpenters."

❖ ❖ ❖

I was fortunate that I was young and strong and I could keep most of the guards satisfied with my work. In contrast, an old slave named Gideon was barely capable of lifting the heavy stones, and I had seen him savagely beaten across his legs with a stick for nothing more than dropping a stone that was too heavy. Once I ran to help as he teetered under the weight of a large piece. Together we managed to move the stone to a cart, and I returned to my own stones, but not before a guard noticed that I had left my own work.

"You are not to leave without permission!" The guard struck me hard across my cheek with his mail-covered fist. I fell to the ground in pain. Blood dribbled from my mouth onto my hand. Hatred flared within me, and my muscles tightened. I remembered the savage crucifixions, the brutal beating of Rufus, the systematic destruction of Sepphoris. The soldier wouldn't expect me, a slave, to attack him. I looked up at him. Could I get past his armor? His neck appeared vulnerable. I trembled in anticipation.

No. That's the kind of attack that he's trained to counter. I must act when he is not expecting it. Misdirection. Wait as long as necessary for him to forget. I won't forget. Even if I have to wait for years.

Suddenly I saw my father standing next to the old Samaritan. The image was so clear and luminous that it was not so much a memory as a vision. My father's hands were at his sides, to show he would not resist the rocks thrown from above. He offered himself as a sacrifice. I understood what he was doing, as I had never understood as a child. Not only would he save the Samaritan from the stones, but he would also save the boys from their cruelty. Then my father spoke to me, as he had on our rooftop. 'The Romans will use whatever force is necessary, Jesus. That is how they control the world. They seek your hatred. But to hate them is to be poisoned by their spiritual illness."

These visions had appeared instantly, taking no time. The soldier stood in front of me. I looked deep into his eyes, searching for any hint of the pain that must be there. Keeping my eyes on his, I struggled to my feet. Was this giant of a man only an ignorant boy throwing stones at a helpless Jew? I thought I saw something behind his face. Simultaneously my hatred faded, like dew in the morning sun. My cheek still stung, but the pain seemed unimportant now.

"Get to work or I'll hit you again!" Even though I was only an arm's length away, he shouted his threat. He was like a boy, hiding behind armor. I looked at him with compassion. "I warn you!" he said.

Without a thought, as if I were being guided directly by the Lord, I turned my face slightly and offered my other cheek for the soldier to strike, while continuing to look at him gently. He stared back at me with a wild look, as if in fear. Somehow I knew exactly what he was thinking. He had seen me help the other slave. He knew that I had done the righteous thing. He was a soldier and was supposed to be cruel. He should strike me again. We both knew that that was his job.

The blow came so swiftly that I never saw it. My head crashed to the ground and the world spun. This sensation in my head, this sensation that I normally called pain, was just a sensation. I chose to ignore it. Although I was dizzy, I forced myself up, struggling to my feet, and once again looked squarely back at the man's face. I felt sadness for him, this cruel human who was hurting himself more than he was hurting me. I turned my cheek to him, the one that he had first struck, not as a dare, but as an offering. Force accomplishes nothing, I thought to him. Try love. Could he hear my thoughts? They come from my father in heaven.

The soldier was shaking now, afraid. I could see his spiritual pain, and he knew I could see it. I awaited another blow, perhaps one that would disable me—or kill me. Instead, the soldier turned and walked away. I collapsed on the ground.

Someone was squirting water on my face. I opened my eyes—it was Gideon. He gently moved my head onto his lap and helped me rinse out my mouth. Then he tore a strip of cloth from his meager shirt and wrapped it around my jaw. He said nothing, but he helped me walk back to my tent and then disappeared. Nobody interfered.

That evening my jaw was aching and my head was throbbing. It isn't so easy to ignore a pain that endures. Gideon came and sat down next to me. "Here, I've brought you your dinner. Would you like me to mash it for you?" he asked. I nodded, and he took two round stones from his pocket, expertly crushed the barley bread between them, and mixed it with the soup. "Now you won't have to chew. May I sit here with you?"

"Of course," I mumbled through my swollen mouth. Gideon curled his thin legs under himself and sat down on the dirt. His bread was already mixed with his soup. I looked at his gaunt, leathery face and saw that he was toothless.

"That guard almost killed you," he said.

"You needed help. You're too old to be loading stones. It's stupid for them to make you do that."

"Smart or stupid, I still thank you." He paused. "I was a tax collector," he said, as if it were a confession.

"Yes, I know." I had heard that he had been enslaved for cheating the Romans. None of the other Jews would have anything to do with him.

"Yet you don't ask me to leave?" he said. "The Pharisees say I'm unclean."

"They're hypocrites," I said. "We're all sinners, and the Pharisees are among the worst."

"I don't understand why the soldier stopped beating you," he said.

"It's painful to beat someone who doesn't hate you."

"You don't hate the Romans?"

"I did. But something happened today. Gideon—that guard, that Roman guard, is a man like you and me. Look into his eyes, if you can. He was created by the Lord. He feels pain and suffering, just as you do."

"He doesn't feel pain. He makes pain."

"No, Gideon, he suffers too. He was raised to fight, and he detests doing anything else. Rome has conquered the world, and there are few battles left, so now soldiers are just building roads and aqueducts. He is a slave too, Gideon, just like us. He is doing a job he hates, just as we are, but he is even farther away from his own people. Even worse, he is a slave working for slaves, for it's the Greek architects who tell him what to do. Today, Gideon, today as he was beating me, I felt sadness for that soldier."

His incredulity was almost palpable. "A Jew with compassion for the Romans?" he whispered, staring at me with wonder. "For the man who beat you . . . ?" he muttered.

Even through my swollen face I sensed that, for the first time, that I was smiling my father's wry smile, the one that had always annoyed me. "It's easy to love your family and to hate your enemies," I said. "Who pleases the Lord more, the man who does what is easy, and loves only those who are kind to him, or the man who loves all of the Lord's creations, even those who persecute him?"

Gideon's face was filled with skepticism, wonder, and awe. Deep in his eyes I could see *his* soul. And maybe, I thought, I had touched it.

7. Magus

IT WASN'T LONG BEFORE I WAS SOLD. MY NEW MASTER WAS A Babylonian named Darius, who was gathering a team of slaves and freemen to work on the large aqueduct that the Romans were building to bring water to the palm groves north of Jerusalem. I was still fearful that my mother would learn of my fate, so I was grateful to be taken away from Sepphoris.

Darius was a kind master; he rarely beat us, and we usually had enough food to keep us healthy. He told us that rested servants worked better than exhausted ones, but in return for decent treatment he expected hard work. That was fine with me. The harder I worked, the easier it was for me to forget. We joined a large number of other workers, most of whom were prisoners of war. We all lived together in a large campground on a flat near the road. The project was to take several years, so we built large tents covered with tanned ramskins to give us protection. I shared a tent with old Gideon, who had been purchased along with me and ten other slaves.

I told Darius that I had been a carpentry apprentice, and soon I was put to work sawing the wooden frames and chiseling the ends so that they would fit snugly with each other. It was good to be working with wood rather than stone, even though the wood was only pine. I lost myself in the work. In the evening I carved small trinkets, little replicas of the aqueduct bridge that we were building, and I was able to sell these to the Roman soldiers. With practice, my carving skills quickly improved. With plenty of hard work, a return to wood, a lenient master, and money in my belt, I felt almost happy.

One night I had the dream again—the same dream, yet different. My father was trying to gather water. He was old, his skin was like leather, and he had no teeth. A centurion in full armor twirled a scourge above his head, and the leather straps grew longer and longer—until they reached my father and lashed him repeatedly on the back. My father was thrown from side to side with each stroke, as if he were a leaf. "That was twenty!" the centurion shouted. I tried to cry out for him to stop, but words would not leave my lips. The soldier kept beating, and warm blood splattered my face. I couldn't shout and I couldn't move. Forty lashes. He will die.

Then, again, I was in his place, surrounded by soldiers. I was on a cross; there were nails through my wrists and my feet. I must bend down to gather water, I thought. My salvation depends on gathering the water. But I could not move. The barbs of the scourge lashed across my chest, across my face, across my eyes. Suddenly I realized, they do not hurt! My eyes had been lacerated, but I could still see. I looked at my wrists, at the nails that penetrated them, and I pulled my wrists off. They can do nothing to me. I bent over from the cross and collected water in a wineskin. The soldiers grew angrier and angrier, and struck me with greater ferocity, but their blows did not hurt.

I awoke. The tent was dark and cold and surrounded by sounds: the snores of the other slaves, the flapping of the leather of the tent in the winter wind, the occasional yelping of a jackal in the hills, and the thumping of my heart.

The next morning, I described the dream to Gideon who had been sold to Darius along with me. "I don't know the meaning," he said, "but there is a man here who understands dreams. I'll take you to him."

I had known that there was a magus among the slaves, but had not known who it was or why he was there. Despite my father's contempt for the magi, I was curious to meet one, particularly if he could explain my dream. Gideon led me through the chilly darkness to a tent about a hundred feet from ours. Hanging on the outside were a strange collection of trinkets, polished stones, and strips of metal with symbols or letters on them that I didn't recognize, religious symbols of Judaism, and of Greek and Roman paganism. I reached to touch a red one that seemed to glow even in the starlight, but Gideon pulled my hand away. "Stones of Zarathustra!" he cautioned. "They might carry a curse." He directed at the tent a few words that sounded Persian, and from within came a reply, also in words I didn't understand. Gideon stepped through, tugging my sleeve to go with him.

Inside, the tent was dark and filled with the sweet smell of frankincense. As my eyes adjusted, I could see the magus in the darkness, a small man sitting in front of a little fire. In the flickering yellow light I could barely make out his pale skin, his narrow nose, and thin lips. He seemed small and unusually delicate for a slave. Despite the large size of the tent, nobody else seemed to be there.

The magus began to chant, "At every offering to your fire, I will bethink me of right so long as I have power." He repeated this twice, and then sat staring into the small flames. I felt awkward, not knowing what to do, but Gideon gestured to me to be patient. Gradually I became accustomed to the darkness. I thought I saw sparks shooting in the eyes of the magus, but I decided that I was only seeing reflections of the fire.

Finally the magus looked up at me and rested his eyes on my face, studying it with compassion, like you might study a wounded fawn in the wilderness. "You are here because you are troubled," the magus said to me solemnly, his tone not that of a questioner but of someone simply stating a fact. "Please, sit down in front of the sacred fire. It will soothe your spirit."

It will also warm me, I thought. The magus pointed to a small scarlet pillow opposite the fire from him, and I sat down. He seemed to slip into a trance. His long straight hair flowed over his elaborate shirt, made of fine twisted linen strips held together by bronze hooks. How could a slave have such a magnificent shirt? The tent too was bedecked in a wealth of possessions. Bits of metal hung from strands of wool and hair. Two small pyramids sat on a short table, along with a collection of carved animals. These forbidden graven images held a particular fascination for me. There was a lion, a bull, and a wolf, as well as several fanciful creatures: one with a neck as long as its body, another similar to a horse but with black and white stripes, presumably creatures from Persian myths. I continued looking around the tent, and then turned back to the magus. My heart jumped when I saw that he had been watching me.

"You are lonely," he said. "You are confused and do not know what to do." Again, it was just a statement of fact. He stared into the fire again, and seemed to reenter his trance. Suddenly his sonorous tones filled the tent. "I humbly pray with outstretched hands for the grace of God's holy spirit that my actions to all may be righteous and that I may gain the wisdom of love by which I may comfort the spirit of my visitor." Though my grief had been numbed by months of hard labor, my tears threatened at the beauty of this phrase.

He opened a small bag, shook it gently, and a small silver ring rolled out and settled onto the swept ground in front of the fire. Silver jewelry? He looked hard at my face and shook the bag again. A small carved bone fell out. It had an odd shape, vaguely like . . . a phallus. No, it must be something else. A third shake yielded a small rolled scroll. And with a fourth shake a small glass amulet came out. I hadn't seen glass since I stole the baqbuq. My attention was riveted on it.

I looked up into the magus's eyes. He was a pale old man, but even by firelight I could see that his eyes were a deep, piercing blue. They seemed to reach directly into my soul. With his wiry thumb and forefinger, he picked up the glass and rotated it slowly. "This amulet holds special meaning . . . for you," he said, again simply stating a fact. He held the amulet up for my inspection. An image of the flickering fire seemed to be trapped inside it. I could feel my heart pounding. "I see love in here," he said, as he stared hard into the amulet, "but it is unhappy love." Could he mean my love for my mother, or for my father, or for Thomas? I was silent. "I see illness," he said.

"That must be the death of my father," I said. I looked harder into the amulet, wondering if I could see it too.

"His death caused great problems."

"Yes . . . great problems." Out of shame, I didn't want him to go further. "Magus," I said, "I have had a recurring dream. Can you tell me the meaning of it?"

"I cannot, but perhaps the divine fire can. Give me your hand." He directed it to a position directly over the fire. The heat was just short of painful. "Now relate the dream," he said, "omitting nothing, no matter how insignificant, or your hand will burn." I described the dream. The heat of the flame brought back details that I had forgotten.

"The meaning of the dream is in the glass," he said. Again he held the amulet between the fire and me. "Look into the glass with me. Look deep. Look hard."

I stared into the glass. The image of the flame seemed to change color. It grew dim and then bright again. Images seemed to move on top of the fire. The magus slowly moved the glass between his fingers.

"I can see your dream in the glass," he said. "I can see your father and you. The image is shifting. I can see within the dream. There is a glow, deep in the glass, within the image. It is the soul of the dream. It is coming out into the room. I can feel it." He paused, and I stared harder and harder into the glass, trying to see what he saw. "Yes, here is the deep meaning," he said, as if recounting it as it unrolled to him. "The death of your father while he was gathering water . . . means that he died before his work was completed. When you moved down to the stream and gathered the water, it meant that his spirit is alive within you. You are in your father's place. His soul has become your soul. You are destined to do the work your father never finished." His voice softened. "The barbs of the scourge hit you but you felt no pain. This means that if you follow your father's true destiny, you will not fail. You cannot fail. His mission will be fulfilled. Your spirit will be invulnerable."

"But what was it? *What* was the destiny of my father?" I asked, excitedly.

"The glass does not answer that question. The image weakens."

I felt somewhat dizzy. Regardless of the pagan methods this magus employed, he had somehow found the truth—I could feel that in my heart. I would fulfill the destiny of my father.

✧ ✧ ✧

It was several weeks later, deep in the night, when I accidentally stumbled and awoke Gideon. "Jesus? What are you doing at this hour? Are you ill?" he asked.

"No, Gideon, go back to sleep. I'm bringing water to Melech, the Ethiopian." That afternoon Melech had been lashed for "laziness." In fact he had been not lazy, but ill, and now he was suffering from both the fever and the beating.

"Again? You can't spend all your nights tending the ill, Jesus! You need sleep."

"This is better than sleep, Gideon."

"Leave Melech be. Cushites aren't worthy of attention. And you'll get sick yourself. That's how people die—caring for others."

"Why do you care so much for me, Gideon?"

"I *don't* care for you. I just want to sleep."

"I'm sorry. I'll try to be quieter."

He turned over on his mat. "That old magus, Simon, has some medicines," he muttered.

I went directly to the tent of the magus and called quietly at the entrance. "Simon, Simon Magus? It is Jesus the carpenter."

His answer startled me: "Enter, Jesus of Nazareth." I had told *nobody* at the camp of my origins.

"Melech has a fever," I said. Simon Magus opened his eyes wide, leaned up from his mat, and looked at me intently, as if he thought me insane. "Do you have medicine?" I asked.

"Does Melech have a rash?"

"Yes, on his chest."

"Are you certain that it's only on his chest?"

"Yes. I helped him wash."

"Does he breathe easily?"

"Yes."

"How long has he been ill?"

"It came on two days ago. At first there was just dizziness. Then today he was beaten. But the rash frightens him. He thinks it leprosy."

"What nonsense. It's only the wilderness fever. It usually lasts three days. By morning it will be gone, vanished as quickly as it struck. Here." He poured a small amount of greenish-yellow powder out of a little bag onto my hand. "Mix it with water and have him drink it. Tell him that the power of Ahura Mazda will drive the evil demon from his soul."

"If he will get well anyway, why should I say that?"

"Just say it. He'll get well quicker if he believes you've driven away the demon. The medicine will reduce the fever tonight and make him more comfortable—so he'll sleep better. Much of the art of curing is simply making people more comfortable while waiting for them to recover on their own."

I went back to Melech. He was now lying on a mat outside his tent, where he had been forced by the other slaves, who feared the spread of his fever. I put the powder into the water and held his head up so he could drink.

"Jesus, you came back! I was sure you had abandoned me. I am dying," he said.

"Drink this water," I said matter-of-factly. "It has medicine in it—from the magus. You'll live."

"Even a man of God can't save me," moaned Melech.

"The magus is not a man of God. But be confident—you'll recover."

"I didn't mean the magus, Jesus. I meant you—you are a man of God. But he is punishing me for eating unclean food." I had noticed that the religion of the Cushites was very similar to Judaism—although what they considered unclean was different. "I've shared meals with Phoenicians and Bataneaeans," he moaned, "and I didn't make the sacrifices. Now God has sent the fever. I'm going to die."

"No you won't Melech. In the morning you will be well. The power of . . . the Lord will drive the evil demon from your soul. You are blessed, Melech. Now go to sleep." The drug, whatever it was, began to work, and soon he was snoring loudly.

The next day Melech's fever was gone, and he went to work. I looked for some opportunity to talk to the magus and I found it that afternoon. "Thank you for the medicine," I said, while being watchful for the guards lest they notice us talking.

"Don't worry about the guards, Jesus. Darius has told them to leave me alone. But there's no need for gratitude," the magus replied. "The medicine wasn't for you."

"Melech says that I performed a miracle. He thinks I saved his life. I told him otherwise, but he doesn't believe me."

"Who is to say what is a miracle?"

That is just what my father would have said, I thought to myself.

The magus continued, "Haoma will reduce fever and pain, but it won't cure a serious illness. I'll give you more when you need it."

"What is haoma? Where does it come from?"

"That is knowledge that I may not share. Pure haoma is exceedingly dangerous, and its source is a secret that only the magi may know."

"Then why did you trust me with the medicine?"

"There aren't many men who would give up their rest to help a Cushite," he replied. "Good thought is strong in you, Jesus. And it is through good thought that Ahura Mazda will achieve righteous order in the world."

"Ahura Mazda? You used that name last night. Is he your god?"

"Ahura Mazda is a title, not a name. It means 'Wise Lord.' There is only one God, the God of the moral and natural order. It's the same God as your Jewish Jehovah, your *Yahweh*. His wisdom was revealed to us through the great prophet Zarathustra."

How ironic, I thought. In my words to Melech I had righteously substituted the words "the Lord" where the magus had said "Ahura Mazda," and now I learned they meant the same thing. "But I thought Zarathustra was the god you magi worshipped."

"Yes, yes, many Jews think that. But we no more worship Zarathustra than you Jews worship Moses. Zarathustra was the greatest of the prophets. During his youth, he was full of compassion for the weak and poor." He looked at me and smiled. "Much like you, Jesus. You would make your father proud, the way you worry over the other slaves."

"You seem to know much more about my religion than I know about yours."

"It was revealed to Zarathustra that there is only one God and that he is a righteous God. And there is only one true religion—the religion of righteousness. Men have sought this religion since the beginning of the world, but their constructs have been only weak shadows of it. Some shadows show more of the form than others do, but each shows something. So we magi have studied all religions, and from each we have learned something—something about the essence of God and how he wishes us to worship him."

I soon discovered that regardless of the injury or illness, Simon Magus had some remedy. One day I asked him, "Did you study medicine with the Greeks?"

"No, no!" he laughed. "Their knowledge of medicine is greatly over-rated. They know much about pharmaceuticals, and they know how to stitch flesh and set bones, but they don't really understand illness. Their book of medicine is called *On Sacred Disease,* written by an ancient named Hippocrates over four centuries ago. It's hopelessly archaic, but the Greeks still follow it slavishly. It supposes that many illnesses are caused by demons, and it prescribes more and less efficacious means for driving them out."

"Most Jews believe that illness is punishment from the Lord."

"Yes, I know, Jesus. Most Jews think illness is punishment for sin, so to use medicine is to counter God's will. It is the cruelest part of Judaism, a deep flaw in an otherwise profound religion. Your Scriptures prescribe some treatments, but they are hardly more than prayers, and even less effective than those in the book of Hippocrates. That's why there are so few Jewish physicians, and never will be. The magi have learned much, culled from the healing practices of many peoples. What I have shown you is only a drop in the sea of knowledge of healing."

"Where did you learn?"

"At the greatest academy of all, the Academy of Zarathustra in Babylon."

Babylon? It was the city the Jews were sent to in exile, after Nebuchadnessar destroyed Jerusalem. It was the city where God sent us in punishment for idolatry. Babylon! No other city was so despised by Jews. An academy of healing, in Babylon?

One Sabbath, the magus and I sat in his tent and shared a meal of bar-ley bread and soup. "Aren't you bothered," he asked, "to eat with one who, according to your religion, is not clean?"

"Oh, no, Simon. No one is unclean, not the am ha'arez, not the gen-tiles. Not even the Pharisees, although if anyone were unclean it would be them. Certainly not slaves, or others who have suffered like slaves. Suffering may be punishment for sins, but God makes us suffer only because it purifies us, Simon. Suffering atones for sins."

"Eloquently said, Jesus. Did you learn that from your father too?"

"About suffering? I never understood suffering, not while he was alive."

The magus said nothing. There were a few moments of silence. I finally found the courage to bring up the subject that I had never discussed with anyone. "I was once possessed by an evil spirit," I said.

"Mmmm?" He continued eating, as if I had not just bared my soul. He swallowed. "And what did *that* feel like?" he asked.

"Not like I expected. I thought it would be painful, but it wasn't. It was exhilarating. I sinned, and yet I felt good," I said. "I committed a crime. It was premeditated. I enjoyed planning it, I enjoyed doing it. I liked the excitement."

"What was it you did?"

"I stole glass baqbuq from the market in Sepphoris. I was caught and was too poor to pay the fine."

"Ah! So *that* is why you reacted so strongly to the glass amulet when we first met!"

"The amulet—yes. I've wondered about that a thousand times. What magic does it possess?" I asked. "The power of God, or of Zarathustra, or of Satan? What magic let you see my dream in the glass?"

Simon stopped eating and smiled. "There was no magic in the amulet, Jesus. I had a collection of a dozen trinkets in my bag. I pulled them out one at a time until I found one that had meaning for you. The pupils of your eyes were as large as the cisterns of Jerusalem when you saw that glass. I knew then that it had special significance to you, so I used it as the focus for the rest of our little seance."

I was astonished, disbelieving. "But you knew about my father, about my dreams! You seemed to know all about me before I entered the tent."

"No, I knew nothing about you other than you were coming to see me. That meant that you had some problem and were seeking help. The most common problems have to do with love, money, or health. I went through each of these, as with the trinkets, until you reacted to one. It is a standard trick. I didn't tell you anything. You told me."

"You were just doing magic?"

"Of course. We magi are famous for it. It's the art of illusion. What I did that evening is called 'mind reading.' It's no miracle, just a skill, and one that can be learned. But I wasn't trying to trick you, Jesus. I was trying to help you. I did it in a righteous cause."

"And how did you know I came from Nazareth?"

"That was harder, Jesus. But I learned you had been arrested in Sepphoris. I know that area—I spent several months there. Your accent told me you came from a small village. I pieced it together from your habits, your way of dressing, the kind of foods you ate."

Why is he explaining his secrets to me, I wondered. But I was also bothered by the fact that I had been so easily fooled. Trying to cover my resentment, I asked, "How could deceit be *righteous?*"

"There is not a religion in the world that has not at some time used magic to attract followers. Some have used it for evil, for power, for control. The righteous use it only for good."

"Jews have never used magic," I corrected. "The Torah, transcribed by Moses himself, prohibits it." Simon's smile conveyed that I wasn't saying anything that he didn't already know. "We Jews hold magic in contempt."

"Contempt?" he said, with the annoying smile of my father. "Yes, Jews hold magic in contempt. I know that." He picked at his food, dipping the hard black bread into the soup to soften it.

After a period of quiet, he broke the silence. "A moment ago you were wondering why I was telling you my secrets. You are right to wonder. I wonder myself. In all my long life, I've told no other Jew. You are a very special person, Jesus. You have a compassionate nature. This quality is not easy to find in anyone, young or old. The slaves call you a man of God— yes, yes I know you don't like it when they do—but they are right, Jesus. I have never met anyone so caring about the dregs of mankind. But even a man of God can benefit from training."

8. The Red Tent

MELECH HAD A SLY SMILE. "COME, JESUS, FINALLY I CAN REPAY you for saving my life." He beckoned with his hand. I got up from my mat and followed him, my curiosity piqued.

We walked outside, through the warren of paths in the crowded campsite towards the hillside where the soldiers were stationed. I couldn't guess where we were going. But as we walked past the Roman quarters, suddenly I realized we were heading for the red tent. I stopped.

"Melech, I . . ."

"You don't have to thank me, Jesus," he said. He took my elbow in his hand, and urged me forward, as if my reluctance were due to his generosity rather than from my own fear. "Since I recovered I've saved all my money from selling trinkets. Finally I can pay you back for your miracle! Don't be shy. I know this is new to you. It will give me great pleasure to be the one who made it possible."

"Melech, you owe me nothing! There was no miracle, I've told you that. I only gave you medicine from the magus. This is unnecessary!"

But Melech persisted, and I followed, out of politeness, I thought to myself. Yet there was also an instinct pushing me forward, more than just curiosity. I became intensely aware of my own body, as if my sense of touch had become heightened. I could feel the skin of my chest and shoulders rubbing against the cloth of my tunic as I walked. My heart seemed to be beating harder.

The red tent was visited primarily by the soldiers, but I had heard that anyone who could pay was welcomed there. Sitting in front was Rahab, an older, heavy woman. I had often seen her around the camps, but hadn't realized her profession. "Welcome, welcome!" she said. "Please wait here a moment while I gather my children." She went into the tent.

"She is rounding up the available girls," Melech explained. "They live in small tents hidden behind this one. Many of the soldiers are away now, so you should have a good selection."

Rahab reappeared at the entrance to the tent. "Now, please come in," she said.

Inside the light was dim, but I could see six women sitting on a bench. I was guided to a padded chair. Flushed with embarrassment, I looked at each of them. Their clothing was loose, partially open in the front. Their faces were grotesquely painted, with heavy dark lines making false eyebrows, and blue and even green blotches on their eyelids. Their lips were smeared thickly with red, and their heads covered with yellow wigs. Their exaggerated smiles seemed as phony as their hair. Sympathy and revulsion warred within me, and embarrassment gave way to desperation. How could I escape?

"Children, introduce yourselves," Rahab requested, and they recited their names: Rebecca, Delilah, Naomi, Sarah, Jezebel and Tamar. "Pick one," Rahab said, as if I were to choose a fish at market. Unable to think of a way out without humiliating both myself and all the women, I pointed to Tamar, who seemed less painted and perhaps more innocent than the others. She forced a big but tired smile, pushed herself from the bench, took my hand, and led me out of the red tent.

I followed her through an array of small black tents. From the sounds emanating from some of these, it was clear that other children of Rahab were busy at their work. Tamar led me to a tent near the end of the row. There was no lamp, and the only light came from small slits in the fabric. She put her hands on my shoulders, and guided me down to a mat on the floor.

"What shall I play?" she asked, with a false coyness. "The lover? The virgin? Or the harlot?"

"Do what you are paid to do," I said, surprising myself with the coldness of my words. It was a strange spirit inside me that was compelling me onward. This was me, but not a part of me that I understood.

My eyes adjusted to the dim light, and I watched Tamar with curiosity, almost detachment, as she showed me what women do to please men. Yet I received little pleasure from her actions. I watched almost as if it were not my body that was involved, as if I were witnessing an event that I was not truly participating in, as if my flesh were detached from my spirit.

Afterwards I didn't even want to look at her. We lay together on her mat, and I held her against me, to apologize for my callousness, to convey some sense of tenderness, to tell her that she had done her job well and that I was satisfied, even though I wasn't. But she seemed to be a thousand miles away.

I sensed that I had done something that men are supposed to do, perhaps something that I could not resist doing. There is no injunction in the Scriptures against lying with a harlot. Yet somehow I felt as if I had sinned.

9. The Red Sea

ON THE PLATEAU THE AIR WAS ALMOST TOO HOT TO BREATHE. The lizards and snakes were in retreat under the rocks—only men challenged the merciless sun. Like the other slaves, I wore wrapped around my head a goat-hair cloth that served as a mask, in the manner of the Bedouins, to protect my eyes from the knife-like glare. Camels were in constant motion bringing water to the flat area where we worked, but there was never enough.

Our work on the aqueduct progressed rapidly. The channel almost reached to the edge of the plateau, where it would join with the many-arched bridge that crossed the chasm. How odd, I mused, that we build a bridge not to cross water but to carry it. I lifted my pickax above my head and swung it down smoothly, crashing its iron head into the limestone. Just a year ago, I remembered, I was tormented by blisters. But now my hands were as tough as the knees of the camels. Simon worked near me, gathering the chipped rock to be hauled off in wagons. He had arranged to have me assigned to the same work team as him. I marveled at the influence he held over our owner, and I enjoyed the freedom, for this group had the most lenient of taskmasters. Still, I worked hard and I liked feeling my body grow stronger.

It was on this scorching day, as I stood stretching my back, that I glanced into the distant desert and saw a shimmering on the horizon. I adjusted my mask to see better. A wide blue lake glimmered in the otherwise dry landscape.

"Simon!" I shouted. "Water! Look!" I rubbed my eyes in amazement. "That must be the Great Sea of the Setting Sun!"

"That's not the Great Sea, Jesus," he said with a wry smile. "It's the Red Sea."

Simon was jesting, but I didn't understand the joke. "The Red Sea is over a hundred miles away, Simon. It must be the Great Sea. But . . . how could we see it from here?"

"Jesus, you told me that you traveled to Egypt as a child. Have you never seen Satan's water?"

"Oh. Yes, of course. Satan's water." To recover my dignity, I just recited what my father had taught: "Satan's water is just an illusion, a reflection of the sky on the ground, made when heat makes it reflect like metal. It has nothing to do with Satan. People just call it that because you can never reach it."

"Persians call it 'desert silver.' To me it is one of the great beauties and mysteries of the desert." He stopped work for a moment to watch the shimmering.

I worked for a while and pondered my confusion. "Why did you say that it was the Red Sea?" I finally asked.

The magus turned his strange blue eyes towards me. "Jesus," he said, "what do you think would happen if we walked right into that water?"

"We'd never reach it. As we walked, it would get further and further away."

"But suppose that we were entering a large desert and we saw this large sea in front of us. What would we see as we crossed the desert? What would the water do? Where would it appear?"

I looked at the shimmer and imagined us walking across the hot sand and rock. "I guess it would be on all sides of us," I answered.

"Exactly right! Think about that. See it in your mind. As we enter the desert, the sea goes back as if driven by a wind, and the waters are divided, and you walk into the midst of what had been the sea but now is dry land. In the distance you see a wall of water beyond your right hand, and a wall of water beyond your left."

I knew the book of Exodus by heart, and the magus was quoting it nearly verbatim. "Are you suggesting that Moses never split the Red Sea, but only split an illusion?" I said, incredulously.

"Jesus, the Jews didn't have to cross the Red Sea, or any other large body of water, to escape the Egyptians—only some marshes and the desert."

"But the Jews would have known about Satan's water!" I countered. "They wouldn't have been fooled so easily." The idea was completely absurd. I was annoyed and a bit indignant at this attack on my religion.

"You were fooled just now," he said, "and yet you knew about it. Of course Moses knew about Satan's water. He had crossed the desert many times. But few of the Jews had ever left Rameses. They lived along the lush Nile—with the desert two days' journey away. Virtually all of them were in the desert for the very first time."

I was dumbfounded. This miracle of Moses was the greatest event in the history of Judaism. It was the most spectacular of God's interventions to protect his chosen people. It was the most wonderful demonstration of his infinite power and his love for us. Even to suggest that it never happened, or that it was only an illusion, was an insult to all Jews.

I looked out over the quivering horizon and thought, it doesn't even *look* like a sea! Anyway, not if you look at it for a long time. Certainly a whole people wouldn't be fooled. In the group there must have been other Jews familiar with the desert. Simon is just trying to make me angry. His contention doesn't even make logical sense.

I had been quiet for a few minutes and was annoyed with myself for not quickly countering Simon's accusations. Finally I said, with an affected sarcasm, "If it really were an illusion, then why did Moses say it was the Red Sea? If he were caught in such a lie, he would have lost his leadership for good."

"He probably never told the Jews any such thing. They just saw that they were heading towards a large body of water. The largest sea in the desert is the Red Sea, so they assumed that Moses was leading them into it. They were probably mystified, and they were certainly frightened. They believed that the Pharaoh's army was in angry pursuit and that they were in danger of being slaughtered. It was going to take a miracle to save them. Just then the sea split right in front of them. A miracle had occurred! They assumed that Moses knew all along that the sea would split. And that's the way the storytellers passed the story down."

"Well, then what caused the pursuing Egyptian soldiers to drown?" I asked indignantly.

"Who says that they drowned, Jesus? Only the storyteller. The Jews never went back. All they really knew was that the water closed behind them. The Egyptian papyri chronicle that same period with no mention of a drowned army. So why didn't the soldiers pursue the Jews?—you are about to ask. I don't know. Perhaps they thought that the Jews would eventually turn around and come back to Egypt. It's not easy to survive on the desert, particularly for such a big group. Rulers have always underestimated the toughness of your people, Jesus."

I swung my pick with added energy, sending tiny chips of rock shooting out in all directions. But my mind was not on my work. I couldn't accept the magus's sacrilegious interpretation of Exodus. I recited to myself the relevant sections of the Scriptures, silently, trying to find the flaw. The magus worked quietly, sweeping up chips with a bush broom. Suddenly I turned to him and said, "You're telling me that Moses used magic to keep the loyalty of the Jews?"

"As I told you before, Jesus, there isn't a religion in history that hasn't used magic for that purpose, although most of them deny doing so. Your people are unusual—they've used magic less than most—but they used it when needed. Your Scriptures are full of examples." He seemed to be thinking with his broom. "Here, how about this. When God first spoke to him, Moses was not sure that he could convince the Jews that he carried the divine word. Now, why was that?"

"Because he wasn't eloquent," I replied. "He said 'I am slow of speech and slow of tongue.'"

"Then how did Moses convince the Jews that he had spoken directly to God?"

"God gave him two miracles to perform, the diseased hand that could be cured by placing it under his cloak, and the walking stick that turned into a snake."

"Why didn't God simply make Moses eloquent? Certainly it was within the power of the Almighty to do that."

I had no good answer.

"Tell me," he continued, "when Moses did these miracles, why didn't Pharaoh believe he was a messenger from God?"

"Because his own magicians could . . . perform the same magic," I said.

"Why didn't God give Moses a better miracle? Like making him eloquent?"

"Perhaps he wanted the Jews to be convinced, but not the Pharaoh."

"You're too clever for your own good!" the magus remonstrated with a laugh. "You're beginning to sound like a Pharisee. Try to be smart, not clever."

"All right, why do *you* think the Lord gave Moses such little miracles, then?"

"Jesus, God didn't give these tricks to Moses. Moses learned them from the Egyptians, perhaps in the Pharaoh's court. Moses used them to keep his own people under control. Of course the tricks were useless in front of Pharaoh, for Pharaoh's magicians were just as good, and probably better."

"Well, then, let me see you turn that broom into a snake," I said rue-fully.

"I could do it, Jesus. But it would take a little preparation."

I stared off at the shimmering in the distance. It really does look like a sea, I thought. I walked over to a day tent and took a drink of tepid water from a goatskin. If it weren't so oppressively hot, I thought, I would have the answers for the magus's accusations. He was a smart man who had studied Judaism, but he didn't really understand our religion. He was just trying to demolish my beliefs. What would my father say? How would he answer the magus? I pondered, and an image came to my mind, of my father nodding, agreeing with the magus about Moses. I pushed the image away. Not only was the magus toying with me, but so was my mind.

For days I could think of nothing other than these accusations of the magus, and I am sure my work suffered. Darius probably thought I was sick. Indeed, my head did feel as if it were swimming, perhaps drowning, as I struggled to find good answers. As I worked, I pondered the other miracles of Moses. Obviously Pharaoh didn't believe the plagues had been brought by Moses. Indeed, his own magicians said they could dupli-cate the deluge of frogs and the turning of water into blood. Aha! The killing of the first-born! Moses couldn't have done *that* by deception. The Jews used the sprig of a hyssop to paint lambs' blood on their thresholds, so the Angel of Death would recognize Jewish homes and pass over them. That midnight the first-born sons of all the Egyptians died. We still celebrate the "pass-over." I'll challenge the magus with that.

No sooner had I imagined myself confronting Simon Magus with the slaughter of the first-born, than I imagined his answer: "The Jews left that night. How did they know that all the Egyptian first-born had died? They didn't even have time to leaven their bread!"

My imagination offered no reply, so I pondered other miracles. What about manna, the wondrous food that God supplied in the desert? What about that, Simon Magus? And in my mind he replied, "What do you think the Jews knew about the natural foods of the wilderness?" And I replied, *nothing.* Anything edible they found would be considered a miracle.

Why was my mind tricking me so?

The one, the great indisputable miracle of Moses had been the split-ting of the sea. Everything else could be explained away, particularly if Moses had some skill in magic. The most spectacular thing he had done, the thing that proved his direct contact with the Lord, had been the part-ing of the Red Sea. It was the only miracle defying explanation that had been performed in the presence of all the Jews. And now Simon Magus had explained it.

No! Moses was not a fraud.

Over the next few days, we finished the digging of the channel on the plateau and then began lining cracks with mortar. Work often came to a complete halt when we ran out of water, and we waited in the day tent. I didn't raise the issue of Moses with Simon during those times, and he didn't mention it to me, but I grew more and more annoyed at my failure to confront him. One day I stepped outside into the hot, fresh air. Simon followed me out.

"The desert is dead," he said, "but beautiful. It's a gift from God. We can show our appreciation by enjoying it."

I was annoyed by the similarity of his words to those my father once spoke. I blurted out, "Moses was not a liar or a fraud. He was our first prophet! He delivered the covenant from the Lord."

"I agree," Simon said. "He was not a liar or fraud."

"But you said he lied to the Jews."

"No, not exactly. I said that Moses used magic to convince the Jews that he brought the word of God."

"Now *you* are just being clever," I remonstrated. "What about the Law? Did it come from a burning bush? Or were the rules made up by Moses? Moses said they came from the Lord."

"Jesus, God speaks in many ways. Perhaps the Law had come to Moses from God, from a voice whispering quietly in his ear."

"Moses said that it was a thunderous voice, not a quiet whisper!"

"Even a quiet whisper can carry a thunderous message." Simon lowered his voice to a whisper. "Moses's greatness is beyond dispute, regardless of whether or not he split the Red Sea. However, even with divinely inspired laws, you sometimes need a little more to convince your people that God has spoken to you. That's why the Greeks use magic. That's why the Egyptians use magic. That's why we magi use magic."

"That's deception."

"If done in a righteous cause, deception can be more honest than truth."

"That makes no sense," I said ruefully.

"According to your faith, truth is God's will. Whatever leads a man to truth—that is what *I* call honest."

The cold of the evening was as severe as had been the heat of the day. Normally we went to sleep at sunset, but there were some embers left in the fire, and Simon Magus and I huddled near it. He believed that fire was a sacred reflection of the Almighty. As I watched the flickering glow dance from ember to ember, I realized that a fire was yet another familiar miracle that I took for granted.

"So tell me," I asked him, "how did the Egyptians turn a walking stick into a snake?"

Of course I had phrased the question in terms of the Egyptians, not Moses, but he recognized my question for the concession that it was. He stood up and walked over to his tent. A moment later he emerged carrying a small sack similar to the one from which he had pulled the glass amulet, and a long bone needle with a leather thong attached. He opened the sack and five hollow tubes fell out.

"These are bones," he said, "carved so that they fit together. They have many uses. Let me show you one." He tied the thong to one end of one of the bones, then threaded it through all four other bones in sequence. He pulled the thong tight, and the five bones straightened out to make a taught rod. "When the thong is tight, the linked bones are as one piece." He tapped it on a stone, and it did indeed appear to be a single stick. "Now watch," he said as he held the rod vertically. He loosened the thong and the bones collapsed onto his hand.

"That's not a very convincing snake," I said.

"Have you ever seen a snake swallow a mouse larger than itself."

"Of course. Its jaws expand."

"And the mouse is pushed down the body of the snake, whole, until it is digested. Imagine that I forced this rod, these sticks, into the gut of a living snake."

"I think I see," I said. In my mind I saw the body of the snake held stiff by the series of bones, the head of the snake hidden in the hand of the magician. He waves it in front of his face, like a magic wand. Then he throws the creature on the ground, releasing the thong. The snake can now squirm and wiggle once again, and as it does so, it draws the end of the thong inside itself. "But a snake doesn't look much like a rod," I objected.

"To be most effective, the magician must have both the snake and a real rod, both painted to look alike. The snake is kept straight, hidden in a tube under the tunic. At the critical moment, the true rod is inserted into the tube, and the snake is pulled out in its place. If someone notices the paint coming off the snake as it wriggles, the magician says 'It is shedding its bark.'"

"If the snake is examined," I said, "they'd find the hidden bones."

"It's part of the magician's skill to make certain that the snake is not examined. A poisonous snake such as a wood viper works best—people don't want to touch it. Of course, after a few days the linked bones will be digested anyway, just like the mouse's bones. The Egyptians often prefer to use a cobra, because it becomes paralyzed when held under its head. Personally I prefer the viper. Any snake held rigid for a few minutes will take a while to start moving."

"Doesn't that destroy the illusion?"

"No, quite the contrary. It makes the illusion even more effective." The magus pointed at a spot on the ground. "You see, the spectator sees a motionless shape on the ground, painted like a stick, and he watches it as it slowly revives." He wriggled his arm, imitating a snake. "He'll later remember that he saw the stick slowly turn into a snake, on the ground, not in the hand of the magician, and that's how he will describe it to others—assuming, of course, that the magician has handled the details properly."

"What do you mean 'details'?"

Simon moved over close to me, and again noticeably lowered his voice, as if he were relating a great secret. "When the substitution is made, the magician momentarily misdirects the observers, perhaps with help from an accomplice. Then he makes the key move: he taps the snake's tail on the ground. This will yield no sound since the snake is soft, but a hidden piece of wood in the magician's other hand, or perhaps on his foot, taps at the same time, giving the illusion that the sound is coming from the snake. He doesn't draw attention to the tap, or it won't be as effective. Nobody is conscious of the tap, but it's essential to the illusion. Then with a flourish the snake is thrown into the air, and the thong released."

I was mesmerized. "It sounds easy." I picked up a stick and poked into the fire with it.

"Oh, no, no, no. It's not easy. The magic must be practiced a thousand times, in front of other magicians, before it can be done before the fish."

"The fish?" I asked.

"The spectator, the target, the person to be fooled," Simon answered. "If you wish to amuse children, you need practice only fifty times. But for Pharoh, for his magicians—no, that needs a thousand. A hundred is not enough. And for Pharoh, you must have the tap. It erases his memory of the substitution, which he may have witnessed inadvertently. Nine times out of ten, the illusion will work without the tap. But especially if the fish is a shark that can bite off your head, nine times out of ten is not good enough."

Slowly, almost without realizing it, I grew to accept Simon Magus's interpretation of the Torah. His depiction of Moses—as a vulnerable man, inspired by the Lord, confronting enormous problems—was more believable to me than the magical wizard I had previously imagined. Simon argued that, despite our protests to the contrary, we Jews had in effect *deified* Moses. Moses couldn't perform miracles—only the Lord can do that. But if Moses could depend on the Lord to perform them whenever needed, didn't that qualify him at least as a minor deity? Moses couldn't perform magic, but he could call on the Lord to perform miracles. What, really, was the difference?

But Simon's vision—quickly becoming my vision—was that there truly is but *one* God. Moses, the human Moses, knew of this God, and tried to teach the Jews about him, in the only way that he could get them to listen.

This vision also answered the question that had bothered me from childhood: Why does the Lord not perform miracles any more? The answer was that he never did, at least not the spectacular water, fire, and earth-moving miracles described in the Scriptures. Perhaps, I thought, he only performs those miracles that my father described, little miracles, the miracles of everyday life.

I took advantage now of every lull in the work to question Simon. His knowledge of religion was enormous. "How did you learn all this?" I asked.

"At the great Academy of Zarathustra in Babylon," he replied.

"I thought that was an academy of healing, to train physicians."

"The deepest illnesses are those of the soul. It does no good to cure a man of his bodily sickness if one does not return righteousness to his spirit. That's the omission of the Greek physicians. The Egyptians make the opposite mistake: they believe spiritualism can cure the body. You Jews are like the Egyptians—you think that all illness comes from sin. It is a serious weakness in your otherwise great religion. The followers of Zarathustra treat the body and soul together. This is part of what we teach at the Academy."

"You've been an instructor there?"

"Until I sold myself into slavery."

"Get up here, Jesus!" It was Darius shouting from the large overhead winch that we used to raise stones. "Simon, you go back to the stone pit! We fell behind yesterday, but today is cool and we can make up for it."

To my great consternation, just as I was bursting with questions for

Simon, our master Darius left the camp and took him along. But just about that time, a new slave was put in my tent, a old man named Fasa, and I soon learned that he professed faith in the religion of Zarathustra. This was my opportunity, I thought, to become knowledgeable about Simon's religion while he was away. When he returned I could show my new knowledge.

I sat next to Fasa during the evening meal. "Tell me, Fasa," I said, "what you know about God."

"We shall not be slaves for long," he whispered back, as if telling me a great secret. "A liberator is coming."

I knew I would soon be released, for my six years were almost completed. But Fasa was a slave for life. What did he mean? I asked him, "Do you mean a Messiah?"

"He will be a son of Zarathustra."

"But Zarathustra has been dead for six hundred years."

"His seed has survived in a lake," he told me. "It has been prophesied, that a pure virgin bathing in that lake will be impregnated, and she shall give birth to the son of Zarathustra, and he shall be named Soshyans. I have heard, Jesus ... I have heard that this has already happened, and Soshyans is alive today. He is coming, Jesus, he is coming." Fasa's eyes shone with excitement. "I can feel it in my soul. He will bring everlasting torture by fire to sinners, to our tormentors, to our guards—to Darius! But the righteous will live together in happiness. Forever." He told me, with a broad smile and utter confidence, that the resurrected adults will remain perpetually forty years of age, and children will all be fifteen.

So, I thought, some Zarathustrians are just as pagan as some Jews.

Nearly three months passed, and my release was imminent. Finally Darius and Simon returned. I was desperate. "Simon," I said, "I have many questions. We must find time."

"Learning cannot be hurried," he said.

"But I will be released in a month! I have so many questions."

"Your education will not stop then, I assure you. You know what I want. You must go to the Academy."

"When I'm released, I must return to Nazareth."

"Nazareth will not be what you expect. Go to Nazareth, if you must. But when you see what is there, remember the Academy."

❖ ❖ ❖

The words of my mother proved true: "This too shall pass." The day of my release finally arrived.

"Stay here," Darius offered. "You are a free man, and I will pay you a denarius each day. You wouldn't earn more in Galilee, and I'll provide food and shelter. In a few years you'll save enough for your own carpentry shop."

"You've treated me fairly, and I am thankful, but I must go," I said.

I had dreamed of returning to Nazareth, of discovering the fate of my family and friends. I was optimistic that my mother had found some decent means of support, perhaps because I felt that my own suffering must have been sufficient to satisfy the Lord. I even fantasized that my disappearance must have triggered a solution to their desperate situation.

Darius gave me a departure present of a silver shekel, worth four denari, enough for food during my travel back home and to pay a tailor to mend my clothes. "Nazareth may not be what you expect," he warned, just as Simon had. "You'll be welcome back here. Don't forget me." I had worked hard for him but was surprised that he showed gratitude.

More difficult was saying good-bye to the magus. "Simon . . . you've been like a father to me. How can I thank you?" I was annoyed at the inadequacy of my words.

"No, Jesus, it's I who must thank you, for you've been a son to me, and a son is far more precious than a father. Here, I have a present for you." He handed me a small leather pouch. I opened it and sniffed the contents.

"Haoma?" I asked.

"Pure crystals. Treat it with care. Keep it dry. Mix it with harmaline and hemp, in a ratio of one to six to sixty-six. Six crystals will suffice for an entire wineskin. This amount should last for many years."

"You told me that pure haoma is dangerous."

"Never taste it undiluted, or you may be driven to madness. Never let anyone know you have it, for it is the most precious secret of the magi. Use it as I taught you, to ease the suffering of the sick and injured. This is a gift of faith and trust." He held my hands in his, and looked at me with a kind but sad smile. "Everyone here will miss you, particularly the sick. There will be nobody to take care of them now."

"You could do it, Simon, far more effectively than I."

"I don't love these slaves, as you do, Jesus. I don't see the good in them. I don't even care about them. My heart has grown hard." He shook his head, as if he hated hearing the words he spoke. I felt sorry for him. How could a man of such vast wisdom and learning, so compassionate towards my needs, not care about the others?

I had wanted to ask him about his indenture, about what tragedy could have pushed him from the high priesthood of Zarathustra to the degradation of slavery, but I had never been able to force myself to raise the subject. I had hoped he would someday volunteer the answer, but now I thought that I would never see him again, and I would never learn the answer. This was certainly not the time to raise the question. Curiosity is like an itch in the middle of your back: it's difficult to ignore, and yet not always easy to scratch.

10. Return

THE BIGGEST SURPRISE WAS THE SMELL, THE FAMILIAR SMELL. I had never realized that Nazareth had such a peculiar odor. As I approached the village, I had anticipated the thrill of seeing my familiar paths and buildings, but I never expected to remember the smell. It was subtle but distinctive, unlike anything I had experienced since leaving. I wondered, is it the soil? The trees? Part is certainly the myrtle in the nearby meadows. Ah, of course. It's the tanneries, those tanneries that my mother hates so much. Myrtle and tannin carried by the light breeze. I laughed at the thought of this peculiar combination. Only a child of Nazareth could love it.

As I climbed the hill to the town, I had a strange perception—that I had never left. The outskirts of Nazareth seemed more familiar than anything from my adult life. Here I was, where I belonged, home—everything else had been a dream. My arrest, the trial, my work on the aqueduct, Simon the Magus—none were as real as this path, that rock, that grove of trees, these things that I knew intimately from my childhood. True, the trees were somewhat larger than I recalled, and the houses seemed somewhat smaller. There was the fruit stand, where Silas's children sold pomegranates. An old woman sat there. I waved, but she didn't wave back.

As I worked my way up the familiar cobblestone streets, other people looked at me in a peculiar way, their expressions saying, what is this stranger doing here? Why is he visiting such an inconsequential town as ours? An old woman—who is she?–stared at me through a window as I walked along the path. Her severe face said, *I see you. Don't try anything, stranger.* I suddenly feared that my years in slavery might have left some sort of mark. Had I picked up a way of walking or a way of dressing, something they could see but I had missed, that made me look suspicious and alien? I grew self-conscious and quickened my pace.

I approached the small synagogue and noticed an old man with a long beard sitting on a reed chair and looking at a book. It must be Rabbi Shuwal. I considered walking around the back, but his eyes suddenly picked up and he stared right at me. It was he, all right, his beard grown whiter, the flesh of his face pale and waxy, and his nose even larger than I remembered. His large chameleon-like eyes bulged from his thin face, and they bored into my own.

"Well, well, well," he said slowly, with an unpleasant smile, as he put down his book. "It is Jesus the bastard, risen from the dead!"

Rabbi Shuwal had always been disagreeable, but as a child I had never fully understood how obnoxious he really was. I said nothing, but glowered back as best I could while quickening my pace.

Even from a distance I could see that our house was in disrepair. No curtain covered the entrance, the clay on the outer wall was gray and cracked, and a hole large enough for a coyote to crawl through marred the side. I approached slowly, fearing the worst. When I peered in the portal I could see nothing but a single ray of sunlight from a hole in the roof. As my eyes became accustomed to the dark, I saw fully the dead carcass of my home, lacking all sign of humanity. No one had lived here for a long time.

I was startled by a sound next door. I went to the wall, jumped up, and held myself at the top to look over. With pleasure I recognized our neighbor, hammering a nail into a plow handle. "Amos!" I shouted.

He looked up to me and his jaw dropped. "No, it can't be! Yes! The Lord our God the Almighty be praised! Blessed is the womb that bore you! Esreth, come here! Jesus is returned, and he's alive, and . . . and he's grown!" He put the emphasis on the last word, as if he were more surprised that I had grown than that I was alive. He was speaking half to his wife, and half to himself.

Esreth appeared from their doorway, looked at me for a moment with an expression of wonder that matched that of her husband, and then said in her matter-of-fact tone, "Get down from there, Jesus! It's dangerous. You look hungry. I'll warm up some soup." It was reassuring to hear Esreth sounding as if everything was right, as if nothing had changed.

I climbed down, and walked around the wall that separated our homes. Amos met me halfway. "Amos, what's happened? Where is everybody?"

"Ah, Jesus, my boy, where have *you* been? You're not dead after all!

How many years has it been? The Lord be praised!"

"But please, where's my mother? My brothers? What's happened here?"

Amos looked at me with sadness. "There's much to talk about," he said. "Come and have some food. Esreth!" he shouted. "Put a piece of meat in the soup!"

Amos and Esreth sat with me, but didn't eat. "This soup is wonderful," I said to Esreth. It was a salty yellow broth with little pieces of bread and globules of chicken fat floating on the surface. "I used to think that everyone in the world ate this soup. But no—it's unique to Nazareth."

Amos began to chatter, nervously, I thought. "Lazarus has moved to Bethany," he said. "Here in Nazareth he was growing more and more sickly. Rabbi Shuwal told us to make sacrifices, and we killed an uncountable number of pigeons, but it didn't do any good. Finally Esreth consulted a wise man."

"A magus?" I asked.

"Yes, I'm embarrassed to admit. The magus said the illness was from damp winters and fumes from the tanners. So Lazarus moved to Judea, where his cousin Martha lives. It's dry there, and his health has returned. He has found lots of work, and he sends us two silver pieces every month."

No mention yet of my mother. I grew afraid to ask. "And where is your daughter, Mary?" I said instead.

"Ah, that's right—you wouldn't know," Amos said. Esreth's eyes filled with tears. She left the table and tended a pot over the fire. Amos continued, "Mary disappeared, about two years after you did. We have no idea what happened to her."

My heart swelled in sympathy and concern. "Perhaps she's still alive, like me."

"Yes, but a girl, that's different. A boy can disappear for several years, and return as a man. But a girl? No, we can only hope now, with no word for so long, that she died peacefully. There's no hope, none, except the hope that she was killed. That's the most honorable end that we can pray for."

At that tragic thought, I could wait no more. I blurted out my guess: "Is my mother dead?"

"Dead? Dead? Oh Jesus no, no, she is alive—and in good health! She'll be so happy that you've returned, and that *you* are healthy."

"Where is she?"

"She took the children and moved to Augustus. There was no work for her here. She is a maid servant with a wealthy family."

"Augustus? You mean Sepphoris?"

Amos laughed. "You have been away for a long time!"

Mother was only a few miles away. My heart beat faster. I could go there that evening!

Amos continued, "Your brother James still lives with her, but Judas Thomas is now an apprentice fisherman on Lake Gennesaret." Lake Gennesaret was the name that older people used for the Sea of Galilee, about twenty miles away. "He was fortunate to get such a position. Zacharias arranged it."

Thomas a fisherman! What wonders! I was impatient to visit my mother, but out of politeness I asked, "Is Zacharias in good health?"

"No, Jesus, I am sorry. Elizabeth died just a year ago, and Zacharias followed her a month later."

"They were both full of years. Their son John? Did he become a priest?"

"He finished his training, thank the Lord, and he served in the temple for two seasons. But he complained about the other priests—they're all Sadducees, you know, and they don't care much for the Law. He says they're letting the Romans control the Temple. I don't know what he really meant."

"He scared me when he visited," Esreth said as she worked by the fire. "The priests fear the Sicarii."

"The Sicarii are assassins," I said, "but they use their daggers to terrorize Roman collaborators, not priests."

"That has changed," Amos said. "According to John, the Sicarii now call the priests collaborators." Amos leaned forward towards me and lowered his voice, so Esreth couldn't hear. "John spoke as if he knew all about the Sicarii. I suspected that they tried to recruit him."

"No . . . ," I whispered back, shaking my head. "John would never . . . that's inconceivable."

"Not as an assassin, but as a spy, to inform them of the inner politics of the Temple, and which priests were closest to the Romans."

"But you said John is no longer a priest?"

Amos resumed his full voice and sat back on his stool. "When his parents died, he went to Qumran."

"Qumran? To see the Essenes?"

"To join. That's what he said he was going to do. He said that he was looking for purity and righteousness and preparation for the coming of the day of the Lord. He was seeking *repentance*. I don't know precisely what he meant by that. I think it had special meaning to him; it had become his favorite word. We haven't heard from him since."

Esreth interjected, "Better the Essenes than the Sicarii."

"They steal some of our best children into their reclusive life. But who knows the will of the Lord? Well, now the Essenes probably have John. But you, Jesus, what happened to you? We all thought you had been killed. Where have you been?"

"I made a tragic mistake, Amos. To help my family, I became a thief." I looked into Amos's sad eyes, but saw nothing judgmental. "I was caught immediately, and tried in the Jewish court of Sepphoris. I have spent the last six years in servitude in penance for my crime, and I hope that the Lord has forgiven me. But I fear that my mother has suffered more than I have. I was anxious to visit her. Amos, Esreth, let me thank you again for your hospitality. Please forgive me, but I must leave for Sepphoris, I mean Augustus. If I leave now, I can get there before dark."

"Yes, of course, Jesus. We understand. But please come back soon."

At the door I said, "Tell me, what is the name of the family that employs my mother in Augustus?"

"Pantera. He's a Roman."

Those words shattered my reality like a sledgehammer smashing a glass amulet. The room rapidly retreated, as through a tunnel, into a dream. Reality was now the face of Pantera, the brutal, cruel face of Pantera, laughing at me.

No one is so easily fooled as he who fools himself. I had truly fooled myself, deluded myself, all those years. How could I have imagined that my theft, my act of evil, my act of stupidity, had somehow solved the problems of my family? In my mind I saw Pantera. I saw my mother. Then I saw Tamar, the woman from the red tent, who serviced soldiers, who serviced me, and I shuddered.

"Jesus, are you ill?" It was Amos, holding me by the shoulder and shaking me gently.

I shook my head in an effort to dislodge the images that possessed it. "Forgive me Amos," I said as I struggled to take control of myself. "I was thinking of my mother. I am impatient to see her." I surprised myself with the calmness, or rather the coolness, of my voice, as I turned away and walked out the door, for there was no calmness within.

No sooner was I outside than the hatred burst from my soul. I felt a power rising within me, and I began to run over the cobblestones, down the path, towards the spring, towards the old Sepphoris path.

I ran faster and faster. The loathing, the despair, the need to act—I had forgotten how overwhelming these passions could be. My rage seemed to give me a superhuman strength. Regardless of Pantera's military training, he cannot resist me. This time, I thought, this time I will kill him.

I had stayed at Amos's table too long. The sky was darkening, and I would be traveling through the woods at night. The houses, the street, were a blur. I ran frantically down the cobblestone path reached the square near the spring. Nobody was there. I turned towards the Sepphoris trail and slipped on a slick stone. My legs collapsed under me, and I crashed onto the street, my head hitting hard on a moss-covered cobblestone.

Lying motionless for a few moments, all I heard was my heart pounding in my ears. I felt as if I had been hit by a thunderbolt. Despite the pain on my head, I pushed myself up with my arms but felt faint and surprisingly weak. My energy had been an illusion. I took a deep breath, wiped my mouth, and noticed with surprise the foam that came off on my arm. I remembered an insane man I had seen in Sepphoris—a man possessed by a demon, they said—and I wondered if that was what I looked like now.

Looking around, I found that I was lying a few feet from the spring with its fountain and trickle of water. My tongue grated against my palate, my mouth was as dry as pumice. I started to get up to go to the spring but grew dizzy and sat back down on the street. My thirst would have to wait.

Something moved and I turned and saw a child, a little girl, standing about thirty feet away, looking at me. I didn't want to frighten her so I tried to smile. She looked away and walked towards the spring. She carried a small water jug with both hands and she held it under the dripping water. The water jug full, she skipped a few steps, and then walked over to the side of the path to look at some blue flowers in a patch of flax. She put the jug down, picked two of the flowers, slit their stems, threaded them together, and carefully added them to a necklace of yellow and red flowers she was wearing around her neck. She picked up the jug and continued down the street towards me, skipping in a zigzag pattern.

As she was passing by the spot where I was sitting she stopped and looked at me again, and then asked, "Are you thirsty?" I nodded yes. "Here, have some water!" She handed me the jug, and I filled my mouth while my eyes stayed fixed on hers. I took only one mouthful, and handed the jug back. She took it, gave me a little smile, turned down the road, and started skipping again. I watched her as she moved back and forth from one side of the path to the other, examining little things every few steps.

Her joy and gentle appearance were so startling, and in such stark contrast to my anguish, that I felt she must be a vision sent by the Lord.

A child, the greatest of miracles on my father's list. A tender miracle. I thought of my father. Then of my mother. And then of Pantera, and my anger began to well up inside me again. It was the same fury that had led to my crime, six years earlier. I was not one man but two: one with lust for revenge, and one who recognized the evil of that lust. But recognizing evil does not give power over it.

Yes, that's why the Lord struck me down in my rage and then sent this child, this vision of peace and love. The message she carried was now clear, severely clear. She had been sent to counter my hatred of Pantera, to remind me of the teachings of my father, of his gentleness, his compassion, and his love. And to remind me that, as a child, I too had received a revelation. My own words rang in my ears: love your enemies. Love the Romans. Love—love Pantera?

But when I was a child, the Romans were only abstract enemies, at least to me. How different now. Pantera was real—a cruel man who had treated my sweet mother like a whore. It is not so easy to love a flesh-and-blood enemy, one who has destroyed the life of your family.

Sitting there quietly on the street of Nazareth, as much as I struggled, as much as I understood the meaning of my vision, I could not overcome my hatred. Every time my mind returned to Pantera, I saw his savage face and heard his cruel laugh, taunting me, filling me with an overwhelming desire to destroy him.

The hatred was too strong. If I cannot control my spirit, I thought, then I must take control of my body. I will not go to Sepphoris, not yet. I must forgo seeing my mother and get away, far away, so far away that I cannot, in a fit of anger, rush to Sepphoris.

Run away? Is that all I can do? Why can't I fight this demon? Why am I so weak? So helpless? Father, I need you! How do I exorcise this demon? Where are you? Are you listening in heaven? Was it you who sent the thunder bolt to stop me, who sent the child to remind me? Help me father! I need your courage. I need your wisdom. I need your spirit. What must I do? Father—please father—whisper to me!

Simon Magus! I can seek help from Simon!

11. Failure

IT WAS EASY TO FIND THE CAMP BY FOLLOWING THE AQUEDUCT.
I found Darius, explained that my family was gone, and asked for his permission to talk to the Magus. "Take all the time you need," he said with generosity. "And remember my offer, Jesus. You are welcome to stay here. You could save a lot of money."

Simon was polishing stone facing for the aqueduct. It was finish work, the kind he loved most. He was working alone, so peacefully that I could almost imagine him a craftsman working for God alone. I approached quietly and watched him skillfully run the pumice back and forth across the face of the stone.

He stopped abruptly and without turning said, "Things were not as you expected." He was speaking in his usual knowing tone. And, as usual, his evaluation was accurate. Was this his insight or just another trick? I couldn't tell, and it occurred to me that maybe he couldn't tell himself.

"No, things weren't as I expected, not at all," I muttered.

He turned and faced me. His blue eyes bore into my own. "Did you find your family?"

"No . . . I mean, I didn't try. I stopped. I was afraid to. I learned that my mother . . ." My throat choked and I felt tears begin to form in my eyes. I turned away from Simon in embarrassment. I felt his arm around my shoulder. As he hugged me, I could not suppress a series of sobs.

"She is with a man you detest," he said gently. "You are consumed by hatred. I understand."

"His name is Pantera. He is a Roman soldier, a hard, cruel man. But I ran, ran away. Help me, Simon. I am lost."

"You were right to return here, Jesus. You were right not to face Pantera. Some day you must, but not yet. But you are wrong to think that you ran away, for you are in the midst of a great battle right now. That battle is raging in the place where the true war between good and evil always takes place: within your soul."

"There is a demon inside me, Simon! It hides, and I forget, but then this rage surges forward and takes control. I don't know how to fight it, Simon. I, . . . I am afraid."

"That demon can only be fought with goodness. I can help you, Jesus. But it will not be without pain."

"Anything, Simon."

"Your first step must be to accept a harsh truth."

"No truth could be worse than what I already know, that my mother has been abased."

"It is harsher than that, Jesus. You must accept your failure. You must acknowledge that the fault is all your own, that all of her suffering was caused by your pride, by your selfishness, by your failure to love."

I stared at him in stunned silence. "Simon, I sacrificed my life for my family. You know the intensity of my love! Yes, I acted foolishly—but how could you call me selfish? I came back here to seek help, not censure!" My anger rose. "Yet you only condemn me!"

"You will not be able to exorcise your demon until you recognize the truth, Jesus. It is you, not Pantera, who is the source of your mother's suffering. I warned you, Jesus, that this would be a harsh truth. I am not condemning you—no, I don't presume to do that. I am harsh with you because I love you so, because you are like a son to me. I want to end your suffering as quickly as I can. I think you are strong enough to accept the truth, as harsh as it is. And I know that you will not achieve peace until you do."

"It is Pantera who is evil, not me! You don't understand."

"I do, Jesus, I do understand. I understand evil much more than you could possibly realize. The evil that sent you into slavery is still within you, and is trying to enslave you itself. The greater evils always reside within. Your enemy is not Pantera, but your own pride and selfishness."

I stared at Simon with shock and disappointment. He looked at me, then turned back to his stone. He had nothing more to say. I had nothing more to say. He slowly rubbed the pumice across the stone.

So, I had made another mistake. I had returned to my teacher for help, only to learn that he dismissed me as ignorant and foolish. I had been wrong in my estimate of his spiritual greatness. Perhaps what I had always taken as his perception and understanding had only been an illusion, one of his tricks. Or perhaps as I had grown older, gaining knowledge and experience, it had been inevitable that I discover the limitations of a man who had once seemed to be the epitome of insight and wisdom.

With no further words, without looking back at Simon Magus, I stood up and walked away. I am not angry, I said to myself, as much as I am sad and disappointed. And alone, all alone. Nobody can help. I will have to plan my future alone.

I followed a rivulet down the hill, where it disappeared into a pine grove. Deep in that little forest I sat down on some soft pine needles to recover my strength, gather my feelings, and figure out what to do next.

I sat there and thought of nothing. I must rest. Why was my argument with Simon so exhausting? Because I love him, I guess. *You must accept your failure.* Simon's words kept sneaking into my heart. *Your enemy is not Pantera, but your own pride and selfishness.*

I watched the needles of the tree sway gently in the breeze. On a nearby pine a small bird, a nuthatch, was walking down the trunk, head below its body, searching for insects. In the peace of the woods, in my exhaustion, as I sat and rested, slowly my anger faded. And I heard another voice, within me, asking *Could Simon be right?* This was a gentler voice. It asked, *Could Simon be right?*

I let out such a large sigh that I laughed at myself.

Now I could see, within myself, what Simon had seen. I was weak and ashamed, but no longer hindered by pride. I worked my way down towards the stream and back to the aqueduct. Simon was just where I had left him, slowly, patiently, polishing the stone. As I walked up to him he stopped work and looked at me with sympathy. I asked simply, "What can I do?"

"Take comfort, Jesus, for your pain will pass. Accept what you've done and the great harm that you have caused. Accept the pain of failure and sin. Accept that it was your fault, not the fault of others. Don't be ashamed, Jesus. All men fail. It is a crisis that God has prescribed for each of us, as a test. Most men, when confronted, refuse to accept their failure. They deny it—they fight it—they blame others. And that is the end of their spiritual enlightenment." I sensed that Simon was talking of his own life. He continued, "For someone who admits his guilt, who takes the responsibility, for you Jesus, it can be a beginning."

"A beginning of what?"

"It is like being born again. You start over, but it is better than that, because you get to keep everything that is good within you. Only the evil is discarded. God is so great that he even loves the sinners. Confess your failure, accept your responsibility, repent, and in penance use your love and your compassion and your wisdom to serve. Accept your goodness, and your failure will die with the past."

Simon said no more. I said no more, but sat down beside him as he polished the stone. Not words, but feelings moved through my soul—no, not feelings, but a sense of spirit, of a reality beyond feelings.

That evening Simon and I sat close to a small fire. He gazed into it, as if hoping to find spiritual enlightenment in the crackling dance of its flames. Fire truly *is* a miracle, I thought, and I can see why the Zarathustrians consider it sacred. I looked not at the fire, though, but at the man who was once again transforming my spiritual life. In the flickering orange light, I studied the shapes and lines of his gentle face and wondered what story they were trying to tell. If I could read those features, would I understand why this man who seemed to care for no one else, cared so much for me?

Simon broke the silence. "You must not return to Sepphoris, Jesus. Not yet."

"I will do whatever you tell me, Simon."

"I passed through a great crisis once, Jesus. And a very wise man gave me spiritual guidance—I don't know why, because I did not deserve it—and he saved my life. And now it is my turn to help you. I ask you to trust me, Jesus, because I am not going to ask something easy of you."

"What was your crisis, Simon?"

"It is better, for now, that you do not know, Jesus. This is not a time for you to think of me, or even of yourself. Your penance, Jesus, is for you to be truly selfless, to devote yourself utterly to others. You must do this with all of your spirit, all of your energy, your skill and intelligence. To regain your soul, you must lose yourself."

"I could stay here and tend the sick."

"No, you must do more. It is not enough to tend the sick. You must go away for another seven years, solely to prepare for this mission. You must study the art and science of healing."

"With you, Simon?"

"No—not with me. My knowledge is more limited than you recognize. You will be a great help to your people, Jesus, but you must bring to them a depth of learning and skill that is beyond my means to teach. You must study at the Academy of Zarathustra."

I shook my head. "I am a slave, Simon—well, an ex-slave. I have no money, and only one skill, carpentry."

"The director is a man named Cambyses," Simon continued, undaunted. "I assure you, when he reads the letter I will write, he will accept you as a worker-student. You will earn your keep and you will study hard. You will begin by learning how to treat the body. You will work harder than you have for Darius, Jesus, because you will be your own slave driver. You must plan to advance, ultimately, to the highest art, to learn to heal the soul. It will not be easy, Jesus, for you will be tempted to leave. You must forget yourself, even your own family. For now you must devote yourself, entirely, to helping others."

I remembered the promise I made to myself, seven years earlier, when I had watched Rufus die under the scourge: *Someday, somehow, I must learn how to heal.* I silently thanked the Lord, for leading me back to Simon to receive his wisdom. I shall become a physician, and devote my life to healing, to relieving others of pain and suffering.

"You know, do you not, Jesus, where this Academy is located?"

"Yes, Simon. Babylon. The city of wickedness."

12. Babylon

BABYLON! TO THE PROPHET JEREMIAH IT WAS *THE ABOMINA-tion of the earth, and the kingdom of the beast.* It was the *abyss* of our exile, where three centuries ago the Lord had sent us to be punished, where we had suffered in captivity for seventy years. *All who go to Babylon shall be astonished and hiss*, said Jeremiah. And now, after three months traveling with caravans, up the Jordan, across Trachonitis to Damascus, skirting the edge of the desert to Antioch, and finally down the lush valley of the Euphrates, working for my keep repairing caravansaries, crates, and camel harnesses, I was finally at the wall of this mythical and hated city.

And I *was* astonished, first by the enormous size of the wall. I followed it for a mile and a half along the Euphrates, passing remains of gardens and marble palaces, all in ruin. Simon had told me the city was ten times larger than Jerusalem, but I thought that an exaggeration until I saw it. I crossed the river on a badly damaged ramp and climbed thorough a gaping hole in the wall, which was more than ten feet thick. Inside, hulks of crumbling brick and rotting timbers were strewn over the landscape like carcasses of cattle killed by drought. What had I expected? Rampant sin? *And I will repay to Babylon and all its people for the evil that they have done to Jerusalem, said the Lord. They will not take from you a stone for a new building, yet you will be desolate forever.* I was filled with awe at the sight of the prophecy fulfilled. I was astonished, but I did not hiss. Instead, gazing at the waste and wreckage, I thought of Sepphoris, and the memory filled me with sadness.

Only the massive Ishtar Gate of the inner wall seemed untouched by

decay. It was embellished with vivid carvings of bulls and lions and drag-
ons surrounded by blue tiles of lapis lazuli. I let this seductive art tantalize
my imagination for several minutes, and I could see why such graven
images are forbidden by Jewish law. No guards protected this monument,
and yet it had survived the looters. It must be considered sacred, I concluded, or else accursed.

A second, inner wall was more than twenty feet thick, but it too was
badly damaged, and I easily found a way through. Within was the heart of
the city, long straight streets obstructed by mounds of rubble. With every
turn I took, with every new sight, the words of Scripture repeated themselves in my thoughts. *They will not take from you a stone for a new
building, yet you will be desolate forever.* And desolate Babylon was,
although in violation of the prophecy its stone had been looted for the city
of Seleucia, twenty miles to the north. This devastation was far greater than
that any army could have wreaked. Babylon the Great had indeed fallen.

Part of a terraced stone building remained, and I wondered if it could
have been part of the famous hanging gardens. No, too small. Where was
the fallen three-hundred-foot ziggurat temple of Marduk? Simon had told
me to look for a square foundation that spanned three hundred feet. "That
was the Tower of Babel," Simon had claimed. "Which strikes you as
odder?" he had asked. "That the tower might truly reach heaven or that
God felt so threatened that he had to confound the builders with confus-
ing languages?" But such questions bothered me no longer, for I had abandoned my belief in the Scriptures as the literal word of God.

At first I thought the city empty of people, but that was an illusion.
There was life, hidden in the ruins like grass growing between cobblestones. Occasionally I spotted children running amidst the rubble, rolling
hoops, or playing catch-the-hyena, as they undoubtedly do in every other
city of the world. Later I discovered that the older neighborhood, called
Esagilia, even had a small but thriving market—one that I was to visit
frequently.

Following Simon's instructions, I found the Academy of Zarathustra on
the left bank of the Euphrates, nestled against the wall in the "New City,"
built six centuries earlier. A dozen buildings stood nearly shoulder to shoulder, creating a virtual wall around an inner courtyard. I slipped between
two the buildings and entered the grounds. In the middle of the yard were
scattered several groups of black-robed men in apparently solemn discussions. At the far end was a gathering of what looked like sick and injured
people waiting patiently by the side of a small building. Moving among
them were more black-robed men, talking to some, examining some. That

must be the clinic. But there were also animals in the group: goats, pigs, dogs, all leashed or otherwise under the control of their masters. I wondered if the same doctors treated man and beast.

One large building standing in the center of the courtyard seemed to be in particularly fine condition. I guessed that it was the building that Simon had called the atheneum. Its sides were decorated with sculpted basins, empty now, but suitable for plants, perhaps in the style of the ancient hanging gardens. Its doors were open and unguarded, and I slipped inside. A tall outer hallway skirted the edge of the structure, and high windows let in light. The walls had floor-to-ceiling shelves on which lay thousands of scrolls. I stood in motionless awe. These scrolls were out in the open where anybody could take them. What priceless treasures! Somewhere among them must be the catalogues of medicines and the manuals of surgery. Others undoubtedly contained compendia of religions. Simon said there were ancient copies here of the Jewish scriptures, four different versions that the scribes had melded into one during their captivity. This bountiful library, I decided, not the Ishtar Gate, was the greatest wonder still remaining in Babylon.

Two men in black robes walked slowly past me, absorbed in conversation in a language I didn't recognize. Not knowing whether they would understand my native Aramaic, I simply spoke out the name, "Cambyses?"

"The director is in the Room of Ancients," one of the men responded in properly inflected Aramaic. He pointed to a half-open door.

I entered a musty room filled with tables, each covered with scrolls piled on scrolls, some made of parchment, some of papyrus, some of copper, many covered with decades of dust. The room was dark, but light from a high window shone on a table near the side. Seated there, bent over a table, was a white-haired man.

"Teacher?" I said in Greek, using the title that Simon had advised.

The man turned. "Just call me Cambyses," he said, in a deep voice out of proportion to his thin, almost withered body. He too spoke perfect Aramaic, as if he could recognize my native tongue just from my pronunciation. He motioned me to wait and turned back to his table.

He continued to pore over his work—and pore, and pore, apparently unaffected by my presence. I watched his small hunched figure for nearly half an hour in that musty room, and decided to rest by leaning back against the wall.

Suddenly off balance, awakened as I nearly fell, I realized that I had dozed in a standing position. To stay awake I decided to count scrolls. I had reached nearly two hundred when Cambyses abruptly turned and beckoned me to approach. I walked to him and held out Simon's letter. He took it, fumbled with it, glanced at it quickly in the dim light, and then looked up at me as if trying to interpret my face. His eyes were gray and tired, his pale wrinkle-covered face framed by pure-white hair. He moved closer to me, as if he couldn't see me unless I were exactly one foot away—the same distance he used to read the scrolls.

Finally he said, in his deep voice, "Simon the Samaritan writes highly of you." The Samaritan? "And I think highly of Simon, yes I do. He also says that you are poor." Had Cambyses read the entire letter in that quick glance? "Unfortunately, so is the Academy. As you can see." He looked down on the floor, and then swept his arm in a grand motion around the room. "This was once the finest, the richest academy in all of Persia," he intoned. "Once this room was illuminated with a thousand lamps. But now Babylon is poor, and we are poor. Except!" He said the word with particular emphasis, and looked intently at me. I leaned my head forward, like an attentive student. He raised one finger and smiled broadly, revealing a complete set of teeth. "Except in knowledge! In this academy we have great treasures more valuable than the stones of Elasser. Our knowledge, our books, and our tradition! Yes, most valuable of all, our tradition. Tell me, young Jesus, do you know where the word *academy* comes from?"

I was proud to be able to answer: "From the name of the gymnasium where Plato taught." I had learned this from Greek traders on my long travel to Babylon.

"No!" Cambyses boomed, the sound rattling off the high dome over the room. "That is what the Greeks will tell you! But why was Plato's gymnasium given that name? The word is far more ancient, young man. The first center of study was founded by Sargon at Accad, the capital of Babylonia. Our academy is a direct descendant. We still have many of the ancient clay tablets."

He looked back down at the floor and began shaking his head. "Alas, our academy may not long outlive the destruction of Babylon. Seleucus Nicator knew he couldn't control this city, so he tore it down. Seleucia, his new city, is built from our stones. But he left us behind—probably hoping we would die with the city. Well, we almost did, and perhaps we still shall. Most of our money is gone. We are withering." He glanced at his own wiry hand. "But we still have our great tradition, our knowledge, and of course our discovery. That was not so easy to destroy. Do you know what it was, young man, that we discovered?" I thought to myself, Egyptian magic? The haoma powder? But I had learned better than to interrupt his rhetorical question with a guess—even an educated guess.

"We discovered that all men worship the same God!" he said. He looked at me hard. I nodded in response. "Ah, I can see you are skeptical. Not only am I wrong, you think, but no great secret can be that simple!" Cambyses was indeed reading my thoughts accurately. "But *you* are the one who is wrong, young man. The greatest ideas are easy to articulate, but difficult to understand, and even more difficult to accept. Yes, it is as easy as that. God has given something to all religions, different secrets to share. This is the lesson we tell all the world. Yet few hear us. If you learn nothing more at this academy than what I have just told you, your entire journey will have been worthwhile! But learn it soon, young man, while you can. We are at the end of a golden age. Think of yourself as lucky to be alive now, while this academy is still here. It may not last much longer." He glanced at the letter, and said suddenly, "So, you want to study the healing arts."

"Yes, teacher. I wish . . ."

"But you can't afford to pay!"

I was suddenly struck with fear that he might not accept me.

"Stop that trembling!" he ordered. His face broke into a welcoming smile. "Don't worry. We're too poor to reject you." He looked at me with sympathy, and I tried to smile in return. "Simon says you're a carpenter. Good. We've been without one for two years now. We have much work for you. The scholars crave students, so they'll be happy to have you here, even if you can't pay them. Nothing flatters a teacher more than to have someone pay attention." I had been flattering him for several minutes now. "There are several empty buildings here. Find one to stay in. Decaying cities never lack for space. But be careful when you wander. Especially avoid the old city. It's full of danger and sin. You may eat in the refectory with the paying students. Ruhollah, who also works for his learning, will direct your work. He's young, like you, but he has been here a few years. Come back here in the morning and I'll take you to him. Now, let's see." He turned away, and returned to his bench and his books.

It appeared that it was time to leave, and I began to back towards the door. Suddenly Cambyses turned around. "Not yet!" he boomed in his outsized voice as he waved a finger in the air. "One lesson. One rule. One law." I waited expectantly. "Only this: *listen.* Merely *listen.*" I listened, and waited, and he returned to his books. He said nothing more.

That appeared to be the end of the lesson, and I began to back away towards the door. But in the corner of my eye I saw a darkness slip across a pile of scrolls on the other side of the room. I quickly turned my head, but there was nothing there. I looked back at Cambyses, but he seemed not to have noticed. Childhood tales of captive spirits in Babylon came to mind. Suddenly the scrolls moved and a large black shape flew out. I inadvertently let out a gasp.

"It's only Moonshadow," Cambyses muttered. "Ignore him."

Moonshadow? The thing had disappeared. I looked around in the darkness. The only motion was Cambyses, hunched over his scroll, slowly writing. Something warm rubbed against my leg. I kicked reflexively, and a large long-haired black cat scurried away across the room. A cat—a domesticated cat! In Israel all cats are wild, and as a child I had received a bad scratch and learned to fear them. Perhaps nothing else those first days made so apparent to me the intense strangeness, the sheer *foreignness*, of Simon's beloved Academy of Zarathustra.

13. The Academy

RUHOLLAH EYED ME SUSPICIOUSLY. "JESUS? THAT'S AN ODD name. You are a Jew?"

"I come from Galilee. A small village called Nazareth." I eyed him in return. He looked to be in his early twenties, maybe a year or two older than me.

"I never heard of it. But you are a Jew?"

"Yes."

"I am Persian," Ruhollah said. "From Sumar. My name means 'spirit of God.'" He looked towards the library. Cambyses, who had just brought me to him, had disappeared back into the atheneum. "We don't get many Jews here," he said, pointing his arm in a sweep around the courtyard. "Am I supposed to arrange for *clean* food for you?"

"Just treat me as you would a Persian, Ruhollah. Think of me as *am ha'arez.*"

Ruhollah laughed. "From the way Cambyses personally escorted you, I thought you might be a Jewish prince in disguise."

"I just met Cambyses yesterday. Was his treatment of me that special?"

"Special? Ha! He escorted you personally. Yet this was the closest *I* have been to him in a year."

"A teacher, a magus named Simon, wrote Cambyses a letter of introduction for me."

"It must have been some letter. Well, first we must get you a black robe."

"You give me that privilege already?"

Ruhollah chuckled. "You miss the point, Jesus. The robe is not a privilege. It is a requirement, to hide distinctions. Here you can't tell wealthy from poor, noble from peasant, or expert from acolyte, at least not by their clothing."

He led me into one of the buildings on the periphery of the courtyard, and we entered a dark room. It was full of intriguing and potentially useful objects: ladders, boxes, empty bookshelves, lamps, benches and tables of every description as well as the more exotic—cages, indecipherable tools, and an assortment of weapons. Several of the boxes were filled with black robes. "Just find one that fits," he said. "Nobody cares what you wear underneath, if anything."

Proudly sporting my new robe, I was led by Ruhollah indoors to a large carpentry shop. Nobody else was there. It was huge. I had never seen anything like it.

"This is yours," he said.

My jaw dropped in astonishment. Mine? No—I didn't deserve it. It dwarfed any carpentry shop I had ever seen. The room held three massive red oak workbenches, each complete with four double-screw vises. On the wall were racks of bits and braces, iron gouges, reamers, files and chisels, calipers, mallets, and a host of tools whose purpose I could only guess. From the ceiling hung wooden cant hooks, frame saws, and hoists. There was a barrel of pumice stones with the full range of roughness. Miscellaneous tools were strewn all around the room. The floor was covered with a thick layer of dirty sawdust. The room reeked of neglect.

"I don't even know how to use most of these tools," I sighed.

"That doesn't matter. Neither does anyone else."

I ran my fingers along the teeth of an iron saw. "This is a fine tool, but it hasn't been cleaned—in years. Who has been using this shop?"

"Anybody and everybody. You look at home, Jesus. Good. Your first job is the dining hall. The roof leaks."

Fixing roofs. That I knew how to do.

And that is how I began—fixing roofs. It was a good way to start, because I quickly earned the recognition and gratitude of many students and faculty. I was determined to make myself valuable, so I worked hard—from dawn to dusk, and for many months I did not allow myself the indulgence of attending lectures. Soon I was also mending benches, tables, reading stands, cabinets, sheds, and ladders. I kept the tools in good repair and even figured out how to use many of them. Gradually I came to feel that I belonged. And I began attending lectures.

I was surprised at the diversity of knowledge that fell under the rubric of *healing*. The academy had scholars who specialized in diagnosis medicine and surgery, in astrology, history, geography, and language, and in even more arcane fields. Experts in obsolescent tongues were particularly valued for their skill in reading the old papyri. "The ancients knew many things that have been forgotten," Ruhollah explained. "Our collection of old manuscripts is unsurpassed. That's because Cambyses often took payment in papyrus rather than gold. *Too* often, some say."

The magi were the experts in religion and thaumatology, the art of miracles, the most difficult and most dangerous skills, taught only to advanced students—and to certain visiting priests. "If they have the gold," Ruhollah said, "they can study anything, even if they aren't prepared." Thaumatology included both magic, the art of illusion, and "true magic," which requires no deception, and was based on the systematic cataloguing of patterns gleaned from observations. "The magi even discovered," Ruhollah explained with pride, "how to breed blue-eyed cats."

"That seems like a worthless achievement," I said.

"Oh, no, Jesus. Blue-eyed cats are in great demand among wealthy Egyptians. Their sale helps pay for our food."

The students at the academy were just as diverse as the faculty. Many were young, but some were older men wishing to refine their skills, probably paying a fortune to come here. There were priests from Egypt, Ur, and even India, and scholars from Israel, Greece, and Persia. Virtually all lecturing was done in Greek or Aramaic, although specialized discussions were held in Persian, Egyptian, and several languages of which I had never heard. Fortunately I had picked up some Greek in Nazareth and from the slaves working for Darius. I quickly became adept at understanding the language, if not at speaking it. Greek spoken by Persians is much easier to understand than Greek spoken by Greeks.

14. Elymas

IT WAS IN MY SECOND YEAR AT THE ACADEMY THAT I WAS approached by Elymas, one of the masters of thaumatology. He was both secretive and severe with students, and he had never allowed me to watch him teach. He was a tall, dark man, who wore the most expensive linens and silks under his robe—and often left his robe open so we could see them. The bright colors of these garments contrasted with the dark pallor of his face. He carried his arms bent, as if he had a slight deformity from birth.

"I have a task for you," he said, as he led me to a locked room in a corner of the east tower, a building across the courtyard from the atheneum. He told me to turn away as he worked the secret method for opening the door. Inside, the room was dark and somewhat musty, reeking with the smell of unfamiliar chemicals. The floor and tables were covered with black cloths, each one hiding some mysteriously shaped object.

Elymas closed the door. He said, "Swear on your god that you will not divulge what I tell you in this room."

"Master Elymas, I am forbidden by my religion to swear in such a way."

"Then swear by my god."

"I am sorry. I can't do that either."

"Damn you Jews! Well then, consider this a trial. If anyone finds out what you learn in here, any bit of it, even the slightest detail, then you will be dismissed from the academy. I'll see to it. Do you understand?" I nodded my head, and swallowed. He seemed reassured by my fear. Then he asked, "Can you carve a finger?"

I shuddered. "Of a live man or a dead one?" I asked.

"No, no, no! I mean like this. . . ." He reached over to a table and pulled a box out from under a cloth and opened the lid. Inside was what appeared to be a ghastly collection of thumbs, forefingers, and fingertips. Elymas finally read my mind, and laughed loudly. "These are made of wood!" he explained. "Here, examine them." He picked several out of the box and dropped them in my hand. They were indeed wooden, carved from pine and painted to look like flesh. The insides were hollow.

"What are these for?" I asked.

"Remember your oath," he said. Had he forgotten that I hadn't made one? "Watch." Elymas picked out a tip and placed it over his thumb; then he took a small red silk from his pocket, waved it in the air, rubbed his hands together for a few moments, and then opened them in front of me. The silk was gone. It must be hidden in the false thumb—but I didn't see him place it there. Indeed, I couldn't even see that he was still wearing the wooden tip, since his hand was in subtle yet constant motion, and his ability at misdirection seemed almost supernatural. I found myself watching the irrelevant spots on his hands that he was looking at himself or pointing to. A moment later the red silk appeared, magically, from his "empty" hands.

"Ah—that was extraordinary," I said.

He pulled the false tip from his thumb. "This is adequate for a silk," he said, "because silks can be stuffed into small places. But none of these tips are adequate for my needs. I need a large hollow, one that fits so well that it won't leak blood."

"Why would you put blood inside?"

"That you don't need to know. Not yet, anyway. Someday you may see blood produced from nowhere and you'll understand. But remember, you must say nothing. For now, just carve me a tip of this same size, but with a larger hollow," he instructed, as he handed me one of the larger ones.

"I'll carve it from pistacea. It doesn't split like pine, so I can make the shell thin. I'll need to make a mold of your finger to work with. If I carve it precisely, it won't leak. But the job will take a while. And I have other work I have to do."

"Forget your other work. Take as long as you need. I'll ask Cambyses to relieve you of your other duties."

"Ruhollah is my supervisor," I said. "I need to ask his approval."

"Forget Ruhollah. Start immediately."

Despite my fascination with Elymas's tasks, I began my serious study of disease and medicine. I started by attending lectures on leprosy, the most dreaded of the diseases of Israel. I learned to distinguish dry leprosy, which is safe and noncontagious, from the virulent wet leprosy, which the masters urged us to avoid completely. "You cannot treat it," said Belanasus, a master of medicine, "so do not try. You will only spread the disease to yourself and others." He talked about the numerous variants of dry leprosy, and prescribed different treatments for each one. Then he startled me by mentioning "the Jewish scroll called Leviticus." It is good, he said, for as far as it goes. "But the Jews are hopelessly confused by the disease. Their fear is so great that they call every skin disease leprosy, even minor abscesses and boils. And they force anybody with a rash to the leper colonies, where they contract the true disease." This is not true, I thought to myself. They only do that sometimes. "The Jews are so intent on their relationship with their god," Belanasus continued, "that they ignore well established medical knowledge. The only medicines the Jewish priests know how to use are wine and strong drink. They are more primitive than the Cushites." All the easier it will be for me to ease the suffering of my people, I thought to myself.

The panoply of medicines I studied included water of Dekarim, barks of various trees, extract of mandrake, pellitory root, maidenhair fern, skunk cabbage, frog spawn, henbane, poppy seeds, goat's gall, and several kinds of mushrooms, fungus, spider webs, and even mold. For many of these there were special methods of preparations, including bruising the live plant several days before the medicine was extracted. Treatments for skin disease included bathing in the smoke of wool, and the application of many kinds of poultices, including boiled hearth bugs. I wondered, who was the first to boil a hearth bug? How could anyone have discovered such strange remedies?

But above all the other medicines was haoma powder. Always used diluted, it could be fed to a patient on bread for relief of pain, or mixed with milk and water for reduction of fever. It not only was a powerful medicine but a potent intoxicant, its magic more persuasive because its effect was quite different from that of wine. "Never take it yourself," Belanasus warned, "even when ill. It makes headaches go away, but it weakens the mind and makes you want more." Its mode of manufacture was a deep secret, revealed to the new magus only when initiated in the ceremony of fire. Even Ruhollah didn't know its makeup, although he freely speculated that its ingredients included harmaline, a crystal extracted from the seed of the harmal herb. Diluted haoma powder was available to the students for use in the clinic. I still had the undiluted haoma

Simon had given me, and only slowly did I come to realize what a trea-sure it was—a treasure I instinctively kept secret.

✧ ✧ ✧

My most intriguing projects continued to be the ones for Elymas. As he learned he could trust me to keep his secrets, his rough exterior soft-ened, and he even seemed to take an interest in my education.

Only in his private, dark room in the East Tower would we have our discussions. Even after two years at the academy, most of the objects under the black cloths were sill mysteries to me, though in fact I knew more than most, because few students were even allowed to *enter* this room. Elymas's assignments to me were always cloaked in a mysterious solemnity. His most complex assignment was the chair—or rather (and this was the great secret) the pair of chairs. He knew what he wanted, but he understood little of the limitations of wood. So to enable me to modify the design, and against his judgment, he had to tell me how the devices would be used.

One chair, he explained, must conceal numerous special compart-ments and devices, including a hidden knife that could be used to cut strings and ropes. A small skin stashed under the seat would supply a sticky resin, used to make objects stick to the back of his hand and other unexpected spots. Secret compartments were to be everywhere, mostly equipped with spring-loaded doors to allow small objects to be hidden. The most complex secret was to be a "servant," a special lever that would thrust a package (the "load") secretly into his hand as it rested on the arm-rest. "It's important that the load be delivered quickly, quietly, without being seen, and without my having to move my arm," Elymas said.

"I can't make anything as complex as that invisible," I objected.

"It needn't be truly invisible, just not obvious. And silent. I can mis-direct the attention of the students with my other hand. The servant can be driven by weights and pulleys somehow. At least that's what I've seen. You figure out the details. I want to be able to trigger delivery either with my foot, my knee, or my head."

I had never imagined that a magician would go to such effort (although it was to be mostly my effort) to devise a sleight. "Why do you want *two* chairs?" I asked.

"The second one is to look identical to the first, but it is to have no secret devices. I must have one that can be examined when I'm not pre-sent. No one but you and I will know that there are two chairs. Build it in the Egyptian style, like this one here." He pulled away a black cloth to reveal an elaborate sculpted solid oak chair, beautifully decorated with carvings of snakes and scorpions. "I want a few defects on each chair, as if they were made in a hurry, or accidentally damaged, but I want the defects to be identical on both chairs. This will be the deepest secret you keep for me. Nobody must suspect that there are two."

"But when you teach this magic, the secret of two chairs will get out. Soon everyone at the academy will know."

"Ah—you don't appreciate the subtlety of it. No, Jesus, nobody will know about these chairs except you and me, not even Cambyses. And if I could build these things without you knowing, I would. I always reserve some magic to mystify and inspire my students, lest they lose their awe. There must always be some things they don't understand. So beware. If the secret gets out, it will get out through you alone. Oh, and one other thing. I'm now going to give you the most subtle lesson in misdirection that you will ever receive. This will be difficult for you, but it will be worth it."

Elymas paused and just looked at me, intent that I acknowledge the importance of the secret he was about to reveal. So I sat there thoughtfully, looked at him with a serious expression, and finally nodded.

"Our relationship must change," he said. "From now on, you must dislike me, at least publicly. I want you to talk sarcastically about my magic; dismiss it as child's play. We'll rehearse what you'll say. I'll even give you some simple tricks that you can expose, so that I can get angry with you. Bear me a grudge. I want everyone to believe that you despise me!"

"I can't do that. I . . . admire you. I respect you. It would be deceitful. Why would you want this?"

"It is not a lie, Jesus. It is only—you know the term!—it is only misdirection! And you will be part of it, a secret part. That is always the most effective. If you hate me, then they will never suspect that you built a special chair for me."

He looked directly at me, and seemed to be able to tell that my resistance was melting. "Ah, Jesus," he said, "you're a good student. Some day you could even be a magician!"

"I only wish to heal the ill," I said.

"Magic is a useful skill for healing the ill. But it is much more than that—much, much more. Stay here at the Academy for a while and you'll learn what's truly important. Kings and ministers learn magic. It is the highest, the greatest, of all the arts, for it gives you power, power to accomplish. When you have mastered magic, you can heal, you can teach, you can lead, you can persuade. You already seem to know something of misdirection. But that is just one of the magician's skills. You have yet to learn of *conditioning*—the preparation of the subject, the molding of him prior to the misdirection. Your feigned dislike of me is, to be precise, an aspect of conditioning rather than misdirection. And there is *timing*. Ah, timing, perhaps the most difficult skill to learn. And *expectation*—knowing your subject better than he knows himself. Take advantage of what he thinks you are going to do. With my designs, you are learning the principles of *technology*, but you seem dazzled by *technique*. That is more than practice, Jesus—you must know the motions precisely. Yes, Jesus, to learn magic takes a lifetime commitment, and the teaching of a master. *Opportunity*, I almost forgot to mention the role of *opportunity*. That is the broad outline, Jesus. Misdirection, conditioning, timing, expectation, technique."

"And *opportunity*," I added.

"Yes, yes, and *opportunity*. You are a good student, Jesus. There is much to learn. Much to learn."

"I will do as you request, Master Elymas. But I do request a special payment."

Elymas seemed taken aback. "In addition to my teaching? You know I have no wealth!"

"I wish to learn the secret of haoma. Show me how to prepare it, so I can use it to heal when I return to Israel."

Elymas glowered at me. I tried to glower back, with as much courage as I could muster. We both knew that Elymas had the power to destroy my status at the academy. I tried to read his eyes. Was that anger I saw? No. It was astonishment.

"You know, don't you, what would happen if anyone learned that I had revealed the secret of haoma?"

He was weakening! I nodded in response to his question, even though I truly had no idea what would happen. My gambit had worked.

"You must never let anyone know the secret," he finally said. "Or even that *you* know the secret. You must promise that you will never admit that you can make the haoma yourself. And above all, you must swear that you will never let anyone, or yourself, taste the pure haoma. Swear to me, Jesus."

"I swear by the Almighty God who made me." *May the Lord forgive me,* I whispered to myself.

He took me into a corner of the room. "I'll show you what even many magi don't know about the great haoma." Those who hold great secrets, once they have leaked just a bit, often release a flood, like a breached dam.

Elymas lit a small fire in a lamp that he kept on a table in one corner.

It flickered with green and blue filaments. "Swear again, before the sacred fire," he said. I repeated my oath, and the flame suddenly shot up above my eyes. Elymas was already teaching me new techniques of magic.

"Now, there is a particular red mushroom," he said, "called the fly agaric. It turns to a greenish-yellow powder when dried and cooked. There is also a flower that the Greeks call laudanium. If you make incisions in the unripe capsules of the plant, a milky fluid with a brownish-yellow color comes out . . ."

I won't divulge the method of preparation any further. Indeed, I wish I had never learned it myself.

15. Zarathustra

NEAR THE END OF MY FOURTH YEAR AT THE ACADEMY, I WAS suddenly surprised to see Cambyses walking down a passageway with a stranger, but a stranger with a familiar gait. It was too much to ask for, but I started running towards them, in hopes that my suspicion was correct.

"Simon!" I shouted. Simon Magus turned toward me, and his face lit up with a pleasure that I could see from a hundred feet away.

"My heart warms as if I were seeing my own son!" he said. I stopped short, and politely bowed. Then I stepped forward and gave him a huge Persian hug.

Simon and I found a private corner of the courtyard, away from the clinic, away from the holes in the buildings that served as shortcuts in and out of the grounds, away from any person or thing that might distract us. We sat on two limestone blocks that had been warmed by the springtime sun. In the distance behind Simon stood the atheneum, the symbol of learning, framing his wrinkled face, his slightly hunched body. He seemed much older, even though it had been only four years since I had last seen him.

We must have spent a quarter hour just looking at each other, exchanging pleasantries, discussing travel and weather. But mostly I was just happy to be with him again. Eventually I began to babble on about my studies. I was proud of what I had learned and felt grateful that he had made it possible, but I didn't want to brag. Simon listened intently, and I finally noticed that I had been doing all the talking.

"What about you, Simon?" I asked. "What are you doing here?"

"Darius set me free, a reward for curing him of a minor illness. I protested, but he insisted, and finally I relented. I thought of you here,

Jesus, and, frankly, I was jealous. I could only think how much I love this academy, the atmosphere, the people, the vastness of the knowledge available here. . . ." He looked over his shoulder towards the atheneum. "Years ago I began a book on the history of magic in healing, and perhaps now I can finish it. No other place has the scrolls, the records, the experts. But tell me more about your studies. What have you learned of true healing?"

"I can diagnose more than twenty kinds of skin disease, and I know how to treat those that can be cured. I can set broken legs and arms, and I assist the surgeons in stitching skin and cauterizing wounds. In the clinic I've treated most of the diseases of Babylonia, and I have read and studied the diseases of Israel and Idumea, Greece, Rome, and Egypt. Simon, I've already learned more of medicine than I ever imagined existed."

"Tell me, Jesus—from which of the Gathas of Zarathustra have you acquired the greatest wisdom?"

I stared at him blankly.

"Just as I feared," he continued. "You haven't read any of them."

"Simon, my carpentry duties have left little time. . . . I've barely had time to learn the uses of medications."

"Potions and drugs—the most trivial of the healing knowledge." He shook his head. "Four years of your life wasted," he said in his characteristically harsh manner.

"I've learned about Zarathustra from Rassam," I said. "I've learned that many of the beliefs of the Pharisees came originally from Zarathustra, adopted during the Jewish exile." I had never conceded this to Rassam, but I was groping for approbation after Simon's rebuke. "I have read the different versions of the books of Moses—the one of Israel, the one of Judea, and the one of the priests."

"Spiritual knowledge is the most essential kind if you are to heal," he said. "It is good that you study the origins of Judaism, but you must learn what others have discovered about God. This is what you've been seeking without knowing it. You must open your eyes, for only then will you no longer be blind."

So with Simon's prodding, I finally began reading the Gathas, the sacred writings of Zarathustra. And no sooner had I taken up this study than I began to understand why Simon was so anxious for me to read them.

God, as revealed to Zarathustra, has perfect wisdom and goodness, as does Jehovah, in striking contrast to the gods of the pagan religions. But in the Gathas, God, called Ahura Mazda, has none of the jealousy or anger that our Scriptures portray. And rather than using prophets to communicate with his people, God expresses his will through a "holy spirit," which can reach every person without the need for prophets or priests.

Simon was right. The Jewish prophets had revealed much about the nature of God, but they had also missed much. They knew God as all knowing and powerful, but had not fully appreciated his wisdom and kindness. I began to wonder if the supposed *anger* of Jehovah might be no more than the anger of the prophets who claimed to be speaking for God. What need had God for anger? A loving and wise God—how could Jehovah be otherwise? That was the God my father Joseph had believed in, a God who talked to us directly, through little whispers.

According to the Gathas, God's three aspects were *Ahura Mazda,* wise lord, *Vohu Manah,* good thought, and *Spenta Mainyu,* holy spirit. But there weren't really three gods, just one, although I had observed that uneducated Persians interpreted these spirits as three members of a family rather than as different essences of a single god. It had been revealed to Zarathustra that the battle between good and evil takes place in the soul of every man and woman—just as my father had taught. If good prevails, then the reward is in the afterlife. However there will be an end to the world, when good will finally overthrow evil. Indeed, Zarathustra believed that this time would come soon. All dead souls will be resurrected and subjected to a final ordeal of fire. To reach Paradise, they must cross a bridge that spans the abyss of Hell. Those who led evil lives will be so tormented by their own evil that they will be unable to cross the bridge, and they will fall to their doom. The righteous will feel no pain, and will cross to Paradise.

Belief in the afterlife was common among both the Pharisees and the am ha'arez. I asked Simon if he believed in life after death.

"How can I not?" he responded. "Jesus, you must either believe that our spirits live on or that we just vanish utterly when we die. Can you truly believe that your spirit will just disappear forever? Does that make sense to you, Jesus? And if you can't accept that, then there must be an afterlife."

"But there was a time when I didn't exist—before I was born. If I didn't exist then, maybe I won't exist when I die."

"Think with your spirit, Jesus, not with your mind! Tell me, you believe that God is righteous, don't you?" I nodded. "Then there must be some recompense for the evil that is done to us in this life. How could God be just if there were no afterlife?"

"My father said that the evil suffer, that they are punished here on earth, and that we would see that if we looked hard enough."

Simon said nothing. His eyes looked sad, his face suddenly pallid. He turned away, as if to hide. "We'll discuss this later," he said, walking away.

There was another aspect of the Gathas that affected my beliefs. Zarathustra taught that God was more concerned with virtuous behavior than with worship or ritual. The Jewish laws, in contrast, seemed to be written to satisfy the arbitrary whims of a capricious God: eat this, not that; pray with these words; wear your tassels this way.

No, the prophets must have gotten this wrong. God wishes righteousness because such behavior is good, not because what he desires is arbitrarily *defined* as good. According to Zarathustra, the sins leading to damnation included pride, gluttony, and sloth. These were vague—unlike the Jewish proscriptions—but their very vagueness gave them added life, a flexibility in their application to a range of situations. These were ideas that even the am ha'arez could easily embrace. Zarathustra also catalogued virtues, such as keeping contracts, obeying rulers, tilling the soil—and others, more general: showing mercy, giving alms, and the Golden Rule.

I began to understand what Simon meant when he criticized me for learning only medications. In the Gathas I saw a basis for spiritual healing. The Pharisees were not just on the wrong path—they were moving in a hurtful direction. Their appeal to Scriptures was misplaced and possibly distorted, for the Scriptures had passed through the hands of scribes and Pharisees. We Jews had lost sight of the true, kind, righteous, and loving God.

❖ ❖ ❖

The warm weather seemed to bring out an unusually large crowd, as if heat produced illness, and along with the patients came a high concentration of animals. I was taking my turn in the clinic, treating everything from fever to ear aches to rashes. The dogs, cats, sheep, and goats kept on discovering each other and reacting with delight and dismay while their owners struggled to control them. From the outside, it was amusing to watch, but for those of us working in the clinic it was somewhere between annoying and infuriating.

The sun set behind the atheneum, and it was time to quit. I was pleasantly surprised to see Simon waiting for me. He suggested we walk along the Euphrates to the old town. I had long ago learned that the dangers of the old town were greatly exaggerated, and I had frequently wandered about the city scrounging for carpentry materials. I looked forward to a quiet walk.

In the middle of the city, the river was paved on both banks with smooth stones. The water flowed rapidly this time of year, and it lapped up against the edges. The yellow sunset sparkled off the water, giving the illusion of gold just below the surface. "No wonder there are legends of river gold," I said to Simon.

"Up in the mountains they do find flakes of gold in this river," he replied. "Small flakes. But not here."

A mockingbird warbled in the distance. I spotted it on a bush growing through some rubble. I had no memory of hearing a mockingbird in Babylon before. Perhaps I had been spending too much time in the academy courtyard.

What was it imitating? I wondered.

And then I thought of my mother.

"Jesus," Simon interrupted, "you've worked in the clinic now for two years. Have you learned how to transfer the evil spirits from the ill to their animals?"

"No, I've never tried, despite the pleas of the patients."

"Because you consider it too pagan?"

"That's part of it. But I am still bothered by the use of deception. I would like to heal without having to lie to the patient."

"Even if that means additional suffering? The transference method works, Jesus, even if we don't know why. After all, we don't know how medicines work either. And how is the practice different from that of the Jewish scapegoat?"

"The transference of sins to the scapegoat is symbolic."

"That may be what you believe, but most Jews seem to believe in it literally. The customs aren't really so different. Most illness is not in the body but in the soul, Jesus. Don't you understand that yet? Most pain is not physical but spiritual. The physician who treats the body alone gives the patient little help."

"I often talk to the ill, to discover the source of their problems, and to advise them on how to maintain their health."

"And you've probably discovered that the ill have no patience for a sermon. They just want to be cured of their physical problems. But they are potentially your best subjects nonetheless. Their illness serves to bare their souls, and the master physician takes advantage of that opportunity."

Opportunity, I thought wryly to myself. One of the magician's skills.

"The physically ill can be cured," Simon continued, "of cruelty, of hatred, of covetousness, of all the sins."

"I've found that it isn't so easy."

"I didn't say it was. Preaching isn't the only way to teach, and it's rarely the best way. Patients listen when they believe in you. Lessons can be slipped in when they are listening but don't know that they're listening. You can alter a man's life with a message that he doesn't even know he has heard."

"By using animals? My father called the magi charlatans and impostors."

"Many of us have, unfortunately, fit that description very well. With any great power comes responsibility and temptation, and many people, even great people, succumb."

"In Galilee the crowds seemed almost to worship the magi. Magic made the magi appear to be gods. Everyone who was sick wanted to see a magus, even if the rabbis warned against them. And the magi healed everybody from the blind to the lame. I know how they can make a coin disappear, or a dove appear, but how could they cure diseases that even we at the clinic can't treat?"

"It's easy to fool people into thinking you're healing them. The Jews are easiest, because they know so little about medicine."

"But the magi did it in crowds, with dozens of people watching."

"It's easier to cure people in large crowds than when they are alone. If you tell a lone person that his pain has gone away, he might disagree. It's quite different in a large group, particularly if you've stirred them into an enthusiastic ecstasy. You look skeptical, Jesus. Imagine the master magus, in the midst of a crowd." Simon moved his hands as if creating such a person in space, and then pointed to him. "He gives a rousing sermon—about good, about evil, about trust in God, in terms that make sense to Jews. Then suddenly he demands, 'Do you have faith?' He repeats the question, louder, louder. 'Answer me, do you have faith?' A few of his colleagues, disguised as peasants, shout out, 'Yes!' He now demands, 'Do you believe?' Now more people shout, including a few Jews: 'Yes!' they shout. 'Yes!' He stirs the crowd, and the crowd roils." Simon almost seemed to be stirring the crowd with his arms. "Then the magus spots an ill man. He points to him, and everyone stares. 'Do you believe that good spirit of God will enter your soul?' What man could say *no*, with the entire crowd cheering? The magus demands of the crowd, 'Tell God that you believe the evil spirits will leave!' They're excited. They roar back, 'We believe! We believe!'"

"What good does it do if you can't truly cure him?"

"But you will! You've put the burden of the healing on the man, on the crowd. If he isn't cured, it's his lack of faith, or theirs. The man will shout out, 'I am cured! The pain has left!' The crowd will rejoice."

"That doesn't mean he's really cured."

"Pain will often disappear simply when the patient believes it *should* disappear. People who are partially blind will imagine that they see better—the partially deaf will hear better. Of course, knowledgeable administration of medicines helps. But medicine won't make the patient take care of himself in the future. Faith will. If he believes he's been part of a miracle, then he'll follow instructions. As I'm sure you've experienced by now, getting a patient to do what you prescribe is the most difficult and frustrating task of the physician. The magic makes it easier, and it is the patient who will truly benefit the most."

"I find this all very difficult to believe."

"Ha! Then let me tell you a story you will *truly* find difficult to believe! One time I cured a fat woman."

"Of what?"

"Of being fat! And I did it in front of a crowd of fifty people."

"You did this, Simon? You?"

Simon seemed taken aback. "Jesus, I assumed you had recognized by now that I was such a healer. I'm not making this up."

No, it had never occurred to me. The itinerant magi were "charlatans and frauds." Simon was a man of learning, wisdom, and kindness.

I swallowed, and said, "Tell me about the fat woman."

Simon started walking along the river, and I followed him, listening, watching his hands sculpt the scene out of the air, watching him excite the invisible crowd. He was the same Simon, but now I was looking deeper into him, seeing something obvious that I had previously missed, something that perhaps he had hidden.

"I had worked the crowd for about twenty minutes," he said. "There were several lepers present whom I had cured previously. They shouted, 'I had faith. I was cured,' on my cue. They were experienced with this. They were true believers in my powers, and they came whenever I was in their village. And then this very fat woman came to me and said, 'My body is overburdened with flesh. My husband looks at me with disgust. I can't control my appetite. Help me!' The crowd had been so responsive that I went ahead. You see, Jesus, I knew that it was really the crowd that would make it all work.

"I put my hand on her head, squinted my eyes, and held her motionless for a half minute. I suddenly shouted at her, 'Do you have faith?' 'Yes!' she shouted back. 'Do you believe that the evil demons can be driven from your body?' 'I do!' I made her repeat her answers several times. Then I shook her head violently in my hand, hard enough that she would not forget it. I shouted, 'Asmodeus begone!'"

"Asmodeus!" I laughed. "I haven't heard that name since my childhood. The men of Nazareth often complained that their wives were possessed by Asmodeus!"

"In the Avesta, he's called Aeschma-daeva, the spirit of concupiscence. You changed the name a little when you adopted it for the hysterical afflictions of your women. But let me get on with my story. I had just shaken the woman's head." He moved his hand in reenactment. "Then I suddenly pushed her back into the crowd and released her—she was caught by several people. I shouted, 'You are cured of your obesity. Asmodeus has been exorcised. Go, and eat no more!'"

I laughed. "'And eat no more'? Did you truly say that?"

"Yes, exactly those words. But now comes the amazing part. She shouted that she had just lost fifty pounds! That she had felt it leave—along with Asmodeus. She declared that her clothing had suddenly become loose on her. 'Look!' she cried as she tugged on her smock. Her dress was indeed loose. I think she must have been sucking in her stomach. She was so convincing that I almost believed her myself."

"Did you know she would react that way?"

"No, of course not. I didn't expect to have her lose weight immediately. It would have been enough for her to walk away believing that the evil spirit had left her, so she could eat less. This was a chance to do good, Jesus. If she truly 'ate no more,' or at least less than usual, she might become a happier woman."

"Suppose she walked away and ate the same?"

"It would have been her failure, not mine, for her lack of faith, for letting Asmodeus back into her soul. But that's one of the tricks of curing people—you don't have to make their symptoms vanish instantly. Announce them cured, but say their symptoms will gradually fade. And, of course, supplement your magic with medicine. Some symptoms are easier to treat than others. The best are headaches, poor eyesight, poor hearing, and impotence. Fear and worry can exacerbate any physical distress. As I said, Jesus, the greatest pains are spiritual."

"My father said that the easiest people to fool are those who want to be fooled." I wondered what my father would think of me sitting here in Babylon and learning from a magus. "He was a man who loved all others, even tax collectors. *Almost* all others," I corrected. "He always held one group in contempt: the magi."

"Perhaps he knew their power," Simon said. "If exercised properly, it dwarfs that of a centurion. And like the power of a centurion, it is easily abused. A skill that can spread hope and righteousness can also be used for evil." Simon's voice quivered, and I wondered if he were thinking of a specific example.

"Do you know of magi who abused their skills?" I asked. "I have heard rumors of a Samaritan poisoner."

"Yes," he sighed. "No—not the poisoner. That was a false rumor. People like to blame illness on others. But I do know of abusers. Evil can be much less violent and yet just as vicious. Yes—I know of abusers." He seemed to be wrestling with something inside himself.

Suddenly he turned to me and said, "Jesus—I was the worst abuser of all. When you told me about the pleasure you found in planning your theft, I knew what you had experienced. There was a period of evil in my life too. As with you, it led to great suffering, and I have done penance."

"Your slavery?"

"Yes, that's why I sold myself. But even that wasn't enough. Ahura Mazda is a forgiving god, but I may have to wait for the afterlife to find true peace." Simon seemed to be struggling with the question of how much to tell. Now that I was on the verge of learning, I wasn't sure I wanted to know.

"It began harmlessly enough," he finally said. "It often does. A woman who was barren came to me and asked to be healed. She had been married for four years, and was without child. She had watched me cure a blind man, and she was convinced I could help her. She was very attractive, and she was begging for help. She said she would do whatever I asked. The temptation was too great to resist. So I told her that I indeed had the power to cure her. I said that I must lie with her three times, and on the third she would conceive her husband's child. I had the wisdom to say that I must have her husband's consent. They dearly wanted a child, and they both agreed."

I was spellbound. The only woman I had known was one behind the red tent, and although I had found that experience unappealing, I found Simon's story arousing. "How could you cure her barrenness?" I asked.

"It's well known by Babylonian physicians that men as well as women are barren, but in Israel everyone assumes it's the woman. I was guessing that it was her husband, not she. Well, I guessed wrong, and she remained barren, but it didn't matter. Healers get their reputations from their successes, not from their failures. However I wisely stayed away from that town afterwards."

"Was this your great evil?"

"Oh, heavens no! I don't even regret that cure. It isn't often that you get to lie with a beautiful woman with her husband's consent and have them pay you for the act. I'd probably do it again. The problem was the temptation that had been planted by my success. I became possessed by my own power. Having succeeded like this, I began to wonder what other women I could maneuver with my healing skills. Alas, it proved all too easy. Soon I had succumbed to lust. I would spot a pretty girl watching my healing and immediately made her my target. I watched her, played to her, worked her so that she would come back to me when the crowd had gone. I could manipulate girls, especially young girls, convince them of my supernatural powers, and I discovered that their feelings towards me bordered on worship. They trusted me, and I found that they were happy to do anything I asked, particularly if I gave them some pomegranate juice spiked with mandrake and haoma.

"You see, Jesus, I too know what it is like to be possessed by Satan. I never thought about them, not really. I was a predator. I had imagined getting caught, but I had never imagined how severe my true punishment could be.

"I indulged my fancies for several years, until one time when a prostitute came asking me to heal her baby, and I recognized her as one of my victims. Her skin had roughened, her hair had become wiry, and her heart had hardened, but I still recognized her. She had been a virgin when I slept with her, as were many of the girls—so beautiful, soft, so accepting of everything I did. Her skin had been like that of a baby. Alas, she had *been* a baby. I had thought that she was too young to get pregnant, no more than twelve, and I was long gone by the time her condition became evident. She told me she had first worked as a servant and then as a prostitute. Her first son, my son, had died in infancy, and now she had two other children with her. They were both dirty and beset with worms and lice. I had destroyed this poor girl's life.

"That evening I wondered how many children I had fathered. I imagined each of them looking like the children of this girl. Where were they? Littering the countryside. *My* children! I didn't know where they were or what was happening to them. They were suffering, and I couldn't care for them. I couldn't even find them. And this is still true. My children, poor, destitute, diseased, unloved, my sons and daughters."

I thought of my mother, and how she had been sexually victimized as a child. A sudden thought flashed into my mind. "Had you ever visited Chorazin?" I asked. "In Galilee." It was my mother's home town.

"Chorazin? Yes, there was a girl in Chorazin." My heart pounded. "She was my last victim. I told her that I would introduce her to mysteries of God that had been kept secret, to a ceremony in which she would anoint me, and I would anoint her, and she would feel the presence of the Lord, a thrill as the holy spirit of the Lord entered her body. I was an angel of the Lord, I told her, and she would remember the time we spent together as if it were a dream."

I cringed at the thought that I might be hearing the details of the seduction of my own mother.

"Isn't it pathetic, Jesus, that I would use such words to work a seduction? Can you imagine a greater profanation? But it was so easy, and so effective. I inverted her natural modesty and shame by invoking the name of God.

"You see, Jesus, evil can give you enormous power in the world of the flesh, the power to manipulate others, if you give it freedom to move within you, if you do not struggle to contain and control it. At first my deceits had been minor, and perhaps even beneficial to my victims, but soon I slipped into the chasm and lost all consciousness of the spiritual world. I lost all sense of righteousness. I lost all sight of the souls of other humans.

"When I repented, after meeting the prostitute, I began a search for my children. The girl from Chorazin was the first I sought. She had indeed conceived, and had moved from her home in disgrace. With help from two of my fellow magi, I finally tracked her to Bethlehem, the City of David. But she was a fortunate one, for she had found a husband. She had just given birth to a boy, and he—my son—was only a few days old. I admired the baby, and inwardly despaired that I would never see him again, for I didn't want the husband to know that I was the father, that I was the man who had seduced the girl whom he so evidently loved. Can you imagine the pain of seeing your own son, and knowing that he would be raised by others, that he would never know you, that he would never love you. My pain was relieved only by the recognition that this child, at least, would be brought up in a good home. I left valuable gifts, more than a stranger should decently leave, and went on searching for other victims. But I found no others."

"Was she the only girl you had—you victimized—in Chorazin?"

Simon seemed puzzled by my question, but he answered. "One girl per village, that was what I allowed myself. For nothing would have exposed me more quickly than the jealousy of a former lover. I was clever, Jesus, too clever."

Simon Magus could not be my father, I concluded, for I had been born in Nazareth, not Bethlehem.

"Finally I couldn't stand the torment," Simon continued. "The thought of my children, lost and ill and suffering. Every beggar I saw increased my torture. I couldn't sleep. My head was in constant turmoil. I confessed my sins to Cambyses. I told him that I thought I could find relief only by ending my life. His response was chilling. He said that suicide was inadequate atonement for my sins. A more severe punishment was required, and he instructed me to find one. He told me that I would know it when I had found it.

"Shortly afterwards I sold myself into slavery for life. I was in my fourteenth year of slavery when you entered my tent. I did what was instinctive to me, and I helped you. Afterwards I watched you care for the ill and the injured. You were the only joy in my life in those days. I saw goodness, and compassion, and love. I saw what I might have become. You thought I was teaching you, but you were teaching me, Jesus."

Simon was looking at me with an expression that somehow showed both immense sadness and immense joy. His eyes seemed to fill with water. I had never seen him cry, and my eyes too filled.

I said, "You know, don't you, that God has forgiven you, Simon."

He said, "Perhaps I do know. Now, for the first time."

We returned to the academy, and I went to bed in the small room that I used just outside the walls. But I couldn't sleep. I had seen into the soul of another human, and having done that, I felt a deep love for him.

But even that feeling of love only reminded me of my mother. I had abandoned her in Sepphoris only because of selfishness and uncontrollable hatred.

I left my room and wandered back to the Euphrates. It was a moonless, dark night, and I found my way through the rubble by starlight. I sat and watched the flow of this muddy river, and I thought of the psalm: *By the river of Babylon, there I sat down and wept, as I remembered my home.*

16. Burial

ONE AFTERNOON I RETURNED FROM THE OLD CITY, WHERE I had been searching for scrap wood and nails. No sooner had I approached the academy grounds than I knew that some great tragedy had occurred. The clinic was closed, every head was lowered, conversation was nil, and many wore white hoods.

Elymas seemed to appear out of nowhere. "Come with me, immediately!" he demanded. He tugged urgently at my sleeve. "There is little time!" His tone was almost frantic, and as I followed him, our rapid walk turned into a run.

"Master Elymas—what's wrong? What's happened?"

His mind seemed to be elsewhere. He had been huffing, and he slowed to a walk.

"Tell me," I persisted.

"Cambyses is dead," he replied, without emotion.

I stopped. "Dead! How?"

"Get moving! Quickly!" His voice was severe, although I sensed panic in his face. He hurried his pace. "Come, come! You have much to do. I am—we are—unprepared."

As I trotted alongside him, I looked around at the courtyard, the atheneum, and the buildings of the academy. It all suddenly seemed much more fragile. "How did he die?" I asked.

"He was found in the library, collapsed over a book."

He led me to his private room in the atheneum. He unlocked the door as I watched—something he had never let me do before.

"What is it you need?" I asked.

"We need four containers, like barley crates. With hooks and eye loops."

"To be carried by a camel?"

"As *if* it were to be carried by a camel," Elymas answered.

"You can buy these in the market."

"I want a false bottom on each one—an undetectable false bottom. They must look old, worn—but they must also be strong. There must be space for . . ." He paused, as if calculating. He looked perplexed. "One crate should have a space about so big." He motioned with his hands. "It must carry about fifty pounds."

"I can reinforce and modify some crates. It won't take long."

He pulled a bag of coins from a drawer and dropped it in my palm. "Purchase anything you need. But hurry. Don't fail me, Jesus."

I knew better than to ask him why the crates were needed. I finished them in two days.

❖ ❖ ❖

I had previously avoided the Persian funeral processions, but this time I was inclined to follow. In the tradition of the Zarathustrians, the body of Cambyses was carried by six bearers; mourners dressed in white came behind. The body was taken to the outskirts of Babylon and placed up on a *dakhma*, a stone "tower of silence" on the top of a hill. The tower had no roof, but was open to the sky above. Cambyses's clothing was slit with care so the knives never touched the body. I watched all this without understanding what was going to occur next. We left the tower, walked to a nearby hill, stopped, and watched.

Within a quarter of an hour I shuddered with revulsion when I realized what was happening. Vultures had been circling the tower, and one landed on it. It climbed awkwardly through the opening in the roof and dropped down inside. It was soon joined by several others. I dared not imagine the scene inside but knew that the body of Cambyses was serving as food for those hideous creatures.

Simon later explained that this was the traditional Persian method of disposing of a body. But with the exception of crucifixions, never before or since had I experienced an event so alien to my Jewish spirit.

I volunteered to be one of the numerous mourners to return forty days later and help remove the remains. When we went back and climbed the tower, we found that the bones of Cambyses were clean and white, as white as the ashes of Sepphoris. The vultures had removed every speck of flesh. I was careful not to touch the bones myself, although I noted that nobody else seemed to mind. We threw them into a deep burial well near the tower. From the clattering sound of the bones hitting bottom, I guessed that Cambyses was joining the remains of many others.

I was surprisingly moved by the death of Cambyses. I had learned that a great leader is not the one who stirs emotions, but one who makes right decisions, consistently right decisions, and who shows the path to truth and righteousness through his own behavior and wisdom. That was what Cambyses had done. That was what my father had done.

And now I had made a decision, and ardently hoped it was the right—and righteous—one.

I finally found Simon in the Room of the Ancients. He appeared to be writing on a papyrus scroll. I approached him with the same delicacy with which I had once approached Cambyses in that room.

Without looking up from his work, without turning, Simon spoke: "Ah, Jesus. So you've found me."

"Are you working on your book?"

"No. I wish I were. No, the elders have asked me to organize the affairs of the academy. But there are few records. I'm trying to figure out whom we must pay and who must pay us. Apparently Cambyses kept records only in his head."

"They say you are to be the next director."

"They?"

"Everyone."

Simon accepted my answer and went back to his work. For a short time he wrote quietly. Finally he said, "Not if I can avoid it, Jesus. I don't want to direct anyone. But I must do what I must. Gangrene has set in. Fortunately they've given me the power to amputate the diseased flesh. My first act has been to exile your mentor of magic, Elymas."

I was momentarily stunned, more by his knowledge of my hidden relationship to Elymas than by the shock of the news. "But why?" I muttered.

"He has been studying the science of poisons. He has gathered a library, a rather substantial library. And a pharmacy. It was all done secretly, for Cambyses had forbade such studies decades ago. Elymas is gone, Jesus. Exiled from the academy grounds. His laboratory has been destroyed, his jars of poisons drained into the desert sands. You have never heard me say this, Jesus, but there are certain kinds of knowledge that should be lost."

"Master—I built some crates! He may have hidden some . . ."

Simon finally turned towards me. He appeared stronger, almost younger, his deep blue eyes full of life. "Yes, yes, I know. We found the crates, Jesus. And their false bottoms. Elymas is not the only master magician at the academy. Don't worry, Jesus. I know that you were unaware of his intent." He looked at me with a kindly expression. "And I understand that you are leaving the academy," he said. "Nothing I can do can persuade you to stay."

"That is what I came to speak to you about."

"There is no need, Jesus. I probably knew you were leaving before you did. Your studies are incomplete, you have only begun your spiritual advancement, and yet you must return to Galilee."

"I must. As you say, I've thought long and hard about this . . ."

"I won't try to dissuade you, Jesus, even though your decision is the wrong one. I know it would be futile, since you will do what you must, just as I will do what I must."

"I am sure the academy will flourish with your help."

"No, Jesus, the academy has been dying for many years, just as Cambyses has. I can only guide the death and assure its dignity. There are those—Elymas isn't the only one—who would turn the academy towards malignancy. There is power in these scrolls, Jesus." Simon swept his arm, again reminding me of Cambyses. "Vast power. I will see to their preservation, so they can be used for truth, for the will of God. The library must survive, just as the academy must die."

He rose from his chair and approached me. I saw in his face, in his eyes, a confidence, a surety that I had never seen before. He appeared to know precisely what he was doing, and what needed to be done. He stood for a moment looking at me, he smiled, and then he took a step forward and again we hugged.

"I may never see you again, Simon."

"Not until the afterlife," he said.

17. Repentance

I SENSED FEAR IN THE EYES OF THE YOUNG WOMAN WHO HAD
just come to my shack—and guilt in the way she tried to hide her face.
She waited anxiously while I tended an old man with a bad tooth. Finally
she interrupted, "Please help me!"

"What's the matter?"

"My daughter is ill—she had an accident. They say you are good at
healing children. Can you heal her?"

"I won't know until I see her," I said without looking up. I tied a cord
around the base of the tooth. "Bring her in here."

"She can't walk. She's too ill to be carried. She's hot with fever. Please
come!"

"Yes, yes, I'll come. Just a moment."

I yanked hard on the cord, the man yelped, and the tooth popped out
of his weak gums. Gradually a smile came to his face as he realized the
aching was gone.

"Rinse your mouth frequently with wine," I instructed. I was confident he would follow *that* prescription. "Now open your mouth," I said as
I pulled his jaw down myself and stuffed a poultice into the wound. "This
is balm of Gilead. It'll help your gums heal. Here's more. Put it on if you
bleed." The balm was made of pine sap, honey, and matted spider web—
not exactly a *clean* mixture, but an effective coagulant.

I followed the woman as she hurried through the streets of old
Sepphoris. Probably another case of child beating, I guessed. The fever
suggested that the injury was several days old.

Her name was Joanna, she said, wife of Chuza, a city official. She led me to one of the wealthier parts of the city and into a large house partially built into a hillside. As I entered, I saw that the walls were plastered both inside and out, a sign of greater wealth than her clothes had suggested. We went through a courtyard to a small dark room lit by several candles. The shutters were closed, probably because of the common superstition that sunlight interferes with healing. A man stood by a bed—the father, I presumed. Lying under a thin white sheet was a little girl, her face badly bruised.

.   I opened the curtains for better light and examined her. She had three broken ribs, infected cuts from a whipping, and numerous bruises near her dull expressionless eyes. Her fever was moderate, not dangerous. As I probed her broken bones I noted that she hardly flinched. She had grown inured to pain.

"Why didn't you call me sooner?" I asked her mother, who hovered nervously in the shadows.

"It was the Sabbath," the father said.

I inwardly seethed at this answer, but said nothing. "What is your name?" I asked the child.

"Rachel," the father replied. "Why do you need to know?" I scowled at him. "Can you heal her?" he asked.

"I can set her on the path to recovery. But you must administer the cure."

"We'll do what you say."

I looked up at the father. "Her wounds are unclean," I said. "I'll give you myrrh to mix with wine for ritual cleansing. Repeat the Shema as you wash them, but be gentle! I'll set the bones and give medicine for the fever, but the most important treatment will be the application of love. It's what she most desperately needs."

"She receives that all the time. Our home is full of love."

"Then how could you beat her?"

The father recoiled slightly, as if trying to decide whether to continue the lie of an accident. Finally he said, "She disobeyed me."

"Was that all?"

"It was willful—and it wasn't the first time. I hit her so she would learn to follow the commandments of the Lord. It was for her own good. She refused to apologize. *Break your child as you would a horse, beat him soundly, or he will grow stubborn and cause you to gnash your teeth.*" That famous passage from Ecclesiasticus was known to many children in Israel. "Be assured," he continued, "the beating hurt me more than it hurt her."

I doubted that. I suspected that the beating hurt *me* more than it hurt him. I restrained my instincts and refrained from insulting the father. I washed Rachel's wounds with wine and myrrh, treated them with balm, wrapped them in clean cloth, and gave her pomegranate juice with a pinch of haoma powder for the fever and pain. I set her broken ribs and wrapped her chest tightly. That was truly the easy part, I thought. The body of this child will recover more easily than her spirit.

I said to the father, "This is only part of the treatment. Most important, you must *never again* beat this child. Violence only toughens her skin. If she misbehaves, show her how it hurts you. Soon she'll want nothing more than to please you—and the Lord."

"Yes, yes, physician, you may go." He thrust two denari into my hand—twice the usual fee—and he turned his back to me.

Judaism is a religion of beauty, generosity, and kindness, I thought. Yet the influence of the Pharisees has led to a perversity that in practice places strict obedience above all the other virtues. I was sick—sick of finding young children broken and injured. Never did the parents listen to my pleadings. Countless times I had mended the wounds of children, helped make them physically fit, only so that they could be beaten again. Eventually they would grow up to beat their own children—and the punishment of the sins of the parents would be passed on to the third and fourth generations.

This event occurred in my third year of practicing as a physician in Sepphoris. After my return from Babylon, I had searched the city in vain for my mother. I finally learned from the Roman militia that Pantera had been recalled to Rome, and I presumed that my mother had gone with him. Although I had been denied my reunion, at least I had been spared the test of confronting Pantera.

Before coming to Sepphoris, I had found a small abandoned house in Nazareth and tried to sell my services as a healer. But my work was cut short by Rabbi Shuwal, who spread the word that it was a sin to be treated by *Jesus the bastard,* who wished to use medications to counter the will of the Lord. So I moved to Sepphoris—I shall always call it this, despite its official name change—where I was unknown and where the Jews were more accepting of unorthodox ways.

I was doing what I had trained for, and doing it well, and yet I felt utterly impotent. I could set bones and pull teeth, but, as Simon had taught, it was not disease that was the source of most suffering. People abused themselves, their families, and their friends. Rather than take joy in the Lord's gifts, they coveted what they didn't have. Rather than rejoice in love, they wallowed in hatred. As I tried to heal, it became more and more obvious that their real needs were spiritual. Perhaps I *had* ended my training too soon. Perhaps, once again, I had squandered my life.

What was I to do? Again I wished for the wisdom of my father. Why had he died before he could answer my questions? If only I could remember all that he had tried to teach—perhaps in his words I could find my answers.

And what advice would Simon Magus have given me? I almost heard his words, *Jesus, you have failed. Admit your failure.* Yes, that's what he would have said.

I don't know if it was thoughts such as these that triggered my departure, or just the burden of an uncountable number of events pressing down like an accumulation of rocks piled too high and suddenly collapsing from its own weight. But one day I was sitting in the doorway of my shack, looking out at the hills, my work for the day finished. And once again I had time to ponder my failed life. My skills were inadequate for tending the souls of my patients. What good was it to polish and finish a piece of furniture if the wood beneath was weak?

I had made my decision before I even knew I was considering it. I gathered my few belongings and prepared to return to Babylon. In retrospect it was only half a decision, for I didn't know what I would do in Babylon when I arrived. Perhaps I intended to study true magic; perhaps I would seek wisdom from Simon, if he were still there—if the academy was still there. It took me less than an hour to gather food for the journey, say farewell to several children I had grown fond of, and depart.

That afternoon I was in Capernaum, a town on the north shore of the Sea of Galilee (recently renamed the Sea of Tiberius, after the new emperor), when I noted a stir among people gathered at the well. I caught the words, *the Baptist.*

"He's no prophet," someone shouted, "for he performs no miracles!"

"He could do miracles if he wanted," shouted another. "He's the Messiah!"

"Then why doesn't he say so?"

"He is a devout Jew! But he speaks with *authority.*"

"He's mad!"

Their words reminded me of those I heard long ago at the well at Nazareth, about Judah of Gamala. I shuddered at the memory. But the Baptist was no violent zealot—I had heard about him even in Sepphoris. He was also known as "the Hermit" and as "the Ascetic." He spent his life in the wilderness subsisting on locusts and honey, and was reputed to be as agile and wild as a desert goat. He wore a shirt made of camel hair to irritate his flesh and to remind himself of the worthlessness of his body and the primacy of his spirit. Only occasionally did he wander near an area as populated as Capernaum, and when he did, he spoke eloquently of *repentance,* and of the Lord's forgiveness.

This day he was preaching some two miles from Capernaum, near the Bethany ford of the Jordan River, close to where it flowed into the Sea of Galilee. It seemed that half the town of Capernaum had been to see him in the last few days. I would not have to go far out of my way to take a look.

I followed the opposing streams of people who were either seeking him or leaving. When I crested the hill, I saw what looked like a giant herd of sheep—the disciples of the Baptist, wearing their characteristic plain white woolen tunics and spread out over the hillside. Down at the river bank, three standing men were just barely visible. As I got closer I could tell from their large girdles and seamless clothing that one of them was a priest and the other a Levite, a priest of a lower order. The third wore a simple tunic with a large leather belt, and had long unkempt hair. That must be the Baptist. I carefully picked my way in between the sitting people and worked my way in closer to hear better. It appeared that the Baptist was being interrogated.

"Are you the Messiah?" demanded the Levite. If he says yes, I thought to myself, there will be another crucifixion.

"No," the Baptist answered.

"Are you Elijah?" the Levite asked with a sarcastic tone. This was also a potentially incriminating question. The book of Malachi says, "Behold, I will send you Elijah the prophet before the coming of the great and dreadful day of the Lord." Based on this, the priests had convinced the Romans that a self-proclaimed Elijah was as much of a danger as a self-proclaimed Messiah.

"I am not Elijah," he responded, wisely. I wondered what he really thought.

"We were sent by the Jewish council, the Sanhedrin. We must return with an answer. You understand that. Everyone calls you the Baptist. Who are you? What do you call yourself?"

The Baptist suddenly extended his arms. With a thundering voice he boomed, "I am the voice of one crying in the wilderness! Make straight the way of the Lord!" I had heard that his voice was mighty enough to break cedars, but I was still startled by its power. Everyone was riveted to attention. Even the Levite seemed somewhat taken aback, if not intimidated.

"Those are the words we expect from Elijah. Are you Elijah?" the Levite demanded. But his weak voice couldn't compete.

"I am not the light, but I was sent to bear witness of the light!" Each word was articulated with strength and beauty, as if it emanated not from the Baptist, but from God himself.

The Baptist crouched in a pose of humility.

"Why do you baptize if you are not the Messiah? If you are not Elijah?"

He began his answer in a quiet tone: "I baptize only with *water.*" But then his voice rose: "But one *mightier* than me is coming . . ." His tone turned humble: ". . . the latches of whose shoes I am *not worthy* to unloose." A pause. Then suddenly he stood up and boomed, "*He* shall baptize you with the holy spirit, and with *fire!*" He swept his hand around the gathered crowd as he intoned, "He will gather the crop—but he will separate the chaff from the wheat! And *burn* the chaff with an *unquench-able* fire!"

I finally understood what they meant when they said that the Baptist spoke with authority. It was not just his power, or his eloquence—indeed most of his words were quotes from Scripture—but it was that he spoke as if directed by the Lord himself. The Baptist's words were appropriate, com-pelling, and persuasive.

Yet I realized that he was walking a thin line. He was protecting him-self with metaphor, but his message was clearly threatening. Everyone knew that the "chaff" to be burned were the Romans and their Sadducee collaborators.

The priest turned to the Levite, and they talked between themselves for a short while. The Baptist was effectively using them as a tool for deliv-ering his own message. But it was obvious that they would not be able to draw him into saying anything that might be a punishable offense.

Suddenly the Baptist shouted, "You *vipers!*" The words reverberated between the hills. The Levite and priest turned to him, but he was looking at the crowd, not at them. "Who told *you* that you could *avoid* the coming *wrath* of God! Repent! Bring forth fruit that proves your repentance!"

Again, each word was articulated with meaning and power—no, with more—with beauty and truth.

"Don't think that because you are *descended* from Abraham that you are *immune!* God can take these stones—" he bent over and picked up sev-eral large rocks from the river bank, "—and turn *them* into descendants of Abraham!" I looked at the rocks and half expected them to turn into peo-ple. "The *ax* is ready to *fall!* Every tree that doesn't bear good fruit shall be *hewn down* and *cast* into the *fire!*" With these words he heaved the rocks into the deepest part of the river.

I was entranced. Was I wheat or chaff? Would I bear good fruit? Were these not the questions I had been wrestling with in Sepphoris, in Babylon, in Nazareth?

I looked towards the priest and the Levite and wondered, are these inquisitors similarly affected by the power and truth that were being spoken? It seemed not. They appeared so frustrated by their failure to draw the Baptist into sedition that they had missed what he had said. None is so deaf. They were probably imagining with dread their return to the Sanhedrin, who would demand: "What did the Baptist say?" And they would have to reply, "'Every tree that doesn't bear good fruit shall be chopped down and burned.'" And the Sanhedrin would say, "If we take that to Pilate as evidence, he will just laugh."

So without looking back at the Baptist, the priest and the Levite left.

The drama over, I was now eager to hear more from this impressive prophet. I sat on the grass and listened as he preached and answered questions. He spoke in metaphors when criticizing the ruling powers, be they Sanhedrin, Pharisee, or Roman, but he was explicit when asked about personal behavior. He alternated eloquent poetry with gentle prose, his tone and his power changing to match his message.

"What must we do?" asked a voice from the crowd. "How can we please the Lord?" Cynically, I wondered if the man who asked this was an associate of the Baptist, placed in the crowd to ask the right questions at the right time.

"Let he who has two coats give to him who has none," the Baptist replied quietly. "Let he who has meat give to those who have none."

No one could doubt his sincerity or his own practice of these preachings. He was going well beyond the usual calls to alms and charity. He seemed to be saying that wealth was intrinsically corrupt. Here is a man, I thought, who is living a truly spiritual life.

Another question from the crowd: "I'm a *publican.*" It was spoken as if a confession. "What must *I* do?" Publicans—tax collectors—were the most detested men in Israel. This was a dangerous admission to make in the midst of a possibly hostile crowd. But publicans were also official agents of Rome. Could this man actually be the priests' conspirator, left behind to elicit seditious words?

"Repent," the Baptist replied. "That is all. Continue as a publican. But exact no more than that which is prescribed."

That was *all?* The Pharisees considered tax collectors to be robbers, forgiven only if they returned twice what they had stolen. But the Baptist simply told him to change his ways—and be forgiven, immediately, wholly. It was that simple. Was *that* the meaning of "repent"? No recompense?

Could anyone, even God, forgive that easily?

Yes. My father could have done so. Certainly the Lord, in his infinite generosity, could do so.

But as I pondered the Baptist's answer, I realized that it was not only deeply spiritual, but also politically astute. In effect, the Baptist was saying, "Obey Roman law." But the publicans were not paid by the Romans; they paid the Romans for the right to collect taxes. They earned their livelihood by the extra taxes they collected beyond those officially sanctioned, fees that made them among the wealthiest men in Israel. If they collected no more than was required, they would have no income. No one would be a tax collector under such circumstances and the entire system would collapse. In preaching strict obedience to Roman law, the Baptist was, in effect, preaching . . . revolution. No wonder the authorities feared him.

Another voice from the crowd: "I am a soldier. What can I do?" The man looked strong enough to be a soldier, but he was dressed in a simple tunic.

"Do no violence for the collection of money," the Baptist replied. "Never accuse anyone falsely. Accept your wages, and take nothing more from the people." In other words, follow the Roman law and accept the mediocre pay of a soldier. Forgo your perquisites. So this would be a gentle revolution, if it truly came to pass. And yet the Baptist was only preaching obeyance of the Roman law.

There were no questions for a while. The Baptist stood motionless, his head down. Then without warning he exploded again, with the words he had spoken previously from Isaiah, but now intoned differently: "Mine is the voice of one *crying* in the *wilderness!* Prepare *you* the way of the Lord! Prepare a *straight* path for him. Every *valley* shall be *exalted,* and every *mountain* and hill laid *low.* The *crooked* shall be made straight, and the *rough* places plain. And *all* mankind shall see the salvation of God."

Before this day, I had always found this passage from Isaiah disturbing. I enjoyed the beauty of the wilderness and I didn't want the mountains flattened and the valleys filled. But when the Baptist spoke those words, I understood the deeper meaning of this passage for the first time. Isaiah was talking not of the physical but of the spiritual world. When the day of the Lord arrives, all spiritual ills will be healed. There will be no rough places, no needless difficulties. *That* was the world I was seeking—and that I had planned to return to Babylon to find.

It was getting dark, and suddenly the Baptist was surrounded and hidden by a group of disciples. Then he was gone, vanished.

The Baptist's preachings rambled back and forth in my mind. He spoke to the poor and downtrodden—indeed, he seemed to have voluntarily joined them. To become spiritually pure and ready for the coming of the Messiah, forgo wealth, he preached. The poor are not less favored by the Lord; they are the ones who are closest to him. Hadn't I once had a similar revelation, when I was a slave? Why had I lost sight of it? Why had I spent so many years preparing to tend to physical ills?

It was growing dark. I had stayed at the Jordan longer than I had intended, so I had an excuse to spend the night in Capernaum. For quiet, rather than stay in the village itself, I slept in the woods to the north.

"Mine is the voice of one crying in the wilderness." The Baptist's words rang in my ears. "Prepare you the way of the Lord!" I couldn't stop thinking of the Baptist's eloquence and his choice of words from the prophets. But most of all, I was struck by *what* he said. Repent and God will forgive. Repentance wasn't just atonement—it went beyond. Repentance was a spiritual metamorphosis that could take place instantly, effortlessly. The "baptism" that gave him his name was a ritual washing that was more a symbol than anything else, a symbol of the change that could take place in the soul instantaneously.

Now it was all so clear. The Baptist had opened my eyes, and I could see what he saw. That was his great power. That was why they said he spoke with authority.

I had not witnessed a baptism on that first day—maybe he had done it earlier, or perhaps the inquisition had interfered with it. Maybe he would perform one tomorrow. I decided to go back, at least for the morning, before continuing my journey to Babylon.

Although I arrived early the next day, a crowd of about two hundred people had already gathered. Still, that was considerably smaller than on the previous day, so I was able to get closer. The Baptist was about my age, and if he truly wore a hair shirt, he wasn't wearing it that morning. He spoke softly, about sins and repentance, and about the day of atonement. It is coming soon, he said, and sinners must repent, change their ways, now, for when it comes and the Messiah appears, it will be too late. "Whoever knows everything but lacks within, lacks everything," he said.

There were long pauses, when he seemed to be praying, and during these moments I thought of my sins, my failures, my mother, my slavery, my wanderings, and my inadequacy. I had spent years studying to be a physician, and yet it was all for nothing. I was lost and crying in the wilderness.

The Baptist spoke quietly. "You are the chosen people—but woe to you if you complacently think that therein lies salvation. Woe to you if your soul depends on the flesh. Woe to you unless you stand ready to march against the forces of darkness."

He lowered his voice even more and the crowd leaned forward as if being closer to him by an additional foot or two would make a difference. "I will take you from among the heathen, and I will bring you into your own land," he said softly. I recognized the words from Ezekiel. "I will wash you with clean water, and you will become clean. From all your filthiness, and from all your sins and your abominations, I will cleanse you. A new spirit will I put within you, and I will take away the stony heart out of your bodies, and I will give you a warm heart of flesh."

The baptisms began. One disciple after another waited his turn, fully clothed, to walk into the River Jordan with the Baptist and be thrust under the water. As the Baptist pulled each out, he joyously pronounced, "Your sins have been forgiven. The holy spirit has become one with you. Sin no more and make ready for the kingdom of the Lord!"

Just as I had never consciously decided to leave Sepphoris, but had just acted as if directed to do so by a greater power, so I never consciously decided to be baptized. I just found myself joining the disciples, waiting my turn, as if driven by the holy spirit that the Baptist had described. Simon Magus had taught me to accept failure, but I wanted more. I wanted my sins forgiven. I wanted redemption.

About two dozen men, women, and children stood ahead of me. When it was finally my turn, I entered the water and walked up to the Baptist, approaching him with my head bowed, as I had seen the others do. He placed both of his hands on my shoulders and gripped them tightly. "Do you repent?" he asked, gently.

"I do," I replied, and then I held my breath in preparation for submersion. I looked up at his face—and recognized him just as his powerful hands pushed down on my shoulders and plunged me into the water.

"John!" I shouted out as he shoved me under, and the river poured down my throat. I gurgled and choked and gasped for air but only sucked in more water, lost my balance and slipped, flailed helplessly and found no grip—but the Baptist's strong hold never weakened and a moment later he pulled me out.

"Jesus!" he shouted back, as I coughed up water, for he had apparently recognized me just as I recognized him, a moment before I almost drowned. "Cousin! Jesus, my friend! I can't believe it! What a wondrous miracle!" he said, as I continued to cough and gasp for air. "I'd heard you were alive, that you'd visited Amos, but then disappeared again. And here you are!" His big smile turned to a puzzled look. "What are you doing here?" he asked.

"I'm being baptized," I said, still coughing up water.

"You should be baptizing *me!"* he roared.

"John—*you* are the prophet! You called for repentance and I heard you. I heard the Lord, through you. So I came, to repent, to be baptized, to have my sins washed away. I didn't even know it was you." I paused then continued, "I can't really believe that it is you!"

"Come, Jesus, I have so much to tell you. It has been long since we've talked. What have you been doing? Where have you been? How did you get here?"

My cousin and childhood friend, John, the Baptist, put his arm around me, and led me out of the river and into the wilderness. His remaining disciples would have to wait until the next day for their baptisms.

18. The Baptist

WE SAT ON THE GROUND AT A SMALL CAMP—NOTHING REALLY
but a blanket, a small shoulder sack, and the charred remains of a campfire.
As John delicately arranged twigs on the old coals, I had my first chance to
study him. His face was brown and lean, like lowlands oak. He had a few
deep wrinkles on his forehead, and his nose was larger than I remembered.
He took some tinder from a little bag and carefully arranged it under the
kindling. Two expert strikes of a flint and he had started the fire. As John
blew gently, I noted that his wild unkempt hair was scrupulously clean.

"I usually like to sleep alone," John said. "In fact, I don't even tell my
disciples where I'm camped. I change my location almost every day. The
isolation is good for my spirit, and also good for my security. The Sanhedrin
would arrest me if they could find me."

"But they didn't yesterday, when they challenged you at the river."

"Ah, you saw that? Before a crowd they must appear to follow the law.
But if they caught me away from the crowds—then they could do what
they wanted."

"Why would they wish to do you harm?"

"Do you ask that seriously, my cousin?" he asked, with a wry smile.

"But you preach obedience to the Jewish law. You're a threat to the
Romans, John, but not to the Sanhedrin. What have the Sanhedrin to fear?"

"What all powerful men fear. The loss of power."

"Power? What power? They, like we, are slaves to the Romans."

"So you truly are that naive, after all. You have much to learn about
rulers!" John roared with laughter.

I tried not to show my vexation. My eyes landed on the soft linen smock he was wearing. "Is it true that you sometimes wear a hair shirt?" I asked, "and that you eat nothing but locusts and honey?"

"I don't know where the hair shirt rumor comes from. My disciples know better, but the stories still spread. The part about locusts and honey is largely true, however."

"Your favorite snack as a child."

John gave a big smile. "You remember? The Lord was kind to declare locusts clean, so we could survive the plague years. But I thank him every day for making them so delicious and nourishing." John's eyes moved up towards the sky, as if he were truly thanking the Lord.

I looked at some of the jars he had taken out of his sack. "Especially when fried in olive oil and dipped in honey," I added. "But now you are a prophet!"

"A prophet? If that were true, Jesus, the Lord would have given me the ability to perform miracles."

"But you *are* performing miracles, John. What you are doing for these people, those are true miracles. You turned their despair into hope. You offered them a new life. You showed them a new world."

"A new world? Have you forgotten? That 'new' world was the one you lived in—you and your father, back in Nazareth."

"But everything has changed since then, John. When my father died, I became lost. I lost sight of what was good. I've been blind ever since."

"Why did you come to be baptized?"

"I've wasted my life." I told him about my crime, my slavery, the academy, and my attempted life as a physician in Sepphoris. But I wanted to know about his life. "Amos told me that you joined the Essenes," I said.

"And so I did. I lived in Qumran from the time my parents died until a year ago. And you say *your* life was wasted! Oh, I learned some things there. The Essenes are devout and they practice the Law of Moses rigidly. I was entranced at first. It took me a long time to recognize how deeply corrupted they are."

"Is it true that the Essenes are preparing an arsenal?"

"Far more than you might imagine. They call themselves 'the followers of the way.' They believe that a war will soon be upon us, a cosmic struggle between the 'sons of light' and the 'sons of darkness.'"

"That sounds like the teachings of Zarathustra."

"The fire worshippers? No, not at all. The sons of light are the pious Jews, and the sons of darkness are the Romans and the apostate Jews who don't observe the Law of Moses. The battle will be brutal, and almost all will die. But victory will be assured by the coming of the Messiah."

"You sound like a Zealot," I admonished.

"Oh, no, no. The Zealots—that's yet another story. The Essenes are peaceful. They won't start the battle. They only plan to do what is necessary to survive it, since the outcome is decided. That's why they are so isolated. They're trying to make themselves completely self-sufficient, with their own farms and craftsmen in every skill. They've even built an aqueduct to bring water to their monastery."

"You said they had become corrupted."

"It is a very subtle corruption. At first I thought the Essenes led an ideal life, with no greed, no acquisitiveness, no selfishness. To be with them you must forsake all your property. Everyone works as hard as everyone else. Everyone gardens and cooks and serves and helps raise the children—people were always bringing us children that they couldn't raise themselves. There was the highest level of discussion and debate—of the apocalypse, of the meaning of the Scriptures. Everyone followed the Law of Moses to its letter. Everyone! Someday, I thought, the entire world will be like this."

"What was it that changed your mind?"

"I believed what they said. And then I realized that I didn't like it. I thought of the world outside of Qumran, the world you and I came from, the world that sent the Essenes its children. That world that would be destroyed in the coming battle—while the Essenes, in isolation, would survive. What a hateful vision. I couldn't accept it. We mustn't let it happen that way. We must try to stop it. I finally recognized that the Essenes had a different kind of selfishness, born of the self-indulgence of living an isolated life when the outside world is full of sin and suffering. Being separate—how could that please the Lord? No—I felt I had to leave, to help, to preach to the Jews."

"By living as a hermit in the desert?"

"That is my weakness, Jesus. If I had the strength I would live in the cities, and spend all my days redeeming sinners. But I find civilization too painful. In the desert I can be closer to the Lord."

"Do you think the war can be avoided?"

"The Messiah *is* coming so—maybe—instead of victory—he can prevent the war. He can bring peace. If we are ready."

"You *know* the Messiah is coming?"

"Doesn't everyone? Don't you?"

"No. How do you know?"

"I don't know how I know. It's just obvious. Isn't it? He's coming. Everything in the world points to it."

"Then where is he? When is he coming?" I asked.

"Soon. I don't know more. But we must be ready. The Jews must be ready."

We talked for several hours. But I was exhausted, and fell asleep.

My father had grown a long white beard. I was entranced with its magnificence. He smiled. He held my shoulders in the powerful grip of his huge hands.

"Father! You're alive!"

"Of course. I never died." He tightened his grip on my shoulders. Suddenly he pushed down, plunging me under water. I struggled, but he held me down with his powerful hands. I could hold my breath no longer and gasped. Water poured into my mouth, down my throat. But I could still breathe!

"You are my chosen!" he said to me through the water. "You are forgiven for your sins. Your soul has been cleansed. You have been chosen to complete my unfinished work. You are my beloved son, in whom I am well pleased."

I awoke to the crackling of a fire. John was sitting next to it, holding a branch wrapped with dough over the heat. "I'm glad you eat something other than locusts," I said. John smiled and handed me a piece of the bread that he had smeared with honey. I pulled some dates out of my satchel and offered them to John. I don't know whether it was the wilderness air or the new life that John had given me on the previous day, but that breakfast was one of the most delicious I have ever eaten.

The sun finally appeared between the cracks in the nearby cliffs, and soon the morning air was warm. "You probably have a hundred disciples waiting for baptism," I said. "You should go to them."

"No, let them wait—the longer they wait, the more excited they'll be when I appear, and the closer they will listen. And when they listen, they understand, they see. Jesus, it is extraordinary."

"They do listen to you, John—and that *is* extraordinary. Where did you learn to speak with such force?"

"You mean the voice, my lion roar? That's just a trick, Jesus—anyone can learn it. Just relax your jaw, open your mouth wide, and get your chest out of the way. Talk with your belly, not your throat. And my rhetoric—that too is just a device, mostly quotes. It's all tricks, except for the message."

"Having the message isn't enough by itself, John. I've tried it. In Sepphoris, there was a man who beat his daughter, and I told him it was wrong. But I could tell he wasn't listening."

"Your mistake was that you were a physician, not a rabbi. You can't just tell them what is righteous. You must convince them that it is the Lord's will."

"But the Lord has never spoken to me. He's never told me it's his will."

"Then how do you know you're right? How do you know that the Lord doesn't *like* his people to beat their children?"

"I just know. Like you know that the Messiah is coming."

"Then the Lord *has* spoken to you."

We returned to the Jordan, and I sat and watched the extraordinary effect that my cousin John had on the people who flocked to hear him. I walked among them and listened to them talk to each other. It wasn't just his voice. He baptized more than a hundred people on just that one day. Each one came away looking transfigured, as if their rebirths had been physical as well as spiritual.

That evening I moved with John to a new camp site, hidden among the gullies in the dry mesas. As it grew dark, I expressed my confusion to John. "It's too much. I'm exhausted. Even when I sleep I don't seem to rest. I'm in a constant state of excitement. I can't bear it."

"The brightness of the Lord is such that no mortal can look directly at him."

"John, this isn't a religious experience. I'm confused and I don't know what to do. I can't go ahead and I can't stay still. Help me."

"Do what I do when I am in turmoil. Go to the desert. Spend time away from everything, until the truth is obvious and you know what to do. Spend forty days and forty nights in the wilderness, if necessary, as Elijah did in the desert, as Moses did on the mountain in Sinai."

"I can't live alone that long in the wilderness."

"I didn't mean it literally. Go to Qumran. It's in the bleakest part of the wilderness, far from anything you've known before."

"And live among the 'corrupted'?"

"Perhaps I was overly harsh. The Essenes are misguided, but they aren't evil. It was while living amongst them that I finally understood what *I* must do. There is something magical about Qumran, something spiritual…. You meet their requirements: you are unmarried, deeply religious, willing to abide strictly by the Torah. They are in need of someone who understands how to build aqueducts—and that's you. They'll accept you, in the hope and expectation that they'll eventually convert you. They lead a seductive existence, and many visitors succumb. Many of their novitiates come to them in a state of turmoil, and they know enough to leave them mostly alone. You need time to think, to sort things out, to pray, to talk to God."

"What if *I* succumb?"

"I don't think you will. Go there, Jesus. You'll discover it easier to find God, to listen to God. Soon you'll know what you must do."

19. The Essenes

THERE IS NO MORE OPPRESSIVE PLACE ON EARTH THAN THE shores of the Salt Sea, appropriately called the Dead Sea by the Greeks, since it kills all fish unfortunate enough to be carried by the sweet waters of the Jordan into its lethal brine. The acrid water is bitter to your lips and painful to your eyes, and it stings your skin at any abrasion. Deep under the lake are reputed to be the remains of the evil city of Sodom, as dead as the fish.

Overlooking this forsaken area is the barren mesa on which the Essenes, the self-proclaimed holy ones, chose to build their home when they withdrew, two hundred years ago, from the "worldliness and uncleanliness" of Jerusalem. On the flat top of the mesa they built the Qumran monastery, making it into a place to live and study, a place to worship, and a fortress.

Steep cliffs of crumbling tufa protected them better than any barricade. Only one narrow road carved through the rock scaled the heights, and it was wide enough for no more than one wagon at a time. Under the watchful eyes of several sentinels, I worked my way up the winding path and finally entered through a gate in the monastery wall. A white-robed guard led me through a series of courtyards to a small room near the watchtower. A young olive-skinned man identified himself as Daniel and asked me to sit with him. I handed him a letter from the Baptist. As he read it, I admired the brilliant whiteness of his woolen robe, unlike anything I had ever seen. This was the famous Essene symbol of ritual purity. The Magus had told me that the secret of this whiteness was to raise the sheep indoors, never exposed to sunlight. As impressed as I was by the cloth, I couldn't help being bemused at the problems they must have encountered in raising sheep indoors.

Daniel looked me over slowly, making me feel distinctly self-conscious. Finally he said, "John of Nazareth says that you've been blessed with a revelation from God, and that you wish to retreat from the sinful world to consider its meaning and significance." I noted that he used the term "God" almost as a name, as had John, rather than using the usual substitution, "the Lord."

He continued, "I can make a recommendation to the elect, but I will need more information. Tell me about your family and your education."

John had warned me to hold nothing back, for if the Essenes determined that I was not completely candid they would reject me, or perhaps imprison me as a suspected spy. So I told them of my life in Nazareth, the tragedy of my father's death, my crime and my slavery, my training at the academy and my failures in Sepphoris. Daniel listened intently, apparently undisturbed by my sins and failures. He interrupted only when I mentioned the aqueduct—and then it was to probe the extent of my experience.

It was clear that my knowledge of Scripture and willingness to abide by the Law of Moses was of particular importance to him. He asked my opinion of obscure passages, and I responded, whenever possible, by quoting adjacent text. At times I was certain he feigned ignorance just to test my knowledge. The examination lasted several hours. Finally he asked, "Do you know the significance of the word *shibboleth?*"

"It means 'flowing stream.' The word was used by the Gileadites at the fords of the Jordan to detect spies. Their enemies, the Ephraimites, couldn't pronounce 'sh.' Anybody who said sibboleth," I said, "was slain on the spot."

He looked at me with a smile. "Are you aware of our requirements at Qumran?" John had told me that if I got to this stage, it meant I had passed the examination. In effect, I had pronounced *shibboleth* correctly.

I responded, "I am prepared to pledge all of my knowledge, all of my strength, and all of my wealth to the community of God. Although, of the latter, I have little to offer. I am poor and own nothing but my clothes, a blanket, and a small satchel of food and herbs."

"You are considered unclean by the rules of the Teacher of Righteousness. However, you may have temporary asylum with the holy brothers—forty days and forty nights. During this time you may sleep in the Courtyard of Atonement and take your meals in the refectory. You will be expected to do your share of work with the holy brothers, but we will allow you time to pray and prepare for your future commitment to God.

If you live according to the Law of Moses and of the Teacher of Righteousness, and you become knowledgeable with his writings, then you may be elected to the first degree of purity and serve as a soldier in the holy army."

He led me outside to a large enclosed courtyard at the north end of the complex. There were several dozen other men, in brown and gray robes, camped there along with donkeys and a few camels. Looming overhead was the tower, with its ever-present guards, who occasionally glanced at the courtyard, but mostly kept a careful watch on the rugged path leading up to the monastery. Daniel told me to wait, and I spread my blanket, sat, and wondered what surprises lay behind those walls.

I had been waiting about three hours when Daniel came back and asked me to follow him. "I am taking you to our holy brother elect Jacob," he said. "He will be your spiritual mentor during your residence. Do whatever he commands, without hesitation and without reservation. For now, he wishes to learn of your knowledge of aqueducts." He led me through a gate, past several fortified buildings, and into the complex of inner courtyards.

Daniel took me into a small storage room at the side of the yard, and I felt relief to be in the shade. From a box, he took a dark goat-hair robe and handed it to me. "Wear this while you are here," he said. "Be sure to use the hood when outside, regardless of the heat."

Back outside, the harshness of the desert plateau was made harsher still by the austerity of the clay and brick buildings and the severity of the sun. I pulled my new hood farther over my head, for protection. But as we turned a corner, the bleakness was suddenly softened by the sound of gurgling water. A water-filled channel, about a foot in width, ran diagonally across the space into a cistern at the far corner. From there water flowed out into two other channels, one of which turned a corner and ran into yet another cistern. Men in gray hoods were at work there, apparently repairing the structure. More channels and pipes branched from this cistern, some entering directly into buildings. Daniel noticed my interest. "The Teacher of Righteousness built this water system," he said. "Until the great shaking, the channels worked without attention, but now they are a constant problem. Unfortunately, the books of the Teacher of Righteousness have no instructions for repairing them."

We came to yet another courtyard, where a small mill stood. It consisted of two cone-shaped stones fitted one on top of the other and a harness for a donkey to power it. Next to the mill was a large bakery and pantry. The kitchen had water running into it through a pipe. I wondered if even the residence of Caesar could boast such an elaborate system. Nearby was a large kiln, and beside it several monks in gray robes were busy making what looked like tall, narrow jars, an awkward shape for food or grain storage. In a corner was a rack holding several dozen such jars.

We entered the Scriptorium, a large room where about two dozen monks, each wearing a pure white robe, stood at high tables transcribing leather scrolls. Daniel indicated that I should wait, and he walked over to one of them.

I noted the care and concentration with which the monks appeared to work, patiently dipping their reed pens into clay inkpots, slowly moving their pens, carefully examining their work after inking in each letter. There was one table as long as the room, and a single scroll was laid out upon it. I knew it must be made of several pieces, but from where I stood I could not see the stitching. The enterprise taking place here was impressive. The copying of scrolls has been a central activity of Judaism for hundreds of years, and was now relegated to the specialists called scribes. But the copying going on before me was greater and more systematic than anything I had ever heard of or imagined.

The monk to whom Daniel had been talking looked up at me. He had a wrinkled brow and tanned face, a striking contrast to his white robe, and looked to be in his early thirties. Daniel beckoned me to come closer. "This novitiate is called Jesus of Nazareth," he said. "He worked as a slave on a Roman aqueduct, and knows their methods."

The man rose from his chair. I was impressed with his height—half a foot taller than me—and his massive shoulders and arms. Not the physique, or the complexion, of a man who had spent all his time indoors.

"We will be pleased to use the tricks of the Romans against them!" he laughed. "My name is Jacob. Come, Jesus of Nazareth. Let us go outside and talk about Roman plumbing techniques."

Back out in the sun, we walked over to a corner of the yard where a puddle had formed near a leaky channel. A crack in the structure had been clumsily repaired. "What do you think of this?" Jacob asked, as Daniel stood near.

I ran my finger over the caulk and scraped off a little with my fingernail. "If I may offer a suggestion," I said, "it appears that your men are applying a dry caulk." I rubbed a bit of it between my thumb and forefinger. "It seems to be properly mixed, but it will hold water well only if allowed to adhere to the stone. That means the channels must be drained before the caulk is applied, and they must be kept dry for at least a week."

I looked up at the severe sun. "Perhaps here it need dry for only three days."

"We have much to talk about," Jacob said. "You may leave us, Daniel. Come, Jesus. Let me show you our masonry shop."

Although the monks worked hard—when they worked—there were long "Hours of Worship" devoted to prayer and meditation, periods when all labor ceased. Then some monks sat quietly in the shade of a wall or building; others gathered in the assembly hall or an inner court for common prayer or readings from the Teacher of Righteousness. These were solemn periods—except for the happy play of the numerous children who flowed around the monastery complex. No attempt was made to quiet them or to force them to participate in the worship. Their happy noise was just another background sound, like the gurgling waters of the aqueduct.

During these periods I was left to pursue my own spiritual needs. But for the first week I made a practice of attending the readings, to learn more about this intriguing cult which had had such a strong effect on John.

If the Teacher of Righteousness had a name, I never heard it mentioned in Qumran. Perhaps it was too holy to pronounce aloud, just as was the name of God, Yahweh, by many Jews. The Teacher was not only the founder of the Essenes and the architect of Qumran, but the most recent and most important prophet. His most important work, the scroll that was read most often, was called, "The War of the Children of Light Against the Children of Darkness." It was an apocalyptic text, but unlike Enoch or Baruch—or anything else in our Scriptures—it was a detailed and precise prophecy of the imminent battle, a virtual guide to God's wishes as to how the Essenes were to fight.

The scroll began with the words, "At the beginning of the undertaking of the sons of light, they shall start against the lot of the sons of darkness...." Then came exhortations, prayers, and prophecies. The war would last forty years, the same sacred period it took Moses to lead the Jews through the wilderness. The army of light would have precisely twenty-eight thousand men in the infantry and six thousand in the cavalry, arranged in a phalanx similar to that of a Roman legion but commanded through the use of trumpets. The army's weapons would include shields, swords, darts, spears, and javelins. The text prophesied that the children of light would suffer a serious defeat, but would ultimately be victorious. A wise prophecy, I thought, to prevent their soldiers from losing hope after a loss.

20. Splinter

EVERY MORNING, EACH MONK TOOK PART IN A RITUAL OF Baptism. They removed all their clothes except for a cloth around their loins and walked one at a time to the cisterns. Standing in the water awaiting them was an elder, and he took each in turn by the shoulders and plunged him into the water—exactly as I had seen John do to his disciples, exactly as John had done to me—except for the absence of clothes. The children and novitiates were allowed to partake, but in a separate shallow pool in the Courtyard of Atonement. That's where I met Matthew.

We were sitting next to each other, drying off in the hot morning sun, after a morning baptism. Matthew had a robust dark complexion, and looked to be about ten years old. His black hair was cropped short, in the style of the monks. He began the conversation.

"You're new," he said. "Where did you come from?"

"Nazareth, although I haven't lived there for a long time."

"I've never heard of it."

"Few people have. Where are you from?"

"Augustus."

"Do you mean old Sepphoris?"

"Yes, that's what the old people call it."

"I worked there for the last three years, as a physician. Nazareth is just four miles to the south—by the dirt trail."

"I still never heard of it. Can you take out a splinter?"

"Let me look at it."

Matthew pointed his foot at me. The large toe had an inch-long sliver of wood embedded just beneath the surface. The end of the sliver had broken off, from his futile attempts to remove it, I assumed, and the skin was slightly discolored—the beginnings of infection.

"Yes, I can heal it. Will you be brave?"

"Of course!" he said, with a slight shudder.

I gently cleansed his toe with a rag and took out a sharp knife from my satchel. Matthew looked at the knife, swallowed, and closed his eyes. I honed the edge on a stone, then held his toe and carefully sliced the surface of his skin, exposing the sliver. I used the point of the knife to gently pry the sliver out. Matthew never flinched. I took a thin paste of haoma from my herb bag, wiped the shallow wound, and wrapped a dry strip of linen around the toe.

"Do you come to Baptism every day?" I asked.

"Are you done?" he said with surprise, opening his eyes for the first time since I had taken out the knife.

"I want you to forego baptism for the next three days," I said. "Keep this clean and dry. Show it to me every day so I can see if it is infected."

"I can't believe that you did that so fast."

"Have you been coming to Baptism every day?" I asked again.

"Yes, so God will forgive my sins."

"Do you sin a lot?"

"Every day. But God forgives me."

"Try to sin less for the next few days. How do you know he forgives you?"

"Oh, I can feel it, every morning, like now. Don't you feel it?" he asked, curious that I had asked.

"Yes, I guess I do." And I did. The refreshment of the rite seemed to extend right into my soul. "How long have you lived here?"

"I came when I was a child. The Romans killed my parents. Some day I'll kill them. I'll kill all of them."

"The Romans stole my mother," I said. That metaphor was the most accurate way I could think of to describe to a ten-year-old what had happened and how I felt.

"Are you going to kill the Romans too?" he asked.

"No," I replied gently. "The Romans want us to hate them. I'm not going to do what they want me to do. When I hate, it feels like having a splinter in my soul."

Matthew looked at me with a combination of curiosity and puzzlement. But he said nothing more.

21. God and Satan

I HAD COME TO QUMRAN TO PRAY, IN THE HOPE THAT GOD would tell me what I must do. And although I spent many hours in prayer, I received no little whispers in return. But John had advised me to be patient, and to work hard at the tasks assigned me.

During the first few weeks, I spent much of the daytime with Jacob, trying to teach him everything I knew about caulks and aqueducts. We walked the entire length of the aqueduct, nearly a mile to the west, where it took water from a waterfall that flowed from the distant mountains. I discovered that I knew far more about the construction, testing, and repair of aqueducts than I thought I did. Many of the previous repairs had to be undone and redone with the proper procedures.

Every day Jacob spent the first work period in the Scriptorium. His duty there was to check the manuscripts, to make certain that each letter was an exact duplicate of the original. "I do not yet have the skill to be a scribe," he explained. "And when I find an error, I tell no one but the master scribe. He then sees to the correction."

I watched as a set of scrolls was wrapped in linen and carefully sealed in large clay jars. "Why do the holy ones work so hard at this?" I asked Jacob. "You are making many copies of the same scrolls. Are you planning on using them as weapons in the coming war?" Perhaps, I thought, the Essenes believed the scrolls carried supernatural power. Moses had invoked the magic of the Ark of the Covenant in battle.

"No, not as weapons," Jacob replied. "But soon the Apocalypse will come, and the Romans will besiege our monastery. They will try to obliterate our religion—especially the writings of the Teacher of Righteousness.

Many of us have memorized the words, but it is difficult to get the lettering precise in our minds. So we are making many exact copies, and hiding them in many different places. Proliferation, Jesus—in proliferation lies security. This way the holy writings will survive."

"The Romans are patient and persistent. They will search every home."

"The Teacher of Righteousness has told us how to preserve and hide the scrolls," he said. "Only the elders know the secrets of their security."

"But what if the elders are all killed?"

"The elders *will* all die in the Apocalypse."

"Then how will you find them?"

"It is prophesied. The Romans will not find them—not all of them. But we will."

I examined Matthew's toe every morning. To keep him from the morning baptisms, where the dressing on his toe would get wet, I suggested that we take walks in the surrounding mesas during that time. It turned out that Matthew knew the mesas very well—not just the trails, of which there were few, but the places where no trails led.

He took me to a high prominence that looked insurmountable. But by using the hand and toeholds Matthew showed me, we were soon at the top. I stood up and let my face feel the strong, dry, hot wind. It was thrilling, and somewhat frightening, to be so high. I had to squint in the bright sunlight, but the view was spectacular. In the distance below us, I could see the entire Qumran complex, and the convoluted trail of the watercourse as it wound its way through courtyards from one building to the next. Far away was the Salt Sea, pale blue and deceptively attractive. The crumbling sandstone, carved into cliffs and gullies by rare but intense thunderstorms, seemed to extend forever. The cliffs were colored with delicate tones of yellow, pink, and gray, punctuated by a great variety of dark spots, like the skin of a leopard.

"Are those caves?" I asked Matthew.

"Yes," he answered. "There are millions. Most are hidden, unless you get right up to where they are. That's where the monks hide the scrolls."

"What? How do you know that?"

"I've seen them. I've been in the caves. The monks think you need ropes to reach them, but I can climb up."

"Do all the caves have scrolls?"

"No. Only some. Mostly the hidden caves.

So, I thought, this is the secret of the hiding of the scrolls. The Teacher of Righteousness did have his genius even in this. For even if the secret were exposed, it would be virtually impossible for the Romans to search every cave, even if they knew where each cave was, and they wouldn't. They'll find some scrolls, but if just one set survived, the Romans would have failed.

✧ ✧ ✧

It was fall, and the Essenes had completed their harvest—from their farms located several miles away in the valley. Food for the winter, and for the war, was stored in jars larger than those for the scrolls. The cisterns were full, and Jacob allowed me to dry out each of the water channels in turn for repair. Three brown-hooded monks were assigned to work under my direction. They followed my orders as if I were the Teacher of Righteousness himself. I was able to lay out a day's work in the morning, with the assurance that by evening the work would be done, exactly as I had specified it. How odd, I thought, to have a former slave now directing work as if he were the master.

John was right: Qumran reflected both the best and the worst of the Jewish worship. The Essenes' pure life, in which by mutual support everyone could follow the Law of Moses exactly, and the lack of conflict and covetousness—these were the best parts, what many Jews strove for. This seemed to be the "ideal life," total fulfillment of the covenant, precisely what most Jews thought God wanted.

But Qumran was to be the last outpost when the Jews were slaughtered, the lone survivor of a Sepphoris-like cataclysm in which the rest of Israel would be destroyed. Forty years of horror, with only a few surviving. Was this to be preferred over Roman domination? Could this really be God's intent? Couldn't we prevent it? *Mustn't* we prevent it? To allow such a fate appeared less like the will of God than a concession to the forces of evil. The Qumran monastery was, in effect, an ark created to survive the coming flood, a flood not of water but of wickedness and evil. God had promised that he would never again bring a deluge. And yet this was what the Essenes were anticipating, planning for, perhaps even looking forward to.

The impure Jews of the outside world didn't exist for them except as potential soldiers. The Law of Moses, practiced here in the isolation that made it truly practical, had never seemed so thin, and yet it was the logical culmination of the separation cult practiced by the Pharisees. John had explained to me his disillusionment with the Essenes, but I hadn't fully understood, not until I had witnessed it myself.

And yet, wasn't the Covenant between God and the Jews as a whole people, not with isolated groups? When the Jews were sinful, they were punished together, not individually. When they broke the rules, their cities were destroyed and they were sent into exile, as to Babylon. These Essenes acted as if they had a separate covenant—that God would treat them differently when the war came—that God would love and protect them while letting the rest of the Jews be destroyed.

Why should all Jews be punished for the sins of a few? Or for the sins of the many? Why should the child be punished for the sins of his father, or of his father's father? Do we not each have an individual soul? Doesn't God love us as individuals, and not just as a *people?*

In contrast to the strict monks were the young children, flowing around the grounds like the water, playing with each other, spontaneous and joyful. Which group pleased God more, I wondered, the ascetics fulfilling their list of duties and rituals, eating only prescribed foods and making prescribed sacrifices, giving rote but unloving obedience—or the children, joyous, happy, thanking God every moment by their love and appreciation of his gifts?

I began to spend more time wandering in the nearby hills, following the tangle of trails that Matthew had shown me and exploring on my own. But even away from the compound, my thoughts returned to those children, my father's favorite miracle. And as I remembered my father, I felt as if he were there beside me. He wasn't speaking or whispering, but just there, in spirit, to keep me from being lonely as I pondered my future.

Love and charity, those were his foremost teachings. *Love your neighbors as yourself.* And I had suggested that perhaps we must also love our *enemies.* Of course, as a child I hadn't really known what the word enemy meant, nor what hatred truly felt like. Even my trip to the devastated Sepphoris had not taught me those words, for I had been too young, and the experience had been too much like a nightmare. I had thought I hated the Romans, but I hadn't really. Only when I met Pantera, the man who had stolen the life of my mother and destroyed my own, had I experienced true hatred.

The wind whistled between the cliffs.

No, Jesus, Pantera did not destroy your life. It was your hatred that did that.

Where did that thought come from? Was it my own, or from the magus, or a whisper from my father? Or a whisper from God?

I remembered Pantera's words: "I have known many Marys." And they set loose a jackal inside me, biting, clawing. Or was it a splinter, causing pain only when I moved? I leaned against the side of the gully and dug my fingernails into the harsh rock. My heart was beating harder and faster, as it always did when I thought of Pantera.

Love? How could you love someone who had caused so much pain?

In my mind I saw my father standing in front of me. He spoke quietly: "Loving others, even those undeserving of love, is not an act of generosity, Jesus. Nor is it an act of compassion. It is an act of self-healing. It is not a gift to another person when you love that person. It is a gift to yourself. You were right, Jesus, when you spoke, as a child, of loving your enemies. I know that now. You *can* love them, Jesus. And you must."

Have you ever had a chronic pain, one you lived with for such a long time, one that you became so accustomed to that you almost forgot it was there? And then without warning it fades? Nothing else changes, but suddenly the world seems to glow with life and health, and you feel exuberance and joy. Nothing has changed, and yet everything is more beautiful. This is far more than the removal of a splinter. At that moment, as I wandered in the hills near Qumran, if felt as if my soul had just been healed of a crippling disease.

It is not a gift to another person when you love that person. It is a gift to yourself.

I sat down and felt the gritty tufa with my fingertips. The sun beat down on my face. I closed my eyes and saw only the warm glow of the sun through my lids. But in my heart I saw the whole world, and it seemed different, changed. Or was I just seeing a part of the world, a spiritual part that I had glimpsed but had never seen clearly before? This was a larger, more wonderful, more beautiful world than I had previously seen. No, the world hadn't changed. Only my vision.

Is this revelation? Enlightenment? Is God talking to me? Or is it my father? Am I receiving knowledge, or am I just seeing the world more clearly?

As I sat there on the warm rock, the *why* of much of my life began to make sense. Job had been tested with deprivation, disease, derision, and misery. I had been tested with hatred. I had failed the test and had suffered. But now I understood that failure, and I could accept it, as Simon Magus had taught. For the first time in my life, I believed that I was beginning to know what God wanted from me. It didn't matter that I had failed. God forgives, completely, utterly, joyously—and instantly. In his forgiveness he shows his generosity and his mercy. God loves the sinner. He even loves Pantera. How could I not do the same?

God is our father—not a stern, disciplining father, but a kind, loving one, our abba. His love for us is boundless, his generosity infinite. All he asks in return is that we love him back. That—not the myriad of rules—is the essence, the deep true essence of Judaism. What he wants is love: love for him, and love for our fellow human beings, who are his creations, and our siblings. We are all brothers and sisters under this one father. Love so pure, that it spreads to Jew and gentile alike, to friend and to enemy. The rituals, particularly the ritual libations, the washings, are only symbols of our purity, just as the baptisms of John are merely symbols of repentance. With love, the symbols are unnecessary; without it, they are irrelevant.

These thoughts suffused my spirit like a spring rain soaking into a parched garden, bringing with it sweetness and purity and new life, rebirth, full of hope and love. I drank it in.

❖ ❖ ❖

Rather than slaughter doves and lambs for their sacrifices, as Jewish law prescribed, the Essenes made a ritual sacrifice of bread and wine. It was hardly a sacrifice at all, yet they treated it as one, one that they could afford to do every day at their communal meals. I was surprised that these "holy ones" who claimed rigorous adherence to the law could consider bread and wine an adequate sacrifice.

I had come to Qumran to ponder, pray, and think, and had a great deal of time to think about these sacrifices, to wonder (as I had in my youth) what satisfaction the Lord took in the burning flesh of rams, bulls, and lambs. Rabbi Shuwal taught us not to ask such questions, for the will of the Lord was impossible to divine. But I had long ago lost my belief in the Scriptures as the absolute word of God.

As I wandered amidst the cliffs of the mesa, I felt a struggle within my soul. I found myself rejecting more and more of the Covenant. I was fearful of rejecting everything I believed, rejecting all of my religion. We Jews were chosen by God, and he had promised to protect us in return for our unquestioning obedience to a set of rules. Even if they were not the *essence* of Judaism, how dare I reject them? I was moving closer to the edge of a spiritual chasm, one that seemed more perilous than the rock cliffs at my feet, and I was growing dizzy.

I left the trail and climbed through a gully towards a yellow-gray mesa. Behind a large wind-sculpted rock I came across a small cave. I worked my way through a crevice, and peered into the darkness. My eyes adjusted, and I saw to the back of the cave. Empty. No scrolls.

Back outside the air was so clear, so severely clear, that the distant mountains looked like they were only a few hundred feet away. I climbed a steep ravine to get a better view. The rock crumbled, and lizards scattered as I struggled to reach the top. But the true struggle was in my heart. The Covenant was the core of everything in Judaism, the essence of all I had been taught to love. And yet it seemed so hollow, so barren, more barren than these grassless hills.

Within my mind I heard the words of Jeremiah: "Behold, the day is coming that I will make a *new* covenant with the people of Israel. I will put my law within their hearts. They will no longer need to teach their brothers and neighbors, for they will know me, from the least of them to the greatest. I will forgive their sins, and I will remember their sins no more."

I had known those words since I was a child. Rabbi Shuwal said they would be fulfilled with the coming of the Messiah, and they had never seemed to me to carry great meaning—but that was because I had misunderstood. They had been waiting in my heart for me to understand them, and now they were clear, so severely clear. Now their meaning burst from my soul, blossoming like petals from a bud of the myrtle bush.

I will put my law within their hearts!

It didn't mean, as I had thought, that Jews would be born instinctively knowing all six hundred and thirteen rules of the Torah. No, it meant that these complex rules would be replaced by a new rule, a new covenant, a new testament, a rule that could be known in the soul, a rule that was simpler yet more demanding, a rule that didn't ask more of the poor than of the wealthy, a rule that transcended all that came before and reflected God's greatness and his love.

I didn't return to the monastery that night. I lay the back of my head down on the rough sandstone and looked up at the heavens, at points of light, twinkling in different colors, surrounded by small luminous clouds moving quietly and effortless among them. My thrill was paradoxically mixed with serenity. I felt completely at ease. I recognized the feeling, but it took me a moment to place it. Yes, it was the comfort of a happy child. This is what God the father wants. For us to be like children to him.

Many thoughts passed through me that night. Time didn't exist. I was undergoing a change, a metamorphosis, and I would never be the same. I wondered if my appearance would change too. *I will put my law within their hearts!* All of the rules could be—should be—abandoned, left behind like a chrysalis. All will be lost, but nothing will be lost. The new covenant is not between God and a people, but between him and each individual soul.

The stars to the east began to fade, and soon the horizon was glowing with a rich orange color. A mockingbird sang a morning song, as if to tell me that I wasn't alone. Perhaps it was the water of the aqueduct that enticed it to this arid mesa. The mockingbird sang again. It was imitating the song of a chickadee. I could recognize it clearly, chic-a-dee-dee-dee. It was different from the original, and yet beautiful.

Was this all there was to speaking with God? It was so simple, so powerful, and so obvious, yet most Jews didn't know it. My father called it bat qol. Why had it taken me so long to learn how effortless it was? My father knew, and so did John. Now Jewish prayer—the ritual chanting, the carrying of prayer shawls, the little box on the head carry-ing the words of the Shema, all ritual, all symbols, all well-meaning—seemed so empty. Revelations were not reserved for lonely prophets; anybody could receive them in abundance, as I had done all through the night. Just talk to God quietly, by yourself, with your spirit, and listen to hear him speak back, gently, with *quiet* thunder.

As these thoughts passed through my mind, I was surprised by the joy within my heart. I knew nothing of the fate of my family, my attempts to help people had been a failure, I had achieved no good in the world, and yet this morning—my spirit was elated. The closest I had felt to this before had been during my slavery, when the soldier had struck me, and I had ignored the pain and turned my other cheek. Then I had chosen to ignore the physical world, and had moved only in the spiritual one. These two kingdoms, the kingdom of man and the kingdom of God, coexist, and yet so many people act as if only the kingdom of man were real. They ignore the obvious. We don't have to wait for the Messiah to bring us lib-eration from Rome. God's kingdom is here, now, for those who see and embrace it!

The sun was directly overhead, embracing me with the full warmth of the day. I removed my robe, and allowed the heat to caress my body. I lay down again and enjoyed the bright pink of the sun through my closed eyelids. I could feel the tickle of beads of sweat as they appeared on my chest, and dribbled down my sides.

I opened my eyes, stood up, and enjoyed the coolness of a slight breeze from the distant sea blowing over my skin. That's the breath of God, I thought. The colors of the plateau seemed particularly vivid, par-ticularly beautiful. It is God's masterpiece, this world, greater than the Temple. Just to be alive, and to be allowed to spend a few minutes in this wondrous place, is a gift that we can never repay. Life is a great miracle. God gives so much, and asks so little.

My mind drifted and imagined an aqueduct flowing through the harsh desert, carrying the cool and soothing word of God to the spiritually parched. "Worship the Lord not with rules and rituals, but in spirit and in truth." I saw myself as that aqueduct. What a wonderful mission of heal- ing that would be! Could God have possibly intended me for this job? No, it is too much to believe. I am arrogant even to think in this way.

I will return and join John, I thought. He understood before I did, and that's why he sent me here. I will help him spread the new joy, the new spirituality, and the new and wonderful worship to all of God's peoples.

Could it be, I wondered, that the Messiah is here, now—and that he is John the Baptist? What is the Messiah, after all, but the man who comes to relieve the suffering of the Jews? Has John thought of this? Has he won- dered? Even if he has, he has been wise to deny it. Men who make such claims are either vilified—or worshipped! Perhaps it is fitting that the self- proclaimed Messiahs have all been hung on wood, for such veneration is truly an abomination in the eyes of the Lord! *Worship the Lord your God and him alone.*

John rails against the sins of the Sanhedrin, the sins of Rome, and the sins of Herod. And so he has become a threat to those who rule. But God cares little for the physical world. His salvation lies in the spirit. Caesar is the ruler of our bodies, as my father taught, and so be it, for the kingdom of God is not of this earth but of our spirits. As the Scriptures say, *Man does not live by bread, but by the word of God.*

Would the Jews listen? They listened to John—at least some did. Others demanded miracles, to prove that John was a prophet. Every true prophet in the history of Judaism had performed miracles, as a sign that he was a messenger of God. The Jews had expected miracles from Moses, and he had performed them. But they weren't real miracles, only illusion, deception, and trickery.

I could *show* John how to perform miracles. God had sent me to the Academy of Zarathustra. Why? To learn medicine? Or to learn the art of magic, so John and I could reach the Jews in the only way that Jews could be reached? I had built many devices for Elymas, and I could build them for John. None of the itinerant magi could perform wonders such as I could! The miracles of Moses would be nothing compared to the miracles of John!

No.

Simon Magus was wrong. Truth cannot be taught through deception. Love cannot exist without honesty. Here in the wilderness I have been blessed with revelations from God, wonderful revelations of the spiritual world, of speaking with God, of love and a new covenant, of God's chari- ty and forgiveness. But now I have also been tempted by Satan. It was he, not God, who tried to trick me into the use of magic. This time I recognized him, and overcame his temptation.

Have I really defeated Satan? I will not know, not until I meet Pantera, and see if I can truly love my own enemy.

"Jesus!"

I gazed up at the sky, which was again growing dark, and as I did, once again I heard my name called: "Jesus!"

One bright star, directly over me, seemed to be looking right at me, twinkling as if with a smile. The voice repeated, "Jesus! Jesus!" Was God calling me by name?

No, it was just Jacob, calling from the next Mesa. Matthew was with him. They worked their way down the gully and up over to me, Matthew in the lead.

"Jesus! Are you all right?" Jacob demanded. "We've been searching for you since daybreak. You are miles from Qumran. You've been gone for two days. Have you had any water?" He looked down at Matthew, who handed me a full waterskin. "I was worried that you'd been attacked by wolves or fallen off a cliff. Matthew said you'd be out here. The wilderness is dangerous, especially at night. Jesus, what have you been doing?"

"Talking to God," I answered, "and confronting Satan."

22. John

IN MY EXUBERANCE I ALTERNATED BETWEEN WALKING AND running. In just two hours I reached the lush Jordan valley. In my excitement I never remembered to look back at Qumran, to see it one last time from the distance, to see if it looked different, now that it had changed my life. Soon I would be back in Capernaum. Would I make it there before John left? I hurried my pace.

I reached the fork where my dirt path joined the pilgrims' highway. Even though there was no festival, the road was filled with Jews on their way to Jerusalem, some for commerce, but most hoping to come close to God by visiting the Temple, as if that were actually where he lived. I felt pity for them. Couldn't they see that God was everywhere? Look, there he is, in the wind; it's his breath! There he is, in the trees, in the fluttering leaves, beyond in the yellow limestone cliffs, here in this burbling stream that feeds the Jordan, in those wildflowers, everywhere, but most of all, in these people, in these very pilgrims who vainly seek him in a distant city. Look at them! They are blind, and they don't know it! If only they would open their eyes, they would see the obvious. Could I help them to do that? How do you help someone open his spiritual eyes?

There is a Pharisee, his regalia proclaiming his self-perceived righteousness. Look at his embroidered cloak, so utterly seamless, with its ostentatiously large blue hem and golden tassels. Look at that jeweled phylactery prominently displayed on his forehead. He too is blind, and yet he fancies himself a leader for other Jews. And many of them accept him in that role. The blind leading the blind! Should I stop and tell him, explain to him what I now know? Would he listen? Would he understand? The truth is so easy to see, if only he would look! He is blind only because his eyes are closed. These are the blind who most need healing. If I could cure just one sick spirit, I would accomplish more than if I were to heal a hundred wounds or to mend a hundred bones.

Don't fool yourself, I thought. It will not be so easy. The Jews are not looking for someone to mend their spirits. They want a military Messiah, one to release their bodies from the bondage of Caesar. I must teach them that the world of spirit is greater than the world of flesh, that *man does not live by bread, but by the word of God.* But will they listen? The temptations of Satan will return, but I must not allow myself to use deception; I must not allow them to believe that prophets have supernatural power, for I must see to it that they shall worship the Lord and him alone. I must have faith, faith that the word of God by itself will be all that is needed. I may stumble, but I will not falter; I will be patient, and not require that God give me signs; I will have faith; for, as the Scriptures say, *do not put the Lord our God to the test.*

Let the pilgrims pass, and go to Jerusalem; now is not the time to mend their souls. I must get back to Capernaum, to John, to tell him of my revelations, to share with him my visions, to seek his advice. I've been away nearly forty days and forty nights—just like Moses!–and I fear John may have withdrawn again to the desert where I will never find him.

I covered the ninety miles from Qumran to Capernaum in just five days and found John baptizing a multitude that was swarming around him like ants about a drop of honey. John greeted me as he would a lost brother. Once again he left half his new disciples unbaptized so we could retreat together to his latest camp, hidden in a dry gully of the nearby badlands.

The sun was setting, the air had already grown cool and comfortable, and soon it would be chilly. We sat on the ground as the daylight slowly faded.

"You seem to be glowing," John said, as he munched on a honeyed locust.

"It was just as you said it would be, John. The Lord—God—spoke to me in the wilderness. He showed me what he had shown you—and more! What he really wants is for us to return the infinite love he gives. That's all that he asks, and yet it's more than we've ever given. It is not just our friends and neighbors that we must love, John, but even our enemies! Only when we expunge hatred from our souls can we be free of sin. Prayer, John, prayer—not burnt meat, not rote rituals—prayer is what can bring us close to him. He's our father, John, our loving *abba.* God wants us to be childlike, full of joy, hope, and love! The kingdom of God is here, now, and the poor are his most favored, for they are the closest to the spiritual world, the only world in which true joy is possible! The time has come for a new covenant, one that is simpler, yet more demanding, than the covenant of Moses."

John had stopped eating and was leaning back with his head on the rough rock. "Jesus, slow down," he said, with an affected frown. "You're gushing like a flooded stream after a heavy rain. Your enthusiasm is admirable, but I'm afraid there's a lot of mud mixed with the torrent. You seem to be trying to agree with my teachings, but much of what you say makes no sense."

"No sense? What do you mean?" I was more surprised than offended.

"You say the kingdom of God is here now, even though the Messiah has not yet arrived. You say that the poor are God's most favored people, despite their suffering. You want to exceed the Covenant, and yet simplify—abandon—it. That's all crazy." I was stung by John's criticism. Wasn't *he* the one usually called crazy? "It is true that God commanded us in Leviticus to love our neighbor, but love our enemies, Jesus? Love those who rape and murder our people? Love those who deny God? Think about what you're saying. To believe that God loves the Romans as much as he loves Jews could only mean that we aren't his chosen people."

"No, John, it doesn't imply that," I responded, perhaps too glibly. "We *are* chosen, we are special, but God created *all* people. We must realize that too." My words sounded inadequate even as I spoke them. John continued to frown. "We must love all people."

"Jesus, the Law of Moses *is* the covenant. It can't be softened at your whim. 'Love your enemies'? That precept is a contradiction in terms—not just spiritual nonsense but logical nonsense. If God loves both Jews and gentiles, why do only *we* have to obey his law? You speak of a new covenant, but the true problem is that we don't obey the law we already have!"

"Closely enough in spirit," I corrected. "God doesn't want us carrying little boxes on our foreheads, containing written prayers. He doesn't want us performing ritual ceremonies. He wants us to behave like his children. He's our great father."

"Father of the Jews?"

"Yes. But also father of everybody."

"Jesus, you're trying too hard to be clever. That kind of cleverness is the same weakness that got you into trouble in school. You're fooling yourself with your own rhetoric. Either we Jews are a people apart or we aren't. Either God chose us or he didn't. Which is it? I can't love the

Romans, and I can't believe that God would want me to. They're here because we've failed God, because he's punishing us for the violation of the Covenant, and only when we repent will all Jews see God's salvation."

"Isaiah didn't say 'all Jews,'" I corrected, for John was paraphrasing the Scriptures. "He said, 'All *mankind* will see God's salvation.' That means Romans too."

"My cousin," John said, "I don't know what happened to you at Qumran. You say that God whispered in your ear, that you were blessed with revelations. But how can you be certain that it wasn't Satan who whispered rather than God? Can you tell the difference? Jesus, you know that you are weak, that you are vulnerable to Satan's temptations, that you are easily drawn into sin. Can't you feel in your soul that you've been led astray once again? Think of your father Joseph, and his teachings. He would have been appalled."

"No! John, these revelations began with him. My father was a prophet, and I was his disciple, only I didn't know it at the time. I've only built on his teachings. This is the fulfillment of his beliefs!" But I struggled to imagine how my father would have responded to John's onslaught.

John got up from his rock and walked over to me. He looked at me solemnly, but also patronizingly. "Jesus, you have a good heart, a strong mind, a fundamentally righteous spirit, and I still love you as my brother. You were a sinner and I baptized you, as a symbol of your repentance. But there's much that you still don't understand. Don't wander astray, like the man who abandons his wife for a young girl who catches his eye. Don't flirt with these dreams of yours. Remain married to Judaism. You are weak, Jesus, and you fall easily into temptation. Strength lies in faith, faith in God and in his Scriptures, faith in the power of the Covenant."

I could feel the power of John's charisma. It lay not so much in his eloquence or in the power of his speech, but in his ability to talk directly to my soul. Could John be right? Was I deluding myself? For a moment I doubted the truth of my revelations.

"Jesus, if you're still willing, follow me and help me spread the revelation of repentance. You'll be the closest to me of anyone. Forget your so-called revelation in the wilderness. The trip to Qumran was a mistake. You're being led astray again, as you were when you stole the decanter. Join with me in teaching repentance and adherence to the Law of Moses."

I sat there quietly and looked at this man of God, this prophet who had saved so many souls, who had baptized me, and who was perhaps closer to God than any man who had come before. All it would take was one decision, one great decision, to have faith in John, in the Scriptures, and I would never have to make another decision again. I could help him in his glorious ministry.

John was a good man, a great man, but as I looked at him he seemed to grow smaller. He had taken one small step beyond the Essenes, who were one small step beyond the rabbis, who were one small step beyond the Sadducees. I could not take these comfortable little steps with him. I had been given the privilege of seeing far beyond the horizon.

John's expression turned sad, as if he had read my thoughts in my face.

"John . . . you are a prophet. Through you I saw that God is forgiving. I asked forgiveness and was baptized. But now *I* have seen additional light in the darkness. Our brotherhood under God the father illuminates all our other law. John, open your eyes . . . a little wider. Can't you see this too? It is so clear, so obvious. If you don't understand, if I can't enlighten you, how can I possibly convince anyone else?"

"I pray to God that you will not convince anyone else."

I was hurt by John's harsh words. He stared at me and I stared back. I desperately wanted to tell him more about my revelations and the joy they could bring to the world. But I knew that John would not listen.

I went over to my blanket and lay down. I stared up at the clouds that moved silently across the dark sky, and listened to the slow methodical chirp of the crickets. They follow no covenant. Were they loved by God? A shooting star flashed across the sky. One of my father's miracles. Was that a sign? No, I shall not require signs, and I shall not accept them. *Do not put the Lord thy God to the test.*

The heat of the morning sun on my face awakened me. How long had I been sleeping? It had been a dreamless sleep. I looked around, and John was gone.

He had disappeared back into the desert. I was dismayed that he would vanish like that, with no warning, no chance to resume our discussion. Had he seen in my face that I could not be brought back to his beliefs?

I must learn from this failure. Even in Qumran I had recognized that Jews would reject a prophet who modifies the law. I must persuade them gently, not by blurting out the truth—as I had with John. I shall not make that same mistake again.

I am here, not to change the Law, but to fulfill it.

I went back to the Jordan, where people continued to come hoping to hear the eloquent ascetic, perhaps expecting to be baptized, only to be disappointed. I was sad to lose John, and also annoyed. I had no more opportunity to show him I was right. And I couldn't even return his blanket.

But at least I could begin my ministry without his opposition.

23. Capernaum

I BEGAN PREACHING WHERE I WAS, IN CAPERNAUM, BY THE Sea of Galilee. As sure as I was of my revelations, I was painfully unconfident of my abilities. John's rejection still smarted. I prepared my words carefully. I wouldn't depend on people coming to me in the wilderness, or near its edge, as John had. Rather I would go to them in the towns and cities.

Finally I felt ready—nervous, but ready. I went to the largest square in the town, a marketplace full of women and children as well as men. There were two wells—one dry, in disrepair, its foundation a suitable platform. I stood up on it, gathered my breath, and announced as loudly as I could, "I bring to you a message of love, of charity, and of hope."

Several people nearby turned to look, but most paid no attention.

"I have been to the wilderness, where I have been blessed with the gift of a new truth, a new revelation from God. Come and listen to me, that I may share with you the joy and good news!"

A few of the people who had been watching me now turned away and went back to their work.

I continued, "The Lord is a loving God. He is a great father and we are his children. He has blessed all of us, especially the poor, the meek, the weak and the oppressed. If only we can accept his love and pass it on to others, we will please him. It is the pure of heart who will see God!"

Not one person was listening. The people in the market continued talking to each other, doing business, collecting water in their jugs. The women were haggling with the merchants and herding their children as if I weren't there at all. They were just ignoring me. To them I must have looked like another crazy preacher. In Galilee, self-proclaimed prophets are as abundant as weeds in a neglected garden.

The message I brought was so easy, and yet it was so hard. Words were inadequate to carry it, because it wasn't just a new idea, but a new world, a new spiritual reality. There it was, I thought, as clear as my own existence, visible to anyone who looked. Even now, I thought, I can see it.

The sun beat down on me as I stood on the old well. Sweat began to trickle down my face. Nobody listened. I strove for John's eloquence and power but fell woefully short. The sun finally set behind the hills. Still, I continued until it grew dark, when there was nobody left to ignore me.

The next day I chose a different location, down the hill in the fishing quarter, near the slips and wharves on the bank of the Sea of Galilee itself. I began differently this time. "I will give you what no eye has seen, what no ear has heard, what no hand has touched, and what has never arisen in a human mind." They were words I had polished for hours. I tried to speak with a tone of authority. "The day of judgment is near. Prepare yourselves for the coming of the Lord. You must repent. You must change your ways."

I was no more successful than on the day before. Towards evening the shore area grew more active with fishermen repairing their nets and readying their boats to go out at night. In the din I had to shout to be heard, and my throat grew tired and sore. The boats slipped out into the water. The light grew dim. Finally I gave up, walked back towards the inn in Capernaum, and worried that I would soon be out of money. I'm a failure, I thought. Have I deluded myself? If I were truly carrying the word of God, surely people would listen.

The sound of rustling leaves above my head caught my attention. I looked up just in time to see a squirrel take a flying leap into space, grab for some branches on another tree, desperately cling on, and then continue along a different branch. Life is going on, I mused, despite the emptiness of my own existence. A finch began its elaborate song, and was soon joined by another finch. What is God trying to tell me? That the world is beautiful despite my failure?

I must not give up. Someday I will understand why I am being put through these trials. I don't know what I'll do, or how I'll change, but I will persevere. Perhaps God wishes me to preach for an entire life, and find only one soul to save, as my father had found me. It is not for me to question the mission he has set for me. I went directly to the inn, where I slept without taking a meal.

I was awakened in the middle of the night by the loud snoring of several men who shared the small room in the inn where I slept. I got up and walked out into the cool darkness. The stars were bright, but one shone with a piercing brilliance that seemed to be aimed right at me. It didn't twinkle, and I realized it must be a wanderer, a *planet*. It was sitting in the midst of the star group called "the fisherman."

I was relieved to be alone, and I thought through each of my failures of the day. I could visualize the faces of the men and women who turned away. I could see their frowns, their sneers, their smirks. I saw myself standing by the crowds, a poor imitation of the Baptist. That's it! I'm doing just what John advised me not to do—I'm trying to be a John the Baptist, and I am not good at it. But I shouldn't mimic his style; I can't do it well even if I wanted to. I'm not trying to throw fear into the Jews. I'm trying to give them a message of hope, of joy. God is kind, infinitely generous, forgiving, not vengeful. I must be Jesus, not John.

The next day I forced myself to return to the square near the docks, and climbed up on a low stone wall that had been built between the beach and the market area. This time I began differently. "You are all blessed," I shouted in as joyous a tone as I could muster. "You are the chosen of the Lord! Those of you who are poor are the most blessed of all." I was sure that almost everyone there considered themselves poor. Then I lowered my voice, as my father did when he wanted to be heard. "Those of you who are oppressed are blessed. Those of you who are humble are also blessed. Those of you who are meek are also blessed. For the Lord your God loves you most of all. You were created in the Lord's image, to love as the Lord loves." I was getting little more attention than I had on the earlier days, but at least I felt that I was myself, and giving the message that I wanted to deliver. And my voice would endure much better at its new quiet level.

Off on the other side of the square, one bushy-haired young man with a short beard seemed to be paying attention, so I raised my voice slightly and directed my words at him. As I spoke, he slowly walked towards me, and as he came closer his face opened into a huge smile. I may not have recognized that face, since it was fifteen years older than it had been when I saw it last, but the smile was unmistakable. I stopped talking, as my throat tightened and tears filled my eyes. I climbed down from the stone wall and opened my arms as my brother Jude Thomas ran towards me, and we hugged deliriously in the square.

Thomas, I don't believe that there has been a more joyous moment in my life! It was as if a shattered world had suddenly been restored.

I was so choked with emotion I could hardly talk. We couldn't let go of each other, and I was surprised by Thomas's strength. Little Thomas, grown up! With a beard! In the rough clothes of a fisherman. I held him at arms length, to look at him.

"You smell like a fish!" I said with a laugh.

"Like many fish," Thomas corrected. "The Lord has been generous to me."

"What has happened to Mother?"

"Mother? She's in good health! She'll be so happy to see you!"

"You mean she's nearby? Where is she?"

"In Cana. She works as a maidservant for a wealthy Roman named Pantera."

At the mention of that name the dry tinder of my soul burst into flame. Pantera—still Pantera—after all these years! But this time I recognized the evil spirit that had entered me and set me afire, and I tried to grab hold and wrestle with it. Satan was once again fighting for my soul. I must strangle the demon, exorcise the evil. But again I saw the face of Pantera, and again my hatred flared. But I pushed the image away—I thought of mother—I looked at Thomas.

"She'll be so happy! So unbelievably happy!" Thomas repeated. He seemed so accepting of her situation. "Everyone thought you were dead. This is truly a miracle, a wonderful, happy joyous miracle! Jesus, when I heard you preaching, I didn't realize it was you. Your words, your gentle manner, drew my attention. Here is a man talking of love, I thought. You reminded me of our father, so I came closer. And then I recognized your voice, not you—you're so much older—but your voice!" Thomas paused for a moment and looked at me. I wondered if I showed any effects of my years of slavery. "After all these years," he continued, "I recognized your voice. This is the happiest day of my life. Where have you been? How long have you been preaching? Tell me about your life! What happened? How did you get here?"

Thomas's questions almost passed me by, for I was still fighting the fury. Within my soul was a beast, forgotten, but not yet put to rest. I pushed Pantera out of my mind, pretended that he didn't exist, but I wasn't winning the battle, I realized, for to forget Pantera was not to love him. And I wouldn't be able to forget him when I saw him, with my mother still in his grip. How would I react when I faced this soldier, this thug, this rapist, for the first time since my arrest? Satan might wait for that moment, when I would be most vulnerable, to overwhelm my goodness, to break through, to unleash fully the jackal I felt clawing within me.

Thomas took me to his little house on the outskirts of Capernaum, nestled close to the woods. I was struck by its similarity to our old home in Nazareth. He gave me a mat to sleep on under the window, just as I had as a child. I lay there as he described his life since I had been gone—how his wife had died in childbirth, and their infant son soon after. He had buried his grief in work, and in just a few years had become an expert fisherman.

"What happened to little James?" I asked.

"He stayed with Mother until he was fifteen. Now he works as a servant in the home of a wealthy Jew in Hebron, south of Jerusalem."

Thomas had been so successful as a fisherman that he had bought his own boat. "It's my sense of the lake," he explained. "You have to think like the fish. I look at the sky, the wind, the rain, and I know where the fish are going."

"And you always called me the clever brother!" I said with admiration.

"I'm not being smart. It's just that the other fishermen are so stupid. They ignore the obvious. The wind changes, and they think only about how the shift affects their sails. They don't realize that the fish watch the wind more closely than they do, particularly the low wind that gives ripples on the surface. The fish know which wind carries insects and which doesn't. They can smell where it comes from."

"Aha. Now I understand why you came to listen to me. It wasn't my words. You were downwind from me and you smelled Nazareth!"

"See," Thomas said, "I told you that you are cleverer than me!" His face opened into a broad smile, and his black eyes shone like those of our mother.

"When can I see Mother?" I asked.

"We'll go tomorrow! Ah, Jesus, she'll be so happy to see you! You know, she always loved you best."

"Nonsense!" I said, embarrassed by his claim. "I'm so anxious to see her, and . . . Pantera." I said the name carefully and watched Thomas for a reaction, but there was none. "But what will happen to your fishing if you leave?"

"I'll rent my boat to Simon—he's another fisherman. He thinks that my boat is blessed. What he really means is that it's lucky, but the rabbis tell them that we shouldn't believe in luck."

"That's because it's pagan," I said. "It means that something other than God drives destiny. The Epicureans worship the god of luck—named Tyche. They say the world was created by a chance meeting of atoms! It is a deeply pagan concept."

Thomas looked at me curiously. "You sound like a scholar," he said. "Where did you learn all that?"

"At an academy. I went there to study healing—but most lectures were about religion. As we walk to Cana I'll tell you about it."

Thomas paid my bill at the inn, and the next morning we started off towards Cana. We spent most of the trip talking about our childhood. I found it difficult to get used to the fact that this strong, intelligent man was the same little boy to whom I told stories back in Nazareth. As we walked along the dirt road, passing the pilgrims on their way to Jerusalem, we talked of the death of our father, and how it had affected both of us. I told him about my crime and my sentence.

"But I still don't understand why you stole the decanter," Thomas said.

"Mother—the family—needed the money, or so I thought. I was just an adolescent, Thomas. Full of vivid imagination." I could not bring myself to tell Thomas, even then, of what really led me to the desperate act. Perhaps he still believed that our mother was really nothing more than a maidservant to Pantera. Nor could I bring myself to ask him about Pantera, a man he thought I had never met.

I told Thomas in detail of my revelations in the wilderness. "Loving your friends, your family, your neighbor—that's the easy part. The greatest challenge is to love your enemy," I said. I looked at Thomas to see if he would find the idea as repulsive as had John, but he only looked back at me and nodded. As we made our way under the hot, high sun, with the sound of a million invisible insects clicking in the yellow grasses, I asked, "Do you think you could love an enemy?"

"Love the Romans? It is a strange thought. I don't know if I am capable of doing it, but I believe you're right. It is something to aspire to. Father taught that to hate is to punish yourself. Love of everyone—it must be what the Lord wants of us. Say, listen to me! I'm talking as if I know what the Lord wants! Does that count as a revelation?"

"If you truly see the correctness of what you said, in such a way that you can never doubt it again, then yes, Thomas, that is a revelation. I have found that I can speak to God almost any time I want, by opening my spirit and letting him in. He doesn't speak back in words, but by revealing truths."

We stood aside to let pass a long caravan of camels — probably on its way to Egypt. We held our breaths to keep the dust out of our mouths, and the smell from our noses. Finally the air cleared, and Thomas said, "You're a *prophet!*"

"But so are you! So is everybody, if only they'll listen when God speaks. And he speaks to us every day."

"You sound like father."

"He *was* a prophet, Thomas. Truly a prophet."

24. Pantera

CANA OF GALILEE WAS A MEDIUM-SIZED VILLAGE NEAR SIDON that overlooked a marsh of reeds or "canes," from whence the town got its name. Thomas took me to one of the largest houses in the town, built into a hillside, with changed levels down its slope. At the highest part there were actually two stories, with a granite foundation and wooden beams for the floors and roof. A servant answered our knock and led us into the main reception room, the floor of which was covered with a beautiful polished blue tile. It was the finest house that I had ever entered. The walls were covered with white plaster and a whole series of windows looked out on an enclosed courtyard. "Tell Mary that she has two visitors," Thomas told the servant. For long moments we waited in silence, my breath and heart suspended.

A few moments later our mother entered the room. Moving with the grace of a dancer, she turned and closed the door, her simple white smock flowing serenely about her. I had forgotten how beautiful she was.

"Thomas!" she said. "What a surprise! It's wonderful to see you again." She walked over to him and embraced him. Then she turned and looked at me, and I felt awkward, not knowing what to say. I stepped toward her. Suddenly she gasped, and put her hand to her mouth. My eyes filled with tears. She stuttered, "Jesus—my son!" I ran to her, like a little boy to his mama, and buried my face against her shoulder.

For many minutes we spoke no words, only held each other and shared our joy. She had endured her hardship like sycamore wood, not only impervious to heat and driving rain, but gaining strength from such exposure. She had gained weight, a sign that someone had taken good care of her, but her face was still lean. Her hair was shorter now, and streaked with gray. Her smile warmed me as the sun does when it shines through an opening in clouds on a wintry day. I felt a pure, warm happiness.

We sat and I told her about the theft and my arrest, but I wasn't candid about the real reason for my crime. "We couldn't afford shoes. I was young and didn't know better. It was a mistake, and I've been punished for it, but you were punished too. I'm so sorry, Mother. What made me suffer the most all those years was the suffering that I caused you."

"You're like your father was, Jesus. More concerned about others than yourself."

I told her about my work on the aqueduct, my studies at the academy, and my failed life as a healer. "But it all began to change, Mother, when I heard John speak, near Capernaum. I repented, and God forgave me, and . . ."

"Your cousin, the 'Baptist'?" Mother looked at me with alarm. "You heard his ravings? I warned Elizabeth, when John was still a child, but she let him do whatever he wanted. She pampered him, and now all he knows how to do is criticize. That's always the kind that becomes an ascetic— the kind that doesn't know what pain and deprivation really are. Is he grateful for what the Lord has given? No. He only wants to reject the Lord's gifts and get everyone else do the same. He's completely lost his mind."

"John may indeed be mad," I said, "but with his help, I heard the voice of God. I withdrew to the desert wilderness, near the Salt Sea. That was where I first recognized that God was speaking to me. His voice was clear and strong—as clear and strong as your words are to me, right now in this room. He talked to me personally and revealed his wishes to me. That was when I learned for certain that Father was a true prophet, and that I was his disciple. But Father's teachings were unfulfilled, and God said that it is my mission to bring them to the Jews."

My mother looked at me very hard and very deep. Not since I left the Magus had I felt someone reading through my body into my soul. I perceived in my mother a depth of understanding and wisdom of which I had never been aware in my childhood. "And what is the message that the Lord gave you?" she asked, without the slightest hint of skepticism in her voice. I was almost surprised that she was taking me seriously.

"The Lord, our God, wishes us to love all people, as he loves them himself. From this, everything else follows."

As I said these words, I realized the time had come to face another test, to prove that my own prophecy had reached into my inner heart. "I would like to meet Pantera," I said to my mother. Could she sense my fear? Could she see the sweat I felt on the back of my neck?

She stared at me intensely, her pupils deep and black and large. "I once hated all gentiles," she said. "Or perhaps I feared them. I had been taught they were unclean. Joseph tried to say otherwise, but I refused to learn. Why was I so resistant? Joseph was the holiest man I have ever known, but it took his death to teach me his greatest lesson. That gentiles could be kind and loving and good. And a Roman provided for me when none of our neighbors would help."

My heart was pounding. I didn't feel prepared, just yet, to discuss her relationship with Pantera.

My mother was lost in thought. "When we took you to the Temple," she said, "as a baby, to offer the pigeons in the traditional sacrifice, they spoke of the wondrous things you would do!" I had never heard that story before. "Tell me more about this message from the Lord," she said, "the prophecy he gave you in the wilderness."

"Among all his people, God loves best those who suffer most. We are his children, and he wants us to behave as children to him, loving and trusting. We must learn to love all of his creations, with simple, unquestioning love. The greatest sin is hatred, hatred of anyone, Jew or gentile, for all men were made by God." I paused for a moment and wondered, do I really believe these words? "The greatest challenge is to love our enemies, to love those who don't deserve to be loved." Was I telling her my revelation, or was I admonishing myself? "Only when we can do this will God be satisfied. That was Father's message, but it took my retreat into the wilderness for me to understand it. Now I'm going to bring that message to all the Jews."

"You speak with authority," she said. "Just as the rabbis said, when as a little boy you were lost at the Temple." She held my shoulders in her arms. "Jesus, Jesus, my son." She backed away and held me at arm's length, as if to see me better. Then she said, suddenly, "You said you wanted to meet Pantera. I am eager for him to meet you. Let me find him. Please wait here."

This was the moment of battle. If I couldn't love Pantera, then my revelation was nothing more than self-delusion, as John, with such certainty, had said.

My mother's recollection of the rabbis in Jerusalem hadn't been quite accurate. I had the event vividly etched in my memory. I remembered waiting at the Temple for my parents, for many boring hours, repeatedly scanning the large courtyard hoping that they would appear, wondering if they were playing some trick on me, wondering if they had truly forgotten me, wondering if they would remember that this was where we were supposed to meet. Eventually I became distracted by a small crowd that had gathered about two men discussing the origin of evil. One of them argued that evil was a punishment sent from God for breaking the Covenant. Yes, that makes sense, I thought. The other claimed that evil was a maliciousness and perversity in the sinful heart of man. That made sense too, when I heard him say it. What would my father have said? There was a brief pause in the discussion and I interjected, "The Law and the prophets are comprised in two commandments: the love of God, and the love of one's neighbors." They were words I had heard my father say.

To my surprise, both men stopped, turned and looked at me. They didn't say anything. They just kept staring. I was embarrassed. Finally one of them asked me, "Do you reject the Torah?"

"The Torah just elaborates on these commandments," I replied, again using the words of my father. "What is hateful to you, don't do to your fellow man. That's the whole Torah. The rest is just commentary."

The man turned to his companion. "This boy is still in swaddling clothes, and yet he has already studied Hillel!" He laughed, and I felt my face flushing red. But before I could object, the man turned back to me with a kindly face. "So what do *you* think is the origin of evil?"

I was being treated by strangers as an adult, for the first time in my life, and it was thrilling. The discussion that ensued was even better than ones I had had with my father, for whenever I was at a loss for words, one of the other participants would inject something relevant. Yet they listened and took my ideas seriously. When challenged, I wished my father were there, but he wasn't, so I gave the answers that I thought he would give. I amazed myself.

When my mother finally found me, she looked relieved, then annoyed, and when I said that I didn't want to leave, she became angry. She and my father had apparently traveled many miles back to Nazareth before they realized that I wasn't with the group. The men defended me. "Your son is intelligent and knowledgeable, particularly for one so young. He would make a good rabbi." He never said that I spoke with *authority*, as my mother remembered.

"Mother! Do you think I could?" As much as I disliked Rabbi Shuwal, to be a rabbi was to achieve the highest honor available to a resident of a village such as Nazareth. My father had been a rabbi, a teacher, to me.

"Jesus, we're poor. You'd have to spend much time studying. We need to have you work like your father."

"That's what I've been doing—my father's work!" I replied, perhaps too sharply.

My mother was embarrassed and angry, and she took me out of the courtyard and severely chastised me, both for getting lost, and for my lack of respect. We quickly found my father, who had been looking for me in the bazaar, and hurried out on the road to try to catch up to the other Nazarenes. He told her that I shouldn't be punished. He took me aside, and told me that I had not acted wrongly, but unwisely. Gradually my mother forgot the worry and the embarrassment, and by the time we were back in Nazareth she was already bragging to her friends how her son had impressed the rabbis of Jerusalem.

I was awakened from my reverie when my mother returned, accompanied by a short, heavy, middle-aged man with a strong Roman nose and kindly blue eyes. "Master," she said to the man, "this is my son, Jesus of Nazareth. Jesus, please show your respect to Pantera of Rome."

Where was Pantera? And who was this man, dressed in the blue robe of a merchant? My mother gestured slightly with her head, as if expecting me to do something.

I gasped as I suddenly recognized the obvious truth. Almost dumbfounded, I could only repeat to Pantera, to Pantera the *merchant,* the words that I had rehearsed a hundred times. "I thank you for taking care of my mother during her time of need."

"Well, you're very welcome. Your mother is an excellent housekeeper, but also a source of wisdom to my wife and me. She has enriched our home enormously, and I thank you for having loaned her to us."

I was still confused. Finally I asked, "Did you know of another Pantera in Sepphoris? A soldier?"

"Oh, God yes!" he blasphemed. "Pantera the centurion. What a brute! How unfortunate that I had to share my name with a man like that. I suppose that's what you get when your parents name you after a panther. I was greatly relieved when he was shipped back to Rome."

That evening I tried to fall asleep in the largest room I had ever slept in, a guestroom in the home of Pantera the merchant. My head sank into a linen sack filled with feathers, but my mind was racing. My soul should have been filled with relief, but I had the disconcerting sense of having been tricked—tricked by myself and by the raging imagination of my adolescence. So much pain and suffering, my own and my mother's—and all for nothing, brought on by my own stupidity. I was outraged.

At what? That my mother had never sinned?

Pantera the merchant. Not the centurion, the merchant! I should be the happiest man on earth. An impossible dream had come true, a dream that I had never prayed for, because it was beyond the realm of the imaginable. Lord, please forgive my mother—*that* I could have asked. But Lord, make it be that she never committed the sin? That she had been telling the truth all along? That I had simply confused two different men named Pantera? No, I never conceived of such a wondrous wish. My mother was innocent. What joyous news!

But what did that make of my life, of my torment? Was it all in vain? Because of my lack of faith, I had wasted many years my life.

Or had I? Perhaps this was God's way of leading me to his ministry—servitude, healing, and the teachings of Zarathustra, John the Baptist, and the Essenes. Each of them had affected me in a profound way. If not for my mistake, I might today be a carpenter in Nazareth. Had it all been pre-ordained by the Lord? Was it through this tortuous path that he had prepared me to be his prophet?

Then again, can almighty God change what has already happened? Perhaps he had granted my greatest wish, a wish so great that it was beyond my imagination. Perhaps my mother really *had* gone to Pantera the centurion—had been his mistress, but God changed the past, as a reward, as a sign that he was pleased with me. Is anything beyond the infinite power of God? Hadn't this miracle happened immediately after I had dedicated my life to him? To the will of God, why should the past be any more immutable than the future?

And then another odd discomfort seeped into my heart. What of my test? I had prepared so strenuously for the difficult moment of meeting Pantera, of loving the man who deserved no love. Now God had denied me the test. In a strange and perverse way, I felt disappointed. I had been cheated of the chance to redeem myself, denied the opportunity to prove my repentance.

But perhaps God knew that I would have failed—that I was not yet ready. Perhaps this denial was a sign of God's love for me. Or just a temporary respite? Would I ever be tested? Could I continue to teach the truth of God, when I was unsure in my own soul? Can a sinner preach the will of God?

Questions, questions, my head roiled with questions. The comfort of my body lying in the soft feathers contrasted with the confusion of my spirit.

It would do no good to think about it further. My father had taught that God's miracles are always such that a skeptic can ignore them. But that doesn't make them any less miraculous. We are surrounded by miracles, and all it takes to see them is for us to open our eyes and notice. My unimaginable wish had come true.

And my test was yet to come.

25. Wedding at Cana

A WEDDING FEAST WAS TO BE HELD IN PANTERA'S HOME, AND Thomas suggested that we assist wherever we could, in payment for our lodging. Nearly two hundred guests filled the inner courtyard, mostly Jewish merchants and tradesmen, but a few Romans and Greeks, and the servants were all very busy. I noticed that the guests were quickly finishing the wine, and the barrel would soon be empty. It would take time to carry the barrel down to the cellar and refill it, so I suggested to Thomas that we fill some empty water jugs with wine in anticipation. Indeed, there were enough water jugs to completely drain the downstairs supply. More could be had from the market the next day, but I was certain there would be enough for the party.

It was a joyous occasion for everybody. As a member of the household of a wealthy merchant, my mother was held in high regard by most of the people of Cana. For her part, she took great pleasure in introducing me as "my son, who is a healer."

"And what can you heal?" a guest asked.

"Many illnesses and injuries. But most important are the diseases of the soul."

"Oh, and can you heal those too?"

Here was my first chance to explain my mission to a stranger. "God—the Lord—has given me a special medicine, for just such illness."

The man laughed. "Has he now? And will you share this secret revelation with me?"

"Love," I said. "It is as simple as that. Our healing lies in loving everyone—not just our family, friends, and neighbors, but in loving our enemies, our oppressors."

He stared at me, and then laughed again. "Thank you for telling me your secrets," he said, and he turned away. I walked over to a group of his friends, and I heard him mutter the word "crazy."

I succeeded no better with anyone else at the party. They politely excused themselves and found someone else to converse with. My message was accepted here no more readily than it had been in Capernaum. From the secretive glances I caught out of the corner of my eye, I sensed that people were talking *about* me, but they didn't want to talk *to* me. One short man left a group of such people and approached me.

"I understand that you are a prophet," he said in a loud voice, for everyone to hear.

I replied, warily, "I have been shown what no eye has seen."

"If you are a prophet, you must be able to perform miracles. So do a miracle for us! But please make it a worthwhile miracle—not just a magi trick."

Many of the guests were watching, so I felt I had to plunge ahead. "We are surrounded by miracles," I said. "This very room is full of miracles. The kingdom of the Lord has arrived here on the earth, for all to see—and all you need to see it is to open your spiritual eyes. All you must do is . . ."

"No, no! A real miracle! Prove you are a prophet by giving us a real miracle."

"What would you consider a *real* miracle?"

"Get rid of the Romans!"

"Our . . . host is a Roman."

"No, I don't mean Pantera," he replied defensively. "He's just a merchant. And he keeps our law. I mean the Roman tyrants. If you are a prophet, tell us when they'll be overthrown. When will the Son of Man come?" To northern Jews, *Son of Man* meant the military messiah, who would lead the army to victory.

"It isn't the Romans that you must conquer, but the hatred in your own soul."

"On the contrary, our hatred is what gives us strength! We'll revenge ourselves on the Romans. 'An eye for an eye, a tooth for a tooth.' We will plunder those who steal from us, and we will kill those who have murdered our people! Would you have us do otherwise, prophet?"

Many of the guests were listening now. "You must not resist evil. If a Roman steals your money, give him more."

"Ha! And what would *you* do if a Roman soldier smote you?"

"If he did it on the right cheek, then I would turn the left to him. If he hit a stranger, I would offer myself as the target."

"You must be new at prophecy," he quipped, "for with your beliefs, you won't live long!" There was general laughter among the guests. At this the man apparently felt he had achieved his goal of humiliating the putative prophet, so he smiled and walked away. My mother had been watching from a corner of the room, and her face was red, with shame or embarrassment or just sorrow, I couldn't tell. I went to her, and she took me by the hands and led me out of the courtyard to a small room.

"None are as deaf as those who refuse to listen," she said. "Don't be discouraged, my Jesus. Have faith in yourself and your words will win over the skeptics. Take comfort in the knowledge that I believe in you."

No words spoken by man or woman have ever been more important to me. Without her support, I might have abandoned my ministry at that moment. She gave me comfort when I was attacked, and strengthened me when I was weak. I never loved her more than I did then.

It was time to toast the newly married couple, and all the guests were asked to fill their wine cups. While I had been talking to my mother, Pantera had ordered a servant to the cellar to bring up more wine—but the servant found the cellar barrel empty. A mild panic ensued, since according to local superstition, without a wedding toast the marriage was not blessed by the Lord. No one knew that Thomas and I had already brought the wine upstairs.

My mother and I noticed the commotion and came back into the courtyard. Pantera was pale with embarrassment. He was talking to the man who had confronted me. The man turned to me and announced, "But here is our prophet and his mother!" He pointed to the water jugs that I had placed next to the wine barrel. "Woman," he said to my mother, "kindly ask your son the prophet to turn the water in those jugs into wine." If this was intended to lighten the crisis with humor, it didn't work. Nobody laughed, and Pantera glowered at him.

My mother looked at me with solicitude. "Jesus, I'm sorry," she said.

"There's no need for concern," I said. "The water jugs are filled with wine."

The room was suddenly silent. Pantera motioned to one of his servants, who fetched a cup, lifted the water jug over it, and poured. There was an audible gasp from the guests when the red fluid trickled into the cup. Only then did I realize that they took it for a miracle. "This isn't a miracle," I protested.

"Bring the cup to me," Pantera ordered. He tasted it, and pronounced,

"This is as good as the finest wine I have owned." The crowd now stared at me in awe. "Let us share the wine and present the wedding toast," Pantera continued. "Then we'll dance and celebrate, for this marriage is truly blessed. But afterwards let us listen to the prophet. I want to know what he calls a true miracle, if turning water to wine is not!"

Despite Pantera's calm, most of the wedding guests appeared almost feverish with excitement. One after another came to me asking for a blessing, a favor, or a prophecy. I told several of them that I had simply placed the wine in the jugs before being asked, yet protestations seemed to do little good. They had witnessed a miracle and weren't about to be talked out of it. The more I protested, the more they seemed to think I had even greater powers.

Responding to his guests' wishes, and possibly because of the general commotion and agitation, Pantera hurried through the ceremonial dancing and then set a seat for me in the middle of the room. Most of the wedding guests crowded around. Pantera quieted the group and addressed me. "Jesus of Nazareth, son of Joseph and my dear housekeeper Mary, many of us heard you speak earlier of your revelations. We wish to listen to your teachings. But please, first tell us why is turning water into wine not a miracle?"

"All of us have seen the magi do tricks like that," I replied. "It can easily be accomplished by misdirection. Those who believe in such miracles are simply believing what they wish to believe. They are fooling themselves, and they miss the *true* miracles."

Pantera nodded in agreement. "Then tell us, what are the true miracles?" I saw him glance quickly towards my mother, who was smiling with pride.

"Suppose I walked on water," I asked the group. "Would that be a miracle?" The room was silent, full of listeners, people who really wanted to hear what I had to say. I was prepared. I knew where I was headed.

A few people silently nodded yes. "Yes, of course," Pantera finally answered aloud, "Walking on water would be a miracle. Provided, of course, that you were really doing it, and it wasn't just a trick." Several of the guests again nodded their agreement with his qualification. A few people were looking at me as if they expected that I would now walk on water.

"Suppose I walked on water every day, and so did everyone else, and we didn't use tricks," I said. "Would you still consider it a miracle?"

"Of course. Water can't support my weight."

"Yet it does so in a boat."

"But that's not a miracle."

"What is it then?"

Pantera paused for a moment, and finally blurted out, "It's just a boat!" The wedding guests all laughed, and then Pantera laughed too.

"When you see the same miracle every day, you lose the sense of awe," I said. "You think, 'that's just the way the world is.' You don't consider it wondrous, although it truly is. Pantera, we are surrounded by miracles, *true* miracles, not tricks like turning water into wine. Rain is a miracle, water falling from the sky, quenching the thirst of the soil. Crops are miracles, providing us food from nothing but seeds, more wondrous than manna from the heavens. People are a miracle. We should be in constant awe of God's power, just from looking at the people in this room." I looked around, from person to person, and then so did several others. "But the more common the miracle, the less awe we feel. Life is the greatest miracle of all." I turned from Pantera and addressed the guests. "Most of you have experienced the wonderful miracle of children. Many parents call their children miracles when they are born, and they are, but then they forget. The greatest gift God has given us is the ability to create life. All that God asks of us is to love his creations." I paused to let this thought sink into their hearts.

The quiet voice of a woman came from the back. "What about the Law of Moses?" she asked in a judgmental tone.

"This is the revelation that I pass on to you," I said, "given to me by God himself as I lay in the wilderness of the desert. The Law of Moses is absolute, and is not to be modified." She seemed mollified. "It is not to be changed, but it *is* to be *fulfilled.* God is our father, not our stern, strict father, but our kind, loving *abba.* His love for us is infinite, his generosity boundless. All he asks in return is that we love him back, him and all his creations. *All* of his creations. That is the essence, the deep true essence of Judaism, the essence of the law."

It was a wonderful but frightening experience to have so many people listening so hard to every word I spoke. I didn't talk as I had at Capernaum, striving for eloquence and power. I simply tried to speak the truth, as simply as I could. When they asked questions, I paused and thought. I didn't think with words, but with images and feelings. I told little stories, parables, just as I had told Thomas as a child.

It was that evening that I first created the parable that not only became my favorite, but the favorite of many of my followers. It was the parable that appealed to them because it spoke a self-evident truth, and yet illustrated the evil of both their prejudices and the strict observances of the

Pharisees. It had as its focus a man who would be hated more than Caesar, a man who would be reviled more than Roman centurions who crucified righteous Jews, a man who was hated because he was so similar to the Jews but was different, a man who was despised because he rejected Judaism. It was about a Samaritan.

"Recently," I said, "a man was walking down the road from Cana to Capernaum. The man was attacked by robbers, who wounded him, stripped him of his clothes, and left him for dead. By chance there came down the road a priest, and when he saw him, he passed by on the other side." Every Jew in my audience knew that the priest was doing the ritually correct thing, since a dead body is unclean and requires elaborate washing of anyone who touches it. And yet every Jew knew, in his heart, that this was the wrong thing to do. "And likewise a Levite, when he was at the place, came and looked on him, and passed by on the other side." Again, ritually correct behavior. "But a certain Samaritan," I continued, "as he journeyed came to where the man was lying, and when he saw him he had compassion for the poor man. He went to him and bound up his wound, cleansing it with fine oil and wine. And then he set him on his own mule and brought him to an inn, and took care of him. And on the next day when he departed, he took out two silver coins and gave them to the innkeeper, and said to him, 'Take care of this poor man, and whatsoever more you spend, when I come again, I will repay you.'" I paused and sat quietly, long enough for my audience to ponder the story. Then I said, "Now of the three, the Priest, the Levite, and the Samaritan, who do you think was neighbor to him that was attacked by the robbers? Who do you think pleased the Lord?" Again I paused and looked around the room. Two dozen faces looked at me. I answered myself, lest there be any confusion, "He who showed mercy to the victim. It was the Samaritan who pleased the Lord. It is such love that the Lord asks of you towards all of our neighbors."

There were looks of surprise, and wonder, but not of disagreement. They were listening to the truth and they understood. I had broken through their walls.

I told other stories and answered many questions. I was surprised at my own quiet power. This is not coming from me, I thought—it is the power of the word, the word of God. I felt possessed by a holy spirit that guided my answers. I overheard one of the guests remark, "He speaks with authority." I felt myself that he was right.

As I lay in the overly-comfortable bed, I felt a deep satisfaction and a spiritual glow. God had given me a sign—he would let me serve as his conduit, and he would bring people to listen. He had chosen me to deliver his joyous message to the Jews, to fulfill the law, to . . .

"Jesus? Are you awake?" Thomas asked, from his bed on other side of the room.

"Yes, Thomas."

"You know, Jesus, Mother really believes that you turned the water into wine. And so did most of the guests."

"But I explained. I told them all that it was just a misunderstanding."

"Well, you may have told them, but you didn't convince them. You performed the miracle on request, just when the skeptic demanded it."

"That was just accident. It was like Moses splitting the Red Sea."

There was a moment of silence from across the room. "Now you really must explain yourself!" Thomas said.

I explained to him what Simon Magus had said, about the mirage and how Moses had taken advantage of it. To my surprise Thomas seemed to accept the explanation without the soul-searching and torment that the revelation had caused me.

"So maybe," Thomas said, "the wine wasn't accidental. Maybe the Lord gave *you* a miracle today, just as he gave one to Moses, because you needed one."

"Then why didn't God just make me eloquent?" I asked.

"Like Moses?" Thomas answered sarcastically. "Maybe the Lord prefers poor speakers."

"John is eloquent."

"And he was so taken by his own rhetoric that he couldn't understand what you were trying to tell him."

Maybe Thomas was right, I thought. Speak not in powerful rhetoric, but in gentle whispers. "Nevertheless, Thomas, I cannot teach truth by deception. Tomorrow I'll explain the wine to Mother, and to everyone who will listen."

26. Leper

NO SOONER HAD I WALKED OUT OF PANTERA'S HOME THAN AN expensively dressed man suddenly ran up to me shouting, "It is you!" He fell on his knees in the dirt and then grabbed me by my ankles, throwing me off balance and almost causing me to fall. He ardently kissed my feet, interrupting himself only to cry, "Oh, Lord, give me your blessing!" I was not so much surprised as I was embarrassed.

"Stop that!" I demanded. "What is it you want?"

He looked up at me and I saw fear in his eyes. "They wouldn't take in a message—they said that you were sleeping, that you shouldn't be disturbed, but I had to find you. There's little time left. My son is stricken—close to death! Please, my Lord, you must come and use your powers! I need a miracle, now, before it's too late! I beg you, oh Lord, please save him!" He reached up, took my arm and tugged gently, as if to emphasize the urgency while maintaining respect.

"What is your name?" I asked.

"Josiah. I was at the wedding feast last night. But my servant came in the middle of the night. My son is dying!"

"Please, calm down," I said. "Tell me quietly, in what way is your son ill? How does he suffer?"

"He burns with fever and he's covered with rash. Please, come with me to Capernaum! I am afraid that it. . . ." He hesitated to say the words; finally he lowered his voice to a whisper and continued, "It's the pestilence." Josiah averted his eyes from me, as if he worried that he had frightened me from coming. "Only a miracle can save him."

"Does the rash cover his body? Are there large boils?"

"I don't know. He may already be dead. Only you can help! I have a cart with two horses ready to leave now–. . ."

"Let me speak to the servant."

"He's only a Nubian—he knows nothing. He's over there with the cart, putting on a seat for you. You must come immediately." He took my arm, and began to pull me gently towards the cart.

I shook my arm loose and walked rapidly to the cart. The servant was a very tired-looking dark-skinned man. "How extensive is the rash?" I asked him.

"It covers his chest, Master."

"Anywhere else? His back?""

"No, Master," the Nubian said, "only his chest." Josiah looked restless.

"His neck? His face?"

"No, Master."

Josiah interrupted: "We don't have time for this! He knows nothing!"

I continued to probe the Nubian: "Are you absolutely certain?"

"I bathed him yesterday. It was only on his chest, but it may have spread by now. He was very hot, Master. He said his head was going to burst. He didn't want me to leave, but I became frightened."

"Does he breathe easily?" I asked.

"Yes, Master, he had no trouble."

"Any boils?"

"No, Master."

Josiah said, "We have fast horses. Bring someone with you if you wish, but we must leave now."

"When did he contract the fever?" I asked the Nubian.

Josiah snapped, "You can ask these questions while we travel!"

The Nubian answered, "Three days ago." He glanced nervously at Josiah.

I continued to talk with the Nubian for several minutes. What he said did not alarm me, but Josiah grew more and more impatient and continued to interrupt every few moments. Still, a clear picture began to emerge. "Has he been to Perea recently?" I asked the servant.

"Yes Master. We returned four days ago."

That confirmed my suspicion. Wilderness fever was epidemic in Perea. The son was suffering from the same frightening but harmless illness that the slave Melech had contracted when I first sought help from Simon Magus. I had been particularly interested in it during my study at the Academy, and I had seen many cases in the clinic and in Sepphoris, mostly among pilgrims.

Satisfied, I turned to Josiah, and said, "Your son will recover. His fever is undoubtedly fading even now, as we speak. By the time you return to Capernaum, he'll be well. I'm quite confident of that. Nothing more need be done." Wilderness fever rarely lasted more than a few days.

"Please come with me, to treat him, I beg you! I'm wealthy. I'll pay anything you ask!" Josiah persisted.

"Trust me." I tried to reassure Josiah with a smile. "Trust in God. There is nothing more to do. In a few days I'll be in Capernaum anyway. Have faith. Go to your son. You'll see. The illness will be gone."

Josiah looked perplexed, and he looked me in the eyes. I saw a man who was accustomed to having his way, and I did my best to return the same look. I must have succeeded, for finally he said, "Jesus, prophet, I thank you." Honorifics to myself notwithstanding, Josiah hurried from Cana.

The next day, Thomas and I began our journey back to Capernaum. Thomas did not trust Simon to maintain his boat adequately, and I was eager to return to the docks with my newly found voice of authority.

As we walked, Thomas asked, "What did Mother say when you explained the miracle of the wine?"

"We talked about God, and about Father, and about the future. She wants to be with us at Capernaum, but she said she can't leave Pantera until he finds an adequate replacement."

"Yes, but did you tell her about the wine?"

"It never came up. We had many other things to discuss."

"Then she still believes that you performed a miracle."

"Yes, I know. Don't fret—I'll tell her the truth. She was so happy. You remember, Thomas, I told them that it was nothing. But they still listened to me. They took in everything I said. They understood and believed."

"In a week they'll have forgotten everything but the miracle."

"Don't be so cynical," I admonished.

I hadn't deceived them on purpose. I had tried to explain.

We were about half way to Capernaum when a man caught up to us on the road. From his heavy breathing I guessed that he had been traveling quickly. Though the day was hot, a large cape made of brown rags sewn together covered most of his body including his face. He peeked at me through a small opening, and he stayed several feet away.

"Master, I feared I'd never catch you. In the sacred name of our Lord, I beg of you to have pity on me!"

"I freely give you my pity," I said. "Is that truly all you wish?" From the way he hid himself, and from his polite distance, I guessed that he had a skin disease.

"You through whom the word of the Lord is spoken! Rabbi! Prophet! Please take pity! I've left my family. I. . . ." He paused as if the words were difficult to say. "Master, if you are willing, if the Lord is willing, make me clean. I am a leper!" He revealed his face, which was covered with dark red blisters.

Thomas backed off, the natural reaction of someone untrained in healing, but I immediately saw that the leprosy was dry. I drew myself closer, examined the man's face, and quickly diagnosed a bad case of rash, probably caused by contact with a poisonous shrub. The blisters on his face were old; many of the scabs ready to fall off. He had obviously been scratching them, and there would be some scarring.

He covered his face again, as if he were ashamed to be seen. "You, who can turn water into wine," he wailed from under his cloak, "heal a poor sinner!"

He must have followed us from Cana, I thought. Whatever his sins, he believed them responsible for his affliction. I could almost hear the magus whispering to me, "Reform the man! Use the opportunity to heal his spiritual illness!"

"Uncover yourself," I instructed. "I have no fear of your disease."

"You truly are a man of God!" he said, as if I depended on righteousness for protection. He slowly removed the hood from his face and let the cloak fall to the ground. The rash also covered his chest, but with blisters that were newer and not yet dry. I took his shoulders gently in my hands and turned him around, examining his arms and legs. His back was clean; he had probably spread the rash with his own hands.

"Have faith, my poor man," I said. "You don't have the leprosy. You are clean. In the next two days the scabs will drop from your face, and soon all of your skin will heal. Repent of your sins and return to your home and to your family. Love them as God loves you."

"Why should God love a sinner?" he asked plaintively.

"God loves all his children," I said, "particularly those who repent of their sins. When you see your family, treat them with gentleness and love. Sin no more." The man raised his gaze from the ground and looked directly at my face. A tear made a track over a red scab. "Have faith in the Lord," I continued. "Your illness won't spread to those you love. Prepare a balm by boiling the bark of the alder tree and use it to wash the rash on your chest three times a day, but do it gently. Don't scratch the sores—don't let anything touch them other than the balm and water." The magi always prescribed a ritual to go with the physical treatment—the more elaborate it was, they said, the more likely was the patient to follow it. So I told him, "For the balm, use only clean water from a cistern, not from a stream or a well. Repeat the Shema as you wash. Don't let the water touch your clothing, or you must begin over again with pure water. When the rash fades, offer a gift at the temple, as the Law of Moses commands." That should do, I thought. Then, almost as an afterthought I added, "And stay away from the oak bush, especially the ones with oily leaves. They could make your skin disease return."

The man thanked me effusively and backed away without turning around.

"I believe you've just performed your second miracle," Thomas said wryly. "Your fame will spread."

I flushed with embarrassment. The diseased man had moved to the side of the road, and was still walking backwards, but I called him back. "Tell no one of this," I instructed. "You are cured, and soon your rash will be gone. This isn't my doing, but only an act of God, who did not intend for your rash to last. Obey the Law of Moses. Love your family and be kind to them. But go your way, and tell no one. I wish your meeting with me to be a secret."

His eyes opened wide, and he nodded slowly. "Thank you, Lord, thank you, thank you. I'll tell no one."

His behavior was almost comical, and I might have laughed if I hadn't remembered my own pain when I was separated from my family. This man had undoubtedly undergone a great spiritual agony, regretting some unnamed sin against those he loved, and feeling that the rest of his life was now forfeit. When he was almost out of earshot, I shouted to him, "And from now on, love all of your fellow men! Love *all* of your neighbors, everybody."

27. Gifts of God

BY THE TIME WE REACHED CAPERNAUM, MY NEW CONFIDENCE had faded. I dreaded my return to the wharves, the site of my humiliating failure. I told Thomas that I would need time to prepare, to carve and sand and polish my words. I offered to attend to his household chores, the baking of bread, the preparation of soup, the cleaning and washing, while he returned to fishing. I would only need a week or so, I hoped.

The week passed quickly and I still felt unprepared, but I forced myself to go ahead. What if I failed again? Thomas and I chose a large open square just up from the docks where a broad collection of Jewish workers could be found, including fishermen, rope makers, tarmongers, carpenters, merchants, blacksmiths, as well as women and children. Thomas went from person to person, talking to everyone who would listen, letting them know that a prophet had appeared and was about to speak at the edge of the square—that he was carrying a new message of joy and hope from the Lord. Somehow he managed to gather a few people to come close.

"Blessed are the poor, for theirs is the kingdom of heaven," I began, in a soft tone. Several people moved closer so they could hear better. "Blessed are you who know sorrow, for you will be comforted. Blessed are the meek among you, for the world will be yours. Blessed are those of you who hunger and thirst after righteousness, for I say to you today that you will be filled. Blessed are the merciful, for you will obtain mercy. Blessed are the persecuted, for great is your reward in heaven."

My small crowd listened for a few minutes, and then two of them began talking to each other, and turned away. Thomas walked over to them, but they shook their heads and left. I continued, "Come to me, and you will find rest. Rejoice, and be exceedingly happy, for great is your reward in heaven!" Several new people joined the group, but even more began to leave.

An hour passed and my audience had virtually disappeared. The wharves were busy, but a small area had cleared around me, as if I were actually repulsive. Thomas had approached most of the people that he knew, and had been able to convince many of them to pause for a few moments to listen, but I could see them soon looking for an opportunity to leave. I never had more than a dozen listeners at a time, and no one stayed for more than a few minutes. Worse, I sensed that they listened only out of politeness for Thomas, for they always slipped away when he was occupied with someone new.

Humiliation threatened to swamp me, but I fought it. What was I doing wrong? Why couldn't people recognize the truth of God? Why didn't they find it exciting, thrilling, as I had, as Thomas had, and as the people in Cana had? Perhaps God was testing me again. Have faith, I remonstrated to myself. Don't demand signs. Persevere.

Another hour passed, and the situation improved only slightly. My voice began to feel hoarse. Thomas brought an old man to sit about ten feet in front of me on a small stool that he apparently carried with him. He sat there without looking up at me, without ever reacting to my words, so I couldn't be sure whether he was listening or sleeping, but at least he gave me someone to address, someone to focus on, someone to turn my glance back to when a passerby obviously ignored me.

"Jesus of Nazareth!" The voice calling out from the other side of the square was familiar, but I couldn't place it. Yet many of the workers apparently did, for they stopped and watched as a well-dressed and obviously wealthy man approached with a purposeful gait. It was Josiah, the man whose son had been ill with the wilderness fever.

"Prophet," he said loud enough for all to hear, "I thank you for saving the life of my son." He walked up to me, bent down, and kissed my feet, as the crowd and I myself watched in amazement. He rose, turned to the crowd, and announced, "My son was dying of the great pestilence!" He turned slowly back towards me, gesturing dramatically, as he continued speaking. "When I was in Cana I went to this man, the prophet Jesus, the prophet who performed the miracle of the wedding feast, the prophet who turned water into wine at the request of his mother, and I asked his blessing. I told him that my son was dying of the pestilence, and prophet Jesus said to me, 'Return to your home. Your faith in me has been rewarded.

Your son shall live.' I returned home, and learned that at that very moment, the moment that the prophet Jesus had enunciated those words, my son had been cured!" He knelt down again at my feet, and I was afraid he was going to kiss them again.

"No, no, Josiah, rise," I said. I took him by the shoulders and urged him to his feet. "Your son was healed by God, not by me. I am here only to bring you his word, the revelations that he gave me in the wilderness. And I say to you that the illnesses of the spirit are far greater than the illnesses of the body. I am here to cure not the pestilence of the body, but the pestilence of the soul."

No sooner had I paused than another voice cried out from the edge of the square. "Lord!" I recognized the ragged brown cloak of the man who had the oak rash, even though his skin was still hidden. "You asked me to be silent," he shouted with remarkable force, "but I can keep the secret no longer!" He kept the cloak covering his body and most of his face. "You told me to tell no one, Lord Jesus, but I must! Forgive me for breaking my promise." He turned towards the growing crowd. "I had committed wickedness towards my son. I beat him for a theft that he had not committed, and he became a cripple. The Lord our God punished me by striking me down with a horrid leprosy. I left my home in despair. But then I asked forgiveness from Jesus of Nazareth, the man who had turned water into wine at the wedding feast of Cana. The prophet put his hand on my head and blessed me." At this moment the man dramatically flung off his cloak and showed himself. "And I was cured of my leprosy!" Not as quickly as that, I thought to myself. And he still had scars where he had scratched his blisters. "I returned to my family, as the prophet Jesus instructed, and I am now the most blessed man on earth!"

Those words truly gave me joy.

The man continued, "And look! My son again walks! I brought my family here with me, to listen to the prophet, to learn from him how to please the Lord!" He pointed behind him, to a woman and three children, one of whom was using a crutch.

Most of the work in the square had come to a stop. Virtually every face was turned towards me now. It was just as it had been at Cana. What should I say?

"It wasn't I who cured these men," I began, "but God! I cannot perform miracles. Only God can do that!"

"Prophet!" came a new voice from the crowd. "Tell us, you who speaks to the Lord. Tell us, when will the Messiah come? When will the kingdom of the Lord come to Israel?"

"Rejoice!" I shouted back. "The kingdom of God *has* come! It is here now, for all of you who have faith in the love and mercy of God and who repent of your sins. Rejoice and be exceedingly happy! Those of you who have known sorrow—you are blessed, for you will be comforted." I was basically repeating what I had said earlier, but the words sounded different, even to me. They were not just a prophecy, but now were illustrating a truth, the experience of a man who had returned to his family. I turned and gestured towards him with my open hand. "Blessed are the meek, for they will inherit the earth! Blessed are those who hunger and thirst after right-eousness, for they will be filled! Blessed too are the merciful, for they will obtain the mercy of God! Blessed are the pure in spirit, for through their purity they will see God!"

A man in fisherman's clothes standing towards the back began talking to his neighbor but was immediately hushed by the crowd.

"What must we do?" a man called out, just as I had heard a man call out to the Baptist. It was the moment to give my most difficult prophecy.

"What must you do? You know that it says in the Scriptures, an eye for an eye, and a tooth for a tooth. But now I say that you must not even *resist* evil. If someone strikes you on your right cheek, turn to him your left. The ancient prophets said that you must love your neighbor and hate your enemy. But I say today to you today that you must *love* your enemies. You must bless those who curse you, do good to those who hate you, and pray for those who cheat and persecute you. For if you love only those who love you, what reward have you earned? Don't even the tax collec-tors do that? And if you honor only your mother and father, what are you doing more than any other sinner? Strive for more, strive to be perfect, as God your father in heaven is perfect, for you were created in his image!"

I paused and I looked around the square. More than a hundred faces were watching me. More than a hundred people were listening, nodding, learning, understanding, accepting—sharing my spiritual vision.

That evening I was elated and dejected at the same time. "They lis-tened to me," I said to Thomas, "but only after they were deceived."

"Why do you care?" he asked. "You spoke to many Jews today. They heard you. What more can you ask for?"

"But it was for the wrong reason. They thought I could perform miracles."

"You tried to explain. I don't think there is anything you could have done to convince them otherwise. They *expect* miracles from prophets—and you, my brother, are truly a prophet. Do you think Moses beat his breast when the Lord split the Red Sea? Your 'miracles' are just gifts from

God. They are his way of enticing people to listen to you. Accept them, as you accept his prophecies."

"What will happen when they discover that I can't perform real miracles?"

"As long as you continue to heal, I suspect they will believe you are performing miracles."

"They don't consider the work of the Greek physicians to be miracles."

"Greek physicians aren't prophets."

"Then I must stop healing. My ministry can't be one of deception."

"Abandon your skill and refuse to help the sick and injured? Is that what the Lord wants of you?"

I had no answer. Thomas knew what I knew—that I couldn't stop healing.

"So what can I do, Thomas?"

"What *can* you do? Jesus, look at what you've already done—even just for me. Before your return I was asleep, spiritually asleep. I didn't even know it. You woke me, and now when you speak I know I'm hearing God himself, through you. Yes, some people ignored you at first. But when they did that it was just because they were sleeping more deeply than I had been. You'll wake them, maybe only a few at a time, but you'll wake them. The man with the oak rash—look what you did for him! So what should you do? Do what you said yourself today. Trust in the Lord."

Thomas buoyed my spirit. "But the ninth commandment says *you shall not lie*," I said.

"No, only that you shall not make false accusations. And the Lord never said you had to correct misimpressions."

I fished through my knowledge of Scripture for a more specific law prohibiting lying. "In the book of Zechariah, God clearly commands, 'Speak the truth to one another.'"

"Zechariah was also talking of a court of law, just like Moses. Besides, you did speak the truth."

"I haven't performed miracles. But everyone thinks I have."

"'Who is to say what is a miracle?' Isn't relieving pain a greater miracle that turning water into wine?"

"You sound like Father, Thomas."

"I was quoting *you,* Jesus, not Father." Thomas's eyes suddenly brightened. "Now I know why the Lord sent you to Babylon! So you'd learn to heal and so be accepted as a true prophet! It's the sign all Jews have been taught to expect. Don't you think that's it, Jesus?"

"Maybe," I said.

The man with the oak rash stationed his family on the road through Capernaum to tell everyone who passed how he had been cured of leprosy by Jesus of Nazareth, and how I had pledged him to secrecy. In town, Josiah continued to spread the stories of his son's cure as well as of the miracle of the wedding feast. Soon everybody who had a sore tooth or an insect up his ear came to seek me out. And just as Simon Magus had said, the sick and the injured were receptive subjects for the revelations of God.

At every opportunity I explained that my miracles were nothing, but my reputation for them continued to spread. The more I protested, the more the people believed that I was just trying to hide my supernatural powers.

One day Thomas told me about a lunatic. "I found him in Moladah," he said, "a little village about four miles from here. He's a crazy man who claims that he's possessed by a devil. He goes into fits and speaks in strange voices. I told him that one word from you, and he'd be cured."

"*You're* the crazy man, Thomas! What makes you think I can do anything for him?"

"I tested him. During a period of calm when he had stopped raving, I told him about your prophecies, your way of talking with God, and your revelation that God loves even those possessed by devils. I said that I was your apostle, your anointed messenger, and that I was authorized to cure for you in your absence. Before he had a chance to object, I told him that his demon appeared to be too powerful for me, and that I could exorcise him for only a minute, but as a test of his faith in you, in Jesus, I would try it. Just then he went crazy again, raving, practically foaming at the mouth. I put my hand on his head, and demanded that the demon leave, and guess what."

"He bit your hand."

"No! The demon left! It actually left. Well, he stopped his fit anyway. He suddenly relaxed, slumped into a pile on the floor, looked up at me with a look of wonder, and smiled. I cured him! He thanked me. But a minute later he went mad again. Foam and everything. Eventually he grew tired and calmed down. I told him he was certainly possessed and I would talk to you to see if you would treat him."

"I don't like it, Thomas. I have enough people to tend here in Capernaum without you searching the countryside for lunatics."

"I watched him carefully for a long time before I approached him. He is suffering, Jesus. I don't know what he did, but I suspect he committed a horrid sin—and blames it on satanic possession. You know, he may be right. After all, what is demonic possession but a soul full of evil? If he believes *you* can drive the evil out of him, then maybe you really can. It's his soul that needs a cure, not his body, and that's what you're good at. What harm can it do? If you fail, it will be because of his lack of faith. It really will be."

"I have no training with lunatics, Thomas. But bring this man to me in private. I'll examine him and talk to him and see what I can do."

Josiah begged me to preach at his synagogue and arranged for an invitation. I accepted with anticipation and trepidation. There I would face a captive but tough and skeptical audience, likely to condemn any wandering from orthodoxy—and one that probably did not believe Josiah's stories of my miracles. But they would listen to me, so, I thought, supernatural feats were not necessary. Let this be a test.

The day arrived, and as the sun set I went to teach at Josiah's synagogue, the largest of the four in Capernaum. It was an impressive stone building, located only a few hundred feet from the lake on a small hill, and built in the Greek style, with white limestone columns on a base of black basalt. Josiah said it was built by a wealthy centurion who had converted to Judaism. Columns topped with elaborately sculpted capitals supported a second story. When I entered, I was surprised to see women and children quietly looking down on the main room from a gallery above.

Ah, I thought, as I sat on a bench. A synagogue is such a comfortable place! The Shema was repeated aloud by everyone together in wonderful sonorous tones. The spices in the oil menorah lent the room a lovely smell that seemed to come directly from God. The rabbi led us all through the ritual prayers, which I knew so well, reading the familiar passages of our Scriptures by the light of the menorah. He asked the standard questions, and the worshippers all chanted together, in unison, the ritual answers. For years, Rabbi Shuwal had taught me that this rote behavior was what pleased God most. What a strange, impersonal concept of God that was. Nonetheless, I admit that I took pleasure in the ritual.

I looked around the room, at the granite reproduction of the Ark of the Covenant in the sacred enclosure near the front door, and at the limestone seats around the walls. Very impressive, I thought, but I still preferred wood. Carved on the walls were a surprising variety of designs, including not only geometrical figures, but also pictures of animals, an image of the Ark, and what looked like magical symbols. Capernaum was well known for its departures from orthodoxy, but this ornamentation struck me as more of a departure from Jewish law than I had expected. Still, was it any worse than giving a doll to a young girl? Perhaps this congregation would be more receptive to my teachings than would more orthodox Jews. Yet I was still very nervous.

Finally the rabbi asked me to rise, come to the front, and teach the congregation about the Scriptures. I walked to the raised platform and turned to face the worshippers. Josiah, in the second row, smiled at me. Thomas stood at the back. They were all facing Jerusalem, I thought, for that was how the synagogue was oriented. In contrast, the chief seats, those occupied by the elders and important Pharisees, had their backs to the holy city. As did I.

The scroll I had chosen was Isaiah, a favorite of the local Jews. I slowly wound the scroll almost to the end, and then read aloud:

> *The Spirit of the Lord is upon me*
> *because he has anointed me to bring good news to the poor.*
> *He has sent me to heal the despondent,*
> *to proclaim liberty to the captives*
> *and recovery of sight to the blind,*
> *to set free the oppressed*
> *and announce that the year has come*
> *when the Lord will save his people.*

"Isaiah spoke these words seven hundred years ago," I said, beginning my commentary. "And our people have suffered while awaiting the prophecy to be fulfilled. We suffered for our disobedience—we were punished with exile to Babylon for breaking our covenant with the Lord. We suffer now under a new oppression."

"Amen" came a voice from the back. Several of the men near the front nodded in agreement. The elders and the Pharisees were more reserved, still withholding their judgment.

"Our women and children beg of us, when will our suffering end? When will the prophecy of Isaiah come to pass? Some of you answer, When the Messiah comes, for then we will smite our enemy and achieve glorious victory." Various amens from around the room punctuated my pause. "But I tell you today that the spirit of the Lord is upon me, and he as anointed me to bring you the joyous news. Your wait has ended, for the kingdom of the Lord has arrived!"

The gathered crowd was as silent as the desert.

"Those among you who are blind"—and I specifically directed these words towards the Pharisees—"shall see!"

One Pharisee stood up angrily and complained to the group: "He treats a man suffering from a common oak rash, and now he claims he can cure the blind!" Several of the other Pharisees nodded in agreement.

"No," I responded, "by 'the blind,' I mean those who close their eyes to the spiritual world of God, those who willfully close their eyes to my revelation!"

"He thinks he is a prophet!"

"I *was* blessed with a revelation of joy," I said. "I say to you today that the kingdom of the Lord has arrived!"

"Now he thinks he's the Messiah!"

"No . . . . But I ask you, who pleases the Lord more, the man who burns the flesh of unblemished lambs or the man who loves the creations of God as . . . "

"Blasphemer!"

In panic, I looked plaintively towards the back of the synagogue, but Thomas had vanished.

There was nothing to do but continue. "I was blessed with a revelation of joy, but you too can speak with the Lord, as I have! Pray, but not like the hypocrites who do so where all can see them. Rather pray in silence, in your homes, even in your closets."

"The Lord has instructed us how to pray!" came the angry reply. "Who are you to tell us differently? Who gave *you* the authority?"

"Don't shut your eyes!" I pleaded. "Don't close your ears! I beg of you, listen to the words that I bring to you from the Lord . . ."

I was interrupted by shouting outside the rear of the synagogue, and the door suddenly burst open. A man rushed in, waving his arms, and shrieking in an ungodly voice, "Let us alone!" He fell on the floor and seemed to move about as if he were being pushed by an unseen force. Suddenly he sprang to his feet, violently pushed aside a dozen men, and came rolling on the floor about ten feet in front of me. I had never seen anything like it. He moaned, gasped, and convulsed like an epileptic. Suddenly he sat up and shouted again, this time directly to me, in what sounded to be the voice of a totally different person, "Let us alone!"

Thomas had returned and stood by the open door. So, I thought, this must be the lunatic. Without thinking about what I was doing, I stretched my arm out and pointed at the crazy man, shouting, "You with the foul spirits! What do you want of me?"

"What do you want of *us,* Jesus of Nazareth?" he answered in yet a third voice, this one ragged and chilling, almost inhuman. How did he do that? Were there really several demons inside him? I had been possessed, but it had been nothing like this! Or had it?

"Let us alone!" he screamed, and then he convulsed with a hysterical, maniacal, cold laugh. He fell over and writhed again on the floor. Everyone but me had backed away. In his original voice he said, "Have you come to destroy us? I know who you are, the holy one of God!"

I felt utterly out of control of the situation. There was only one thing I could do, so I did it. "Hold your peace, evil demons!" I shouted. I walked up to the man, who was spinning and convulsing at one location now. I put my hand on his head and jerked it suddenly, in the manner that Simon Magus had described when exorcising Asmodeus from the fat woman. "Leave this man! Get out of him!" I shouted.

The man abruptly fell silent, and I worried for a moment that I had injured his neck. But he stood up slowly, looked at me, and then fell to his knees, obviously exhausted. "Jesus of Nazareth, holy man, my savior!" he said, grabbing my legs and kissing at my feet.

"Your sins are forgiven," I said, as I pulled him to his feet. "Blessed are they who have suffered, for they will be comforted," I told him. "Blessed are they who hunger and thirst after righteousness, for they will be filled."

I turned to the congregation, half of whom were intently staring at me, while the other half were riveted on the formerly possessed man. The Pharisee who had been most severe with me had left, along with several of the elders.

"Blessed is he who knows pain and sorrow," I said, looking at the former lunatic, "for he will be comforted." Now every eye was upon me. Even the former lunatic nodded at my words. "Blessed are the merciful, for they will obtain mercy. Blessed are they who have sinned but are now pure in heart, for they will be forgiven. And blessed are they who believe without demanding signs, for they shall themselves hear the voice of God!"

I was not invited back to this synagogue. Josiah told me that the elders considered my sermon blasphemous. But I continued teaching to large crowds on the docks and back at the marketplace, and I did receive invitations from three of the smaller synagogues.

Several of the men who had been at the synagogue now came to the outdoor gatherings. The most faithful was a tailor named Jairus, who often brought his wife Ruth and their daughter, whom they called 'little Anna." They sometimes brought their work. I would teach, and they would sit and stitch and listen.

One day Jairus came to me in despair. "My daughter is dead!" he sobbed. "Why her? She was young, and beautiful, and . . . righteous. Why did the Lord pick her? Please tell me, Rabbi! Why little Anna?"

"What happened, Jairus? I saw little Anna here just yesterday, and she had looked healthy to me? Tell me, was there an accident?"

"My Lord, she did not awake this morning. We shook her, and slapped her, but her soul had departed during the night."

"Had there been any sign of illness?"

"No, Lord. We had no warning."

"How do you know she is dead?"

"Her heart no longer beats," he said. "Rabbi Barak made the holy pronouncement. Her body has been prepared, and she will be buried today." His sobbing became severe, and he seemed to lose control.

"Please, Jairus, take me to her. I must see her and examine her." His daughter was plump, and I knew it was easy for the untrained to miss a pulse or heartbeat in such a person. At the Academy I had seen cases of premature pronouncements of death, and I knew Rabbi Barak well enough to mistrust his medical skill.

As soon as I arrived in the house, my suspicions were confirmed. There had been no settling of the blood, and Anna's face was still pink. I checked her heartbeat and could hear nothing. No pulse. I moistened my lips and put them close to her mouth, I sensed a very slight breath. I tapped at her knee and she kicked slightly—and Jairus gasped. "Rejoice!" I announced to Jairus and Ruth. "She's only sleeping." From my purse I took some pungent salts and held them to her nose, and a moment later she was sputtering and coughing, and soon she was wide-awake. Jairus's wife hugged her daughter while Jairus rushed outside.

I heard his words through the open door: "The prophet Jesus of Nazareth has brought little Anna back from the dead!"

I rushed out after him, and was greeted first by cheers but then by a reverent silence as the crowd, gathered for the funeral procession, dropped one by one to their knees. "No!" I insisted. "Rise to your feet! She was not dead. She was only sleeping!"

"My Lord, I thank you for the miracle you have wrought today!"

"Jairus, it was no miracle. Don't call it that! I merely awakened her." I looked at the crowd and found all looking directly at me. "This was not a miracle!" I insisted to them. "Tell no one that this was a miracle! Little Anna was only asleep! I only woke her."

I examined little Anna at length, but could find nothing wrong with her—except that she was hungry. I gave Jairus some of the pungent salts and told him how to use them if she ever appeared to die again. When at the Academy I had heard of an illness called sleeping epilepsy, but I had never seen a case of it there. I still don't know if that was what had afflicted little Anna.

As I feared, my pleadings were in vain. Soon the word spread throughout Capernaum that I had raised the dead. My protestations only made my reputation stronger. Thomas heard one of my followers mutter, "He is hiding his even greater powers from the Romans, until his appointed time has come."

28. The Virgin

IN THE MIDST OF MY CAPERNAUM MINISTRY, THOMAS AND I
received word that our mother was ready to join us. Josiah generously
offered to let her stay in a room in his large home. We were about to leave
for Cana to get her when I came down with a frightful cold. So I took a
rest from teaching for a week, stayed indoors, studied the Scriptures,
prayed, and recovered, while Thomas went to Cana. I wondered what my
disciples would think if they saw me unable to cure myself of a cold.

I was well by the time Thomas returned with our mother. After our
joyous greetings at Josiah's home, a maidservant took her to a room to rest.
Thomas remained with me.

"Did you explain the water and the wine to her?" I asked him.

"I tried, Jesus, but she doesn't believe me. You must do it yourself. But
it's worse than you think. The stories of your healings have spread to Cana.
She now believes that her son is a prophet who can cure all illnesses."

"I'll talk to her as soon as she's rested."

"I'm not yet finished—you haven't heard the worst. She's been telling
people that you weren't the son of Joseph."

"She's never hidden that fact."

"But she says that she was a virgin when you were born."

"Save me from the abyss! It's the Messiah myth! I must speak to her!"

The maidservant let me know as soon as my mother was awake, and
I went in to see her. We embraced again, and she started to tell me about
her journey. I interrupted, and told her that there were some things I had
to explain. I couldn't allow myself to put it off any longer.

"Mother," I said, "I can't perform miracles. I didn't turn water into wine that night in Cana. It was just an accident, a misunderstanding, not a miracle. I had placed the wine in the water jugs beforehand. I tried to explain at the time, but nobody wanted to listen. I think Pantera knew all along."

"And I suppose that you didn't cure the son of Josiah, or the leper, or the man possessed by the demon, or little Anna."

"No, I didn't, not as miracles anyway. I studied healing in Babylon. Each of those cures has a natural explanation."

"Jesus, did you know that I was a virgin when you were conceived?"

"Mother, please. Thomas told me you've been saying that. But you were just a young girl. You didn't know what you were doing. Some man took advantage of you. Surely you understand now that you were just a victim of rape?"

"Rape? No! Jesus! No man knew me. What put that into your head? I was a virgin when I married Joseph!"

I looked in her eyes. She seemed to believe what she was saying. But some man had certainly taken advantage of her when she was too young to know better, too young to defend herself. I had seen many such cases at the Academy clinic. I couldn't believe that a child who had suffered such a trauma would have no memory of it when she grew to adulthood, and yet that appeared to be the case. I couldn't understand. "You were raped!" I insisted.

"No I wasn't. I was still a virgin. When you were born, it was a virgin birth."

In frustration I said to her, "Don't try to make me into the Messiah. I'm just your son, Jesus. Please believe that."

"Why are you afraid?" she asked. "Why don't you want me to call you the Messiah? Aren't you bringing spiritual liberation to our people? Aren't you carrying the word of God?"

Rather than respond "yes" to her questions, I said, "But I am *not* performing miracles!"

She looked at me with the sweetness of a mother looking at her child, and asked, "Are you in danger?" She nodded her head, as if she had suddenly understood something. "Of course. They'll kill you, as they did Judah of Gamala. You wish to heal, bodies and souls, and you can do that only if you don't threaten the Romans. I understand, Jesus. Being identified as the Messiah wouldn't help, but would only interfere."

"Mother, I'm just your son. I'm no more than that. Please accept that."

"You're my son. I accept that."

29. The Rock

THE SUMMER ENDED ABRUPTLY, AND WE HAD OUR FIRST blustery day of autumn, the kind when mothers bring their children indoors, when the sun only occasionally peeks through to remind you that it's hiding behind the clouds, but also the kind that my father loved. "On days like this," he would say, "you can feel that your face is alive."

And the rest of my body too, I thought to myself as I shook off a shiver. I wondered for a moment whether I should even bother going to the lake, for surely nobody would come to an outdoor sermon in weather like this.

But I was wrong. Waiting for me were about two dozen disciples, come to listen, to learn, to pray, to be reborn, or for whatever reason only they knew. Perhaps some of them came simply to enjoy the wind.

Most of my followers were from the class the rabbis contemptuously called the am ha'arez, the people of the land, the group to which Rabbi Shuwal had once consigned me. Am ha'arez! The epithet carried the implications of ignorant, irreligious, and immoral. In the minds of the Pharisees, each of these was the inevitable consequence of the other. Ignorance means not knowing the Law of Moses, and if you didn't know the law, then you were irreligious, regardless of your love of God. And if you were irreligious, you are immoral, regardless of how you treat your fellow man.

For every Pharisee in Israel, there were a hundred am ha'arez. The latter accepted the Covenant in principle but broke it every day—not always willfully, for sometimes they were honestly mistaken about the law. And yet frequently the am ha'arez broke the rules because they found them too burdensome. Although they had their sons circumcised and they eschewed pork, they didn't wear the tassels and prayer boxes prescribed by the Torah, or totally avoid work on the Sabbath. They couldn't afford to, for they were too close to starvation. Nevertheless I knew that most felt guilt for their perceived shortcomings.

Among those who came to the lake were the very poor. They were unskilled laborers when there was work, beggars when there wasn't. I had asked Josiah if he could supply food for the most desperate of my followers, and he set up meals of fish and bread to follow my sermons. But whether the am ha'arez came for my teachings or for food, I didn't know and I didn't care, for at my side they were like children, eager to learn, guileless, not full of the caustic wit and arrogance of the Pharisees at the synagogue. Too poor to support their own families, they joined my family, and I taught them to call each other brothers and sisters under the fatherhood of God. In my congregation all were equal, all were equally loved, all could find fellowship and acceptance. Their poverty was not a sign that they had been abandoned, I taught them, for wealth in this world is inconsequential. We were placed here only as a test, as was Job, and if we worshipped God with love, our reward would come.

These were the most extraordinary days of my ministry. At the time I felt that there was some kind of magic within me, because I could tell that I was helping these people—or rather, that God was helping them, using me as his tool. That magic seemed to radiate to those around me. Tortured men came to me and I eased their pain. Distressed woman and children found comfort in my words. My blessing was so great that others could sense it, and share in it, almost by just being with me.

But how I squandered that blessing!

There was one person whom I particularly noticed, a powerfully built young man who came often but always sat as far away as he could while still listening, as if he were hiding from the others. Nonetheless I could sense his concentration when I talked about love and forgiveness, and his great interest when I spoke of hope and the presence of God's kingdom on earth. He was so responsive that at times I directed my sermon towards him, thinking that if I made a difference in just this one life, that my ministry would be a success. I asked Thomas if he knew the identity of this lonely disciple.

"That's Simon the fisherman," he said. "The man who rents my boat. He comes to hear you frequently, except when he's trying to fish."

"Trying?"

"He's the worst fisherman I've ever seen at Capernaum. He has no sense of where the fish are. And he spends more time squabbling with his partners—his brother Andrew and two cousins James and John—than he spends looking for fish. He is one of these people who fails at everything he tries. His wife left him last year, and he's grown more and more despondent. You actually met her once and helped her mother, an old white-haired woman. Whatever you did, you made her feel better, because she got up out of bed and made you soup."

"Yes, I remember now. I think she got out of bed because Simon brought a group of strangers home."

"Nevertheless, you impressed him. He looks somewhat sick himself. He may be hoping your sermons will cure him too."

"He's never come to ask for anything. He's never even approached me."

"I think you should appreciate, brother, that some of your disciples are afraid of you. They are sinners and you are in direct contact with the Lord."

"But I teach that God is a loving father."

"All their lives they've been taught that the Lord is a vengeful master. For some of them, that's not an image that's easily undone." Thomas pointed past my shoulder. "There he is."

Simon was walking over to a stump near the shore. He sat on it and bowed his head, as if he were feeling nauseated.

"I'll go talk to him now."

"Don't expect too much, brother. Simon was a failure as a husband, he's a failure as a Jew, and he'll probably be a failure as a disciple. Oh, by the way, his partners call him Peter."

"Meaning 'rock'?"

"It's a nickname he got as a child. Andrew told me the story. Simon accidentally sliced his finger with a sheep knife. He couldn't find anybody to help him, and it was bleeding badly, and all he could remember was a saying about rubbing salt in a wound."

"Oh no! He didn't . . . ?"

"Yes, that's what he did."

I winced. "Some people always learn the hard way."

"When his rabbi said Simon was 'dumb as a rock,' his schoolmates picked up on it."

"Why does he still use the nickname?"

"He liked the image of strength. He was a small child."

"He's small no longer. He looks like he could lift a camel."

"Such are the miracles of God."

I approached Simon, who was still staring at the ground. As I stood in front of him, he looked up suddenly, and seemed startled and embarrassed by my presence. "Follow me," I said quietly and began to walk away. I felt that a vigorous walk was the best treatment for depression. Simon sprang to his feet, caught up, and walked a few feet behind me, like a servant. I turned my face to him over my shoulder, while walking, and said, "Your name is Simon." He looked surprised, as if he thought that God had told me his name. I moved to the side of the path, and he came up alongside me and fell in with my steps. "You're troubled," I continued. "You're unhappy, and ill. Your wife has left you and you blame yourself, yet you feel that you haven't been treated fairly."

"You see into my soul, Rabbi!" Simon replied. "I miss her. She called me stupid, so I beat her. Not that badly, Rabbi. No more than she deserved. But still she left me."

"Violence is an abomination in the eyes of God," I said. "When you hurt another, God always sees that you suffer yourself more than the person you hurt."

Simon stopped walking and just stood still. "Rabbi, I'm not worthy that you talk to me," he said, almost crying. "I'm a failure. I'm despised by everyone." Simon's hulking body looked surprisingly weak and fragile.

"Not by God," I said, "and not by me."

"I spend my time with sinners, dissolutes, and drunkards," he continued. "Then my head throbs as if it had been pounded by stones. My family hates me, my partners hate me, and I hate them. I no longer know why I continue to live. The world is dead to me."

"And God punishes your hatred with illness. But I know why you have been coming to my sermons, Simon. Because you seek to repent."

"Yes, but ..." He averted his eyes again. I said nothing, while I waited for him to finish his sentence. "...But it's hard. I try, and then I get angry. Rabbi, you ask us to love our enemies. I can't even love my friends! They make fun of me and they talk behind my back. They call me slow witted— and a lousy fisherman."

"To me, Simon, you appear to have the strength of a rock." He looked up at me as if startled by the metaphor. "Most men are like the grass of the field," I said, "and their glory is like the beauty of the wildflowers. But when the Lord sends a dry wind blowing, the grass withers and the flowers lose their blossoms and fall away. People are no stronger than the grass and no stronger than the flowers, and they too wither and fade." Simon nodded, as if he knew this from his own experience. "But," I continued, "the word of God is unlike the grass and the flowers, for it is strong and endures forever."

"That's beautiful," Simon said.

"That's Isaiah," I replied. "You should learn more of the Scriptures."

"I can't read," Simon said, with shame.

"Then come with me and I'll recite the Scriptures to you, for they're full of beauty and wisdom. You think the world is dead to you—that you are dead, and you are! But only as a seed is dead, with a spirit of life that is struggling to push out and to grow and be reborn. That's why you continue to live, because despite your failures your spirit is ready to be reborn. You need only let it out, let it burst the shell of hatred that holds it back."

"I am withering like dry grass," Simon said, aptly repeating back the metaphor from Isaiah, "in the hot wind of the Lord." He may be illiterate, I thought, but he has a good memory. One day he could make a good preacher.

"No, Simon," I said. "You are a rock lying in the field of grass." Simon looked up again. I bent over and picked up a large stone. "It was rejected by stonemasons who thought it worthless, for they didn't recognize its strength." Simon examined the stone carefully. "But this is a rock that can serve as the cornerstone of a great structure!"

"Lord, people call me 'Peter'!" he beamed, as if he thought I didn't already know.

"And Peter will you be to me! You'll grow to be an example to others, like a great stone on which they stumble when they're disobedient to the Lord. Simon, whom I call Peter, a rock of the Lord, my rock. Lay aside all malice, lay aside all hatred, lay aside all excess. Rid your soul of all hypocrisy, of all envy, of all evil. Be like a newborn baby who craves only the milk of God's truth to make you grow! You are reborn!" I put my hands on his shoulders. "With love and humility you have repented. Today, right now, your health will begin to return. Abstain from the fleshly lusts that Satan uses to torment your body and to war against your soul. Drink no more of strong liquors, not one more drop. Open your heart to God, your gentle and loving father."

"My lord Jesus! You give me hope, but I'm a weak man. You cast out my devil, but he'll come back."

"God will strengthen you. He'll make Simon Peter as strong and stable as a rock. Trust in God, let his truth guide you, and he'll make you perfect. But you must be sober and be vigilant. Satan is like a roaring lion that stalks people to devour. You must be cautious and steadfast!" His face brightened. "Do you feel the freshness entering your soul?" I asked.

"Yes, yes, it feels—clean! Rabbi, what do I do next? What should I sacrifice? Should I be baptized?"

"A bath would be a good idea, Peter. But remember that your rebirth is spiritual. God will help, but you must completely and utterly forgive those who have sinned against you—without qualification. You must abstain completely from liquor, lust, and the filthy sins that have consumed you. Go back to your wife, to your brother, and to your partners, and bring with you love instead of hatred. Be kind to them, offer them anything of yours that they want, and seek their forgiveness."

Peter seemed to be thinking for a moment, and then he blurted out, "I forgive them, Rabbi. I do. And I'll seek their forgiveness. I'll turn my other cheek. I will! I'll do it now!" He turned, and started to run away.

"Stop, Peter!" I called. "Wait. Pray to the Lord. Stay with me a while. Let your love grow. Think about your wife, your brother Andrew, and your partners, James and John, how they are creations of the Lord, as are you." He reacted with surprise, probably because I knew their names. "Don't rush to them. Go only after you've prayed, and after you've gained control of your weaknesses. It may take your loved ones a while to see the change, for it's all deep within your soul. Be prepared for their skepticism, and be patient. When you do go, go clothed in humility and strengthened by love. Now you should pray. Express your love for God, and your desire to please him, and seek his help. Talk to him about your failings, and about your hopes. Seek strength from him to do what's right. If no words come to you, then just think about him and his love for you. Think about the wonderful gifts he's given you in the past."

"Gifts that I squandered," he said as he fell to his knees. He bowed his head and then looked up, but his eyes were closed, his hands tightly clasped. He mumbled quietly to himself. I couldn't quite understand what he was saying, but his prayer sounded sincere and spiritual. I walked away quietly, sat on a log, and watched him from a distance. He stayed there for a long time, but I didn't want to leave. I was curious—no, excited. Nearly an hour passed. Peter's knees must be hurting badly by now, I thought. He moves as if he is really talking, really listening. I felt chilly and realized that a fog had moved in off the lake. A slight drizzle dampened my shirt. I neither wanted to leave Peter here, nor to interrupt him.

Suddenly Peter stood up, leapt in the air, and clapped his hands above his head. Ignoring me completely, he ran directly towards the road to Capernaum, breaking several branches with his massive body as he crashed through the brush. It was an energetic, joyous eruption of spirit, a spirit that had been utterly invisible in the sad, heartsick man I had approached an hour earlier. What I was seeing, there in the drizzling fog, was the enormous power of God's love healing a tortured spirit.

Within a week Peter claimed that his health was restored. Shortly afterwards he reconciled himself with his brother and partners. The change to them must have been dramatic, for they began coming to my sermons, particularly when the fishing was poor. Peter's headaches continued, but a small dose of haoma in wine seemed to relieve them. His one failure may have been his wife. He never mentioned her, and I believe she never came back to him.

One afternoon after I had finished a sermon and had tended to several ill, Peter brought his partners to talk with me privately. "My brother Andrew has been talking to God," he said, "but God hasn't been answering his requests."

I turned to Andrew. "What are you asking of the Lord?"

"Rabbi, we are poor fishermen. We work hard, but we go unrewarded. I asked the Lord to help us with our livelihood, to bring the fish to our nets—so that we can better serve him."

"You're like a foolish child," I admonished. Peter nodded as if he agreed with my censure of Andrew. "Do you think that God doesn't know what you need, even before you pray? Do you think you have to tell him?"

Andrew looked embarrassed; James and John stood by, saying nothing. Finally Andrew said, "I was asking for no more than the daily catch that he gives to other fishermen. I'm not being selfish. Is even this too much to ask for?"

I smiled. "Andrew, if the Lord wanted you to catch fish, he'd fill your nets to the verge of breaking! Nothing is beyond his means, or yours, if you have faith!" I leaned over, picked a wild mustard flower, and pulled out one of its tiny seeds. "If your faith was no greater than the size of this mustard seed, you could move that mountain—" I pointed to a hill by the lake, and then to the other side, "—over there!"

"How do I get such faith?"

"Be like a little child," I said. "Trust in God, your great father. He will provide. Look around! Look at the lilies in the field, and see how they grow. They don't fish or farm or labor. Yet look at them!" I pointed to the nearby hillside that was in its full spring glory, and waved my arm in a grand gesture. "Solomon in all of his magnificence wasn't arrayed like these! If God clothes the grass like that, think how much more finely he will clothe you! Don't search for food or drink, but rather seek the kingdom of God, for it is in your spirit that you are most wanting."

James looked confused. "Are you telling us that we should abandon fishing?" he asked in a dubious tone.

"No. But Andrew, you must recognize what is important and what isn't. The kingdom of God is here, in front of you, and you can enter any time. If the Lord denies you fish, it's because you are more concerned with the world of money than with his kingdom of the spirit."

Peter returned to me the next day. "Andrew is skeptical," he said. "After we left, he asked me, 'If the Lord could move a mountain, why can't he provide us with a good catch?' I tried to explain to him that the Lord could do that if he wanted to, but Andrew wouldn't listen. Rabbi, you do miracles for the sick. Do you suppose you could do one for me—I mean, do you suppose that you could do one for Andrew, just so he could see what I see, that you are truly a messenger from God?"

"I can't perform miracles, Peter. Only God can do that. And he performs them only when he chooses. Many of my followers believe because they see my healings, but more blessed are those who believe without seeing signs. I can't provide faith for Andrew. It must come from within. Do your best to help open his eyes, so he can see what you see, so that he will know that we are surrounded by miracles, so that he will enjoy the faith that you have."

I wondered, had Peter requested this miracle for Andrew, or had he really asked it for himself?

The numbers of my disciples continued to grow. Several had been former disciples of the Baptist, including Philip the merchant and another man named Simon, who had once been a Zealot. "You're winning over the disciples of John," Thomas said, optimistically. "You'll soon have as many as he has."

"Tell me Thomas, do you think there's any risk in having a Zealot among my disciples?"

"A former Zealot? No, I don't think so. You attract all kinds, beggars, thieves, debtors, and harlots. The Pharisees take comfort in the fact that your disciples are mostly the scum of the earth."

"They are the salt of the earth, Thomas, a valuable spice sometimes mistaken for dirt."

"They come to you, Jesus, because they find love."

"And also because they find food and medicine."

"And you accuse *me* of being cynical! Is it possible that you don't really understand your own power?"

"I don't know, Thomas, I truly don't know."

I still taught occasionally in a synagogue, although rarely on the Sabbath. On those occasions, Thomas had the sick and injured sit in the front of the congregation rather than in the rear. I took pleasure in seeing these seats, once the dominion of the wealthy, become the realm of the poor and weak. I ministered to them in the middle part of my sermon, so that I preached both before and after.

After one rather successful Sabbath at a small synagogue on the edge of Capernaum, I noticed that a lame man who had entered with a crutch was leaving without it. I picked it up and brought it to him. "Brother," I said, "your faith in God will help you to walk, and your legs will grow stronger as you use them, but don't leave your crutch just yet. It will take a while for your legs to strengthen fully."

"Rabbi, that's not my crutch," he replied. "It was given to me by a man when I entered the synagogue."

I immediately suspected Thomas. I confronted him and he confessed.

"But I don't see what's bothering you," Thomas said. "It's only a way of making your cure more vivid. I always talk to the patients first, and I give them crutches only if I think their disability is amplified by sin. 'Those with crutches,' I tell them, 'are more likely to be treated by the Rabbi.' I ask them to leave the crutches behind when they go, and the rest of the congregation sees them leave the crutches behind. It's *always* worked, so far."

"It has always worked? How often have you done this, Thomas?"

"This last was the fourth. You didn't notice the first three. I meant to tell you, Jesus, I really did. Please don't be angry."

"Angry?" I caught myself. Yes, I was angry. I took a deep breath and tried to relax. "Thomas, what you did is blatant deception!" I said with exasperation.

"I didn't think of it that way," he said timidly. "You really do cure these people. But the healing is mostly spiritual, hard for others to see. The crutch is just a way to create a bit of drama that people will remember."

"Thomas, Thomas, my little brother Thomas! Don't you see that it's wrong to practice willful deception?"

Thomas looked at me sheepishly. "But I thought that *if done in a righteous cause, deception can be more honest than truth.*"

"No, Thomas. That was the Magus speaking. God wishes us to move beyond the corruptions of previous religions, of previous prophets. It's bad enough that my disciples ignore my denials of miracles. The worship of God must be based on honesty and truth." Thomas looked dejected, and I wondered if I had been too harsh. To cheer him up, I said, "Besides, don't you appreciate the danger?"

"That we'll be exposed?"

"No—that the man will keep the crutch and walk out with it. Those who saw him arrive without one may think my preaching made him lame!" Thomas laughed weakly.

30. Loneliness

YOU PROBABLY THINK IT IS A WONDERFUL THING TO BE CALLED by God for a divine mission. And perhaps, if God gave power and strength commensurate with the weight of the task, it would be so. But overwhelmed as I was at times by the pain and suffering that I couldn't always cure, burdened by the demands of sinners begging for help, and constrained by my own weaknesses, there were times when I could bear no more. In desperation I told my disciples that I had to leave, to retreat to the wilderness for prayer, to talk to God. But what I really needed was solitude and rest.

Nothing helped me revive so much as spending time in places tended only by God. In the forests, the hillsides, or the desert, I found beauty, strength, and renewal. Evil seemed absent, left behind in the human domain. I wandered alone, feeling not the pain of others, but the greatness of God's world, this innocent world cared for by God alone. I had told my disciples that I was going to pray, and indeed, wasn't this communion with God's world a form a prayer? Yes, although my disciples might not have recognized it as such, for I didn't sit and mutter words, but only indulged myself in the wonder of God's creations. I might sit quietly on a fallen laurel trunk and listen to the clear whistle of the blackbird, the chatter of squirrels, or just the wind through trees imitating the sound of a brook. I might lie on the grass, looking through a bouquet of white poppies at the clouds drifting slowly above. I might run through the woods, exulting in the sense of being alive.

And yet I never wandered for long without my solitude drifting towards loneliness. How strange to feel so empty when surrounded by riches, like Adam in the Garden of Eden. God knew Adam would be lonely, and so he created Eve. But how did he know? Alas, how could he not know—for, I pondered, is there anyone more lonely than God, the being who has no equals?

Rabbi Shuwal had taught that God was powerful and all knowing, strict and remote, almost a bully, somewhat like the Rabbi himself. When he told us to love God, he meant a respectful love, a deferential love, a fearful love, a submissive love, a cold love. But one moonlit evening, as I walked through the woods, contemplating for the first time God's loneliness, I felt a new kind of love towards God, one that included compassion, a love that had warmth.

My reverie abruptly ended when I realized I was being watched. In the fading light I spotted a tall man in ragged clothes, looking very much like a bandit, standing a hundred feet down the path and staring intently at me. I had heard of highwaymen who beat victims too poor to satisfy their rapacity. I stopped walking but dared not back away. Would God protect me?

Why did I fear? Maybe I was destined to bring this man to repentance. He took several steps closer to me.

"Jesus of Nazareth!" he shouted. His voice was strong and yet it had a gentle edge. He began to walk closer.

"Yes, I am he," I answered. My heart beat faster. "Peace be with you! And who are you?"

"I am Dositheus, a disciple of the one who is called the Baptist." As he drew close, I could see that his clothes were made of many scraps of clean cloth crudely sewn together, held to his body by a broad leather belt similar to that worn by John.

"You followed me here?" I asked, my fear gradually turning to curiosity.

"To bring you a message." Dositheus lowered his voice and said, "And to lead you to the Baptist."

"To John? Where? Is he near?"

"He wishes to meet with you. I may tell you no more. Come with me." Dositheus turned and walked away at a quick pace. I followed, as he apparently assumed I would. We went through the woods, down the sloping hillside to the road leading to Magdala. So, I thought, John has emerged again from the wilderness and wants to meet with me! But why this stealthy approach by Dositheus? Was John calling me to him only to censure me again? Much had changed since our last meeting. Had John heard of my ministry in Capernaum?

We followed the road for about a mile, climbed past an olive orchard, and then Dositheus, with exaggerated mystery, led me back into the forest to a small opening beyond the orchard. No sooner had I entered the clearing than Dositheus quietly and suddenly vanished. I should learn how to disappear like that, I mused. About fifty feet away I spotted John, standing by himself in the growing darkness, looking more like a ghost than a prophet. I walked closer to him.

He had grown thinner and more gaunt. Was that just the desert life, or had he truly become an ascetic? This time, in addition to his characteristic heavy belt, he appeared to be wearing a rough camel-hair shirt. I wasn't sure what to say. I thought of the commotion there would be in Capernaum if the disciples knew that John and Jesus, the two prophets of Nazareth, were standing together on a hillside just west of their city.

Beware of the sin of pride, I cautioned myself.

John broke the silence. "I've heard of your miracles," he said without sarcasm.

"They are nothing."

"The blind can see, the lame can walk, the lepers are made clean, and the deaf can hear."

"And the good news is preached to the poor," I said.

"Yes. 'The good news is preached.' Many people ask me about you."

"What do you say?"

"I say that you are the lamb of God."

"What does that mean?"

"That Jesus heard the voice of God speaking to him in the wilderness. That Jesus speaks the words of God, that God has given you the spirit without limit."

"Thank you, John." What had brought John's turnabout? "I hear the word of God in you also. I tell the people that you are a prophet, and that you are much more than a prophet. I say that among those born on this earth there has not been anyone greater than John the Baptist."

"And you also tell them that he who is least in the kingdom of God is greater than John."

"Only to show how great is the kingdom of God. You have good spies, John."

"I don't have spies. But I do hear about you, as I'm sure you hear about me—from the many disciples that you have enticed away from me." If this was a reproach, his tone was lacking in bitterness.

"If you preached in the towns as I do, they would all follow you, and I would have no disciples left. But I've lost followers to you too, John. You and I both preach the word of God."

"We both preach repentance. I emphasize the Law of Moses, and you emphasize love, but we are more similar than we are different. I can't love the Romans, as you say you do, but I admire your courage. Courage, yes, that's needed now. Jesus, there's something we must discuss." He paused as if considering what to say, or in what tone to say it. Finally he said, simply, "The Council in Jerusalem, the Sanhedrin, plans to kill me."

"Kill you? John, you must be . . ."—I almost said "crazy"—". . . mistaken. You're no Zealot. The crowds you attract are enormous, but . . ." I visualized John as the Sanhedrin must see him, the leader of a multitude that would do anything he asked, and I thought, maybe they do have reason to fear. "Besides, the Sanhedrin don't have the authority to execute."

John smiled wryly. "If the Sanhedrin wish me executed, the Romans will accommodate them. That's part of their unspoken agreement. And the Sanhedrin want me dead."

"How can you be certain?"

"Let me just say that I am certain. There are people at the highest levels who send me word."

"Your attacks on Herod were unwise," I said. All of Galilee knew that John had castigated Herod for divorcing his wife and then marrying Herodias, who was already married to his half-brother Philip, all in flagrant violation of the Law of Moses. In criticizing Herod, John had crossed the dim but dangerous line dividing religion from politics.

"My disciples ask me about him, and I must be honest. How can I preach repentance while he flaunts his sins?"

"You can be honest without being candid."

He squinted at me in an expression of disbelief, as if to say that he didn't comprehend my words. Then he shook his head and said, "No I can't. There's no difference between truth and candor."

I was embarrassed by his righteousness. But then I recalled his dissembling with the Levite, when I had first seen him on the Jordan.

"Beware, Jesus! They won't stop with me. You are a greater threat to them than I am. They might even come after you first, since you preach in the towns and are easier to find."

"Nonsense! John, I preach love of enemies!"

"As long as you call them enemies, you are a threat."

"I doubt they know that I exist."

"They *do* know, Jesus, be assured of that."

How could John know all this? Was he guessing? "Is that why you came? To warn me?"

"In part." John seemed to relax again. In an almost conversational tone he said, "I hear that you've begun baptizing."

"That's true. The ceremony gives a sense of rebirth to those who have repented. Once their sins are physically washed away, they are less likely to revert. A ritual washing is something all Jews can understand."

"They will call you Jesus the Baptist."

"And you will be John of Nazareth."

John's lightness of mood suddenly transformed again. His face seemed to darken. "If they arrest me, Jesus, I'll tell my disciples to follow you." These words bothered me, more than anything he had said previously. I suddenly realized that John truly expected to be murdered.

"If they arrest me, John, I'll tell my disciples to follow *you*," I responded. But I don't think I believed, at that time, that this would ever happen.

We stood there looking at each other in the moonlight. Cousins and childhood friends from the same obscure village in Galilee were now prophets carrying the message of repentance, and both were feared by the Jewish authorities. Even my father would never have imagined this. Thanks to the danger John felt, he had recognized that I too brought a message from God. And yet, even with so much in common, we had nothing more to say to each other. We stood for a moment in awkward silence, and finally John turned and walked away. I watched him cross the field and vanish into the woods on the other side, and wondered whether I would ever see him again.

31. Disciples

THE WEATHER WAS CLEAR AND WARM AND FISHING HAD BEEN poor—optimal conditions for a large crowd. They were also optimal conditions to bring out large numbers of the sick and invalid, who swarmed around me begging to be cured. Peter worked his way to the front and asked if I would prefer to preach from his boat, with everyone listening on the shore. I accepted. The sloped beach would provide a perfect amphitheater, and the quiet offshore breeze would carry my voice.

When I finished, Peter rowed the boat towards the beach. That was when I noticed that Thomas had been frantically trying to catch my attention. As the boat plowed into the soft sand I asked him, "What is it?"

Thomas leaned over and spoke softly, but I could feel his excitement. "I think it is time for God to reward your fishermen! Jesus, listen to me. I've seen conditions like this only twice in the last ten years. A long period with a dry south wind. Cold water and no fish. By accident I happened to be near Bergesa on the eastern shore the first time. The local fishermen were hauling them in by the cartload."

"In Bergesa they take catfish, the unclean fish with no scales. Of what interest is that to us?"

"There were carp. And sardines. Thousands of them! They must have crossed the sea because of the unusual weather. All the edible fish of the Sea of Galilee seemed to be concentrated there. The Bergesans were throwing them away, leaving them to rot on the beach. Those pigs only saved the catfish! I almost cried. Then two years ago conditions were similar. On a hunch I sailed to the east shore. My catch was fantastic, I had a filled boat, and everyone else at Capernaum was empty. That strong dry south wind hasn't been back since then."

"You are suggesting that we show the fishermen where to catch fish?"

"Peter and Andrew are good disciples, but they still wonder why God doesn't reward them. They would quit fishing and work in our ministry, but they still have doubts about the power of God. I believe the Lord has sent us this opportunity. We should not deny his help."

I turned towards the wharf where Peter was tying the boat and called out to him. He stopped and walked over to me. "Peter," I said, "let us launch out across the lake so you and your partners can put down your nets for a catch."

"Rabbi," he said, "we were out all last night. We're exhausted. There are no fish in the entire Sea of Galilee."

"Have faith," I said to Peter. "Today you'll see the generosity of God! Call to your partners and go out again. I'll go with you, as will Thomas. Let us go and catch fish!"

Peter looked at me with bewilderment, but finally he called out, "Andrew, James, John, we're going out again. The Rabbi says we'll catch fish."

It took us two hours of strenuous rowing into the wind to get to the eastern shore, and I wondered at Peter's faith in me—or at mine in Thomas. As we approached the shallow waters, Thomas gave the signal, and I told Peter that it was time to fish. Peter stood up in the boat as the others balanced it, and with an enormous heave he flung the stone weights of the dragnet in a high graceful arc towards the deeper water. The weights splashed nearly simultaneously and began pulling the delicate ropes of the net, like a huge spider web, suspended at the top by wooden buoys, down into the water. As soon as the net was out, Andrew began hoisting the sail, and the four fishermen, aided now by the south wind, dragged the net towards a spit that projected out from the shore.

We had not gone a hundred feet when the wooden floats began rocking and bobbing. The look of wonder on Peter's face was exceeded only by Thomas's broad smile. "Pull, my brothers, pull!" Peter shouted, and the men strained their muscles to make certain that they swept up the entire school of fish in their net. As they hauled it into the boat I could see that it was teeming with carp and sardines, flashing like streaks of silver as they glinted in the sun. Such a catch was extraordinary at any time, but in daylight—and on a day when there were "no fish left in the entire Sea of Galilee"—was miraculous.

Peter and Andrew cast the nets again and again, and each time were rewarded with full catches. Each time they discarded the inedible catfish and put the clean carp and sardines into holds in the boat. Once the holds were filed, they piled fish between the thwarts, where the creatures squirmed over our feet and between our legs as the wind took us home-ward. Peter was exultant, but when we were about halfway back to Capernaum he grew suddenly quiet. He looked at me periodically. Thomas was sitting next to me, and he whispered, "I think we've caught our fish."

"Yes, I think we have," I replied. I laughed louder than he had expect-ed, and Thomas gave me a peculiar look. I explained to him how the magi used the term *fish* to refer to the victims of an illusion.

But this memory also brought on a sudden twinge of doubt. Were we showing the fishermen the power of God, or the deceit of men? Were we using a God-given opportunity to draw them into his ministry, or were we just tricking and manipulating a group of naive fishermen?

The next day the fishermen approached me. Peter began: "Rabbi, we've all now recognized that the Lord doesn't want us to be fishermen. He's been telling us that for a long time, but we only understood yester-day. We'll sell our boats and give the money to the poor." He paused, as if waiting for a response from me, but I said nothing. "We wish only to be your disciples, to help you in any way we can, and to learn from you how we can please our father in heaven!"

I looked towards his partners. "Andrew, James, John, is this what you truly want?" They nodded. "More than anything else you could ever imag-ine desiring?"

"Yes, Rabbi!" they said, almost in unison.

"Then the four of you will join Thomas in my ministry. Henceforth we are all brothers under God. You will still be fishermen, but you will catch men rather than fish! Come to me," I said, as I walked closer to them. They looked at each other, and walked up to me, and I embraced each in turn, then we all embraced together.

With a core of dedicated men, my ministry grew quickly in size and influence. We soon became the major center of charity in Capernaum. It gave me particular pleasure to feed children, many of whom came alone. At first I thought that they were orphans, but I learned by talking to them that they were sent by parents who were too ashamed of their poverty to come themselves, parents who feared their neighbors would interpret pri-vation as God's punishment for hidden sin. I made certain that the chil-dren were well fed and that they took some bread home.

Our success was a sign, I finally decided, that God was pleased with what we had done.

Other wealthy people beside Josiah seemed to find us a comfortable conduit for giving alms. Thomas took care of collecting the money and buying the food, but soon the daily purchases grew to be a major burden on his time. "We need a treasurer," he pleaded.

"What about Peter?"

"Jesus, we need someone who can count! Someone who won't be cheated. Matthew would be a better choice." Matthew was a former tax collector who now came to my sermons every day. Thomas brought him to me, and I explained our needs.

"My master, my lord, my savior, please take my health, take my life, but don't ask me to be a publican for your disciples!"

"Matthew, I only ask you to keep the money safe and to buy what we need. I'm not asking you to collect taxes."

"Rabbi, when I left the customs house to join you, I promised myself that I would never again work with money! You spoke to me when you said, 'Where your treasure is, there also is your heart!' I had given my soul to mammon, and you redeemed it for me. My Lord, I'm not a strong man. I've forsaken my wealth for you. I've repented, as you taught. I'll do whatever more you ask, but please, if it pleases you, I beg of you, lead me not into temptation."

So we had to find someone else. I finally suggested to Thomas a recent disciple named Judas Iscariot. "He appears to be well educated," I said.

"Peter told me that Iscariot was once a thief."

"Actually, that's why I thought of him," I said. "He may have had useful experience handling large sums of money."

"Your unquestioning trust in people will get us in trouble, my brother. And doesn't 'Iscariot' mean 'assassin'? That's another bad sign."

"We don't believe in signs, do we, Thomas? Besides, I think the name only means 'man of Kerioth' in the southern dialect."

As I approached, Judas Iscariot rose to his feet. He was an impressive man, tall and strong, and perhaps a bit proud. Although he had exchanged his expensive clothes for a simple tunic and sandals similar to mine, his clear skin, fine teeth, and groomed hair still conveyed an aura of aristocracy, if not nobility.

"Judas," I said, "I understand that you were a thief."

"Yes, Rabbi, a very successful one. I was wealthier than Josiah."

"I too was a thief, Judas." He looked at me with surprise and disbelief. "I stole a glass baqbuq, when I was fifteen years old. I was immediately caught. I thank God for that, for otherwise I might have continued to steal."

"Alas, I was not so blessed," Judas said. "I was never caught because

I broke no laws of Rome, only laws of God. I never threatened anybody or harmed their flesh. I stole through trickery and deceit. It was a subtle crime, and very effective. I was a man of the law—I mean the Roman law—and I knew the law better than anyone else. I wrote contracts with provisions that people didn't understand. I manipulated people and prices and circumstances. I was very clever, too clever, and though I rationalized my deceptions, deep in my soul I knew I was sinning. I obeyed the Law of Moses—I almost became a Pharisee!–but as I grew wealthier, my happiness diminished. My only pleasure was in cheating people, but such pleasure is short-lived. I was surrounded by people who loved me for my wealth, but was loved by no one. Successful in everything I did, I was a failure. Given everything I desired, I lost all desire. I floundered in the depths of despair. I wanted to hang myself, but I didn't have the courage."

"You have courage, Judas. You have repented, and you have found forgiveness."

"Through you, Rabbi. My revelation was in Capernaum, when I heard you speak the words of God and discovered hope. Hope! My life was gangrenous, and I could see only death, but through you I was reborn, I began life anew, like a child." Judas's face brightened as he seemed to contemplate his future. But below the surface I sensed a fire of determination and passion.

"How will you serve God with your new life, Judas?"

"I aspire only to passing your revelations on to others. I have learned of God's love and forgiveness, and I wish to teach—particularly the wealthy, since they do not understand their sins and they think wealth is a reward from God. As you said, 'It is easier for a rope to pass through the eye of a needle, than for a wealthy man to enter the kingdom of God.' But first I must serve the poor—to purify myself in the truth that you teach.

I was deeply moved. I felt that Iscariot might be the disciple who was most similar to me. "Judas," I said, "I need your assistance. We are feeding more than two hundred people each day . . ."

"Rabbi, forgive me for my selfishness. I can help serving the meals, organizing them if you wish. I can purchase the food—"

"And manage our purse, Judas?"

He appeared startled by this suggestion. "Thank you, my Lord. Your trust in me will be repaid."

"Speak to Thomas, and he will tell you what is needed."

"I'll do so immediately."

As Judas walked away, I noticed the darkness of the sky. Storm clouds had been moving rapidly overhead all day, but now their thickness had totally blocked out the sun. They churned and convulsed above, as if the sky were boiling. To the am ha'arez such baleful signs signified the arrival of something evil.

32. Storm

THE SEA OF GALILEE HAD GONE MAD. A FEW DAYS EARLIER IT
had been my ally, providing food, water, and cool companionship on hot
days, but now this friend was furiously out of control, possessed by a
demon, demented, determined to destroy anybody or anything foolish
enough to wander close. Wave after wave crashed on each other like
mountains doing battle with other mountains, their foaming peaks fighting for dominance, the winners shattered by the onslaught of yet further
impacts. Then the true storm hit. Day turned as dark as night, and sheets
of water blown by unpredictable winds plunged from the turbulent skies,
lit intermittently by bright white flashes and accompanied by thunder
whose virtually continuous roll drowned out the crash of the surf. Hail
pounded the foolhardy few who had left their shelters to check the condition of their crops or the security of their boats. The tiny houses of
Capernaum had never looked so fragile, as they sheltered huddled families
who recited the passages from the Scriptures that told of God's promise
never again to destroy the world with a flood. God had sent rainbows to
remind us of his promise, and even I wondered, when had I last seen one?
However, it wasn't Judaism but paganism that made best sense of this raging storm, for the chaos outside felt like nothing less than a battle between
gods.

I had been preaching near the Jordan River when the storm struck
suddenly from the south. It dwelled for more than a week before moving
off to the north, where it continued to feed the river. The Jordan over-
flowed its banks, and soon the Sea of Galilee rose almost a foot. Only gradually did commerce recover, as did my ministry. The fishermen were the

last to resume their work, for it took many days for the waves to spend their energy futilely pounding against each other and the shore. Finally the water calmed and a heavy fog settled across the lake, blanketing all vision and muffling all sounds. The exhausted sea was finally at peace.

Thomas came to me in a state of agitation reminiscent of the storm. "The dock near Bethesda is submerged!" he cried with evident excitement.

"Yes, much of the shore is flooded," I said

"No, no, you don't understand. It's perfect. And the fog will help. It's just perfect. It will be the greatest miracle since Moses split the Red Sea!"

In retrospect, I was ripe for Thomas's suggestion. As I had tried to reach out to more people, particularly Pharisees and educated Jews, I had often become mired in lengthy explanations. The truths were so simple, but they could be understood only through the heart, not through the mind. Every bit of logic and law argued against the love of enemies. I confess, it didn't even make *logical* sense to me. It was equally difficult for my disciples to believe that the kingdom of God had already arrived, when Israel was still subjugated by Rome. How could I get Jews to forget their logic and open their spirits? In order to understand, they would first have to believe. But how do you get someone to do that?

God seemed to have provided the answer: miracles. They were so effective and my attempts to deny them so futile that I finally stopped resisting. "Gifts of God," Thomas called them. All my attempts to explain that my healings were not miracles failed—in fact my denials only seemed to strengthen the belief I was hiding even greater powers. So, despite my initial protestations, belief in my supernatural ability soon grew into a central tenet of the faith of my followers.

Yet doubts and guilt continued to haunt me. Why didn't the Baptist require miracles? The answer, I finally decided, lay in the simplicity of his teachings. His was a reaffirmation of Judaism, and he could boom it out with drama and impact: Repent, and obey the Law of Moses! Do what the priests and rabbis say, only with more urgency! And John did have *his* gift from God, his powerful voice and persuasive rhetoric, which he himself had termed a "trick."

My teaching was new, deeper, and more subtle than John's, and to many Jews it seemed a denial rather than an extension of what they had been taught. My little miracles, my healings, had served to break through into the hearts of potential followers, and also to reaffirm the faith of my disciples.

Thomas reminded me of the tortuous path that had led me to my ministry. From the lessons of Simon Magus, to my study of healing at the Academy, and to the construction of illusions for Elymas, I had received a strange education for a prophet. Why would God lead me along such a strange path unless he planned for me to use all of these skills?

The time had come, Thomas argued, for me to perform a great miracle. And God had provided just the required natural occurrence, as he had for Moses.

I stood at the edge of the lake, with the water gently lapping at my toes. It had taken us less than two days to make the preparations. Soon the moon would rise, but the fog was still thick, and I hoped that Thomas's navigation skills were as good as he claimed. On his boat were the key disciples, the group I hoped would grow into the core of my ministry, the men I called my "apostles." None of them except Thomas knew I was here. They thought I had retreated into the forest to pray.

I had lit the lanterns along the shore and wrapped my bare feet with woven goat hair, in the manner of fishermen who work on wet docks. I tested the traction, and indeed, my feet did not slip. I looked out into the fog over the lake. Thomas should be here soon, with the boatload of disciples. But could he really navigate well enough to find the dock in the fog-shrouded darkness?

Two hours passed and the fog grew brighter. The moon must have risen, I reasoned. As I waited, thinking about our impending miracle, I became more and more concerned. We had broken the first rule of magic, for we hadn't rehearsed. "You must practice a thousand times, before other magicians, before you try it in front of Pharaoh!" Thomas and I had discussed what to do if something went wrong, but without trial, how can you know? And now I became more nervous as I imagined an ever-wider range of possible disasters.

Were those sounds? A voice from the lake? The mute sloshing of a paddle? Everything was so muffled I had difficulty distinguishing true noises from the thumping in my ears. I decided to go out, carrying my lantern, just in case. I began my slow walk on the submerged dock, guiding my way by feeling with my toes the stones that Thomas and I had arranged on it. I looked back over my shoulder at the dim lanterns peeking through the fog, the lanterns that Thomas was using to guide the boat to the point of our rendezvous. One was out on a prominence that reached several hundred feet into the lake; the other was on a rock a few feet from the shoreline, about a quarter of a mile on the other side of the submerged dock. We had carefully marked these spots so that a straight line between them would pass just by the end of the dock. And now, I hoped, Thomas was moving his boat along that line.

Suddenly through the moonlit mist came the clear words, "Wake up! Wake up, Peter! Matthew! Judas!" I recognized the voice of Thomas.

Then silence. I peered into the white darkness but could see nothing.

"Wake up!" Thomas shouted again. I could hear him more clearly now.

"Where are we?" It was the voice of Peter.

"In the middle of the lake," Thomas said. The bigger the lie, the more likely is it to be believed, the Magus had taught. "The fog is thinning," he continued, "but I fear a storm is coming. There's been lightning. We're far from the shore, and I'm worried." I could hear the commotion as Peter woke the other apostles. "Oh Lord, we beseech you, protect us!" That prayer from Thomas was my cue. I covered and uncovered my own lantern three times, as a signal, and extinguished it by placing it down on the water-covered dock. I continued walking slowly out on the pier, feeling the boards with my toes to keep in the middle. The fog had begun to thin from above, and the vague shape of the moon hung like a lantern on a ceiling, but its diffuse light made the fog above the water all the more impenetrable. Even though the dock was less than two hundred feet long, I soon lost sight of land, although I could still make out the flicker of the two dim lanterns glowing in the distance, one on each side. I was wearing a long white robe to increase my visibility. I found the end of the pier, looked with satisfaction at the buoy, and backed off about ten feet from the end. The sounds of the commotion on the boat grew closer. Finally I could make out its vague shadow-like shape in the whiteness of the fog.

"Look! It's a ghost!" It was Thomas, shouting to the other apostles. They weren't all quite awake, and they stirred about in a comical sort of way. Thomas was supposed to have said, "Look! It's Jesus!" But he seemed to be inspired when he saw me glowing in the moonlight. Several of the apostles, particularly Peter, truly believed in ghosts.

I raised my arms in a gesture of love and peace, the movement that I used when I entered a home or wished to quiet an unruly crowd, a gesture that they would recognize. "Peace be with you!" I called to them. "Do not be afraid! It is me—Jesus!" I walked slowly forward to the end of the pier, and curled my toes around the front edge. For a moment I wondered if it truly looked like I was walking on water. The waves were larger out here, and I was grateful for the traction of the goat hair.

The plan was that Thomas would bring the boat close enough that I could step on board, but if it started to drift into the pier, I was to push it off with one foot so it wouldn't hit. Thomas was working an oar, and I could now clearly see Peter's face, his mouth agape. He said, in a tremulous tone, "Lord, if it is really you, order me to come out on the water to you!" He was the most superstitious of the apostles, and it seemed he truly thought he was seeing a phantom.

I looked at Thomas through the fog. We each knew what the other was thinking. He shook his head—too risky. But the position of the boat was perfect. "Come!" I said, and stepped back a foot from the edge.

As Thomas steadied the boat, Peter stepped out directly from it onto the end of the pier. His eyes opened wide, and he said, "It is as firm as the earth!" He turned back to the boat, as if he were welcoming the other apostles to join him, and I feared that I had made a mistake, and as he moved he slipped off the left side into the deep water. "Help," he shouted, as he splashed in and flailed his arms—like many fishermen, Peter was a surprisingly poor swimmer. "Save me Lord!" he screamed as I rushed to the end of the dock, being careful not to fall off myself. I reached out for him with one arm and for Thomas with my other. Thomas grabbed me, and I grabbed Peter, and I stepped on the boat and pulled Peter aboard. Thomas pushed the paddle on the end of the pier, and the boat eased away from the dock.

"What little faith you had, allowed you to take several steps," I told Peter, so everyone could hear, "until you doubted. Why did you doubt?" Actually he had shown no doubt at all, but I needed an explanation for his fall.

"Had I had the faith of a mustard seed," he said, paraphrasing my parable, "I too could have walked on water. And I did, for a moment! Truly you are the Son of God!"

"Don't call me that, Peter!" I admonished. "It's blasphemous!" That term was used by pagans to mean a god descended to earth in human form. "We are *all* the children of God, but that's different. The gentiles will think you worship *me!*" However, I feared that Peter had *intended* the pagan meaning. I realized that I was in danger of becoming an icon, a worshipped statue, a graven image, a false God.

Judas Iscariot had moved to the stern of the boat and sat by himself. No expressions of wonder came from him as they had from the other apostles. He didn't kneel in the thankful prayer with the others as we approached Capernaum. I couldn't evaluate his mood, for every time I looked at him, he seemed to avert his eyes.

After my walk on water, my apostles seemed to find miracles not just in my healings, but in everything I did. The most remarkable example occurred one afternoon when we were crossing the Sea of Galilee in three boats. Peter and Andrew were each handling a boat, and Thomas, as usual, captained mine. We had become separated from the other boats, and there was a storm to the south. The water got a little choppy, but Thomas said there was nothing to worry about, so I napped. But Nathaniel, who was on my boat and wasn't a fisherman, became fearful, and against Thomas's strong admonitions, he woke me. I have very little memory of the incident, because apparently I went right back to sleep.

When we arrived at Gadara I discovered that Nathaniel was telling the apostles who had been on other boats that I had "calmed the storm." I overheard him telling Peter, "This man gives orders to the winds and waves!" I asked Thomas what had really happened.

"You were sound asleep," Thomas said, "and Nathaniel was badly sea-sick. He saw the lightning to the south and became frightened. I told him to relax—the storm was distant and moving away, but he wouldn't believe me. 'Look at Judas Iscariot,' I said to him. 'Judas isn't worried, so why should you be? The storm will pass.' Just then a big wave washed some water into the boat, and Nathaniel panicked. So he ran over to wake you, as if you knew something about the sea that I didn't. You weren't sleeping very well, and when he called you to awake, you said, 'Be still! Be quiet!' or something like that. He was in such a panic that he grabbed you by the shoulders and shook you. You opened your eyes and looked at the waves. For a moment you must have been concerned too, but then you looked at me; I smiled and shook my head. So you said to Nathaniel, 'Why are you so frightened? Have faith,' and then you went back to sleep. Needless to say, your words didn't calm him very much. He came back to me. 'Listen to the words of the Master,' I instructed him. 'Have faith.' Well, soon the storm quieted, just as I expected, and Nathaniel thinks you did it. You know, Nathaniel wasn't there when you walked on water. He felt badly that he had missed it. Well, now he has a miracle that he witnessed himself."

A crowd was gathering around Nathaniel, and Thomas and I moved into a position where we could hear him. "We were crossing the Sea of Galilee," he stated with elation, "and behold, there arose a great tempest in the sea." I had never heard him sound so eloquent. "The ship was covered with waves, and it filled with water, and we were in jeopardy."

"The perception of a landlubber," Thomas whispered to me.

"He's a good speaker," I said.

"And so we went to the Master, and awoke him, saying 'Lord, save us. Don't you care if we perish?'"

Thomas whispered to me, "By 'we' he means himself."

"And the Lord said to us, 'Why are you fearful, oh you of little faith?' Then he arose and he rebuked the winds and the sea, saying 'Peace! Be still! Be quiet!'"

"Actually," Thomas whispered to me, "he seemed very upset when you told him to be quiet. He must have thought about those words for a long time before he decided that they were addressed to the storm."

"And there was great peace and calm," Nathaniel continued.

"About a half hour later," Thomas added.

"Shhh!" I said, afraid that somebody besides me would hear Thomas.

"And then we thought," continued Nathaniel, "'What manner of man is this? For he commands even the winds and the water, and they obey him!'"

"Nathaniel looks like a new man now that he has his own miracle," Thomas said as we walked away.

"And it has turned him into an effective preacher," I said. I looked back to the crowd, and noticed that Judas Iscariot was looking directly at me. I was disturbed by his expression. "Perhaps I should talk to Nathaniel, and tell him I had nothing to do with it."

"And take away his miracle? Don't be cruel. Look at him! He's captivating more than thirty disciples! He never could do that before. It's all in the cause of righteousness. It'll do no harm. Besides, the story will grow more vivid and dramatic with each retelling. This will make it certain that you won't have to do any more miracles, but that you can emphasize your revelations and teachings." Thomas knew how to appeal to my soft spots.

But the calming of the storm wasn't the end. The disciples saw miracles everywhere.

We were far from the Jordan Valley, far from the place where the Baptist was reputedly preaching, so I was surprised to see Dositheus enter our camp. It was Dositheus who had brought me to John that night near Capernaum. He didn't look well. He was tired and uncharacteristically unkempt, and he had an air of desperation.

"Peace be with you," I said as he approached. "You are troubled," I continued, in the mode I had learned from Simon Magus.

"Yes, I've been traveling day and night since I left the Jordan."

"John is in trouble," I said, without knowing how I knew it.

"It's as you say. He's been arrested by Herod Antipas. We believe that he's being kept in the dungeon in the fortress of Machaerus."

"Why do you come to me?"

"John foretold his arrest. He prophesied that he would be assassinated. We don't even know for certain that he's still alive, but he said in his prophecy that he was not the Messiah, but had been sent ahead of him. He said, 'After me comes a man who is preferred before me, for he was before me. The Lord sent me to baptize with water, but the man who is before me and is after me will baptize with the holy spirit.'"

"Did John tell you who this man was?" I asked.

"He said simply that the man would be evident to all of Israel."

So, I thought, John had not truly kept his end of the bargain. He alerted his followers to the impending arrest, but hadn't identified to whom they should go. Of course, if he had identified me as 'the one,' then he might have lost all his disciples immediately. But, I asked myself, had I done my part? Had I told my disciples to go to John if I had been arrested or killed? No, I had simply indicated my respect for him, and kept the intention that if something happened to me, that I would honor our pledge, if there were time.

"Tell me," Dositheus said, "tell us, for I speak for all the disciples of the Baptist, are you the one that John spoke of, or should we look for someone else?"

I had to be careful, for Dositheus might be expecting a particular response. "I can't tell you," I said, "for John's prophecy meant that you would be answered with signs, not words. Talk to those who have followed me. They will tell you that the lame walk and the lepers are made clean. Talk to the apostles who were with me when I walked on the Sea of Galilee, and talk with those who saw me command the storm to calm. Blessed you will be when you recognize these signs and lose your doubts."

33. Bread and Fish

SOON MY CROWDS SWELLED TO ENORMOUS SIZE, AND I assumed that many of them were followers of the Baptist, although I never saw Dositheus among them.

But as the crowds grew, it became more and more difficult to sustain them with food and healing. Rather than being surrounded by lilies of the field, I sometimes felt that my group was more akin to a swarm of locusts.

I had been preaching to an extremely large gathering on a hillside for three days, and every day the crowd had grown. We hadn't anticipated such a large group. Fortunately our purse was full, and I sent our treasurer Iscariot to forage. We were down to our last seven loaves of bread and a few fish when he returned with a large wagon-full of provisions that had cost us nearly two hundred silver shekels. It was just barely enough.

Afterwards Iscariot came to me looking somewhat troubled. "Philip and Andrew are telling the people that you performed another miracle!" he complained. "They say that you fed all of your followers with only seven loaves of bread. They say, 'See the miracle! Surely this is the prophet who was to come to the world!' I told them that I had just arrived with a wagon-load of food, but they won't listen to me. You must not let them lie to the crowds!"

"Philip and Andrew aren't lying," I said. "They believe what they say. They didn't know of your mission. Why do you suppose that they don't believe you?" Iscariot had become somewhat of a loner, and was not close friends with any of the other apostles.

"Perhaps because I've been denying some of your other so-called miracles, such as your calming of the seas!" Iscariot looked at me severely. I did my best to look right back at him, to cover my embarrassment. "You must tell Philip and Andrew the truth. They're making fools of us all."

"What harm is done by their faith?" I asked. "Word of our mission is spreading. We've never preached to such a large group before. Thomas tells me that the people talk among themselves about the power of love and charity and the arrival of God's kingdom."

Iscariot virtually exploded. "There are Zealots in the crowd who are trying to enflame them all, telling them to rise up, telling them that they have found the new king of kings, and that a sign has been given that you are the Messiah! Philip and Andrew are falling right into their hands. You can't teach truth through lies! How can you, of all people, ask such a question? I came to you because you carried the wisdom and truths of God, or at least so I thought. Is this part of the revelation that you heard in the wilderness? Part that you never told us about before? That you allow your disciples to believe in your own divinity? How do I know what to believe, when you allow such deception?"

Iscariot could have no idea how deeply he was cutting into my heart. "You speak with wisdom, Judas," I said. "I must do more than speak the truth, which I've always done. I must also correct others who are in error and who propagate their mistakes in the name of my teachings. I must not allow deception, even when I'm not at fault myself. I'll talk to Philip and Andrew and explain the truth to them."

Iscariot's frown loosened somewhat, although his lips remained tightly closed. His eyes stared intensely into mine. He seemed taken aback by my concession, as if he had not expected me to agree and had been prepared to argue. Finally he bowed his head and said, "Forgive me, Rabbi, for doubting you." I smiled at him, and he smiled faintly in return, and walked away.

I sought out Thomas, who, it turned out, was looking for me. "Thomas," I said, "I need your help. I'd like you to talk to Philip and Andrew about yesterday, and the miracle of the seven loaves."

"Yes, yes!" Thomas said. "Jesus, guess who was listening to you yesterday!"

"This is important, Thomas. We must stop Philip and Andrew from describing the feeding as a miracle. Iscariot is disturbed. You should probably talk to him too. We can't let doubts arise among the apostles."

"You'll never guess!" Thomas persisted. "Who would you like to see more than anyone else in the world?"

"Thomas, I'm in no mood for games. Who was it?"

"Lazarus! Our childhood friend! He sat at the edge of the crowd, and listened to your sermon for the entire afternoon."

"How do you know? Did you talk to him? Where is he? Why hasn't he come to see me?"

"I think he's frightened of you, Jesus—fascinated but frightened. I did speak to him. He said you don't seem like the same person he once knew. The crowds talk of your great powers, of your miracles, and he doesn't know what to make of it."

"He'll see I haven't changed. I can't wait to see him, Thomas."

Thomas led me to the home of a nearby carpenter where Lazarus was staying. When we arrived he was helping saw a large beam, working with his host in the traditional manner, to pay for his room and board. I immediately recognized his bushy eyebrows, and even the way he move seemed familiar. But I couldn't help but stare at his utterly bald head. He saw us coming and quickly put his work aside. He looked a little nervous as we approached, and I felt a little awkward myself. We stood about five feet apart and stared at each other.

"Lazarus, it's so good to see you again," I said. "You haven't changed one bit." Then I added, "From your eyebrows down, that is."

Lazarus laughed. "My head is ritually clean!" he replied. "I hear that you can restore lepers and bring the dead to life. Can you cure baldness?"

"That's harder. Not even the prophet Elisha could do that. However, I can guarantee that you will never again be infested by lice." We both laughed, and then we hugged. He was the same Lazarus, and I was the same Jesus.

We sat on the grass under a nearby sycamore tree, and exchanged stories of the last fifteen years. "My reputation as a miracle worker began in Cana," I told him, "from a misunderstanding. The guests thought I turned water into wine, when I hadn't." I described the events of that day, and how they too were misunderstood. "As long as I preach the revelations of God, everything healing I accomplish is interpreted as a miracle. And almost everything else I do too. Just two days ago, when food arrived, my disciples thought a miracle had occurred."

"I was there. Your words reminded me of your father, but you—standing there with a thousand worshipping disciples."

"I'm trying to reach as many people as possible."

"I heard about you even in Jerusalem. 'Jesus of Nazareth,' they said, was 'leading a force of a thousand disciples.' It sounded like a rebellion. I wondered if it was you."

"My preaching is to the spirit, Lazarus. I have no interest in this earth."

"I've looked at your crowds, Jesus. You could ask your many followers to march, and they would do whatever you asked. There was a Zealot who spoke after you left. These are dangerous times."

"I couldn't counter Rome even if I wanted to, and I don't want to. Remember Judah of Gamala? The Romans can crush any uprising, even if it included all of Israel."

"But it isn't Rome that fears you most. It's the Sanhedrin."

"They are slaves of Rome, just as we are. They are powerless. Rome has castrated them."

"Don't deceive yourself, Jesus. I've lived in Bethany for eight years now, and I've watched the politics of Jerusalem from up close. Like clever eunuchs, the priests can manipulate their Roman masters to their will, as long as they don't ask too much. And removing you wouldn't be too much."

"Is that why you came, Lazarus? To warn me?" As John had warned me?

"No, Jesus. I came to seek your help. Do you remember my sister Mary?"

My heart leaped. "Yes, of course! When I visited Amos two years ago he told me how she had vanished. I was very saddened to hear that. I always admired her spirit. She was a special friend."

"And she always liked you. But that's why I've come. I've found her. She is living in Magdala."

My heart suddenly thumped harder. I wondered if Lazarus could hear it. "How is she? What happened to her?" Lazarus frowned. I asked, "What's the matter?"

"She won't talk to me." He paused for a long time. "She has become—a courtesan. She is presently one of the mistresses of a wealthy Pharisee named Simeon."

We both sat silent for several moments. "But why won't she speak to you?" I finally asked.

"From shame, I think. I hope. She's suffering, Jesus. But I thought—maybe she would speak to you. You were closer to her than I was. And now, after hearing you speak, I'm even more optimistic. You told a parable about a prodigal son who left but was welcomed back. At the end I wept. I wept! I felt that you were talking about Mary. If she could hear you say what I heard you say today, it just might bring her home."

"You said she is in Magdala? That's less than a day's journey away."

"You'll go? She calls herself 'Magdalene' now. Please, Jesus, see if you can talk to her. I love her so much, but I feel so helpless."

"Of course I'll go."

"What about your flock?"

"Let them wait. I must go to Magdala." To find Mary. Mary the no-longer child. Mary the courtesan.

34. Magdala

I WAS AWAKENED BY THE CHEERFUL WARBLING OF LAKE FINCHES. The sun peeked through the low pines to the east and quenched the chill in the air, and the first breeze of morning chased ripples on the water's surface. I stood up and stretched in the cool light of the early morning. A new day had begun and there was work to be done. I was eager to leave the south of the lake and to travel to Magdala, to see Mary.

Mary! My imagination was fired. What could she be like? Would I recognize her? Had she been crushed by her life? Or grown hard—like the courtesans of the red tent? Was there anything left of the little girl of Nazareth? Could I do anything to help her? She was living in a reputed center of licentiousness and sin—Rabbi Shuwal had called Magdala the "Babylon of Israel." Was that why she had gone there?

I knew little about her master, Simeon, other than the fact that he was a wealthy Pharisee, that he was smart and articulate, and that he loved beautiful women. Lazarus had somehow arranged an invitation for me to visit at Simeon's home. But would Mary be there?

I woke the rest of my group—Thomas, Peter, Andrew, John, James, and Judas—and urged them to hurry. It took most of the day to walk the Tiberias road to Magdala.

We reached the city in the early evening. As we entered the town walls, I was mildly disappointed to discover that Magdala was similar to most of the other towns on the Sea of Galilee—fishermen, merchants, women, and children were working, talking, playing. So what had I expected to see—semi-naked harlots plying their trade at sunset in the town square? We easily found the large home of Simeon, and were greeted at the doorway by a Greek slave, who led us into the main room. I paused, and surveyed the half-dozen guests. No Mary.

"Peace be with you," I said.

"Ah, you must be Jesus the Magus!" said a large, muscular man who was lying on a sofa in the rear of the room. I wondered if he knew how much his use of the term Magus bothered me. He slowly rose and walked toward me.

"And you must be Simeon the Skeptic," I countered. "I know the teachings of Zarathustra well, but I'm hardly a magus. I preach the word of the Lord our God."

"And I know the rhetorical methods of the Greek sect of Skeptics, but I'm hoping to learn, not to argue." A broad smile fit in with his friendly tone. He beckoned me with a sweeping gesture of his arm. "Please enter my home as a welcome guest." Then he suddenly frowned. "But alas, we're almost out of wine. Perhaps you could transform some water for us?"

Even I was amused by his gentle humor, which was more like teasing than sarcasm. "My miracles are nothing," I said. "Don't believe what you hear."

"I don't. But I am glad to hear you say so."

Simeon introduced me to his guests, which included members of the local council, a rabbi, and two other Pharisees, identifiable by their prayer shawls. No women were present. Simeon offered me a chair, a gesture of honor, and my apostles sat on the floor with the other guests.

For dinner, Simeon served *muries,* the heavily salted fish of Magdala. I could taste little but the salt, and had to wash my mouth frequently with wine. While we ate, Simeon politely kept the discussion off the subject of religion. He asked me about my family, and then probed into my background. I was leery about giving this friendly man information that the Pharisees could later distort, so I just answered in generalities about my youth in Nazareth. I felt a little tipsy from all the wine, and I wondered if Simeon had served the salted fish in order to make me drink more.

"Your mother says that three kings visited you just after you were born, presented you with gifts, and announced that you would be the king of the Jews." Inwardly I groaned. It was truly possible that my mother was saying such things, although I hadn't heard that particular story.

"My mother told me that I was a handsome baby, and that some strangers expressed admiration, but they were certainly not kings. Had three kings indeed visited it would have been the biggest event that ever occurred in Nazareth, and I'm sure I would have heard about it."

"Ah, the love of the mother," Simeon said. Many of them think their children are gods!" Simeon's guests laughed, but my group was silent. Thomas scowled, and Simeon took notice. "Forgive me, teacher!" he said, turning back towards me. "Sometimes my wit vaults past my hospitality." Simeon seemed to enjoy alternating between overly polite and solicitous conversation, and a sharp interrogation. But I was getting accustomed to him, and I enjoyed the stimulation. The discussion reminded me of debate at the Academy.

After dinner Simeon invited me to say a few words on a subject of my own choosing. I chose to tell the parable of the Good Samaritan, to illustrate the faults of the Pharisee tradition of strict observance of the law to the exclusion of love and charity.

"That's well and good," said Simeon when I had finished, "but let me tell you the story of the Good Pharisee." The group was in high spirits, partly due to the free flow of wine, and they turned to him with anticipation.

"A certain man went down from Jerusalem to Jericho," he began, copying my words closely, "when he fell among thieves, who stripped him of his good clothes, wounded him, and departed, leaving him appearing dead. For he had been a sinner, and this was his punishment from God. And by chance came a priest, and when he saw that the man was a sinner, he passed by rather than touch the uncleanliness. And this pleased God, for it didn't interfere with the punishment he had given, and because the priest obeyed the rules of the covenant that had been laid down by the Lord. But a certain Pharisee, as he journeyed, came to where the man was, and when he saw the sinner, he had compassion for him. But rather than touch the uncleanliness and displease the Lord, the Pharisee went on his way, and when he arrived at his home he prayed to the Almighty that the Lord forgive the man, and he went to the Temple and offered two doves as a sacrifice. And the Lord was pleased with the sacrifice, and with the Pharisee for obeying the covenant, and so he showed mercy on the sinner, and his wounds were healed and his purse restored." He affected a self-satisfied smirk. "You see," he said, "you can reach any conclusion you wish with little stories."

I smiled back at him, and said, "A sower went out to sow his seed, but as he sowed, some seed fell by the roadside—and it was walked on by men and devoured by birds. Some seed fell on a rock, and as soon as it sprang up, it withered away, because it lacked moisture. And some seed fell among thorns, and the thorns sprang up with it and choked it. But other seeds fell on good ground, and sprang up, and bore fruit in abundance."

Out of the corner of my eye I saw a woman pass quickly by a door-way. Her hair was golden, a traditional sign of a prostitute. None of the others seemed to notice her. I wondered whether it was Mary, and whether she had been listening.

I continued, "Likewise it is true that when truth falls on closed ears, it's like the seed that falls on hard ground, and nothing will grow from either. And pray, Simeon, that you will never use your wit to hinder the truth."

"Truth!" Simeon responded. "Now there's an elusive concept. To me, truth is the nature of the will of God. That which agrees with his will, that is what is truthful."

"And how do you believe we learn the truth?" I asked.

"Through the revelations of the prophets."

"What of the oral tradition?"

"That's commentary on the law. It doesn't change it."

"Perhaps then you'll accept some commentary from a simple carpenter?"

"Yes, of course—although you are hardly a simple man, Jesus of Nazareth. But please, grant me one request: no more little stories."

"Do to your neighbor what you would have him do to you. This is the entire Torah."

"So," he said, "you were a student of Hillel. Well Hillel was no prophet. Yet even so, he was never so mad as to preach love of the enemies."

Simeon was more familiar with my teachings than I had expected. "Who are our enemies?" I asked rhetorically. "The Romans? The Samaritans? Or the am ha'arez? The very name of your sect, Pharisee, means 'those who stand apart.' You've become a religious caste, a group that disdains even the poor classes of your own people."

"Who is this 'simple carpenter' who knows about castes," Simon asked rhetorically to the guests, "a word little used outside of India?" He turned back to me. "The Lord said, 'As I am separate, so be you also separate.' No, teacher, we Pharisees stand apart only from impurity. That is a proper segregation, one that the Lord wishes. I am ready to stand together with anyone—anyone!–provided that he obeys the will of the Lord."

"But you've built a wall that can be scaled only by the wealthy. You drive away the poor, or, more accurately, you drive yourself away from them. You say you stand apart as does the Lord. But does the Lord stand apart? In what does he not exist? Did not the Lord create everything, the land, the rain, the animals, the people—all people—including those you despise? Yes, let us be separate from all those things that do not contain God. But from what is that?"

"And yet," said the Pharisee, with a puzzled expression on his face, "I hear that you claim to preach strict adherence to the law yourself."

"Yes, in fact I preach a *stricter* adherence, for I preach adherence to the meaning behind the law, which is more difficult, and yet easier. The law says that you shall not kill. I say that you must go further, that you may not even be angry with your neighbor."

"To forsake anger? Is that what you believe the Lord wants from us?"

"That is part of what the Lord revealed to me. But it's only the beginning. Above all, the Lord wants us to love him with all our heart, and with all our soul, and with all our mind, and with all our strength, just as he loves us. But beyond that, he wants us to love all of his creations. There are no greater commandments."

"That is, indeed, a severe interpretation of the Shema," Simeon said. "To love our enemies, as you describe, would be more difficult than following the other commandments."

I took this thoughtful reply to be a concession. "Simeon," I said, "you now understand what has been revealed. You are yourself now not far from the kingdom of heaven."

I sensed a change in mood of the room, and in some of the faces of the men who were listening—they were looking at me intently, but their expressions had softened. Others entered the room, against our agreement to bring equal numbers of guests. I wondered if they had been listening outside. Some were craftsmen, some were women, and some were servants.

"It isn't the wealthy," I continued, now addressing the larger group, "but the poor who are the most blessed, for they are closer to God, and it is they who will know God. It isn't those who are treated with mercy on earth, but those who are merciful themselves, who will receive the mercy of God." I looked towards the curtained doorway. "Blessed are you who are righteous yet who are reviled and persecuted. Rejoice, for great is your reward in heaven."

I became aware of a gentle sensation on my feet. I looked down, and there was a woman with long shiny black hair. I couldn't see her face, only that glistening hair, hair that brought back a childhood memory of my mother. She was looking down at my feet, and then she took hold of her own hair and gently wiped them with it. What was the meaning of this bizarre act? Was this something that Simeon had planned? I didn't know how to react. As she rubbed my feet I realized they were wet. I thought I detected a quiet sob from the woman. Was she crying? Could those be her tears that she was wiping from my feet? She looked up at me for a moment, and for that moment her eyes met mine. For that tiny instant my attention was riveted to those eyes. Were those the eyes of Mary? The face seemed hard, her lips showed no smile, but her eyes were filled with water. She quickly looked down, and more tears landed on my feet in a gentle splash, only to be wiped away once again. Suddenly I felt the softness of her lips pressing against my feet. My confusion and self-consciousness was suddenly washed away by a sense of compassion for this woman, strangely mixed with erotic excitement over her simple acts of tenderness.

"In this synagogue you may join with the men," I said to her. She paused for a few seconds, and then abruptly rose, and keeping her face turned away from me, she left the room and disappeared behind a curtained doorway.

I suddenly realized that the room had been silent for a long time. Everyone was staring at me. I flushed slightly with embarrassment. Simeon leaned over to me and quietly whispered, "Teacher, I must warn you. Everyone looks, and they think, 'He speaks of righteousness, yet he doesn't even know what kind of woman he allows to caress him!'"

"Then they have something to learn," I whispered back, "for I am not fooled by the removal of a wig." I guessed that the woman at my feet had been the one with yellow hair, and from Simeon's nod, I surmised that I was right. Simeon seemed strangely bothered by the incident, and I surmised that not only was it not of his planning, but that the woman had performed an act designed to upset him. But was it Mary? I hoped so, but that hard face made me fear that it wasn't.

In a voice loud enough for everyone to hear, I said, "Simeon, do I have your permission to tell one more story?"

"Rabbi," he replied, "speak as you will."

I addressed the entire group, but I kept watch on the curtained door, hoping that the woman was listening. "Once there was a certain creditor, and he had two debtors. One owed him five hundred pieces of silver, and the other owed him only fifty. And when neither had anything to pay, he forgave the debts of both. Now tell me," I asked, looking directly at Simeon, "which of them will be more grateful?"

"I suppose the one with the larger debt," he hesitatingly answered, as if he were anticipating a trap.

"You're correct," I answered. Just then the woman reentered the room, her face still down, hidden by her long black hair. Her thin smock hung loosely on her body, revealing more of her shape than most guests would consider proper. She was carrying two small alabaster jars.

"Is that the end of the story?" Simeon asked. "If so, what is the meaning?"

The woman sat down at my feet and opened one of the jars. The powerful fragrance of the valuable spikenard ointment suffused the room. She dipped a small white cloth in the perfume and dabbed my feet with it. *I am the anointed one,* I thought. But this time I controlled my reverie. "See this woman," I said to everyone, "who loves so much." The double meaning was intended to startle. The woman didn't look up. "She has washed my feet with her tears, and wiped them with her hair. Now she anoints me with perfume. Whosoever fails to love, that person will not be loved by God, and will not be forgiven. But this woman who loves so much, through her love have her sins been forgiven."

"This is a waste!" The shout came from the back of the room. "That ointment is worth three hundred pieces of silver!" It was Judas Iscariot! "Jesus, why do you allow this waste!"

"Judas," I said calmly, although I felt offended at his rudeness, "there is less than an ounce, worth less than thirty pieces of silver, and she's used only a little. I suspect that this spikenard is all that she owns." I looked down at the woman, who was still dabbing my feet.

"Whatever it's worth, it would be better sold, and have the money given to the poor."

"Just as you gave your wealth, Judas? How many souls did your generosity bring to the kingdom of God? The poor are as numerous as the clover, and a little silver gives them no sustenance. Let this woman be, dear Judas. It's more fitting that love be shown to the living rather than to the dead." Judas retreated. I was annoyed that he would self-righteously criticize this poor woman, but I also worried that his insolence was a further sign of disillusionment.

The woman had stopped and was looking up at me. "God will wipe away all tears," I said. I looked deeply into her face for the signs of the child I had known. The facial features were there, the high cheekbones and the thick eyebrows, the cinnamon-colored eyes, but there were fewer similarities than differences. It is painful to see a face grown callous from the loss of hope. Yet she had been gentle in anointing my feet. Could I entice further softness out of this hard person, as my father had coaxed the softness from hard wood?

Deep in the black pupils of her eyes I imagined that I could see the child who had been lost. Gazing into the eyes of another human, I thought, must be the closest we come on earth to seeing God himself. "Mary," I whispered, on an impulse, "I must speak with you."

"I have been listening to you and no one else all this evening," she said quietly. From her answer and her voice, I knew, finally, for certain, that she truly was Mary. Did she know who I was?

"Let us leave now, together."

"Jesus, I am a sinner." She knew.

"God forgives sinners. He loves all his children. Come outside with me."

"If we leave together they will talk."

"As they will no matter what we do. But *we* must talk." I took her hand and led her out of the room. I motioned to Thomas to remain behind, and left without looking at anyone else. Thomas restrained the other apostles.

35. Mary

MARY AND I ENTERED A SMALL COURTYARD BEHIND THE HOUSE. I put my hand gently to her chin and tried to raise her face towards mine, but she resisted. "You are unhappy," I said to her. "You feel lost and confused, and you don't know what to do." I held her by her shoulders. "I see love in your face, Mary, but I also see pain."

"Please," Mary said, "let me go. I must go. I shouldn't have come out here. I am cursed." She pulled away from me and started to run.

"With seven demons?" I asked. Lazarus had told me of a myth that had spread about her in Magdala. Mary stopped.

"Can you see them?" she asked. "Can you see into my soul?"

"You are driving them out, Mary. I can see them leaving. They can't endure the love that's growing in your heart, your love of God. When you repent, you exorcise the demons yourself."

Was this really the same Mary with whom I had played as a child?

I looked around. Nobody had followed us out to the courtyard. "Quick!" I said, taking her hand again. "Let's make a run for it! If we're gone by the time they come out, they'll never be able to find us!" I tugged gently at her hand. That finally brought a smile out of her, a smile that hadn't changed since she had been a child—a smile that excited me.

She looked directly into my eyes. "You follow me," she said. "Let me take you, this time, to a secret place." She squeezed my hand, and we ran together out of the courtyard. I felt surprisingly little guilt at my rudeness to Simeon. I knew I had to take advantage of the opportunity. A single soul is worth more than the entire world.

A moment later we were in a dark alley, and then winding through a warren of narrow streets in the poor section of Magdala. Soon we passed from the edge of the town onto a trail that led directly into the woods. Running through the woods at night brought back my memories of the horrid tragedy of Sepphoris, but this time the trees seemed like friends. The woods opened to a field, and we followed a hedgerow to a woodshed. In the back was a small addition, with a door and a window.

"I live in a room in the house of Simeon," Mary said, "but I keep this too, so that at least sometimes I can be alone." She pushed aside a curtain that covered the door, and I began to follow her inside. She motioned me to stop. "Don't come in," she said. "It's better outside. I only want to get something. This shelter is only for bad nights." I started to imagine what would make a night "bad," but I didn't like my thoughts. She disappeared into the shed for a moment and reappeared with her hand behind her back. She smiled again, and then proudly held a worn doll in front of her.

"It's Deborah!" I said. "You still have her, after all these years! I wouldn't have believed it." The poor little battered doll still had its smile too.

"It was the best gift anybody ever gave me," she said. "You were the only person who was truly kind and loving to me."

"You're unjust to Amos and Esreth. They are good people; they were good parents."

"For a boy, perhaps. They gave all their love to Lazarus," she said. "All they wanted from me was obedience so I could be marketed as a dutiful wife."

I was surprised at her bitterness. "Mary, I'm sure they loved you. They were heartbroken when you disappeared."

"Please call me Magdalene. Mary is the name they gave me, and I changed it when I left."

"Mary is a beautiful name."

"It means 'stubborn.' I hate the name. I'm sorry, Jesus. I know it's the name of your mother. But now I am Magdalene." She walked away from the house and sat down on the grass a few feet away, just as a young girl might. I walked over and sat down next to her. The grass was cool and slightly damp with evening dew.

"How can you blame your parents so much?" I asked.

"You don't know, do you?"

"Know what?"

Magdalene's sad solicitous smile made me feel like a naive child. She looked as if she were thinking, trying to decide how much to tell me. Finally she said, "They betrothed me when I was twelve, just after you vanished. I know they didn't tell you who I was to wed, or you wouldn't have defended them."

"Was it someone I knew?"

"Yes, but you are too good—too innocent—to suspect. You wouldn't guess if you tried for a hundred years." Mary looked intently at me as if she wanted to watch my reaction. Finally she said, "I was to be the bride of . . . Rabbi Shuwal."

"My Lord, keep me from the abyss!" It was rare that I was driven to profanity, and I shook my head in disbelief. "That can't be! How awful! How could they do that to you?" Mary had been right. I was too naive to have guessed.

"My parents said I was a sinner, and that he was a man of God. They said that he would teach me to be righteous, to follow the rules, teach me to do what they had failed to teach. He quoted the Scriptures, 'An unbroken horse turns stubborn, and an unbroken child turns rebellious.' And he offered them thirty shekels of silver."

"To break you. The price of a slave. From where could he obtain such money?"

"He's far wealthier than any of us ever guessed. He clearly didn't send all of the tithe he collected to Jerusalem. I was so frightened. Even now I shudder to think of that man taking me in his arms." I shuddered too as I pictured the small, delicate child being held by that repulsive man. But was he really worse than what she later encountered? "Now you understand why I ran away," she said.

"I understand completely. Yet I still can't believe that Amos would do that."

"My father wasn't evil. I was just a commodity, like every other girl in the village." Mary's perspective was certainly different from mine. Could she be right? But then she added, "There was another reason too, but I'd rather not tell you."

"Tell me only what you wish," I said. I knew better than to press too hard. "Where did you go?"

"From town to town. I told people I was an orphan, and some of them were charitable. I worked as a maid for a poor couple, but they were even stricter than my parents were. I soon found only one profession that gave me freedom. In one night I earned enough to feed myself for a month. I knew it was sinful, but I felt that it was the best choice. Life as a prostitute isn't as bad as you might think. It's probably better than a bad marriage, because if someone is truly awful, you don't have to go back. And it was only part time, at least at first, while I was still young."

"You still are young," I said.

Mary smiled, a wonderful glowing childlike smile. "I'm glad you think so," she said, "but I no longer command as high a price. I never regretted running from Rabbi Shuwal. But what happened to you? Did you run away too?"

Surprising myself with my candor I told her not only about Pantera the centurion, but even the relation I had imagined he had with my mother. I had not shared that thought with Lazarus, nor even with Thomas, and I still didn't want to, so I pledged her to secrecy. "Secrets hurt, Jesus," she counseled. "Why do you bury this within yourself?"

"It's hard to explain. I'm more ashamed that I thought my mother capable of sin than that I sinned myself." I looked at her and wondered what secret she was keeping from me. She looked away, down at the moonlit grass.

I went on to tell her about my thievery, my capture, and my servitude. She listened with intensity, asking probing questions, wanting more details, questioning me about my feelings towards everyone I mentioned. She particularly wanted to know about Simon eeeeeeeeee w e and the Academy, but I went on. Whenever an opportunity presented itself, I changed the subject back to *her* life, particularly the recent years, but about these she was reticent.

"It isn't that my life was painful," she said, "but it was lonely. That is the worst punishment that God can give—not disease, not death, but loneliness. For most Jews I'm unclean, unworthy of attention, undeserving of friendship. They will come and spend a night with me, and sometimes whisper sweet things in my ear, but in the morning they leave, and don't want to speak to me, or even look at me. To be an outcast is worse than to be a slave. I sometimes think I would have been happier had I married the rabbi."

"But you don't think that for very long, do you?"

She looked at me with a smile. "I don't know. Only as I grew older did I begin to realize what I was missing. Jesus, there's no love in my life. Without love my freedom is hollow." She laughed sardonically. "Children! That's what I wanted most of all, but I couldn't bring a child into my miserable life. I couldn't share my wretched existence with someone I loved. Isn't that odd? I don't have a child, yet I know that I would love her. No one to love, that's my punishment, my cruel punishment for my sins."

"God does punish the living, and sometimes he is too cruel."

"All these years," Mary continued, "and still all I have is the child you gave me, my Deborah." I saw a glint of the moon in what appeared to be a tear in the corner of her eye. Yes, I thought, she can still cry, as she had when she anointed my feet. That's a sign that she is not lost. "What happened after you left the Academy?" she suddenly asked.

I told her of my return to Nazareth, of my continued misplaced hatred for Pantera, of my encounter with the Baptist, my decision to preach, and my revelations while visiting the Essenes. "What does it feel like when God talks to you directly?" she asked.

"It feels no different from any other time. I believe that God is talking to us always, all of us, every day, every moment. Mary, Magdalene, God is talking to you right now, if only you'll listen." Mary gave me an odd look. "We're all blessed, blessed every moment of every day, every moment of our slavery, of our exile, of our pain. Of our loneliness. God loves the poor, the weak, the frail, those who suffer. He loves sinners. That's what I learned in the wilderness."

"Your eyes sparkle when you say those words," she said. "You look very happy." So did she, at that moment, and when she was happy she was beautiful.

"I *am* happy," I answered quickly, surprising myself. "The message of God is truly a message of joy for the world. Our pain is self-inflicted, because we ignore the kingdom of God. I hope to spread these truths, that love of God is all that we need for salvation, and that the deepest expression we can give to that love is kindness, charity, and love of God's creations. Sometimes I feel that it's my destiny. I'm spreading the seed of the Lord's word. Much of it falls on thorns and dry ground, and it saddens and discourages me. My faith is tested every day."

Again I looked into her cinnamon eyes, and she looked back. Her pupils seemed to grow larger as I watched. As worn as her body was, there was only beauty in those eyes, beauty of spirit. "I feel a glow inside me," she said.

"That's your soul," I told her. "It has been cleansed. God is generous and charitable. He forgives instantly and completely. You have been born again."

"Does that make me a virgin again?" she asked with a smile. I became aware that her shoulder was now touching mine. Had she moved, or had I?

"To me you are a virgin," I replied.

"You are the only one who matters now." Mary called Magdalene spoke softly. "Sow your seed on my good ground, and I will bear you fruit."

I thought that I had experienced the love of a woman, in the red tent during my slavery, but I was wrong. The gentle touch of Magdalene, the touch of a woman expressing love for me, a love that I could return, was new to me. I felt the joy of truly feeling, knowing, sensing, experiencing the life and the soul of another human.

❖ ❖ ❖

The sun eventually rose up above the lake, and I walked slowly back to Magdala to try to find my apostles. Mary would follow, she promised, to join me in my ministry, as soon as she had paid some debts and set her affairs in order.

I don't know whether it was the fresh spring henna flowers, the cool breeze off the water, or just the beauty of the shifting patterns on the cloud-cluttered blue sky, but I felt wonderful. Images of Magdalene, memories of her touch, of her smell, the sensation of her soul, filled my thoughts. I asked myself, what should I do? What would my father do?

A congregation of chickadees descended on a cedar next to the road. I stopped to watch these plain little birds hopping from leaf to leaf, weaving their way thoroughly through the branches, happily twittering as they searched each leaf for insects. These are my favorite birds, I decided. And this is my favorite path. And this is the most beautiful region of Galilee.

Had I ever seen the soul of another person before? I once thought I had, of my father, of my mother. But those visions seemed dim compared to what I now experienced. To know the soul of one other person, to perceive it as vividly as if I were holding it in my hands, is to know God's true greatness. This is what love is, the clear vision of the soul of another person. God's most wondrous creation, isn't heaven, isn't earth, isn't even life, but the human soul. God gave us the ability to see and feel and know that soul, directly and clearly, and that ability, so similar to the gift of prophecy, is the gift of love. I had been preaching God's word, and yet I was only now beginning to think that I understood its full meaning. I had seen love before only darkly, as one sees an image in a metal reflection, but now I was seeing it face to face. With all that I had learned previously from God, with all that I thought I had understood, yet without this love I was nothing!

What would my father do now if he were me? He whispered in my ear. He shouted in my ear. I started walking faster, and then I broke into a joyful run. Yes! It is all clear, so clear! I will ask Magdalene to marry me.

But what if she refuses? And she might. She is just crazy enough and unpredictable enough that she might. Unpredictable—yes she is unpredictable—how I love her unpredictability! And her craziness! I must persuade her, somehow.

As I approached the home of Simeon, guilt over my rude disappearance the night before slowed my pace. I noticed several people standing in front of the house, excitedly talking, or arguing, about something, and I feared it was me. As I got closer, I recognized Thomas among them, and I waved to him.

"Jesus, you're back! Where were you?"

"With Magdalene, with Mary. She wishes to be a disciple, and I've told her that she can come with us." Thomas seemed distressed. "She'll join us in a few days, as soon as she takes care of some affairs."

"Jesus—a great tragedy! I don't want to believe it, but . . . Dositheus came last night. He says that . . . John is dead—murdered . . ."

My head grew dizzy and my knees suddenly weakened, and I sunk to the ground. I shook my head, hoping to dispel my dizziness. "How? What happened?" I asked, looking up at Thomas.

"All Dositheus knows is what is being said by the Levites, who learned from . . . who knows. But the details are too bizarre to be believed. They say that Herod had John beheaded because his stepdaughter Salome had done a dance, and taken off her clothes, in front of her father! He offered her anything she wanted, and she asked for the head of John, on a plate!"

My heart was thumping. I did not want to imagine the grotesque scene, but a vision of John's severed head floated before me. I pushed it out of my mind. I must think clearly. "It was Herod's wife—Herodias," I finally said. "It was her revenge for John's attacks. She put Salome up to it."

"Unless Herod put her up to it himself."

"Promise to daughter or not, he would not have done it if he hadn't wanted to."

So much was happening so fast. What were the politics behind this murder? What forces were at work? What were the dangers? John had correctly prophesied his own death, but I hadn't believed him. But how could I foresee a threat when I had so casually dismissed John's own prophecy of the impending murder?

John and I had taken the first step towards reconciliation. Had he truly recognized that our teachings were similar, or had he just taken an expedient path, to join forces when he felt endangered? His last words to me had been a warning—what did they mean? Did he know more then he said? What did he mean when he said the Messiah was coming? Why did he seem to know of the secret councils of the Sanhedrin?

Whenever there is death, there are too many unanswered questions.

36. Nicodemus

THE TALL MAN HAD HOVERED NEAR THE EDGE OF MY DISCIPLES for several days, but this was the first time he came near me. The freshness of his tunic, clean yet lacking the wear that comes from washing, made me wary. Although he was lean, his muscles looked soft; the pale color of his hands suggested that he spent most of his time indoors. His unblemished face strengthened my suspicions—he was less likely a farmer or a fisherman than a spy. His tall forehead and almost Roman nose suggested mixed blood. For his approach he had selected a moment when Thomas and I were alone.

"Rabbi, I am a Pharisee," he said quickly, as if anxious to get his admission out of the way. "My name is Nicodemus." The name startled me, for a Pharisee named Nicodemus was known to be a member of the Sanhedrin. "I need to meet with you privately," he said, "on a matter of gravest urgency—and secrecy." From his assertiveness and proud demeanor I decided that he was indeed the well-known Nicodemus.

I glanced at Thomas, who appeared to sense a trap, and almost imperceptibly shook his head to advise "no." But my curiosity won out. "Come late tonight," I told him.

Soon after midnight Nicodemus entered my tent. He bowed his head slightly towards me, revealing thinning hair. Quickly he studied the interior. From the movement of his insatiable eyes, I guessed that whatever achievements he could boast came from alertness and craft. "Rabbi," he said, as he looked back towards me, "I know that you are a teacher sent by God, for no man could perform the miracles that you perform unless God were with him." I tried to read his face and I saw him doing the same with mine.

"My miracles are nothing," I said diffidently. "The Lord has chosen me to bring good news to the poor, to set free the oppressed, and to announce that the time has come when he will save his people. You call me Rabbi. Have you learned from my teachings?"

"Your true miracles, Rabbi, *are* your teachings. Your magic, that to me is incidental. It serves well by attracting the poor and uneducated, who are in most need of learning and comfort. But in me your words ignite a rapture that betrays their source in God." He seemed to be probing for sensitive spots, seeing how I responded to a variety of approaches.

"Tell me what it is you've learned in your ecstasy," I asked with barely suppressed sarcasm.

"Woe to us Pharisees," he intoned with passion, "for we are hypocrites, who pay to God our tithes of spices and silver, but neglect the deeper law of justice, mercy, and honesty. We are whitewashed tombs, clean on the outside, but full of bones and decaying corpses within." This was an accurate paraphrase of my own diatribe of the previous day. His self-chastisement made me smile, and that seemed to encourage him. With ardor worthy of my apostles, he continued, "We're like dogs sleeping in cow troughs—we don't eat, but neither do we let the cows feed!" He had listened well.

"What does the Sanhedrin wish of me?" I asked, consciously betraying my deduction of his identity in order to verify it.

"I come tonight not as a representative of the council, but on my own, to make myself known to you as your disciple, to seek your wisdom"—then his voice dropped—"and also to give warning." Ah, I thought, now comes the threat.

"I've broken no law," I said. "What have I to fear?"

"Herod."

This answer was unexpected, and for a moment I lowered my guard. "Does Herod Antipas even know that I exist?"

"You are more famous than you suspect, Rabbi. Yes, he knows of you, although his education is recent. He appears to be suffering anguish over his murder of the Baptist. He alternates between such depression, and a mania in which he contends that he is the anointed one, the Messiah, the Christ."

"Herod the Messiah? You're not serious!" Immediately I regretted speaking such words. I must exercise caution. "Antipas isn't even a descendant of David." And that was only the most neutral of his shortcomings.

"He's hardly even a Jew," Nicodemus elaborated. "His father was Idumean and his mother Samaritan. Although he chooses priests, he's not even allowed to enter the inner court of the Temple himself. But genealogies aren't as simple as many think. There are numerous half-brothers and remarriages. Herod is convinced that he has a connection to David. He says he feels it in his blood"—Nicodemus was giving the impression that he heard Herod say this in person—"and he's determined to find it. Believe me, Rabbi, find it he will, even if he must 'correct' the birth records to do so. You know, it's not easy to understand the minds of potentates, even incompetent ones. He is not like his father, Herod the Great, who was cruel and brutal, but did win his position through military victory and diplomatic skill."

"He delivered Israel to Rome without a battle. Is that what you term 'skill'?"

"I call it diplomacy. Rome would have taken Israel regardless, and he avoided war. Judge him vicious if you wish, yet he was a man of ability, a quality that his son didn't inherit. Nonetheless, Antipas aspires to assume the father's eminence. You and I understand that he truly cannot know that he is not the Messiah, because he does not understand what it means to be great. He knows only the prophecy of Nathan, that a descendant of David will build a temple, and that his dynasty will last forever. His father built the Temple, and Antipas believes that the dynasty is now his, that the Lord will restore control over Judea, and the Temple, to him."

Had those words Nicodemus uttered been overheard by a credible witness, he could have been condemned for treason and executed. Let me be wary, I thought, lest his candor induce similar looseness in what I say. "Why do you warn me?" I asked. "Why do you believe I need fear this man?"

"Herod still rages against the Baptist. In his fits he rants that he has failed to destroy him."

"The Baptist does live on—as a martyr," I said, "and the cult of Baptism grows, led by Dositheus." And as a rival to my own following, I thought.

"It isn't the new cult that causes Herod's fear, Rabbi. He's heard of your miracles, and he thinks that you may be the Baptist reincarnated."

"He must be insane!" I cried out—and immediately regretted my words.

"He's possessed of demons that even you couldn't exorcise. Rabbi, he hears that you calm storms, that you walk on water, and that you cure men who have been blind and deaf since birth. Only a resurrected prophet could perform such miracles."

"So, he believes that John was a prophet, and yet he murdered him. And he believes that I am John—yet he still thinks that he, Herod, is the Anointed One?"

"As I warned, his is a dangerous madness." Nicodemus smiled, but almost too quickly, and it made me feel nervous rather than comfortable.

"Nicodemus, my miracles are exaggerated fantasies spread by overly enthusiastic disciples. I pose no danger to Herod. I even cautioned the Baptist, when he was alive, not to attack the personal life of Herod, and you can be assured I won't challenge Herod or his reported sins myself. How could I be a threat to him? I abhor the Zealots, and I love the am ha'arez. I've promised God that I will never seek civil power. You are a member of the Sanhedrin. Tell Herod that he has nothing to fear from me."

"Herod distrusts the Sanhedrin. He knows that we oppose his hegemony. He won't listen to reassurances from us, and certainly not from me, for as a Pharisee, I'm a minority in the council."

"It might help were he to recognize that my miracles are the imagination of the credulous."

"I count Herod among the most credulous, or he would not believe your miracles in the first place."

"Any more than you believe in my miracles. So why do *you* come to listen to me?" I looked at Nicodemus, this man who addressed me with reverent titles yet spoke with such frankness. Although I still couldn't guess his motives, with every candid thought that he shared I felt a deeper trust in him.

"As you undoubtedly guessed, I came to observe you at the request of the Sanhedrin. They know that I'm familiar with magic. They asked me to watch and to listen and to report."

"And what will you report?"

"That you are only a rabbi, and that they have nothing to fear."

"*Only* a rabbi?"

"That's what I will tell them, my Lord. Yet I was speaking truthfully when I said that you bring me to rapture with your teachings. I know that you speak the word of God."

"Though I attack the Pharisees?"

"You criticize out of love, as a father chastises his son. You do it because you know that the Pharisees are within your reach. It's the Pharisees who will join your movement, not the Sadducees, not the Zealots. It's the Pharisees who will preserve your teachings as a prophet, as oral law, or . . . " Nicodemus paused and smiled, as if he had just had an idea. ". . . or as a new book to the Scriptures. It's the Pharisees who can accept change, as I have. We are looking for salvation, for the Messiah. The Herodians thought you were a Zealot, but I will truthfully report that you detest violence and have a distaste for politics."

"What about the rest of the Sanhedrin?" I asked. "Will they cause me problems?"

"It was Herod who brought you to their attention. Until recently their concern was the Baptist. None of them knows that I am meeting with you personally, or telling you of my mission. I do this at considerable risk. I would be stoned for revealing the secrets of the council. You must not speak of my visit to anyone."

"I'll respect your wish, Nicodemus. Yet some of my followers will know of your visit, and will want to know why you came. So I'll tell them that you came as a supplicant, to learn the path to the kingdom of God."

"You'll be speaking the truth. What is it that you'll tell them that you taught me during this visit?"

"That as Pharisee, you are inwardly dead, and must be born a second time in a spiritual rebirth. I'll say that you had difficulty understanding, but that even the Pharisees can be saved, and therefore I spent a long time explaining it to you."

"Good. I'll be back to learn from you, and to bring you anything useful I learn. I'm a landowner, my Lord. I know it's more difficult for a wealthy man to enter the kingdom of heaven than for a rope to pass through the eye of a needle, and I know that you tell the wealthy to abandon their riches and to follow you, but I think I will be more useful to you if I continue as a member of the Sanhedrin. I have powerful friends. There are many besides myself in high places who despair over the corrupt spiritual life of Israel. A small flame can start a large conflagration. So I'll abandon, for now, only this small token of my wealth. I hope you find it useful." He handed me a small but heavy bag, and I placed it unopened on a table.

"Thank you for your trust, and for your faith," I said. "God be with you." Nicodemus disappeared through the door of the tent into the darkness. A few moments later Thomas entered my tent. "Please sit," I said to him. "We have a problem."

"Yes, that Herod believes you to be the Baptist."

"How did you know?"

"I was outside during your discussion. I assumed that you wanted me to listen. Did I do wrong?"

"No, I think not. I have no secrets from you." But I had become care-less. Suppose someone other than Thomas had overheard us?

I opened the bag Nicodemus had left and counted thirty pieces of sil-ver. "We now have a friend in the highest places, just as the Baptist once had." I returned the coins to the bag, and held it out for Thomas. "Give this to Iscariot." But as Thomas reached for it, I reconsidered and pulled back. "No, on second thought, perhaps we should keep a separate purse. Let us be wary of Iscariot."

"Let's be wary of Nicodemus too," Thomas advised. "He strikes me as a man with political ambitions."

"You're right, Thomas. The more successful we are, the more cautious we must become."

37. Messiah?

WHERE WAS MAGDALENE? SHE HAD TOLD ME THAT SHE NEEDED
time to settle her affairs, and as I had promised, I had waited at Naberin,
a small town about six miles north of Magdala. But two weeks had passed
and still she hadn't come. I wanted to search for her, but Thomas convinced me to let him go in my place. A day later he came back.

"She's gone, Jesus. Simeon says she vanished, just after you left. He
thought *you* would know where she was. I asked everyone I could find,
but without success."

"Did you find her shack?"

"Yes, just where you said. Many of her things seemed to be there—a
mat, some clothes."

"Was there an old rag doll? With a head carved from pistacea?"

"A doll? I don't remember. I didn't notice."

I was sick with anxiety. I could think of little else but Magdalene during the day, and I dreamt of little else but her at night. Somehow I managed to continue my preaching, but if my soul was in it, my heart certainly
was not.

It was a warm but cloudy afternoon when I first spotted her—at least
I thought it was her—sitting up on the hill, at the farthest edge of the
crowd, listening. I had been preaching my "list of woes," and I quickly
ended my sermon and headed towards her. But I was besieged by disciples
seeking individual blessings and healings, and by the time I reached the
spot, she had disappeared. I searched frantically for her but without success, and I wondered for a while whether I had seen a vision.

But the next day she appeared again, sitting by herself at the edge of my crowd of disciples. This time I asked them to take a few minutes to be still and pray, and I easily walked through the crowd to where she was sitting. It *was* her. Her head was bowed in prayer, but as I approached she suddenly got up. I stood a few feet from her, surprising myself by my nervousness. "Mary—Magdalene—I've thought of nothing but you," I said. "Where have you been?"

"I've been here, Jesus, for the past week." She looked down as if embarrassed. "I have been listening to you preach."

"Why didn't you tell me? I've looked all over."

"I've come to learn, with the others. There are thousands with you today."

"Alas, there are so many that I can't even remember their names. Or even notice when a new one has joined! But you should have come to the front."

"I'm the newest of the new ones. It is proper that I sit at the back."

"Come with me," I said, and I reached for her hand. But before I could take it, she backed off a step. "Magdalene, I want to be alone with you. Come to my tent. I . . . have so much I want to tell you."

"No. We . . . we must not be seen together."

"What? Why?"

"I'm a harlot. A common harlot." She looked at me with an expression of guilt. "They're laughing at you in Magdala—because of me—the way you went off with me."

"You are a child of God," I said. I put my hands on her bare shoulders. They felt soft and delicate in my hands. Her hair flowed gently over my fingers. "If they laugh, it is because they don't yet understand that. So come with me."

"Not to your tent . . ."

I lowered my hands from her shoulders and took her hand. It seemed tense. "Then to the forest." She relaxed slightly, and smiled, and followed me as I led her to the trees.

"Where in the forest?" she asked.

"I don't know," I replied.

We scrambled over some rocks, walked through a heavy thicket of pine, climbed up a steep slope, and finally came to a flat clearing. I didn't understand Magdalene's behavior, but in the dark woods the problems of the human world seemed less important. We came upon a grassy field speckled with white, blue, and yellow flowers. The sun disappeared for a moment, and Magdalene looked up at the clouds. "I think it might rain," she said.

"I hope it does," I said. "You would look beautiful wet." Magdalene laughed. I leaned over and picked a lily of the valley. I passed it under Magdalene's nose for her to smell, and she smiled. I reached up and threaded it into her hair. How I loved the touch of her hair.

She reached up and removed the flower, and smelled its fragrance again. "I'm frightened," she said, as she sat down.

"But there's no longer any need," I said, as I joined her on the cool grass. "Magdala is behind you. You'll never see Simeon again."

"It's not Simeon," she said, somewhat sullenly.

"What is it?" I waited quietly.

Finally she said, "It's you, Jesus."

"Because of what happened to John?" I knew that she had heard, since I had spoken about his sacrifice in my sermons.

"No, it isn't that. Yes, I fear for you. But I am also frightened *of* you."

"I—I don't understand. Is it my miracles?" She fidgeted slightly. "Is it because I speak with God?"

"No—I understand *that.*" She was quiet again, and I waited. "It's hard to explain," she said.

"Then don't try. Let's just sit here together."

I'm going to lose her, I thought. And I don't know what to do about it. I looked at her, her gentle yet strong—almost tough—face. She had closed her eyes. What was behind those eyes? What was she thinking? Oh, how I wished I could really read minds! She was such a mystery to me. How could I be so infatuated with someone I understood so poorly? After a few minutes I broke the silence. "You can go back, Magdalene."

She sighed. "No, I can't. It's already too late." She opened her eyes and looked at me. "That's why I'm so scared. Now that you've come, I can't go back."

"Why does that frighten you?"

"Because I don't understand it. I thought I knew where I was going. I thought I could make my own destiny. But my life was wretched, Jesus. Wretched—and I didn't know it. Now I can't go back. And yet things went so quickly. Too quickly."

"You'll come with me?"

"Yes, Jesus. But don't expect anything. Let me stand in the distance for a while. I don't know what is happening."

"Neither do I, Magdalene. I'm frightened too," I said, with a slight quiver in my voice. "Every day I seem to understand less and less."

We arrived in Capernaum, with Magdalene traveling with my "flock," as Thomas had begun to call my large itinerant troupe of disciples.

Whatever fear she had, it either seemed to fade with time, or become better hidden. I was determined to rush nothing, for I truly had no idea where I, or we, were headed. Every day she and I spent some time alone together, usually in the woods, sitting, talking, enjoying God's little gifts. I felt something natural, something spiritual—divine—happening between us, but slowly, and I was not going to force it in any particular direction. My old plan to propose marriage, conceived on the morning after I had found her, now seemed selfish and irrelevant.

I told Magdalene almost everything, even my unhappy experience in the Red Tent. The only things I held back were the miracles. I didn't know what she had heard of them, or what she thought. Did she really believe that God had given me supernatural powers? Was that part of what she feared? Or had that drawn her to me? Several times I imagined explaining to her what had really happened, and how I had given up my attempts to tell my disciples that the miracles were not real.

But then I remembered the walk on the sea, and I tried to imagine how I would justify the willful deception of my closest disciples. The more I thought about what I had done, the more I felt a deep shame—shame and guilt that I didn't have the courage to expose.

But I knew I had to confront the Messianic fantasies of my mother. So immediately after our return to Capernaum, I asked her to come and sit with me for a while. I picked a quiet spot behind Peter's house. "Mother," I began, "why do you persist in calling me the Messiah? You know that it's not true." I felt relief at just getting those words out.

"Because you say it isn't?" she replied. "Don't you realize the importance of your own teachings? How can you not see what you're accomplishing? Just look at how many people listen to you, how many follow you wherever you go!" She was right. The ministry was growing huge. New crowds formed effortlessly wherever we went.

"I learned from a stranger that you say I am fulfilling prophecies from the Scriptures."

"And you are. ' For unto us a child is born; unto us a child is given; and the government shall be upon his shoulder, and he shall be called wise counselor, the almighty God, the everlasting father, the prince of peace.'"

I had never heard my mother quote Scripture before. "What has that to do with me?" I asked.

"You were born in Bethlehem, Jesus. 'The Lord says, Bethlehem, though you be little among the thousands of towns of Judah, yet out of you will he come forth who is to be the ruler in Israel.'"

This must be another fantasy of hers, I thought. She is inventing memories that fit prophecies. "Mother, I was born in Nazareth, not Bethlehem."

"Jesus, your mother certainly knows where you were born better than you do! It was on a trip for the census. Didn't I ever tell you? You are fulfilling all the prophecies. 'The Lord himself will give you a sign: a virgin will have a son, and will name him Immanuel.' And you know that I was a virgin when you were conceived, Jesus. That was surely a miraculous event."

"We've discussed this before, Mother. Nobody at the time thought you were a virgin," I said. "Not even you. And your quote from Isaiah refers just to a young girl, not necessarily a virgin."

"I was young. At the time I didn't even know what it meant to be a virgin," she continued, caught up in her own thoughts. She seemed to be looking up to heaven, speaking to God rather than to me. "Only after I married did I understand. Then I told Joseph that I had been a virgin. He believed me." She looked down at me with so saintly a smile that I almost believed her myself. "And I've had dreams, Jesus. An angel came to me," she continued. "His name was Gabriel, and he told me that I was to give birth to a son, and that this son would be great, and that the Lord our God would give him the throne of his ancestor David, and that his kingdom would never end."

"Mother, you aren't a descendant of David, and so therefore neither am I."

"Your father is."

"But you say you were a virgin. Then Joseph isn't my father."

My mother stopped, momentarily confused but determined as she pondered this fault in her logic. Finally she said, "We were married when you were born. So according to the Law of Moses, he is your father, and that makes you a descendant of David." She smiled smugly.

This is pure sophistry, I thought. To her I said, "The Messiah was to be called Immanuel. If I am the Messiah, then I have the wrong name!"

"Immanuel means 'God is with us'; Jesus means 'God saves.' It's almost the same. Jesus was the name that the angel Gabriel gave me."

"You once told me that you named me Jesus because of the miraculous proposal from Joseph, who saved you from shame. This dream of Gabriel, when did you have it?"

"After you returned and found me in Cana. And many times since. But I believe that I had it before. I think I must have had it when I was pregnant with you, but I didn't remember it until recently."

As I had feared, this conversation was going nowhere. "Mother, don't you realize that I don't fulfill half of the requirements of the prophecies, unless you twist their meaning completely around?"

"Jesus, forget the prophecies. You don't take them seriously anyway, so how could I possibly convince you?" She was certainly right there. "Now let me ask you some questions. Do you believe that the Messiah will come?"

"Yes."

"And how will he be recognized?"

"He will carry the word of God. He will announce the arrival of God's kingdom. He will end the spiritual sufferings of our people."

"Then why don't you recognize that you are the Messiah?"

I had no good answer.

She continued, "You've said that God speaks to you, and he does so every day."

"As I believe that he speaks to all his children, if only they would listen."

"And your role is to teach them how to listen. You said that he has given you a special message, a truth that you are to bring to the rest of his people. You believe in this truth, and you have taught it to me, a message of love, forgiveness, hope, charity, and humility, and that in these lie the salvation of the Jews." I was surprised by her clear articulation of my teachings. "Then, Jesus," she continued, "you were chosen by God to be the spiritual savior of our people. So you are the Messiah." She stopped and looked at me. I looked back. I was speechless. This discussion hadn't gone the way I had planned.

I finally said. "Let's continue some other time. I love you very much, mother."

"Not as I love you, Jesus. You are the greatest gift that God has given any mother."

38. Betrayal

I HAD SEEN NICODEMUS SEVERAL TIMES IN THE CROWDS SINCE his first visit, but he was always near the edge and he had not come to talk to me personally. He was simply collecting my sermons to pass on to the Sanhedrin, I assumed. It came as a surprise, then, when he appeared again in my tent late one night.

"Peace be with you, Nicodemus. Is this visit also to be secret?"

"You will not have to ask that, Rabbi, when I tell you the bad news I bring."

"Is it Herod again?"

"No." Nicodemus looked hesitant, as if he were afraid to proceed.

"The Sanhedrin?"

"Rabbi, one of your disciples. He has appeared before the High Priest, Caiaphas." Caiaphas was rumored to be very close to Pontius Pilate. He was a clever and dangerous man. "He came to betray you."

At these words I felt weak and I sat down on a bench. Suddenly I said, "Judas! It was Judas Iscariot!"

"It was indeed he," Nicodemus replied. "You knew?"

"Just a guess. But I've done no wrong. Nothing that I do is secret. There is nothing that one can say that I haven't said openly myself."

"He says that you are using trickery and deceit to fool your followers into thinking that you've performed miracles."

"Lord help me!" I muttered. I felt nauseated. It was the illness of guilt. I took a deep breath, put my forehead to my hand, and shook my head in despair. Nicodemus sat by passively. I looked up and tried to read his face. Suddenly I wondered if I had, in fact, done something illegal.

"Have I committed a crime?"

"Rabbi! Do not misunderstand! I come here only to warn you, not to criticize. The council hasn't learned anything from Iscariot that it didn't already know. I had already reported that your miracles were nothing more than the magic widely practiced by magi and Greek seers. There's nothing illegal! Your man hasn't given them any useful information. I came only to let you know that there is a traitor in your camp."

"What do you suggest I do?"

"There's no need for you to do anything. But if you wish to influence the Sanhedrin, you now may have a more effective method—more effective than using me. As long as we keep our knowledge of his treachery a secret, this traitor can be a tool. I'll come to you more often now, so I can relate to you what Judas tells the council. And you must tell me what you tell Judas, so I won't be accused of misleading them."

"There isn't much that I will tell Judas anymore."

"I think it wiser to treat him as before. There's little danger in a spy if you know what he's doing. It's better not to let him suspect."

"Thank you, Nicodemus, for your wisdom, and also for your courage and faith. We must have faith that God will preserve us."

"My father had a saying, Rabbi. 'Trust in the Lord,' he said, 'but don't forget to tie your camel.'"

As soon as Nicodemus had left, I sought out Thomas—as much for his comfort as for his wisdom. I told him everything that Nicodemus had said.

"Does Judas ever talk to you, Thomas?"

"No—but he hardly talks to anyone. Shall we alert the other apostles of this betrayal?"

"We must do nothing that could betray the confidence of Nicodemus. Judas is like juniper wood, ready to warp and splinter if handled roughly, but responsive if treated with care. I think I am to blame, for not being open and honest with him and the other apostles. I want to win Judas back, Thomas."

"That's risky, Jesus. Do you appreciate how dangerous this is? Two spies are reporting everything you do to the Sanhedrin."

"Nicodemus isn't a spy, Thomas. He is helping us."

"Nicodemus only helps himself, brother. We can't count on him. And we must learn more of what Judas intends."

"Then you must win his friendship. Does he know of your role when I walked on the Sea of Galilee?"

"I'm sure he doesn't. It seems to be the one miracle that he hasn't figured out."

"Then tell him that you don't believe it either. Tell him that the only miracles you believe are the spiritual ones."

"I'll play the doubter—just as you did for Elymas."

"Judas has no friends among the apostles. If you criticize me, he may open up to you."

No sooner was I alone than I was again torn by anguish. Iscariot was just telling the Sanhedrin the truth. Was this "betrayal"? Did I need fear the truth? Had not Thomas and I just devised yet another new deception?

And yet—the danger was real. Herod, the Sanhedrin—these were powerful forces that I didn't understand. John had been murdered, and now the focus of their attention was on me.

What had I been doing? Where was I headed?

My ministry was an enormous success. Every day I could see the rebirth of spirits, the healing of deep wounds, the peace brought by God's kingdom. My soul burned with a passionate fire, one that seemed to ignite those around me.

But was smoke from that fire choking my judgment?

❖ ❖ ❖

"Something troubles you," Magdalene said simply, as she stepped behind where I sat and began to massage my shoulders and neck. It was the first time that she had visited me in my tent. I sighed with pleasure and relaxed into my chair. "See, I can heal too," she said, "but my real powers of healing, like yours, are for illnesses of the spirit. Tell me what's bothering you."

"I wish I could, Magdalene. Let me only say that I'm troubled by a disloyalty."

"It must be Iscariot," she said quietly as she kneaded my shoulders. Was it so obvious? I said nothing. "Ah," she continued, "I feel from your muscles that I'm right. Jesus, don't try to keep secrets from me. It's useless." Her hands massaged me with surprising strength. "However, I'm not surprised," she continued. "Judas appears troubled that you allow your disciples to believe in your deceptions."

She continued her massage, as if nothing had happened, as if she hadn't just told me that she knew of my deceits, as if she didn't care. I took Magdalene's hands from my shoulders and turned and looked at her.

"You know?" I said. I could feel the tears coming to my eyes. "How? How do you know?" I asked.

"The way I know most things, I guess. I watch people. I try to understand them. Judas is clearly in torment. Nothing bothers him more than to hear Peter, or your mother, brag about you turning water into wine, or your walk on the sea."

"No, no, I don't mean Iscariot. I mean the miracles themselves! You know about them?"

"Your miracles?" She appeared puzzled. Then she looked into my eyes, as if trying to discover the nature of the torment inside me. Suddenly she seemed to understand. "Oh, my Jesus! Did you think that I took your magic to be real?" She smiled as if I were her silly child. "You performed magic for me when we were children. You explained to me how the magi did their tricks. No, I don't believe that you can calm storms or walk on water. You never said you could, and I certainly don't believe those wild stories spread by your disciples. I don't know how you walked on the sea. But you do seem able to cure people, at least for some illnesses."

"My training in healing is real. But the other miracles—they were tricks, deceptions." I looked deep into her eyes. She returned an expression of so much compassion that I felt as if I were melting. "I'm a fraud! In my sermons I talk about a perfect person, a man who shows no anger, a man who doesn't look on women with lust, a man who doesn't lie. Magdalene, I'm not that man. I'm an impostor, a charlatan!"

"My Jesus, you are nothing of the kind. No, you are not perfect, but you are a good, kind, and wise man with much to teach, an example for us all to follow. If you used deception, Jesus, I am sure that it was no more than necessary." She turned me around, placed her hands back on my shoulders, and began to knead my muscles once again. "Your apostles spread stories of your magic feats, but nothing is more wondrous than what your spirit conveys, what your words accomplish. You talk about true and false miracles. The miracles you perform—the spiritual ones—are all real."

"Magdalene, Magdalene, Magdalene! The loneliest man in the world is a man with guilt that he can't confess. Until now I did not realize how lonely I have been."

"You need never be lonely again, Jesus." Gently she pressed her lips to my neck. "How do your shoulders feel now? Shall I anoint your feet with perfume?"

39. Warning

"I FIND THE CARVINGS PRETTY, BUT HOW CAN YOU STAND THE smell?" Nicodemus held his nose as he surveyed the figures of pomegranates and palms that were carved on the ceiling and walls of my room. I was a guest in the home of Asher the Phoenician, and Nicodemus had somehow managed to find me despite my attempts to keep my location secret.

"Quite the contrary, I find the fragrance of cedar quite pleasant," I replied. "It's a lovely wood, soft, yet resistant to insects. Asher makes a profession of importing it from his homeland in Lebanon. The gates to the inner Temple are also made of cedar, you know."

"The best wood is seen and not smelled, I still say."

"But I think it must be the odor that repels insects. You'll grow used to it, I'm sure. Take off your cloak and sit down." Nicodemus pulled his arms out from his expensive Cilician cloak, slipped it off, and put it on the floor, where it stood of its own accord. He was wearing a white linen tunic with blue-dyed embroidered fringes at the bottom. It was elegant and expensive, a suitable disguise, I thought, for one who does not want to be known publicly as a disciple of Jesus. He sat on a bench and folded his hands on his lap in the manner of a rabbi about to begin a lesson. Nicodemus never traveled without a purpose, and I wondered what brought him to me this time.

"Tell me, Nicodemus, how did you manage to find me here in Nain?"

"It wasn't difficult. I know you try to keep your travels clandestine, but everything you do is widely talked about. You left Tyre and Sidon a week ago, and now you're passing through here on your way to the Jordan valley. In the meantime you're staying in the home of your latest secret disciple, a gentile no less!"

"Some gentiles already follow the spirit of the law better than many Pharisees. They too wish to worship God, but I think they've always been repelled by the Jewish rules."

"Not the least of which is circumcision."

"Not the least of which is the requirement that all other gentiles be treated as unclean," I said, "including their families and friends. I preach that all are clean who obey the spirit of the law."

"Yes, even the occasional Pharisee."

"And what brings the occasional Pharisee to me this time?"

Nicodemus bit his lip, as if unsure how to begin. He paused, and I waited, and finally he said, "As I've said to you before, I see the true threat to your ministry coming not from the Pharisees or from Rome, but from Herod. Rome merely wants its taxes, and it keeps the peace to enhance those taxes. Emperor Tiberius is happy to let us Jews worship any way we please. We tell him that images on Roman coins displease God, and soon he lets us manufacture our own coins. No, the real danger of religious suppression comes not from Rome, but from Herod."

"Nicodemus, you know that I've sought to avoid conflict with Herod."

"And you know that I've tried to help you. But he won't ignore you, regardless of our advice. His paranoia grows every week. Some action is necessary." Nicodemus paused, as if I would find his next remark unpleasant.

"What do you have in mind?" I prodded.

"Many of the Sanhedrin, including myself, fear that Herod seeks the kingship of Judea. Privately he already uses the title King, even though he is only tetrarch of Galilee. He takes the prophecy of Nathan to apply to himself, as if he deserves to be the full ruler of all of Israel. If he convinces Tiberius to appoint him king of Judea, then I fear for us all, for all of Israel."

"Do you truly think he could persuade Tiberius to do that?"

"Arimathea recently visited Tiberius in Capri. He reports that Tiberius is unstable, bordering on insanity. What is clear to me is that Tiberius has slumped into total incapacity. His primary interest appears to be fornication, and his only other concern is getting enough taxes. Regarding government, all he cares about is making sure it maintains him as emperor. In such a state, he may be vulnerable to a man like Herod."

"I'm not concerned with government," I said. "The kingdom of God is not of this earth." Somehow, sincere as they were, my words sounded pretentious.

"It is truly a kingdom of our spirits," Nicodemus agreed. "Even the Pharisees abdicate politics." My face must have reflected my skepticism, for he quickly elaborated, "But Rabbi, the Pharisees are in an awkward position. We've acknowledged the rights of the Romans to levy tribute, and to take the census for taxes. That's because we're primarily interested in salvation, in the eternal life, not in political control. But it's one thing to proclaim a kingdom, and another to welcome citizens into it. I find it distressful that so few Jews listen to you, Rabbi, and more painful that even fewer understand. You deserve to have all of Israel listen to your teachings. Some of your disciples have been with you for months, but many have left you to go back to their mortal lives, only because you've refused to declare yourself publicly as the Messiah, as the Christ."

"Publicly? What do you mean? Nicodemus, I refuse to declare myself even privately as the Messiah!"

"For you know that your apostles would tell the world. Yet you *are* the Messiah. I know that. You know that. Many of your people know it too, and they would tell others if only you gave the word. It's now clear that the Baptist was Elijah, if not in body then at least in spirit, and the prophecy that he would return just before the Messiah arrived has been fulfilled. You speak continually of 'the son of man' and what he brings, what he will do, what he requires. Forgive me, Lord, but your refusal to declare yourself—this is nothing but some strange pride on your part, a kind of courteous deceit. You reveal to us that the kingdom of God is here, now, but you refuse to give this revelation a living meaning! Admit that you are our king, the king of our spiritual lives. Allow us to spread the joyous news to others."

I looked at Nicodemus and he stared right back at me. I can't do what you ask, I thought to myself, because I am not the Messiah. Let me now say so, directly, forcefully, out loud, to Nicodemus: *I am not the Messiah!* But the sentence stayed within me. The words didn't come out. We stared at each other. What's wrong with me? Why can't I speak this aloud? Why can I not perform this simple act?

Is it that it is not the truth? Is it God who has paralyzed my tongue? Is it that God is whispering to me: Do not lie?

Am I the Messiah?

My mother has long believed that I am. So does Nicodemus—at least he says he does. Is it Nicodemus speaking to me now, or is it God speaking to me, through Nicodemus? Could it be true? I am bringing the kingdom of God to the world—at least I am teaching them that it is here—

and that is the role of the Messiah. But would *the* Messiah be only partially successful, as I have been? Would he have had to use deception, as I have? Would he be so unsure of himself, and not know what to do?

"Nicodemus, I'm confused. Please don't press me. If I were to declare myself the Messiah, I would be arrested by Herod and beheaded like the Baptist, or crucified like Gamala."

"Ah, that won't happen if you are careful. Remember, you are not alone. First you must get out of Herod's reach. You can do this by taking your teachings beyond Galilee. Come to Judea. Teach there, in the Temple. In Jerusalem you'll be safe from Herod, for you'll be out of his tetrarchy."

"Safe from Herod, but in the clutches of the Sanhedrin! That's like escaping the lion by running into a den of wolves."

"Leave the council to me, and to the Law. They can't condemn a man without a trial, without hearing him and finding out what he's done. And you've broken no laws. I've told them that. They accept that. They'll send interrogators to trick you, so you must be careful, but you're not easily tricked. As long as you don't attack Rome or proclaim yourself above Caesar's authority, the council can do nothing. But if you remain in Galilee, you'll be subject to no law other than the whims of that madman."

"What do you want in all this? You fear Herod, but how can this help you?"

"I only wish to see the teaching of the truth of God spread throughout Judea. Rabbi, with the strength that you will bring to Judaism, Caesar will have no need to appoint a king. There is no need to undermine Herod politically, if your teachings are fulfilled."

"Nicodemus, your information has been helpful, and your insights have been valuable. You are the thirteenth of my twelve apostles. But to do as you ask requires that I put a great deal of faith in you and in your judgment."

"Rabbi, it is I who place my faith in you. My candor already puts my life at risk. But don't take my advice. Do what you know is right, not because I suggest it, but because God reveals it to you. If you don't think that you should go to Judea, to Jerusalem, to preach the word of God in his holiest of all cities, then I don't wish you to do so either. I trust completely in whatever revelations you will receive."

"I need to think about what you've said, Nicodemus. Stay with me for a while here in Nain."

"I can't do that. I must never sleep when I'm in danger, and when I'm near you, secretly, that is—the council doesn't know of this trip—then I'm in danger. I must begin my return trip to Jerusalem tonight."

"Who else knows you've come?"

"Only Arimathea. My household believes I am negotiating to buy silk from the caravans that pass through the Jordan valley. I'll tell them that I've had another unsuccessful trip. I am very particular about my silk, you see."

"God be with you, Nicodemus. I thank you for sharing your knowledge and your wisdom."

"I thank you, my Lord, for showing me the path to righteousness. Let me give you this modest gift, and take leave." Nicodemus handed me a large package wrapped in dark cloth that he had hidden under his cloak, and before I could open it he left through the heavy cedar door and once again disappeared into the night. I unwrapped the package and found a bolt of the most brilliant white wool I had ever seen. At night its whiteness reminded me of clouds lit by the moon. To produce this, I thought, they must have kept the sheep not only indoors, but also in the dark!

Nicodemus was always persuasive, and to counter his influence I had developed the habit of following any discussion with him by seeking advice from Thomas. So early the next morning Thomas and I took a vigorous walk along a path in the fields behind Asher's home.

"Whew!" he said, as we walked side by side. "It's good to get away from the smell of cedar."

"At least you agree with Nicodemus on something," I said.

"So what was the purpose of last night's visit?"

"To warn me. He says Herod's insanity has grown, and that I'm in imminent danger. He advises that I go to Jerusalem."

"That could be dangerous too, Jesus. You have over a thousand followers. The Romans might think you were leading an insurrection."

"We could go alone, unannounced. Besides, I've always made it clear that I have no concern for politics."

"But that's not true any longer, is it?"

"What do you mean by that?" I asked sharply.

"Don't you see?" Thomas said, affecting a matter-of-fact tone. "You're already involved in the politics of Jerusalem. Nicodemus is using you, not just to undermine Herod, but to increase the influence of the Pharisees within the Sanhedrin. And you are letting him use you to do that."

"Thomas, that's all fantasy. How could he be using me? His power in the Sanhedrin is no stronger now than it was the day we met."

"I wouldn't be so sure," Thomas said. He kicked the base of a tree, and seemed to hurt his toe. "He's setting up something. I don't understand it yet, but asking you to move to Jerusalem is part of it."

"Thomas, we can't ignore the Jews of Jerusalem. We both know that I must go there—that I've always planned to go there."

"Eventually, yes, of course. But your time hasn't come, not just yet. You've been preaching for barely two years."

"We'll be cautious. We'll go without the flock. I'm anxious to preach there, to see what response I'll get, to see if I can counter the Pharisees of the Temple."

"Please, Jesus, don't make that decision. At least take more time. Think about what I've said. There's much more to be lost than to be gained. Jerusalem will wait."

"I don't have the luxury of time. If I remain, Nicodemus says I'm sure to be arrested."

"There are places besides Jerusalem that we can go, places that are much safer. You've talked of Caesarea Philippi, up north. That's out of the tetrarchy of Herod. We would be safe there."

I suddenly noticed Thomas's use of the word *we*. I had been thinking only about my own safety, but I should have realized that my apostles, indeed all my disciples, were at risk along with me. All the more reason to leave Galilee.

But Thomas's suggestion of Caesarea Philippi was a good one. It was a largely pagan city with only a small population of Jews. I could get away from the crowds, and have a chance to think—about Nicodemus's other suggestion.

40. Messiah!

IT WOULD BE NECESSARY TO LEAVE MY FLOCK BEHIND, SO secrecy was called for. So the next evening, at dinner with my apostles, I announced that before sunrise we would depart for the north. I told no one else, except my mother, who chose to stay at Capernaum, and Magdalene, who chose to come. Peter and Andrew objected to the trip, but I insisted that God had commanded me to make the journey. Five days later we were there.

Thomas had kept a record of disciples who would provide our small group with food and shelter, and there were several such people in Caesari Philippi. When we arrived we strongly emphasized that our presence must be kept secret. And, to my amazement, the secret was kept and my hoped-for privacy was achieved. I encouraged the apostles to walk by themselves in the surrounding countryside, to think and to pray about the future. Most of all I wanted to be alone with myself.

The most beautiful time for me was after midnight, when the warm summer night became exceptionally quiet and yet even distant sounds traveled for miles. I chose to walk in the wooded foothills of Mount Tabor, finding my way by the dim light of the brilliant stars, and by the feel of the ground under my sandals.

It had been in that discussion with Nicodemus in Nain that I had realized, *maybe he is right.* Maybe I truly was meant to be the Messiah— not the Messiah of Rabbi Shuwal, swinging a sword and bringing retribution to the enemies of Israel—but the Messiah that my father believed in, the man of peace who beat swords into plowshares and brought the lambs into brotherhood with the lions. Why had I gone forward to be baptized by John? What was the unfulfilled role of my father that I would fulfill? Was it to lead our people to a spiritual liberation? This was indeed what I had been trying to do for the past two years.

What arrogance, I thought—even to think that *I* might be the Messiah!

But no—just the opposite. The thought requires a deep humility, I argued to myself. Such responsibility is beyond grasp, beyond imagination, beyond awe. It is a task for which I am not worthy—and yet–
. . . Even Moses felt inadequate when chosen by God to deliver the Jews from Egypt. God asks only the impossible, and it is only with his help that his demands can be met, only through his miracles, true miracles, through his strength. I must trust in God. I must have faith.

My father suddenly appeared before me, in a memory from my youth. "Messiah is alive today," he said. I asked why he didn't announce himself. My father answered, "Maybe he doesn't yet know he is the Messiah."

Why had these words come to me just then, for the first time in twenty years? Was it to remind me that God doesn't announce his intentions through burning bushes, but through inner revelations? Through little whispers.

Perhaps I am indeed—the Messiah.

I thought those words as a tiny splinter of the moon suddenly appeared over the distant hills, and the countryside grew alive with its colorless glow, as if a powerful spirit were enveloping the world. I could see the mountains, the valley, and the distant forests.

The Messiah. I am the Messiah.

There was no doubt. It was revealed to me in the quiet way that God reveals all his truths.

The next night I brought my apostles with me to the same spot on the top of the hill, to see the moon rise over the countryside. I hadn't said anything to them or to anyone else of my latest revelation. I wanted no talking, just peaceful meditation and prayer, until the moment would arrive when I would let them know. I was wearing a new robe, made for me by Magdalene out of the white cloth brought by Nicodemus. I motioned to the apostles to sit on a small rock on the hilltop, and then I walked a short distance towards the bright glow on the horizon that indicated the moon about to appear. The appearance of the first bright sliver of the moon drove shivers across my skin. I stood up, turned away from the moon, and walked to my apostles, silhouetted against the moon.

"Who is it," I asked them, "that my disciples say I am?"

The apostles appeared surprised by the abrupt question, the first words they had heard from me in several hours. They looked to each other in a quandary. Half a minute passed, and I asked again. "Who is it that my disciples say I am?"

Finally Matthew said, "Some say that you are John the Baptist."

"Others think that you may be Elias!" said Andrew.

Why did they not give the proper answer? Although it was now obvious to me, was it still not obvious to them?

"It is said," James spoke, "that you are Jeremiah." *No!* I thought to myself.

Iscariot spoke up. "Some people say only that they know you are a prophet."

"But who do *you* say I am?" I asked, trying to hide my impatience. Thomas was standing in the back of the group, looking perplexed. I glanced at Peter, who had been quiet. "Peter! Who do you say I am?"

He looked back with an expression that seemed to say, What do you want me to say, my Lord? What answer are you searching for? In my own mind, I responded, the *truth.* Just respond with the truth!

Peter must have heard my thoughts, for his face suddenly lit up. "You are the Messiah!" he said, seemingly astonished by his own answer. "You are the Christ!" he repeated, using the Greek term, as if to add importance to his thought.

"You are blessed, Simon Peter," I said. "You did not learn this from me, nor from any man, nor from anything on this earth. It was truly revealed to you by our heavenly father! This is why I call you Peter! For your faith is like that of a rock, and it is upon such faith that I shall build my ministry."

"Master! Lord! We've been waiting for this moment! I had prayed that you would announce yourself!"

"Peter, I did not announce myself. It was you—you who recognized the truth." I turned to the rest of the group. "We are at the gateway to heaven, and I am doing little more than carrying the keys. We are on a joyous journey to that gate."

As we walked back to Caesarea, the apostles appeared to be bursting with energy. All but Thomas walked ahead of me, and I was pleased by their evident joy, a sign from God that I was pleasing him. Thomas walked alongside me, and was surprisingly quiet. I assumed that he too was relishing the peace of the moment.

I overheard Peter describing to the others how he would announce to all of Caesarea that the Messiah was among them. Panic surged though my body, and I rushed to catch up with him. "No, Peter, no! You mustn't tell anybody of your revelation tonight! God has told you that I am the Messiah, but you may tell no one else."

"But we must!" Peter said. "I've seen hundreds, thousands, leave us—because they don't know who you are. They'll travel the wrong road—they'll never get to the gate—they'll be lost to the kingdom of heaven." He looked at me pleadingly. I shook my head. "Why do you demand this of us? How can it be righteous to deceive?"

"My time has not yet come," I said, glancing at Thomas—but he was just staring at the ground. I turned back to Peter. "These thoughts don't come from God, as your earlier ones did, Peter. They come from your hot temper, not from your spirit. Listen carefully to my words." Peter looked at me like a pouting child who had just been chastised by a parent. "There is severe danger ahead. The Sanhedrin fear that I threaten their power. The Pharisees consider me their enemy. And Herod Antipas—wishes me dead."

"You foresee all this? That they will kill you—as they killed John?"

"Peter, even if they were to kill me, remember, death is nothing, for the kingdom of God is not of this world. If you lose your life for God, you will find eternal life. Even if God were to ask you to be crucified, the most horrid of all deaths, even then you must take up the cross with joy, carry it with happiness, and die not in agony but in exultation that you are fulfilling God's will."

The mood of the group was much more somber after this discussion. Thomas and I walked together, this time ahead of the rest. A cool breeze had begun, and I wrapped my new white tunic tightly about me.

"They walk quietly now," I said to Thomas. "Perhaps they're praying."

"They're fearful," Thomas said. "They believe that you predicted your own death, your own crucifixion."

"Is that how they took it? Well, if so, perhaps it will do some good. I couldn't have them announcing to the world that I am the Messiah."

"It is a dangerous time for the ministry. But what you did was necessary. You had to do it."

"You mean, declaring myself the Messiah?"

"You had to—go ahead and call yourself the Messiah."

I looked hard at Thomas, but he just stared straight ahead at the path. In the cool moonlight it was hard to read his expression. "Do you doubt, Thomas?" I waited, but he said nothing. "Surely you understand, if anybody understands. Don't you believe me?" My voice undoubtedly reflected my inner hurt.

"Believe you? Jesus, you know that the Messiah legend doesn't really exist in the Scriptures. The rabbis have selectively chosen unrelated passages, quote them together to create a prophecy that isn't there." Thomas was only repeating back to me words that I had said previously, to him, to our mother, to others.

"No—no—of course, Thomas. I know the prophecies don't predict anything. The rabbis cite the Scriptures only to justify what they already know, what they feel, what they are told in their spirits—that he Messiah is coming. Even our father believed that, Thomas. John knew he was coming, not because of the prophets, but because he could feel it. This is not a deceit, Thomas. I am trying to be honest, absolutely honest. Think of everything that's happened in the last two years. You know the message I was given, a message to spread to our people."

"You misunderstand me, my brother. I do believe in *a* Messiah, just not in *the* Messiah. Since I was a child, I've believed that someday the Lord will give us a leader, a prophet, who will relieve our pain, and I've come to believe that you may well be that prophet, Jesus. But to call yourself *the* Messiah gives me fear, for that title is full of explosive implications. Most Jews are expecting a military leader who will lead them to victory, not a prophet who will emancipate their spirits. Can you, Jesus, be the spiritual Messiah—without becoming the political, the military Messiah?"

"Yes, Thomas. Otherwise I would not have said anything tonight."

"And the Romans are watching for that military Messiah, so they can destroy him. And there's something else, Jesus. When you told us—or rather, when you let Peter tell us—that you were the Messiah, it didn't carry the same authority as your teachings. This is a dangerous path we're slipping down. I fear now, Jesus, I truly fear." He shook his head in despair.

It was now Thomas who was speaking with authority, and I who was listening. I began to fear too. I was on a path that I had not foreseen. I was silent. I just walked, and prayed, and pondered what Thomas had said.

We arrived back at Caesarea just as the sun rose. The town was alive with its early morning activities, children waiting at the spring to fill skins with water, merchants hawking bread, the ringing sound of blacksmiths. Everything was the same as it had been yesterday. And yet everything had changed.

We had been staying in the home of farmer named Joah. He had already left for the fields, and his wife was preparing the morning bread. Magdalene was outside churning butter.

"Where have you been?" Magdalene demanded, as I approached.

"In the hills, thinking, praying."

"You pray with your twelve by your side?"

"This time they came."

"But not me?"

"The apostles were with me. But prayer is a private matter, not to be shared among people, even those who love each other."

"Yet *they* were invited."

"There are times when I must be with them."

"Sometimes I think you are no better than Rabbi Shuwal."

"Magdalene!" She had never been that harsh with me before. She looked down at the butter churn, and jerked the plunger up and down with greater force and speed. "You know that you're more dear than anyone else in this world," I said. "I would never hurt you—I would never even offend you."

"You believe that matters of religion are too important for a woman."

"I tell you more of what is in my heart than I tell to any man. Magdalene, that's why I wanted you to come with me to Caesarea Philippi. There's nobody else who understands me so well as you do. There's no one else who shares my most intimate secrets." Then unrehearsed and unexpected words leapt from my heart: "Magdalene, there is nobody else I want to marry."

Magdalene looked at me. The pupils of her eyes seemed to contain the world. Her lips seemed to quiver slightly. But then she turned her head down and looked at the ground. "It's not marriage I wish," she said. She seemed to suppress a low, ironic laugh. "It's just that I can't bear to be excluded."

"I'll never exclude you!"

"You did last night."

Was Magdalene right? Had I, without questioning my own actions, treated her as the rabbis had, as a woman and therefore unworthy of lessons—the chattel of a man, to be excluded from the main hall of the synagogue and from discussions of religion?

I thought of the prayer I had been taught by Rabbi Shuwal: *Thank you, Lord, for not having created me a woman.* If the distinctions between clean and unclean were to be forgotten, if Jews and gentiles were to be treated alike, if slaves were to be loved as much as the free, then could women be treated as inferior? The revelations of God come without warning, in strange and unexpected ways.

Magdalene interrupted my reverie. "Ah, my Jesus, I see in your face—in your silence—that you *do* understand. That's why I love you so much. Because you alone can really understand."

We sat together quietly. I was convinced that Magdalene could read my thoughts, for she seemed to be taking care not to disturb me. Could I read hers? I had never been very good at that. I became aware of her touch, of her breathing, of her . . . crying? "Magdalene, what's the matter?"

"Jesus, I'm sorry that I was hateful."

"You weren't hateful. No. You are the strongest woman I've ever known. And I love you so much more because you're honest with me, because you tell me what your are truly thinking."

"Right now I feel like the weakest, frailest person in the world."

I tried to lift her head so I could look her in the eyes, but she resisted. I tried again. "Magdalene, something is still bothering you."

Without looking up, she said, "Jesus, I . . . I've been keeping a secret from you."

"There's no need to tell me, Magdalene, not unless you feel you must. Your secret isn't important to me."

"I want to be that honest person you just told me I was."

I held her, and said nothing.

She finally looked up at me. She spoke quietly. "Just before I ran away, my mother found Deborah—my doll, the doll you gave me—hidden under my mat. She confronted me, called me a liar and a cheat, and cried that I had violated the fifth commandment. She was about to tear Deborah in pieces as I watched. I was desperate. So I cried out, 'No! I am the sinner! Let me do it! Let me destroy the graven image myself.' So she handed me the doll."

"And you . . ."

"I ran from the house as fast as I could, clutching Deborah. I shouted back at her that she was the Witch of Endor. I ran into the woods and hid Deborah in the Wolf's House."

I almost laughed, but I held back—and instead hugged her. "That's why I loved you so much, Magdalene, even then!" I said.

But Magdalene wasn't laughing. As I held her, she sobbed, but kept on with her story. "My parents came searching for me, but I led them away from the woods. They caught me and brought me home."

"And beat you?"

"I wish they had. They treated me as an outcast, as if I had been expelled from the family. They left me food, but wouldn't eat with me, not unless I would bring them the doll. They seemed desperate, but I was desperate too. That was when my parents went to the rabbi. He told them that I was in danger of forever losing my soul, and that my sins would reflect on the family. And that was when he offered himself as my savior. My husband."

I sat there with Magdalene, pondering the story she had just told. My gift, my secret gift to her, had led to her estrangement with her parents, to her life of suffering, to her life as a prostitute.

"Jesus, I didn't want to tell you, for fear you would blame yourself."

"Magdalene, I have sinned many times in my life, but even now I am only beginning to understand the harm caused by my deceits."

"No, Jesus, it wasn't your fault. I couldn't live the life that my parents wanted for me. If it hadn't been Rabbi Shuwal, it would have been someone else, equally unbearable. Now I'm happy. I'll be your mistress for as long as you want."

"You will be my wife."

"You deserve better. I am, I was, a harlot."

"You are a child of God, whose sins have been washed clean." I regretted the words, for they sounded too formal, too rote, too rehearsed. With Magdalene I wanted to use words that I had never used before. She would have only the freshest thoughts. "Magdalene, it's I who am unworthy. It's I who have sinned. It's you who must forgive *me.* Never again will I exclude you. Never." She looked up at me, and although she remained silent, I could sense she understood. "I will make a prophecy! In less than a year a child will be born, born to parents who will love him like no child born before or since, a child who will make his parents happier than they could possibly imagine. It will be the most wondrous miracle of all time."

I could feel my spirit glowing, and I could feel the glow of Magdalene's, and as we sat there together I felt that our spirits had joined.

"We'll name him Joseph, after my father," I suggested.

"Unless we name her Deborah," Magdalene whispered.

Later that morning, as I sat with her, I finally said, "Magdalene, on the slopes of Mt. Tabor, on the night before last, I had a revelation."

"You understood that you are the Messiah?" she said.

"How did you know?"

"Jesus, I . . . I always knew you were the Messiah."

"You never said so to me."

"I was afraid. Afraid for you, and for me. I didn't want you to be the Messiah. Maybe I was hoping that it wasn't so, that it would change, or that you wouldn't let yourself follow that destiny. I wanted you for myself, Jesus. Even now I fear that I'll lose you."

"Magdalene, oh Magdalene! You needn't worry. You will never lose me. I know that as strongly as I know anything."

41. Transfiguration

SEVERAL DAYS LATER PETER CAME TO ME WITH A DISTURBING vision that he had shared with James and John. They had returned to the foothills of Mt. Hermon, to the site where I had taken them several nights earlier, but this time just the three of them alone. Peter said that they had fallen asleep on the mountain, and then had been awakened by my sudden appearance. He said that I had appeared, glowing like a ghost, "in heavenly glory," and that Moses and Elijah were there too.

"Peter, what you had was a dream."

"Forgive me Lord for disputing you, but it wasn't a dream. Dreams aren't shared, and James and John were there, and they remember it all exactly as do I. My Lord, don't you remember being there? Do you have some reason to want me to forget what happened?"

"You say you saw Moses and Elijah with me?"

"Their clothes were dazzling white, as were yours, more white than anyone could wash them."

"How did you know that they were Moses and Elijah?"

Peter was stumped for a moment. He put his hand to the side of his head, as if lost in thought. Finally he said, "I just knew. It too was a miracle, that this knowledge was conveyed to me as we watched you discuss the coming glory of God."

"What did we say?"

"That you would soon fulfill God's purpose by . . ." Peter paused, and looked at me intently.

"Go on."

"That you would soon fulfill God's purpose in Jerusalem. You said that you would be hung on wood, you would be crucified, until you died. But then you would be raised from the dead. My Lord, what did you mean?"

Now I was lost momentarily in thought. I had not had the dream for a long time, the dream of my crucifixion. How many times had I had it? I didn't know. But the memory was vivid. I saw myself on the cross, I remembered my feeling *it does not hurt!*

"What did you mean?" Peter asked again. I looked at him and realized that he was referring to his own hallucination, not my dream.

I shook away my vision. "You mean it wasn't revealed to you? Then why didn't you ask me last night?"

"Lord, we were frightened. We feared your brilliance. You were more dazzling than the sun. We were all blinded by your brightness."

"You were blinded but yet you could recognize me and Moses and Elijah? Yet another miracle?" Why did I persist in pointing out the logical inconsistencies in Peter's vision, as if they would have any impact on his belief in its reality? Sarcasm would accomplish nothing with Peter. He had grown inured to it during his youth.

"We offered to build you tents, three tabernacles, for you to rest in."

"Peter, you don't even understand what you're saying." It was just like Peter, to see glowing ghosts appear out of air, and then to think that they would need shelters! Indeed, something strange had happened to Peter the previous night, something he shared with James and John, but what could it be? Suddenly I had a conjecture. "Peter, have you been treating yourself with haoma?"

"My Lord, the medicine that you have brought to tend our spiritual woes is truly a miracle!"

"Did you have spiritual woes last night, before your visions?"

"You know all, my Lord! You read deep into my heart and my soul!"

"Then tell me the truth, for surely I already know! Did you use haoma yourself, at full strength, unmixed with bread, and did James and John?"

"It is as you say, my Lord. This medicine of the spirit brings us closer to God than does prayer!"

"Peter, listen carefully, for I am about to give you a command that I want you to obey with all your heart and all your strength. Never again shall you take the medicine haoma yourself, and never again shall you allow other apostles to use it themselves. Never again! You may use it weakly, a small amount in soup or on bread, but only to treat our disciples who are ill with fever or pain, as I've taught you. You shall not use it yourself for your physical woes, and certainly not when you feel spiritually weak or ill." I felt I couldn't trust Peter with anything less than total abstinence. "Keep the mystery of the haoma secret, for it does not bring the enlightenment that you believe. It is only intoxication. Talk to God through prayer and prayer alone, for only prayer brings the blessed intoxication that comes directly from God, and it is only the intoxication of prayer that pleases him. I do not want you to remember your vision of last night, of me and of Moses and Elijah, and you shall not describe these visions to anybody. Tell James and John to come to me, so I can instruct them likewise."

I felt sorry for Peter, for he had taken such joy in his hallucinations, but I knew that I had to put a strict and absolute end to the abuse of haoma. There was no way to predict what visions the drug would bring, and there was great danger that the dreams would be interpreted as carrying great import, possibly greater import than true revelations from God. Many pagan priests had used such drugs, for they were a sure way to fool an initiate into believing that a great spiritual experience was under their direct control, and many men had been misled to false spirituality and false worship through abuse of this and other potions.

I am the Messiah. As I spoke the words of that revelation to myself, they seemed to clear the haze that had obscured my vision. The retreat to Caesarea had fulfilled its purpose. Everything was falling into place. I knew what I must do. I must go to Judea, to Jerusalem, just as Nicodemus had advised. We would gather our resources at Capernaum, and move our ministry to Judea.

Yet I still feared the Sanhedrin. Although they were Jews living in my own land, to me they were as mysterious and unknown as the peoples of India and Africa. Nicodemus said I had nothing to fear, but I worried that even he had underestimated what they could do. They had recently called on the Romans to destroy a Zealot band that had been preaching openly in the Temple. The Romans had destroyed their refuge, the Siloam tower, by smashing its underpinnings with battering rams. What few Zealots survived that attack had been crucified.

Thomas suggested that he go to Jerusalem ahead of me, with a select group of apostles, to gauge the mood of the city.

42. Jerusalem

I COULD NEVER REMEMBER WHICH WAS THE LAST HILL, THE ONE that would afford the wondrous view. Mile after mile passed, and still there was another to climb. Then suddenly it was there, Jerusalem, spread out on the horizon, the immense city walls like huge arms protecting the sprawling houses, and the towers of the Temple ablaze with fire. I hadn't seen that illusion since I had been a child, when my father explained to me that I was seeing only the reflections of the sun in the gold leaf of the towers. Gold, on a building? Back then I believed that the Temple was not man-made, but had been built by God himself.

Even from the distance I could sense the vitality and variety of this most wonderful of all cities. Nearly a hundred thousand people lived there, and during the Feast of the Tabernacles the population virtually doubled. Herod the Great had begun restoration and enlargement of the Temple when my father was a child. Despite the fact that this work was done in a Greco-Roman style, Jews venerated the structure as the legitimate successor to the Temple of Solomon. Every time I looked at it, it seemed miraculous that so large a structure could have been built by humans. It was overwhelming, glorious, a fitting monument to God. Even were it not for the commanded pilgrimages, every Jew should come to Jerusalem, I thought, just to see the Temple.

Someday, my father had confidently predicted, I would have the pleasure of bringing my own son to see it. My son! Until now, that had been an abstract idea. For the first time in my life this dream seemed possible, even inevitable. I thought of Magdalene, and a soft feeling of joy spread throughout me, replaced a moment later by a sweet loneliness.

Buried deep within the heart of that Temple, in the chamber known as the Holy of Holies, was the Ark of the Covenant, and within that Ark were the original tablets of stone with the ten commandments, chiseled by God himself. My father had once told me that he suspected the Ark was no longer there but had been lost, perhaps during the invasion of Nebuchadnezzar the Babylonian. The reason no one but the High Priest was allowed to enter the Holy of Holies, my father speculated, was to preserve the secret of the loss, so that only the High Priest would ever know.

So my father had told me that he believed the priests lie, even about the most sacred matters! I had never articulated that thought before. What other ideas had he implanted in my mind?

And I no longer believed that God had carved the ten commandments on that stone, did I? Moses had done it himself, during his forty days and forty nights on Mt. Sinai. What will I teach my son, I wondered, when I bring him here to the Temple? Could I allow him to believe the myth, the lie, of Moses? No, he'll know the truth. I'll tell him how our people had once believed the myths and fables, but how we had learned that the glory of God was greater than these petty deceptions depicted as miracles. By the time I bring my son here, everyone will know the truth; the era of illusions will have ended. The glorious religion of Judaism, the worship of the one true God, will have been fulfilled.

I was wrong. The temple is not a fitting monument to God. It is a graven image, a false icon, no better than Mount Gerizim of the Samaritans, no better than the golden calf of Aaron. It would be better to tear it down than to allow our people to believe that this carved wood and stone is somehow holier than anything else. No more lies, no more sacrifices, no more catalogues of prescribed and proscribed rituals. The hour will come when all men will worship God their father, not in idols, but in spirit and in truth.

The priests, the rabbis, have been mockingbirds, singing a beautiful but distorted imitation. The Jews haven't yet heard the pure, glorious, unaltered psalm of the song sparrow itself. It is God's gift to me, I thought, that I have the pleasure, the honor, the joy of bringing that beautiful song to the Jews.

❖ ❖ ❖

The Feast of the Tabernacles, the celebration to remember the forty years spent in the desert during the Exodus, was nearly half finished by the time I arrived in Jerusalem. The pilgrims were into their third day in their special tents, the *tabernacles,* decorated with the festive lubab made of twigs of palm, myrtle, and willow, symbols of rejoicing. Jews, even the permanent residents of Jerusalem, were eating all their meals in these tents to recreate, in this tiny symbolic way, the life on the desert.

I arrived in the afternoon. Soon the sun would go down, and the city would be aglow with the lights of a thousand menorahs. I was anxious to find my apostles, so I quickly worked my way through the commotion and entered the Temple grounds through the double Huldah gate, which was faced with cream-colored marble, and overlaid in places with gold. There, set high in the pillars, were notices forbidding entry to all who were not Jews, on penalty of death. As a child I had felt privileged to pass that point, although now it was obvious to me that many crossing that threshold were not Jews at all. Just past the gate was the area known as the Court of the Gentiles, its name informally reflecting what I had just noticed.

The courtyard spread before me like a spring pond, filled with the most wondrous variety of life–Jews from all over the world, from Parthus, Mede, Elan in the East, Rome in the West, Babylon, Crete, Arabia, Egypt, and Cyrene, all identifiable by their clothing. Nowhere else, not in Babylon, not in the markets of Sepphoris, was there such a mixture of colors and cultures. Nowhere else was there such a mixture of wealthy and poor.

Then I noticed something new, something I did not remember from my childhood visit to the Temple. The poor were not begging, but were standing in their meager rags, some on crippled legs, others evidently blind or ill, crowding around stalls, holding coins in their thin hands. Commerce, in the Court of Gentiles? I had heard of this, but had forgotten. I waded into the crowd, gently pushing myself to a position where I could see the tables. Two men, dressed no better than beggars, were examining pigeons, apparently trying to decide which to purchase. Pigeons are the least expensive animal offering, and are used for everything from the first-born child sacrifice to purification of incurred uncleanliness.

A merchant said to one of them, "These are temple pigeons, unblemished, the finest sacrifice for the Lord, especially blessed by a Levite, and for you, only two denari." That was more than four times the price of a pigeon in Sepphoris. I didn't believe that the bird was any more unblemished than any other. The Temple courtyard had become not only a site of commerce, but a venue for blatant cheating as well.

But why should the poor be spending their money on sacrifices at all? What is the correct price for them to pay for a bird that will be burnt on an altar in a misguided attempt to please God?

I watched a blind man being led to a table to exchange a coin, paying a surcharge so he could give to the priest a coin that held no image of

Caesar. Cynically, I guessed that the priest would receive half of that surcharge.

My cynicism grew. Why can't men and women worship God as well at home as in Jerusalem? Why must they trek to this idol? These pilgrimages to Jerusalem, "required" for the faithful—were they not just a way to increase the commerce, and the profit?

Off in one corner a substantial crowd had gathered around a man who was standing on a stool addressing them. To my delight and pleasure, as I worked my way in, I recognized the man as Peter. I moved close enough to hear his words. "The kingdom of God on Earth has been proclaimed!" Peter shouted. I listened for a while, and judged that he was doing a credible job of delivering my sermons. In some ways he seemed to be a more natural orator than I.

"Is that Jesus of Nazareth?" a man standing next to me asked. I was momentarily confused, and then realized that he was referring to Peter.

"No, I think it's one of his apostles."

"One of his *what?*"

"Apostles. An emissary, like an ambassador. One of the teachers that Jesus trained to send out in his place."

"Why doesn't Jesus come himself?"

"You'll have to ask Jesus," I said.

We listened together for a while. "This man is good," he said.

"Are you a believer?"

"No, but I enjoy listening to him. He speaks with authority."

"Then why don't you repent?"

"I may someday. I have a family to take care of now. Perhaps if I hear Jesus himself."

"You should come back tomorrow then."

"Oh? Do you know something? Is Jesus coming here!"

"Bat qol," I said, "just a feeling. What have you heard about this fellow Jesus?" I asked.

"That he does magic. He heals. But he does it on the Sabbath, and that worries me. How can he be a man of God if he violates the Law of Moses?"

Now wasn't the time to argue. Instead I said, "I understand that he's not doing miracles anymore, Sabbath or otherwise. He wants people to listen to his teachings, not just come for a show."

"That would be a pity. I've never seen a real miracle."

That evening I made myself known to my apostles, and the next morning I wore my pure white tunic and assumed their place in the courtyard. A large, polite crowd gathered about me. My apostles had done an effective job of attracting listeners. I began with my popular "Blessed are they" sermon, and then I told several parables. Never before had I preached to so many strangers who listened so attentively—without needing to first convince them of my ability to do miracles. I realized that the courtyard was full of people who had come to hear the word of God, people I did not have to distract from their daily jobs. I came daily and was gratified by the burgeoning crowds.

But after the Festival of the Tabernacles was over, I lost my audience. Apparently most of them had been pilgrims who returned to their home villages. Lazarus, with whom I was staying in nearby Bethany, said that the pilgrims came in a mood of religious fervor, and had been eager to find preachers to listen to. The regular residents of Jerusalem were much tougher. "Be patient," he advised, "for it may take time to break through their crusts."

Several other men preached daily in the Court of the Gentiles, men who called themselves prophets. One appeared to be a former disciple of the Baptist. Another seemed to be a lunatic who spent half his time talking to empty space, claiming it was God himself. And a third was a thinly disguised Zealot who one day disappeared—arrested by the Romans, Lazarus speculated. These men seemed able to draw as many listeners as I did.

Magdalene arrived to stay with me in Bethany, and she did her best to encourage me, as did Thomas. My apostles came each day to the courtyard to form a core of listeners, in the hope of attracting more. And a few people did come, but nothing like the crowds I had been able to attract among the am ha'arez of Galilee. Was I speaking to the wrong people? Was my message not meant for the sophisticated Jews of Jerusalem? I couldn't believe that. Yet although I carried joyous revelations from God, I did little better than the other courtyard "prophets." So what was I doing wrong?

43. Magic

M‍Y PREACHING WAS INTERRUPTED ONE DAY BY THE ARRIVAL OF a famous magus, a man named Elymas—the same name as that of master magician of the Academy—but this Elymas was said to come from the island of Paphos. Word of his imminent appearance served as a giant broom, sweeping the Court of the Gentiles virtually clean, sending the hoards to watch him at his chosen site at the garden of Gethsemane, across the Kidron Valley from the Temple. There was no reason for me to stay in the empty courtyard, and I joined the crowd to satisfy my curiosity.

Elymas had positioned himself on the hillside, in the heart of a garden of olive trees. He had a long white beard, equally white hair, and was dressed in a magnificent robe that flowed like a river as he swept his arms through the air. Looking at this voluminous clothing, I wondered what hidden objects he kept in it that would soon "miraculously" appear. I worked my way up the hillside and a little off to the side, the better to observe his magic.

Something about the way he turned his head struck me as familiar. I moved closer yet. His arm—the way he held it crooked—I had seen only one person do that before. Could it be? The longer I watched, the more I became convinced that this was indeed my former master, Elymas of the Academy of Zarathustra. He had come down a long way from his prestigious position at the Academy. Or had he?

He began by handling some supposedly poisonous vipers. I doubt he could have guessed that in his audience was a former student who had attended his lecture on draining the poison from living snakes. He produced blood from a melon handed to him by a man in the audience. He turned a clay pigeon into a live one, which flew off. That trick is based on the fact, unsuspected by most people, that a pigeon becomes completely docile and quiet when confined to a small sack, so that it is as easily handled as any passive load.

Once the people in the crowd had lost most of their skepticism, Elymas began his healings. He chose three men to come forward, one on crutches, one blind, and a third with a deformed arm. Probably paid actors, I guessed. From the totality and immediacy of their cures, I concluded I was right.

His grand cure, the one for which he was apparently famous, was to be the physical removal of an evil spirit from the naked chest of a diseased man. He bared his arms—to prevent blood from splattering on his robe, he explained. The man lay quietly on a bench as Elymas washed his hands. Then he turned to the man, and suddenly thrust his fingers into the man's chest, as blood spurted out, and the crowd gasped. I too marveled—not at Elymas's healing powers, but at his mastery of illusion. It was the first trick whose sleight wasn't obvious. I couldn't figure out any way the blood could have been carried there by his empty hands. The bleeding slowed, and Elymas now cupped one hand over the man's bare chest, and pulled out strings of rotten flesh. Where did that putrid meat come from?

Suddenly I remembered the wooden finger tips I had carved, the ones that had to fit tightly enough to hold blood without leaking. The crowd was cheering now as the man arose, wiping the blood off his skin with a rag. But when he wiped I was looking not at him, but at Elymas—in particular, at his hands—and for just an instant I could see an unnaturally long thumb. A moment later it was gone.

Elymas continued by asking God to tell him the woes of those in the multitude. He then called out the names and ailments of many in the group, a trick that could have been easily achieved with help of a few accomplices talking to the crowd as they had gathered.

Elymas concluded by collecting donations of coins, jewelry, anything of value, which he said he would sacrifice to the Lord to cause similar miracles to occur "within the year" to all who made the sacrifice. "The Lord will repay a hundredfold to those of you who show your faith!" It was the most blatant sacrilege and religious perversion I had ever witnessed. I found it distressing to watch the poor and crippled parting with their meager possessions. Dozens of people threw their possessions into the wooden "ark" that Elymas opened: coins, belts, sandals, and even tools. Most of these people could ill afford these sacrifices.

I wanted to run to Elymas's altar, to announce that he was a fraud, to expose him. But I was exhausted from my own failure in the Court of the Gentiles, and I doubted that I could successfully counter this crafty and experienced magician.

Why had Elymas succeeded in captivating the faith of these people—when I had failed? Why had they succumbed to this charlatan, this man willing to manipulate their religious instincts for his own gain? How could he convince them that *he* was a messenger of God? And was Elymas any worse than the priests and rabbis themselves, who not only benefit from the required sacrifices, but who also collect a ten- percent tithe from the income of virtually all Jews? This was the money that had gone to construct the Temple; this was the money that Rabbi Shuwal had used to try to buy little Mary Magdalene. Wasn't this tithe just as perverse as the rapacity of this magus?

It was not I who was enamored of the use of magic and illusion. It was the Jewish people. They would not listen—unless attracted with signs, miracles, and prophecies fulfilled.

I had used calculated deception only once—for the walk on the Sea of Galilee. And ever since, I had regretted that act, because it had trapped me in a fabric of lies. I could tell my disciples that the water at Cana had already been replaced by wine, that the fish and loaves had been delivered by Judas—but I could not explain to them that I had knowingly deceived them with my walk on the Sea. That act had been a mistake—perhaps even a sin. And yet that was what the Jews seemed to require.

Yes, there were those other deceptions: my healings. Jews ascribed all cures to God, so as long as I healed, I was credited with miracles. Even the priests and rabbis invoked God when they set bones or prescribed medicines. I could not even *deny* these "miracles," for if I admitted my training in Babylon, Jewish patients would consider my treatments a sinful disregard of God's wishes.

Someday complete honesty will be possible, I hoped. But as I surveyed the minuscule group of disciples I had attracted at the Temple, I thought, the Jewish people are not yet ready for it.

Still, I resolved not to use willful deception. Through the grace of God, I had received training as a healer. In Capernaum I had used my skills to ease suffering, and my followers had interpreted my work as a sign. Perhaps it was. And because they took it as a sign, they listened to my revelations, understood the deeper meaning of the law, and were healed in spirit.

Yet in Jerusalem, I had forgotten all that. I had spent too much time preaching and not enough tending to the illnesses and hurts of my people.

Perhaps it was yet another kind of arrogance to depend completely on my poor skills as an orator. I decided to make use of the gifts that God had given me.

I continued preaching at the Temple every day, but on my way there and back, I stopped just outside the city walls. There, at the fountain of Siloam, my apostles announced that Jesus of Nazareth, a great *healer,* would treat the infirm—after a brief sermon.

And once again I was treating rashes, headaches, fever and wounds—with herbs, medicines, careful advice, ritual prayer, and love of their fellow creatures. Before and after and while I healed, I taught them to forego hatred, to love and forgive, and to see and feel the preeminence of the spiritual world. When besieged by the lame, blind, and otherwise incurably ill beggars, all I could offer was hope—hope that God loved them too. And even without a cure, many of them became faithful followers who came to the fountain every day. As at Capernaum, even the lame walked better, and the partially blind saw better, once they accepted my reassurances that their affliction was not God's retribution for sin.

As my reputation grew, so did the crowds that came to listen to me at the Temple. They came to see the man who did the healings of Siloam—but after they saw me, they stopped and listened. Frequently I attracted more than a hundred listeners, not yet the thousands of Galilee, but a new beginning. And I began to see among my faithful not just the poor and the am ha'arez, but merchants and tradesmen, and even—more frequently—the occasional Pharisee.

44. Stoning

I NEVER SAW THE BRICK THAT SMASHED INTO MY FACE. AS I began to fall off the stand, I reached out to stop myself, but there was nothing to grab. I remember feeling embarrassed when I landed on two men who had been sitting at my feet, and I remember feeling the coolness of the cobblestones against my jaw, seeing the pool of blood accumulating near it, and thinking, I must move, for blood is unclean. But I can't move; my strength is gone. The small crowd is shouting, but I don't understand why. What is happening? I can't even turn my head. Something strikes my back. More shouting. A rock hits my forehead. More blood. They are stoning me. I must protect my head, I must get up, I must get out of here. They will kill me.

Powerful arms grab me under my arms, and pull me rapidly over the worn stones of the pavement. Is that you, father? No, it is Judas Iscariot. Judas, I didn't know you were so strong. I sent you to Capernaum—what are you doing here? Now my legs are lifted. It is quiet. I am indoors. Finally I can rest.

I had never expected to be physically attacked in the Court of the Gentiles, on holy ground, but I had been naive. The crowd had been unusually large that day, perhaps two hundred. Soon, I hoped, it would be thousands, as it had been in Galilee. But—I now wonder—how many on that day were hired thugs?

On the day of the attack, I had been preaching about the kingdom of God, how easily we can enter it; how it is a world that exists everywhere, a spiritual kingdom that knows no death. "These truths were revealed to me by God in the wilderness," I said.

"No! It was Satan!" came a shout. "You are possessed by Satan himself!"

"I'm speaking the truth," I said. "Why don't you believe me?"

"He's a Samaritan!"

"How little you understand," I said, "if you think that an insult."

"He's a foreigner! A devil! He told us that he's possessed!"

"Possessed with the holy spirit—that's what I said. God speaks to you—through me!"

"He says we won't die! " came a roaring voice, as powerful as that of the Baptist. "But only if we obey him! Abraham was the mightiest of the prophets, and *he* died! This blasphemer thinks he is a god! But we know there is only one God!" Did this man not understand, or was he distorting my words purposefully? He pointed at me accusingly. "You place yourself greater than all the prophets—and yet *they* all died!" He turned towards the crowd and shouted, "Men of Israel! We have here a man who thinks he cannot die!" I suspect that was the cue, for general shouting followed, and then I was hit by the brick.

❖ ❖ ❖

I awoke on a mat in a familiar room—in the home of Nicodemus's friend—and my secret disciple—Arimathea, who had a small house in Perea just on the other side of the Jordan River. I wondered for a moment why I was there, until the throbbing of my head reminded me. Magdalene suddenly appeared over me, her sweet smile illuminated by the light of the oil lamp in her hand. She put the lamp on a table, and wiped my face with a cool wet piece of cloth. From her gentleness when she approached my temple, and from the sharp pain when she reached it, I knew that that was where I had been hit.

"It's good that you're awake," she said. "Is the pain bad, my dear Jesus?" I shook my head to indicate no, but it throbbed when I did. "Well, I don't believe you. Your face is badly swollen. Can you see out of your right eye?" I nodded. "Good. Nicodemus sent a Greek doctor, and he said that he didn't think your skull was cracked." Magdalene gently wiped my face again with the cool cloth. It was splotched with blood. "They might have killed you."

Through unsteady lips I muttered, "That's what they were trying to do."

"Don't talk, Jesus. Just rest. This bruise on your head is a badge of honor, like the one you told me your father Joseph once received. The pain will pass. Nicodemus said to tell you that you'll be reborn."

His words made me smile, and that hurt too. "Where is Judas?" I asked.

"Oh, yes, Judas—it was Judas who saved you. He told me he had been watching you, from the other side of the courtyard. You're lucky he was there. But he's gone now. We don't know where."

"He was supposed to be in Capernaum."

"I guess that the Lord blessed you by bringing him back early. How do you feel? Are you hungry? I've made some Nazareth soup." I shook my head. "Then rest. Try to sleep."

Two weeks after the attack, Thomas finally found Judas and brought him to me. "Judas Iscariot, my brother," I said. "I thank you." But my warmth elicited no smile.

Judas pointed to Thomas, and said sullenly, "Send him away." Thomas withdrew immediately. Judas scowled at me. "Why do you keep your location secret?" he demanded. "So your disciples won't see that you can't heal yourself?"

"Judas, I only seek quiet while I recover."

"Your apostles spread the rumor that you escaped unhurt. Yet even they don't know where you are."

"Judas—you risked your life for me. Is that a bruise on your forehead?" Judas turned away, as if to hide it from me. I asked him, "But why were you there? You had gone to Capernaum to see Josiah, to . . ."

"No, Jesus. That was *my* deception." His voice quavered. "I stayed behind—to expose you!"

"But you rescued me. . . . You saved my life."

"I was waiting for a miracle," he said, his voice almost breaking, "for a false healing, and then I was going to expose you." He lowered his face to his hands. He sobbed quietly, and without looking up said, "But you never did. Not in the Temple courtyard."

"Miracles aren't important," I said. "It's love of God and men that I wish to teach."

Suddenly Judas looked up and snapped, "You can't perform miracles!"

"What . . . what do you mean?"

"You know what I mean! You never calmed the sea. It was no more of a miracle than when you fed the multitude with food I brought myself."

"I never said that I calmed the sea—or produced the bread and fish. . . ."

"But you let them believe it. Andrew and Peter *still* believe the lies. You make fools of those who trust you. How can you?"

"If Andrew and Peter refuse to believe the truth—is that my fault?" Judas glowered at me, and I felt uncomfortable. "And what harm is there in it?"

"And when you walked on the sea . . ." Judas said, "I saw you do it, and I don't know how you did it, but I don't believe it was a miracle. It was a trick, some sort of illusion."

"Walking on water is nothing, Judas." My own voice quavered now. "God surrounds us with miracles, true miracles. Children are miracles. Life is a miracle. Love is the greatest miracle of all, and yet..."

"Hypocrite!" he screamed. "It's all deceit! You're a liar! A fraud!"

I was trembling now. "I never lied, Judas."

"But you *let* people believe lies. You let others say things that weren't true. You lied with your face, with your smiles, with your actions. You lied through your apostles."

"I believed and I still believe that I was bringing to you a great truth from God, one that he had given me personally."

"And I believed that too," Judas said in a whisper, as if he were in too much pain to speak aloud. "For a long time, I believed that too. That's why I came to you in Capernaum. I had heard of your miracles, but they meant nothing to me. I didn't care about magic. I knew that there were means of healing that I didn't understand. Magicians and false prophets can cure illness. But I came to you because you spoke a truth that hadn't been uttered before, at least one that I had never heard. It was a truth that saved my life. You spoke with more than wisdom. You spoke with authority."

"My words now are the same as they were then."

"Oh, no, but now I know. You are clever with words, Jesus of Nazareth, too clever. Now let *me* speak with authority. You can't speak the truth while living a lie. You can't give us the word of God while allowing deceit to fester unabated around you! You've *used* us, used everyone, everyone you pretend to love, for your own purposes."

"What purposes are those?"

Judas shook his head. "I don't know." He spoke now in the voice of an exhausted man. "I honestly don't know. Maybe that's why I've stayed with you for so long—to find out. I don't understand you. I no longer understand anything. I once thought that you sought power, but now— no, you don't seem to. You allow us to call you the Messiah, but—I don't know. I'm confused."

"I proclaim the kingdom of God on earth."

"Is the kingdom of God a kingdom of deceit?"

"Judas, you're very angry, and I understand that. Let me assure you that I face great difficulties that you don't recognize, that you don't understand. The guidance of the Lord sometimes leads us through tangled and tortuous paths. Remember the suffering of Job, and how it too made no sense? Now you know the physical danger I'm in. You've seen it yourself. Did you appreciate the threat, before I was stoned? I believe that the Lord sent you to save my life, and perhaps to do more, although I know not what. It's a time when we, you and I, must depend on faith. Don't do anything rash. Pray to God for understanding, and for compassion. Cast out anger, and allow your soul to be filled with love. Trust me, Judas. Trust me and I can help you to understand."

"I wish I could. I wish I could trust somebody."

"Then trust in God, Judas. Ask yourself what is true, what is real, whether the spiritual world of God is here, now, as I have taught, and whether God wants us to love all his creations. Aren't these revelations as clear to you as they are to me? Isn't God speaking to you, too? I've served as a conduit for God's word, but you can pray to God yourself. Let him talk to you and he will, in little whispers. Don't let my presumed failings make you doubt your own revelations. You came to me not because I was perfect, but because you knew what I was saying was true. None of that has changed. Have faith in God, Judas, faith in God. Don't despair because you've discovered that I too am a sinner. Men can strive for God's ideal, but they will always fall short, despite their most sincere efforts. Without sin, men wouldn't be human. Only God can be perfect. God knows we'll fall short, and when we do, he is merciful. It's in this mercy that he shows his great love for us. Stay with me, Judas. Be my brother."

Judas sat in silence for a long time. As I watched him, I thought I could sense his anger fading, or rather transforming into a mixture of confusion and hurt, like that of an adolescent who has just discovered his parents aren't perfect but can't decide whether he still loves them or not.

"Rabbi?" he finally said. "Rabbi, I'm lost."

"Don't be afraid, Judas, for it isn't me, but God who is your shepherd, and God is all powerful. He won't let you fall astray. Pray, Judas. Pray, and have faith in God."

After Judas left, I reflected on our meeting, and worried that I hadn't been completely candid with him, for I had neither explicitly admitted nor denied his accusations. But, I thought, perhaps caution had been appropriate, for neither had he been completely candid with me. He had said nothing about his visits to the Sanhedrin.

It was I, not Judas, who was truly lost. Once the Sanhedrin had determined that my crowds were growing, they had decided to eliminate me. They knew the critical time was before I had gained enough of a following to protect me. They had correctly gauged the spirit of my followers and had concluded they could safely attack me.

And if I attempted to return to the Temple or to preach anywhere nearby, they would do so again. I would be killed. But to remain away was to abandon my mission. How could the Messiah, the spiritual Messiah, not be victorious at the Temple?

Should I return and be attacked again? Does God intend me to die—to be a martyr—like John? Have I followed this tortuous path to Jerusalem simply to be crushed by stones?

Bat qol, Father, Lord, God, speak to me! Tell me what I must do. And give me the courage to do it.

In Jerusalem I had become known for the bright white robe I wore. So I felt confident that nobody would recognize me when I donned a coarse tunic made from brown goat hair. The swelling on my face had gone down, and the bruise looked like little more than sunburnt skin. I felt physically strong and eager to get out. It was my spirit that was still suffering, and maybe . . . maybe the fresh air and exercise would help.

And indeed, as Thomas and I wandered around Perea and the other villages on the outskirts of Jerusalem, nobody paid us any attention. Once again I was an ordinary person, and it felt restful. Once again I could watch craftsmen work in their shops, watch the farmers in their fields, and watch children play in the streets. Nobody disturbed me. No beggars came for food, no sinners came seeking forgiveness, no cripples came to me hoping to be healed. A burden had been lifted from my shoulders. And yet—my life had never seemed so empty.

"It's over," I lamented to Thomas, as we wandered through the streets of Perea. "I can't return to Galilee for fear of Herod, and I can't preach in the Temple for fear of the Sanhedrin. They would not let me escape a second time."

"I warned you not to trust Nicodemus," Thomas said.

"Nicodemus admits he misjudged. The decision to attack me was made when he was absent. It is a mistake that he said he will never make again. But he says that he can't guarantee that another attack will not be made. In fact, he predicts it, if I dare return to the Temple."

We came to the shop of a glassblower. On his bench he had an assortment of bowls and plates and jewelry. I picked up a blue ornament and admired it as it sparkled in the sunlight. The glassblower walked over to us, looked up and down at my robe, and said with a sneer, "Six denari. If you can't afford it, don't touch."

"I'm sorry," I said, putting it down. "It reminded me of one my mother once owned."

We walked together silently. It had started with that piece of glass. Was this now the end? Ever since the attack, I had prayed and listened. But no answer had come.

Suddenly Thomas spoke: "We need a miracle, Jesus!"

"Yes, I know, Thomas. But how long must we wait for God to provide it?"

"God has provided!" Thomas said excitedly. "We just haven't been listening!" He clapped his hands, looked up to the clouds, and said, "Thank you, Lord!"

"Thomas, what is it? What have you thought of?"

"It's just as I already said, Jesus. We need a miracle. And God has provided. He has given you the training and experience. The rest is up to us. It must be something that will rouse the crowds, something as wondrous as the walk on the sea."

"You mean another deception?"

"It is the only sign that the Jews of Jerusalem will understand. That's why God prepared you . . ."

"For deceit?"

"He prepared you as he prepared Moses, and Elijah, and all the prophets. They used illusions and magic—and so must we. It's what the Jews expect and demand. Who are we to question God's ways?"

I sighed deeply. "Thomas, my illusions have caused nothing but trouble. And besides, even were I to perform a 'miracle,' it wouldn't be enough. They would attack me again, and it would take a *true* miracle to keep the rocks from crushing my head."

"They dare not attack a man with a thousand disciples."

"I have fewer than a hundred truly faithful."

"You still have thousands in Capernaum. The Passover pilgrimage is near. With a great miracle, they would all come. In the crowds, there is safety."

We continued walking together quietly for a while. Thomas seemed to be thinking hard. Then he said, "You'll raise a man from the dead."

"I've already done that—or at least they say I have. It wasn't enough."

"The daughter of Jairus, who was sleeping? It was enough in Capernaum. Do you forget how many new disciples came to you after that? But it didn't happen here, and the Jews of Jerusalem don't believe it. You have to do it right. It can't just be a sleeping child. It has to be more vivid."

Thomas appeared lost in thought. "Brother, I think I have it," he finally said. "Imagine that the man had been dead for three days and his body was already rotting—it could be smelled outside the tomb. The dead man was not one of your apostles, or disciples, not a beggar or traveler, but a man who lived near Jerusalem, someone known to the local residents. It would work! Your disciples would flock from Capernaum to Jerusalem for the pilgrimage, and local Jews would triple the size of the group. Surrounded by a flock of thousands, you could reenter Jerusalem without fear."

"Whoever we use," I said, "will be arrested and interrogated. He would have to be someone whose total loyalty we can depend on."

And with those words, I slipped into my penultimate sin, for I already knew that I would do as Thomas suggested. I had lost hope, and Thomas had rekindled it. After a mere month of despair, I had already lost faith— faith that God would provide an answer, in his own time. The sin was already committed, and all that was left were the details.

"Nicodemus?" I asked.

"No," Thomas replied. "Nicodemus couldn't be the resurrected man. We're not going to fool the Sanhedrin, Jesus. They'll know it was magic, and if we use Nicodemus, it would only expose him."

"Then who, Thomas? I can tell from your smile that you have an answer."

"Lazarus."

It was the solution. He was known to be a friend of mine, but the closeness of our relationship had been kept secret so that my frequent residence at his house wouldn't be suspected. Would he do it? His gratitude for the salvation of Magdalene seemed endless, and he professed belief in my teachings, but he had never shown a true passion for them. This was asking more than letting us use his home. How would he react? I didn't know. It was dangerous. This would be a true test of his faith.

I let Thomas develop most of the plan, although I made critical suggestions and changes. Only when it was complete did I present it to Lazarus. He sat and listened to the details and nodded. I was surprised at his easy acquiescence. "You have no doubts? You enter this with no hesitation?" I said.

"If this is what must be done."

"It is. There's no alternative. We wouldn't put you in danger,

Lazarus, except as a last resort."

"Don't worry about me, Jesus. The Sanhedrin are cowards. They'll attack you on their own ground—Jerusalem—but they won't dare send their thugs to Bethany."

. "They may call for your arrest."

"Let them. They're vicious—I'm still shocked over how you were attacked—but Nicodemus is right about one thing: if I'm arrested, I'll be in open court, and they'll have to follow the rules. Unless they have witnesses, they'll be helpless. So I doubt that they will actually arrest me, because it would only help spread the story."

"What about your cousin Martha? Can we trust her?"

"Let's just do it all when she is away," Lazarus said. "She is a devoted follower of your teachings, but the fewer people who know, the better."

The plan went almost as expected. I traveled to Ephraim, leaving Thomas and Magdalene at Lazarus's home. After a few days, Thomas came and appeared before a gathering of disciples to announce to me that Lazarus was "sick," and that I must hurry to Bethany to cure him. But then I announced that I knew Lazarus had died shortly after Thomas had left Bethany. I delayed a bit longer, sending my apostles on ahead, so that they could verify that Lazarus had already been buried and so that they would have time to let people know that I was coming. Nicodemus and Arimathea had arranged for the tomb and burial.

When we finally returned to Bethany, Lazarus had been "dead" for four days. We arrived at the prescribed time—but as we approached his home, I was startled to see Martha running towards me, followed by a desperate looking Magdalene. A crowd of more than a hundred people were there, for Thomas had spread word of my imminent arrival.

"Lord!" Martha cried out, falling to her feet. "My brother is dead!"

Magdalene caught up, put her arms around Martha, and tried to calm her. To me she said, "Martha came back yesterday unexpectedly, only to find that her cousin Lazarus had died and already been buried." She looked towards me plaintively and shrugged her shoulders. Once again, we had not anticipated everything that could happen. And this time, poor Martha was the unintended victim. I was determined to end her suffering as quickly as possible.

"Lord," Martha cried out hysterically to me, "if you had been here, my cousin Lazarus would not have died!"

"Your cousin will rise again," I said.

"I know. On the day of judgment he will rise," she sobbed.

"No, Martha. You need not wait. I bring his resurrection and return his life today! Do you accept my revelations?"

"I believe that you are the Messiah!" she said.

This pronouncement was an unexpected stroke of good fortune. It was heard by more than a hundred people, each of whom might report it to a dozen others. This was going much better than I had hoped, with the clear exception of Martha's suffering, which I was anxious to end.

"Show me where you've buried him," I directed. Thomas had argued that I shouldn't ask this—that a man about to use the powers of the Almighty to raise the dead would hardly need help locating the body. But I felt that the illusion would be more convincing if I pretended that I didn't know the location.

Lazarus had been entombed in a cave, since raising him from an earthen grave would have been considerably more difficult. The entrance had been closed with a large wheel-shaped stone. I asked some of the assembled crowd to move it—another request for aid that a true miracle worker wouldn't need. But get the crowd to participate as much as possible, Simon Magus had once advised.

Every eye was on the entrance to the tomb. Suddenly a woman shrieked. Others in the crowd just gasped. I was glad nobody was looking at me, because I barely suppressed a laugh. Lazarus had appeared, bound in burial clothes, and with a cloth tied around his face. On his hands he wore thin lambskin gloves stuffed with pieces of rotten meat. Nicodemus and Thomas had overdone it a bit, and poor Lazarus was so bundled up that he could hardly walk. All I need now, I thought, is to have him trip on one of his own rags, fall, and crack his skull. I met him halfway. "Loosen his wrappings!" I ordered.

Thomas, who had been waiting by the tomb, came up and untied the wrappings. Everyone else seemed afraid to approach. As soon as he was free, Lazarus ran to me, fell at my feet, kissed them, and overacted a bit, but the gathered crowd seemed to love it. I pulled off the lambskin on his hands, and stuffed it into a pouch under my white tunic. I took Lazarus by his shoulders, raised him to his feet, and said to everyone, "Did I not tell you that you would see the glory of God if you believed?"

If I hadn't been so caught up in the excitement myself, perhaps I would have noticed what Thomas saw: Iscariot, standing to the side, ruefully watching our show.

Nicodemus advised that I leave Bethany immediately. He had to report the event to the Sanhedrin, and he was certain that they would launch an investigation. From that day on, I could travel in only one of two ways for my protection: in very large groups or in secrecy.

The word of Lazarus's resurrection spread like a wildfire throughout Jerusalem and the surrounding countryside. According to Nicodemus, the Sanhedrin interpreted the miracle to mean that an insurrection was imminent. And perhaps it was, although not a military rebellion of the kind they expected. It was time to proclaim myself the Messiah publicly, and to return to Jerusalem. I met with Thomas and Nicodemus at the home of Arimathea to plan this important step.

"Your entry should be triumphant!" Nicodemus advised. "You'll enter the city on a donkey, so that all will know that you are the prophesied king of the Jews. Your fearlessness in entering the city will prove to all that you are indeed the anointed one!"

"And the crowds will protect you," Thomas added.

45. Hosanna!

A MULTITUDE OF MEN IN BLUE AND WHITE PASSOVER ROBES flowed like a river through the winding streets of Jerusalem, crying "Hosanna!" Women wearing red and yellow smocks sat scattered among the rooftops like hillside wildflowers, and they shouted "Hosanna!" From doorways and windows voices sang out, "Hosanna! Blessed is the King of Israel! He comes! In the name of the Lord! The kingdom of King David! Praise the Lord! Hosanna!" As I rode the donkey through the narrow streets of Jerusalem, children wearing brightly colored shirts ran alongside throwing palm leaves on the pavement in front of me. When I stepped down from the donkey, old men pulled off their tasseled woolen cloaks and threw them on the street for me to walk on.

Hosanna! The word thrilled me, frightened the Sanhedrin, and worried the Roman militia into making special preparations. Originally just a verse from the book of Psalms, the word was now recognized by all as the greeting for the Anointed One, the Christ, the Messiah. The multitudes were singing, in effect, "Save us, we implore you, save us!"

My entry into Jerusalem was joyous and exhilarating, triumphant, greater than I had ever imagined it could be, and I felt I had Nicodemus to thank. His genius was evident and impressive. He had coordinated my trip from Perea, through Jericho, and along the main paths of the Passover pilgrimage. At every crossroad he had stationed a disciple to tell the story that the Messiah had appeared, that he had raised a man named Lazarus from the dead, and that soon this Messiah would be coming. My disciples recounted my miracles, the signs, the prophecies fulfilled. They announced to all that I had been born in Bethlehem, the City of David, the prophesied birthplace of the Messiah. They promised that when I reached Jerusalem I would proclaim the arrival of the kingdom of God on earth. They invited all the travelers to wait and join me in my triumphant entry to the holy city!

Many, perhaps most, of the pilgrims ignored these men, but those who listened were enough to clog the roads, causing delays and spreading excitement and anticipation. When I finally approached Jerusalem, on the prophesied donkey, the donkey that Joseph of Arimathea had supplied at Bethpage, there must have been ten thousand men, women, and children marching with me, stretching a quarter mile ahead and behind. Word traveled twice as fast as the procession, and as we crested the ridge of the Mount of Olives, I could hear cheers from the walls of Jerusalem, even though I was still a half-mile away.

Nicodemus told me later that he had organized twenty men to distribute palm leaves to children of Jerusalem. These men would also throw their cloaks ahead of my donkey's path, and shout "Hosanna!" as I approached, enflaming cheers from the gathered crowds. He must have spent a small fortune on the palms and cloaks that were trampled on that day.

The procession moved so slowly that on that first afternoon, we barely had time to weave through the city. Our plan was to excite the crowds about my planned appearance in the Temple courtyard on the next day. As the sun set, a man carrying a jar of water beckoned us to follow. That was the prearranged signal, and we entered the door of a house; from there we were quickly whisked out a back door and led down narrow streets out of Jerusalem. Nicodemus advised that we stay outside the city except when the crowds were sufficiently large to provide protection, for the Sanhedrin had readied their thugs, in case they caught me alone.

The next day, a short march to Jerusalem was enough to attract sufficient disciples for safety, but not so many as to slow my entrance. That was as I wanted it, for I had an ambitious goal to accomplish. We entered the Temple grounds through the Huldah Gate, and although it was still quite early, the Court of the Gentiles was already crowded. The moneychangers and pigeon sellers had arrived before sunrise. I walked to a spot between two of the tables. The moneychanger standing beside the first table watched me approach with more interest than apprehension. After all, I was bringing a big crowd. The other moneychanger was hunched over his table, neatly arranging coins from many regions next to Hebrew ones to show his rates.

"May I give you some of the Lord's coins in exchange for the idolatrous icons of Pilate?" said the first moneychanger in a patronizing tone. "I have pretty coins with pomegranates and figs on them that are sure to please the Lord, and I'm willing to take and dispose of the pagan icons of Tiberius, in exchange for only a tiny fee." Then he moved closer to me, and said in a whisper, "If you tell your followers to come to me exclusively, I can make it worth your while."

"Get out of here!" I shouted, and he backed off. "God called his Temple the house of prayer for all nations, but you've made it a place of business and cheating and thievery." A few in the crowd shouted *Amen!*

The moneychanger glowered at me defiantly. "I'm here to serve the Lord!" he barked. "Get out of here yourself!" The crowd watched with curiosity. Had I expected the moneychanger meekly to admit guilt and leave? Perhaps, overawed by my triumphant entry on the previous day, I had expected the crowd to back me up, to cheer and shout, but except for a few scattered *amens*, they remained silent, looking curious, expectant, and bemused. In the next few minutes I could lose this crowd—or win it. My God, tell me what must I do next. What should the Messiah do next?

Without looking up, the moneychanger at the adjacent table said gruffly, "We don't cater to beggars. If you have no coins to exchange, don't block the table." Somehow this man, his way of speaking, reminded me strongly of Manasas—the moneychanger who had arrested me, and who had been my first slave master. My temper suddenly flared. Without taking time to think whether I was being seized by the holy spirit or by Satan, I grabbed the man's table and with all my strength threw it over, hard against several other tables that were also upset. Coins flew into the air and men jumped out of the way. Even after the fallen tables stopped clattering, coins continued to tinkle on the stone pavement, and several men dove to their knees to grab them.

"Liar!" I shouted at the moneychanger. "Cheat! Thief!" He backed off, startled, confused, and speechless. I turned to the tables of the other moneychangers. "Robbers!" I shouted at the others. "Bandits! You are all bandits!" Several of them started to collect the coins on their tables and hurriedly dump them into the folds of their wide belts. "Those of you who buy and sell in this sacred courtyard will be cast out like Satan!" I still couldn't bellow like the Baptist, but my voice had grown stronger. "It is written," I cried, "'My house shall be a house of prayer,' but you have made it . . ." I paused for effect, and looked around the crowd, making eye contact with as many as possible in the few seconds I allocated myself to collect all my power. Then I boomed, "You have made it into a den of thieves!"

The crowd behind me cheered, whether for their hatred of the cheating moneychangers or just out of the excitement, I don't know. I walked purposefully over to the stalls of the pigeon sellers. In anticipation they grabbed their cages, but I managed to pull a few cages away and smash them to the ground. "Out!" I shouted to the sellers, and as if on cue, a dozen pigeons flew free as the wooden cages crashed open. "Out!" I shouted again, "do not defile the house of the Lord!" The pigeons fluttered up past the Temple walls to the top of the Antonia Tower, and again the crowd erupted into cheers.

There was a stir towards the edge of the courtyard; several Roman militiamen had appeared. This was a critical moment. I had to quiet the crowd. Summoning up the spirit of John the Baptist, I relaxed my jaw, opened my mouth wide, and in the most powerful voice I could muster, I sang out one of my most famous and best sermons, one I knew to be attention-riveting: "Woe to you, scribes and Pharisees and *hypocrites!*" The crowd did calm, as they strained to hear. "Woe to you!" I continued, "for you shut the door of the kingdom of heaven against men, and yet you will never enter yourselves! Woe to you, scribes and Pharisees, hypocrites all! For you pay your tithe, even in such things as mint and anise and cumin, but you ignore the weightier matters of the law, of judgment, mercy, and faith! You are blind men who think you can serve as guides to others. You strain a gnat out of your wine, but you drink a camel! Woe to you, scribes and Pharisees and hypocrites! You clean the outsides of your cup, but inside it is full of extortion and excess! You are blind men! Clean the *inside* of the cup, and the outsides will be clean also!"

The crowd *was* riveted, and the militia was watchful but seemingly satisfied, and as I spoke, more and more people gathered at the edges of the mass of listeners. The militia, to my delight, never even allowed the merchants to reopen their stalls.

I had accomplished the extraordinary goal that I had set for myself. The Court of the Gentiles had been *cleansed.* It was a fitting beginning. More than a thousand men and women strained to hear my words. Over a thousand men and women seemed to welcome me as the Messiah.

That evening Thomas took me aside. "Peter is telling a strange story, and you've got to stop him. He's already told a crowd of disciples about it. He says that you cursed a fig tree and it died."

"I did *what?*"

"You heard me. You cursed a fig tree and killed it."

"I haven't the vaguest idea what you're talking about."

"Apparently after you left Jerusalem on the first evening, after your entry, you stopped to pick a fig from a tree and it was barren."

"Yes, I remember that."

"Well, now the tree is dead, all the way down to the roots. Peter is telling everyone who will listen that it died because you were angry with it."

"It sounds to me like a stunt *you* might have pulled."

"No, Jesus, it's not my style. I would never have you lose your temper at a tree, or punish it for such a trivial offense. And the tree really is dead," Thomas said. "I went to see it myself. It looks to me as if the roots were soaked with a strong poison. I assumed you had somebody do it for you."

"Without consulting you, Thomas? No, never. Besides, there's no need to use magic any more. I can't imagine . . ."

Suddenly Thomas said, "Nicodemus! It must have been Nicodemus. He poisoned the tree, and pointed it out to Peter. I'll check, but I'm sure I'm right."

"But Nicodemus wasn't even with me when I looked for a fig."

"No, but his men were, leading you out the secret exit of the city. Jesus, Nicodemus has his men spying on you, and then he does things like this!"

"He doesn't spy. Nicodemus coordinates the secret disciples. When they tell him what happens, that isn't spying. Besides, we don't know for sure that it was he who killed the fig tree. But I'll tell Peter to stop talking about it. I'll remind him that we teach love and kindness, not retribution and anger. And, Thomas, I'll try to control my own temper better from now on. I can't teach love and kindness through violence. I apologize for my violence in the courtyard."

There was a small smile on the corners of Thomas's lips. I had suspected that he was unhappy with my apparent loss of temper with the moneychangers. Later that evening I spoke with Peter, and asked him to stop spreading the story of the murdered tree.

46. Court of the Gentiles

My arrival at the Court of the Gentiles on the next day was greeted with a great cheer. I had no trouble passing through the multitude, for they parted like the Red Sea as I slowly walked among them. I had instructed Peter and Andrew to set up a platform for me, not by the arcades that formed the outer walls of the courtyard, but in front of the Temple itself.

No sooner had I stood up on the platform and looked down on the vast and colorful crowd than a wondrous quiet spread like a wave across the yard. They were waiting—waiting to receive spiritual nourishment. And I was there to feed them. I began, "Blessed are you who hunger and thirst after righteousness, for you shall be filled! Blessed are they who are persecuted for their righteousness, for theirs is the kingdom of heaven!"

I spoke for nearly two hours, to the most diverse and responsive crowd I had ever addressed. I told of my revelations, about communion with God, and how they could speak to God themselves. Soon I would ask them to pray, I thought, and then I could take a rest.

But suddenly a powerful voice from the middle of the crowd rang out, "Who gives you the right?" I continued speaking, but as soon as I paused, it came again. "Who gives you the right?" My listeners turned to a man dressed in a white cloak about a hundred feet from me. I couldn't see his face, although his voice seemed to thunder across the courtyard. "You tell people that they can speak to God whenever they want, and that he will speak back. What right do you have to say these things? Who gives you such right?" I knew what he wanted: for me to claim that my miracles were my credentials. Then he would compare me to magi, seers, and other pagans.

"Do not seek the man who is in contact with God," I shouted back, not to him but to the entire crowd. "But seek instead God himself, for this you can do whenever you wish, through prayer!"

"What right have you?" the voice shouted again. I had learned that trick of rhetoric at the Academy: to repeatedly ask the same question as if I had not answered it. Whenever I paused he yelled, "What right have you?"

I had anticipated how the Sanhedrin would counter my success at the Temple with righteous heckling. Their pawns in this tactic would be Pharisees, many of whom were experienced lawyers. And this man must be the first. But I was ready.

"Let me then ask you one question," I shouted back to the voice, "and if you answer, I will answer yours." Now he had to be quiet for a moment. To defeat a man who cares not for what you say but only wishes to disrupt, you must use rhetorical methods as powerful as his. "My question to you is this: Who gave John the right to baptize?" I knew that John was revered by many in the crowd. If the heckler said that John had no credentials, he would be booed out of the courtyard. Yet he couldn't admit that John was anointed by God without leaving open the possibility that others besides the priests and the recognized prophets had divine blessings. He remained silent.

Yet to some extent he had been successful. He had interrupted my sermon, and forced me to quiet him. There would be many such hecklers, I knew. I would have to quiet them all quickly, while keeping the crowd on my side, or my teaching would go nowhere.

After a quiet period of prayer, an older man with white hair and beard spoke out. He had worked his way close to me. "Rabbi," he began, "we know that you speak the truth, and that you teach the way of God." His was a patronizing approach, but I knew it could be just as dangerous as that of the challenging heckler. "We know that you don't care what men say, but only about the word of God. Tell us, therefore, what you think about giving tribute to Caesar?"

This was a trap that I had expected, for I had encountered it before in Galilee. If I counseled nonpayment of taxes, I would be considered an open rebel against the Roman rule, and the soldiers would be forced into action. And yet if I said taxes should be paid, I would look like a Roman collaborator. How could I keep my spiritual authority without fomenting rebellion?

"Show me the tribute money!" I demanded. The crowd waited while he fumbled in his belt, and then he held up a coin. "Pass it to me!" I shouted. It moved from hand to hand until it reached me. I took it, held it up, and carefully examined it, while all watched. "Whose image is this? Whose name is on this coin?"

"It is Caesar's," he answered.

"Then, give to Caesar the things which are Caesar's." I contemptuously flung the coin into the crowd near him. "But give to God those things that are God's." This was a righteous answer, and yet not a rebellious one. The kingdom of God does not interfere with the kingdoms of this world. As I had promised God, mine was a spiritual ministry, not a political revolution.

Had I won the debate? Yes, for my response would spread among my disciples, and they would learn. But I had lost, too. As I looked around, I saw a trickle of people leaving. And in the far courtyard I could see hundreds of Jews streaming up the steps to the Portal of the Priests, carrying their recently purchased pigeons, clutching what were undoubtedly "clean" coins, going to pay their Temple tax.

I had cleansed the courtyard, but the Jews still carried their tribute to the priests. I had attained prominence in the courtyard of the Temple, but it appeared to be a small achievement. I could capture the attention of a thousand Jews, but my ministry would be a failure unless I could reach farther, much farther.

Alas, I continued to win the arguments, but to lose my crowd. The Pharisees hacked away at me slowly, like patient woodsmen slowly chipping at a tree, even when unskilled, doing damage. They interrupted my sermons, forced me to change the subject, and engaged me in intellectual points of Scripture, whereas what most Jews needed was not a debater, one who always had the right answer, but a spiritual leader who could show them how to remove hatred from their hearts. Even my challengers' weakest arguments served to interrupt the flow of my lessons and to wear me down. Eventually the soldiers allowed some merchants to set up their stalls again. They looked prepared, and I doubted that I could overturn their stands a second time.

"Thomas," I said, "I need your help."

He brightened considerably at my words. "Of course, Jesus. Of course. Let's go to the garden." I must have looked distraught, for he said, "Don't worry. We'll be safe. We've changed locations every day, and I'm sure nobody knows we are here."

We had stayed in four houses in four days, since my "triumphant" entry into Jerusalem. This one was the home of a wealthy merchant, a friend of Nicodemus and a secret disciple of mine. The house was in Gethsemane, just across a deep ravine from the city and less than a mile away. A few hundred feet from the house was a magnificent orchard and garden that was watered by an elaborate aqueduct system. In addition to the trees, the wealthy residents of Gethsemane maintained an extraordinary garden of flowers and exotic plants, making it the most beautiful area near Jerusalem.

I wandered through the flowers, enjoying the smells, unsure how to tell Thomas the fateful news. In the silence, Thomas began.

"Jesus, you mustn't concern yourself with those you lose," he said. "Many who came four days ago were there out of curiosity. But I can sense that the solid core of disciples is growing. More and more people are coming back—I recognize them. Think of the importance of each soul that you have saved, and take joy and encouragement in that. You are in the Temple courtyard every day teaching God's word to hundreds of the Jews of Jerusalem." He paused, and looked discouraged that his words weren't cheering me. "Jesus, your time has finally come!" he said.

"But I don't have enough time," I replied.

"Patience, brother! Other prophets were ignored too, at first. Think of Jeremiah . . ."

"We've been betrayed by Iscariot," I interrupted.

"That's not new."

"He's agreed to lead the Sanhedrin to where we are staying, to where they can arrest me. They'll pay him thirty pieces of silver for my life."

Thomas's face had turned white. "Blood money? Judas? Give them information, yes, but lead the Romans to arrest you? I never thought. . . . Was it Nicodemus who told you this?"

"Of course."

"You can't trust Nicodemus," Thomas said.

"He simply brings the information."

"I wouldn't be so sure that it wasn't his doing."

"Thomas! Nicodemus risked his life for me. And his story makes sense. He said that Iscariot is distraught over the resurrection of Lazarus. He appeared before the Sanhedrin and called me an impostor and an agent of Satan."

"We should have ostracized Iscariot when he first betrayed you. We must do it immediately."

"There is no need for haste, Thomas. He doesn't know where we are tonight. And we must be careful not to expose Nicodemus."

"Jesus, your life is at stake!"

"We must keep our movements totally secret from Iscariot. The only safety we now have comes from Nicodemus. He'll give us whatever warning he can."

Thomas was silent. We walked together in the garden, surrounded by dark forms, stars, and magnificent smells.

"Tell me, brother. How long do you think we can continue to preach in Jerusalem and still evade capture?"

Thomas pondered my question for several seconds, looked up, and said, "Until the Passover pilgrims have departed."

"That's right. In a few days they will be gone. And when they leave, so will our protection. We will all be arrested, tried, convicted of blasphemy, and executed by stoning," I said, surprising myself with my calmness.

"Or crucified for rebellion," Thomas said, with a shudder, "like the Zealots of Siloam."

"We must withdraw," I said. "Our triumphal entry to Jerusalem was a mistake, because we didn't allow enough time to win over the city. The heckling of the Pharisees has proven too effective. We must have a stronger following when we return, enough to counter the Sanhedrin and their henchmen."

"We mustn't give up yet! We can station your apostles around the courtyard," Thomas suggested. "They can try to keep the Pharisees from approaching you so they can't interrupt."

"In Galilee we had individual Pharisees oppose us. Here they are organized. There are many more of them here, and their attacks are planned and coordinated."

"You can preach outside the city, where you can't easily be trapped."

"If I abandon the Temple area it could be seen as a defeat, as proof that I'm not the Messiah. Unless . . . unless I leave to return to the am ha'arez, to those who can't make it to the Temple. Thomas, I believe that this is what we must do. Leave Jerusalem, perhaps head south to Idumea, to people who haven't heard my revelations."

"If Herod is truly bent on your destruction, my brother, then you won't be safe even in the most remote wilderness of Israel."

"He has no jurisdiction in Idumea."

"But the Sanhedrin do. If Herod supplied forces for them to suppress a blasphemous rebel, then Pilate might accede, if only to avoid involvement in what he considers a religious dispute."

"Thomas, how can you be sure you're right?"

"How can you be sure I'm wrong?"

My heart sank. It was no longer my ministry that was at stake, but my life. *Our* lives.

I suggested, "We could retreat to Bethesda . . . or back north to Caesarea Philippi."

"Because they're in the tetrarchy of Herod's brother Philip? You think that makes them safe?"

"Herod and Philip been feuding for years. Philip considers his brother mad. He wouldn't have us arrested and turned over to Herod. We were safe there before."

"Herod Antipas is a man who offered half his tetrarchy for a dance from Salome. Now that Jesus can be considered a political force, Herod might offer just as much for your head as he did for John's, and for *that* much, Philip would accede to even a 'mad' brother."

Thomas was right. I wouldn't be safe anywhere in Israel. Nor would my disciples. Nor my brother. Could I retreat to Syria? To Rome? And preach to non-Jews? The hopelessness of my situation began to overwhelm me. How did I become so trapped? Was it the resurrection of Lazarus, or the triumphant entry?

No, it was my success. What tragic irony. Just as I was frustrated by my failure to reach more Jews, my success at reaching so many was bringing my ministry to an end.

The night felt darker and colder. The stars had disappeared. Even the flowers seemed to have lost their fragrance. It is over, I thought. A few days ago I felt the exultation of a triumphant hunter. Today I felt the fear of the cornered prey.

The dread returned, the overwhelming hopelessness of the dungeon of Sepphoris, the despair of knowing that I had slipped into the mouth of the abyss.

I looked towards Thomas, hoping for comfort, but I could not see him in the darkness.

Father, I cried silently. What would you do?

My Lord, my God. . . . Help me!

✧ ✧ ✧

Back in my room, I huddled under a woolen cover, but it seemed to offer no warmth. I could smell a physical illness beginning to envelop my body. Or was that the smell of death? I shook my head vigorously. I can't let this happen. There is something I am supposed to do, but what? My mind refused to see solutions. It seemed to be paralyzed, allowing me to envision only horrid endings: Herod slicing my neck, stones crushing my skull. . . . I understood again, as I had in the prison of Sepphoris, the intense dread that people can feel, the paralysis of despair that can drive them to take their own lives. My Lord, my God, help me!

I am on the cross, surrounded by wailing disciples. A group of boys throws rocks at me. Nobody tries to stop them. Warm blood streams down my face, coming from my scalp, where a crown of thorns pierces my skin. My chest is sliced with gashes from the scourging. I look down at my lacerated flesh. Now I know what to do, I thought. I have been trained as a physician, and this time I know how to treat these wounds, how to relieve the pain.

Pain? What pain? It doesn't hurt.

I suddenly leapt from my mat. Had I been asleep? Was that a dream, or a vision? Or was it a whisper in my ear? "Thomas!" I shouted out. He immediately appeared from the next room, as if he too had been awake. "Thomas!" I said, "I know what to do!" He said nothing, but just looked at me, his despair mixed with confusion and not yet mitigated by my sudden surge of hope. "I must be crucified!" I said.

✧ ✧ ✧

I held Magdalene's hand as I led her to the garden. Once again outside, I was surprised by the warmth of what had started as a cool evening. The moon had risen and the trees and shrubs shone in a pale, colorless light. Magdalene and I sat on a bench. Her hand shivered. "Are you cold?" I asked her.

"No, Jesus. Afraid."

I squeezed her hand gently. "Magdalene," I said, "Iscariot plans to betray my location to the Sanhedrin." She sat motionless and silent. Neither her hand nor her face gave indication of her thoughts. I continued, "I must perform one last miracle. There's no alternative." Still she said nothing. "I want you to understand. You must understand. Because the danger is great—as you already sense." She didn't even look at me. "Magdalene?"

"Jesus, you don't need to perform miracles." She spoke quietly, without turning, and withdrew her hand from mine. "I think you are deceiving yourself. If only you would learn from your own wisdom."

"What do you think I must learn?"

"Truth—the power of truth. Deceptions are unnecessary. It's when you are honest, totally honest, that you are compelling—that you speak with authority—that you speak the words of God. You know that. Forego deception, Jesus, please, I beg of you."

"Every religion has used magic, many of them for evil. I use it only for righteousness. But never again will it be necessary, not after this." I still held back, afraid to tell her the nature of the miracle I intended.

"Jesus, my dear Jesus!" She shook her head sadly. "You talk as if your ministry is a craft, like cooking or carpentry. But you are on a divine mission. Even if you needed it in the past, magic isn't necessary now."

"Without it, my ministry will end in failure."

She turned to me with a warm smile. "No, Jesus, that's not possible. Even if your ministry came to an end today, it is already a success. What can be greater than saving a soul, than showing a single human being the face of God? And that's what you have done, Jesus, not just once but countless times! You've done it for me."

"Herod will kill me."

"We can disappear, Jesus. You have many friends. The Sanhedrin will never find us."

"Abandon my ministry?"

"Abandon your ambition. Save just one soul at a time—as your father did."

"Oh, Magdalene! How can you measure the despair that fills the souls of Israel? How can I balance the small good I've done against the infinite good that is calling out, yet to be accomplished?"

"Jesus, my Jesus, you have so little faith! You have ignited a fire, a small fire, but one that will never be put out, one that can only grow. There is no need to fan the flames."

"The Messiah was to have his mission accomplished in his lifetime."

"Damn the prophecies! They're meaningless, Jesus! You know that!"

"Magdalene, I was sent here with a mission. It's all so clear now! John said that he knew the Messiah was coming, that he felt it in his heart. Now these are things that I feel within my heart. Magdalene, you know what pain is, you've recognized it in the eyes of those who came to my sermons. Their eyes were full of hatred, hatred of the Romans, of the Syrians, of the Samaritans, of other Jews. The Sadducees hate the am ha'arez, the Pharisees hate the Sadducees, the Zealots hate everybody, and they all suffer. They all seek material salvation, for they don't recognize that the kingdom of God is already here! Without God's message of love, the Jews will follow the lead of the Zealots to violence and obliteration. I foresee this! We can't wait for a small fire to grow. There isn't time. The Jews are slaves—not to Pharaoh, but to the priests. When they sacrifice at the Temple, they aren't worshipping God, they're worshipping a golden calf. I am Moses, and I am carrying the ten commandments, and my people have become idolaters. I must . . . I must split the Red Sea. God has given me the means to spread his truth throughout Judaism in one great stroke. Magdalene, I beg for your faith in me again."

Magdalene sat there with her head down, her shoulders forward, looking very fragile and vulnerable. Had she tried one last means of persuasion, to draw on my love for her, she might have succeeded, but before I could be overwhelmed with my concern for her, she spoke out. "Jesus, I think that you are wrong, but I'm not certain. Do what God tells you to do. I will pray, pray to thank God for what he has given me, and pray because I am frightened, very frightened."

47. Crucifixion

MY FINGERS CURLED AROUND THE BLOCKS OF ACACIA WOOD
as I tried to pull myself higher, to relieve the pressure of the ropes cutting
into my arms. When I attempted to relax, my arms pulled my chest tight
and I had difficulty breathing. I recalled what I had learned in Babylon,
that crucified men actually suffocated as they slumped in exhaustion.
How stupid of me, I thought, not to have put more care into the design
of the wrist blocks. If only I had smoothed the corners a little, made them
easier to grasp, I would be so much more comfortable now. The sedecu-
la, the small block on which I am partially seated—now I understand
why it is there: to support the victim and thereby drag out the ordeal for
as long as possible. I should have increased the size of that block and put
it at a better angle. Now I suffer for my negligence. I will hang on this
cross for five more hours before relief comes, and they will be difficult
and painful hours. Perhaps that's best, I thought, so that I will be convincing in my feigned death.

Nakedness is meant to be part of my humiliation, I thought, yet it
doesn't bother me. It is a symbol of my unity with the oppressed and forsaken. It also makes most witnesses avert their eyes, and I am grateful for
that too, lest they see that I don't suffer enough, lest they uncover the
deception.

The crowd, so large, violates the prophecy of Isaiah: that the Messiah
"was taken from prison and from judgment, and was cut off out of the land
of the living," meaning that no one cared about him when he was killed.
But there is my mother at the foot of the cross, in torment, and I feel pain
for her suffering. There is Magdalene too. She isn't weeping—she knows

what I'm doing. But my poor mother doesn't, and she suffers unfairly, for now. She kneels at the foot of the cross. Magdalene tries to comfort her. Mother looks up at me, and I see the love in her eyes, mixed with pain. How can I be so cruel! I want to tell her, "This too shall pass," but I dare not speak.

In just a few hours we will both have relief. I'll call out, "I thirst," and Thomas will press strong haoma to my lips in the guise of wine and vinegar, enough to render me unconscious and apparently dead. I'll be taken to the tomb of Arimathea, and in three days I will appear before all, risen from the dead. Everything so far, everything, has gone according to plan.

❖ ❖ ❖

On the previous day had I told Judas where I would spend the night, and then sent him out on an errand. As expected, my arrest occurred shortly afterwards. I was then taken to the home of Annas, the eighty-year-old former high priest and father-in-law of the current high priest Caiaphas. What is happening, I wondered? If this is a courtesy of the Sanhedrin to Annas, I can't afford it. Time is short, and I must be taken for crucifixion well before the Sabbath begins.

Home for the residence of Annas is perhaps too modest a word, for the building is more like a palace, the floors covered with polished blue and white tiles, the walls with elaborately embroidered cloths, the ceilings with carved oak beams. So this how the tithes of the faithful Jews were spent. All for the glory of God, Annas probably would say. I was conscious of time passing as I stood before an empty couch, my arms held stiffly behind my back by the hazzan, who had warned me, "Be polite to Annas, or you'll regret it." I had every intention of being polite.

Finally Annas entered, wearing a blue robe embroidered with gold and encrusted with jewels, the colors making his aged skin look even paler. These are just his everyday garments, I thought to myself. His fancy priestly garb is locked in the Antonia Tower, under the control of Pilate.

"So, Jesus of Nazareth! You are probably wondering why you were brought to me." He looked me over carefully and then sat down on the couch. "I know in detail about your teachings," he said, "particularly about your secrets, those things you do not tell your disciples."

"I have always spoken openly to the world," I said. "I taught publicly in the synagogues and in the Temple, where every Jew could hear me. I've said nothing in secret. Ask those who have heard me what I said to them."

Suddenly I was struck on the cheek by the hazzan. "Don't answer the high priest that way!" he barked, and he wrenched my arms more tightly behind my back.

"Lay your hands off him," said Annas. "Release his arms. This man preaches peace. I don't fear him." The hazzan looked surprised, but he did as he was ordered. "I *have* asked those who heard you preach," Annas said. "Believe me, I have. I've talked to many people about your methods, and they tell a story different from yours. They say to me that you had secret teachings that you gave only to your closest disciples, your so-called apostles. In private you explained the true meaning behind the parables, and these words were not for ordinary Jews to hear. Nor were they for us to hear, but hear them we did. Yes, hear them we did. Do you deny having secret teachings?"

Finally I understood. He was referring to the meetings I held with my apostles to make certain that they didn't misunderstand my parables. I always intended my words to be spread to all the disciples. Annas must have learned about these sessions from Iscariot, for Nicodemus wouldn't have reported them without letting me know. I couldn't truly deny the accusation, so I decided to say no more.

"You've lost your voice, Rabbi? Or should I call you Messiah? That's what the mob now calls you, isn't it? You know, I am truly the Messiah myself. Don't be surprised at what I say. The word only means 'anointed one,' and as high priest I've been anointed to the service of the Lord. You may call me 'Christ' if you think the Greek term is more elegant. I prefer the Hebrew myself. But being anointed doesn't give the power to rule, does it?" Was Annas expressing his own impotency?

"I'm really quite familiar with your teachings, Rabbi," Annas continued. "You have compassion for the poor and you rant against the oral law. But the oral law isn't mine. It's the invention of the Pharisees, and you are right in your complaint that it causes problems for the poor. It's the meaning behind the law that matters, not the repressive myriad of little rules. You and I agree on that. See, you are much closer in spirit to us Sadducees than to the Pharisees. They preach hatred and separation. We Sadducees try to live with the Romans. Ours is a religion of love and acceptance, much as you preach. But if you think that means we submit to the Romans, then you've misunderstood us in the same way that both the Zealots and the Sicarii have misunderstood—and underestimated—us."

Why was Annas telling me this? Alas, I had not planned for this delay.

Annas continued, "You know that you are playing directly into the hands of the Romans, the great enemies of our people, don't you? Is that what you intend? Still speechless? It appears that you've entered deep water, but before you've learned to swim. Rabbi, let me teach you some lessons, lessons about the world that go beyond your limited vision. The Romans are barren people, nothing more than sophisticated looters, cut-throats, butchers, and rapists. Their religion is crude and pitiful. They've produced nothing of value in the world, except perhaps for their engineering. Yes, they build great roads and aqueducts, but that's only because they need them for their tyranny. That's all they know, how to bully! They are a muscular but pitiful people. Their roads are as straight as arrows because they plot them on maps and then build them; they have no more awareness of the land then they have of the people they despoil. They enslave peoples whose spiritual accomplishments are far greater than their own, and I don't mean just the Jews, Rabbi.

"The Pharisees say we Sadducees have befouled ourselves with Roman ways. They are naive. The Sicarii accuse us of 'collaboration,' and they attempt to assassinate us in the streets. Those fools think they can defeat the Romans with brutality, but *that* is the only skill the Romans have truly mastered. Fight them with brutality, and the Romans will always triumph!" Annas looked at me intently. "Do you understand what I am saying, Rabbi?"

Yes, I thought to myself, but I don't understand why you are saying it, or why you address me so respectfully. I looked around the room and noted that there were no Romans present, just Jews. Please hurry and finish, I thought, and let me get to my trial!

"The only effective counter to Rome," Annas continued, "is a strong Jewish power, a strong Sanhedrin. When you, Rabbi, undermine us, you serve only to endanger Judaism. Don't you realize that? You play into the hands of the Zealots, who wish destruction of our authority, to create a void that they hope to fill. They are anarchists, and you must appreciate that if they ever achieve what they want, it will be the end of Judaism—an apocalypse beyond their imagination! You have preached that you could tear down the temple in three days. I know you are speaking figuratively, but the Romans could do it, and they would do it, brutal thugs that they are, if the Zealots ever gained power!

"Ah, I can see you asking yourself, what is the alternative that this old, foolish priest thinks can save Israel? Collaboration with the pagans and eventual despoiling of our covenant? To become like Samaritans? No, Rabbi, we're much smarter than that. To defeat the Romans, truly, deeply, permanently defeat them, you must understand their ways. And *you* haven't even begun this study. Neither have the Pharisees. But we Sadducees have mastered it. So let me give you a quick lesson. See if you can learn, Rabbi, and then you'll understand why I asked that you be brought to me.

"The Romans don't abide by divine rule, although that's not surprising, given the immaturity of the gods they claim to worship. Nominally the Romans are ruled by Caesar, but one man can't control an empire as vast as theirs. No, their true secret is what the Greeks call the Roman 'bureaucracy,' government by organization. Whoever controls the bureaucracy can get whatever they want, provided of course that they don't draw the attention of Caesar. And to understand the bureaucracy, Rabbi, is to control it, because so few really understand it. You may not appreciate that, but it is true. See, I'm not a foolish old man! We Sadducees have been filling the bureaucracy with Jews, and soon we will again rule. We'll win the conflict, without Rome ever recognizing that they were engaged in battle!

"Are you beginning to understand, Rabbi? Are you beginning to appreciate the difficulty of the problem, and the subtlety of the solution? I am an old man as full of wisdom as you are full of youthful ambition. Do you understand yet why I'm talking to you? Your foolish extremism will accomplish nothing. But you could help us, and that means help your own people, those you 'love,' even the am ha'arez! I'll give you my advice, the advice of a wise old man. But are you wise enough to take it?

"I can save you, Rabbi, and you can help us. You see, your message of loving the Romans is just what we need. Let us all live together, gentile and Jew, without hatred, as long as the Romans let us worship our own God. It will help us to save the Jews from the Zealots, the Sicarii, and from destruction. Don't you see?

"Here's what I propose. Confess to me, express remorse, and I'll see to it that you won't be tried. Work with us, and you'll live. You could even flourish. Tell your disciples that we are the legitimate rulers. Teach them to accept the Romans and to forego their hatred. That is your 'revelation,' isn't it? Tell them that they can worship the Lord while working with the Romans. Help us counter the Zealots and the other extremists, for they are the true danger, not Caesar. We will defeat the Romans, slowly but surely, through infiltration and control of their government. Unless, that is, we first defeat ourselves, by falling victim to our own hatred, and becoming as brutal as the Romans themselves. Surely you understand this. Help us keep it from happening!"

I never claimed to understand the politics of Israel, but I must confess, I was entranced by Annas. His arguments made sense, and he correctly perceived the dangers of hatred and violence. Had he come to me a few weeks earlier, I might have acceded. But my plans had progressed too far, and success was within my reach. I would not change now.

"What do you say?" Annas asked. "My son-in-law Caiaphas acts in front of the council. He cannot give you a second chance. If I send you to him, you are doomed."

"I am innocent of all crime," I said. "Proceed and be done."

Annas issued a loud and exaggerated sigh. "I pity you, Nazarene, for the holocaust that you bring on yourself. Your martyrdom will bring nothing. I had thought you were a smart man. Caiaphas warned me that my hope was imaginary. Now I must send you to him. You'll be tried, and convicted, and executed. We must do without your help."

When I have succeeded, I thought to myself, Annas could become a useful counselor.

Annas wrote something on a piece of parchment, handed it to the hazzan, and ordered him to take me to his son-in-law, the current High Priest. Again, I was rudely pushed through the dark and empty streets; again, I was brought into a strange building, this one with tall Greek columns on the front, their tops leafed with gold. This must be the building where the Sanhedrin meets, I thought, now that Pilate has forced their "voluntary" move out of the Temple area.

The interior was like the courthouse of Sepphoris, but larger, and expensively decorated with gold, marble, and purple cloth. What seemed like hundreds of oil lamps lit the room. Do they keep them burning all the time, I wondered? The hazzan gave Annas's letter to a guard, who took it behind a curtained doorway. Again, time passed as we waited standing in front of a large table.

Finally a group of about a dozen men entered. The hazzan jerked me to a more submissive pose while they took their places behind the table. Caiaphas was easy to identify. He sat in the middle, wearing a tall headpiece with gold trim and a white robe with golden tassels. I soon learned that the others were members of the council, priests and elders.

I stood before the group for more than an hour while Caiaphas interrogated me about my teachings and demanded answers that I knew he had already received from Nicodemus. I was worried about time, and it was important that my sentencing not be delayed too long. Ask me the question about kingship, I thought. Don't put it off. Don't bother trying to tire me. I won't disappoint you. But instead they brought in a series of witnesses, several of whom I recognized as men who had come to my sermons. They testified, more or less accurately, about my teachings. Some of the witnesses testified at variance with others, giving me the impression that these were not paid informers but true disciples with poor memories. So Nicodemus was right—they would do their best to give me an honest and fair trial before they condemned and executed me.

Finally Caiaphas said, "I've also been told that your disciples call you the king of the Jews." Ah, I thought. At last. "Are you creating a new kingdom in Israel?" he asked. "Is this part of your teachings?"

I broke my silence. "My kingdom is not of this world," I said.

"*Your* kingdom? So, then, you claim that you are a king?" Caiaphas was on the edge of his seat, as if he thought he had tricked me into a confession.

"Yes, I am a king. It is just as you say."

Caiaphas sat back on his chair. His face broadened into a smug, superior smile that reminded me of the expression of a camel. "That is good, very good. Thank you for those words. I hadn't expected that you would be so clear. Until now, based on the testimony of witnesses, you've been guilty only of blasphemy, and for that we have the right under Roman law to stone you to death. However now you've gone further, much further, for to proclaim yourself a king is a civil crime, not a religious one. Ha! You are a common revolutionary, a rebel, a Zealot, a *bandit.* You've committed the crime of sedition, and your punishment will be delivered by the Romans, not by the council. You'll be tried by Pontius Pilate, found guilty, and crucified. And with crucifixion, you will be shamed. Humiliated! Discredited!" He carefully articulated the words, as if he were taking particular pleasure in each. "Disgraced! Yes. That's better. Much better than stoning." His eyes squinted over his broad smile as he mused over the cleverness of his move. Little did he realize that we had counted on it.

Having elicited my "admission," he sent me to Pontius Pilate. The council guard led me again across Jerusalem, this time to the fortress of Antonia, the tall castle that sat at the northwest boundary of the Temple. I had seen its towers many times from within the Court of the Gentiles, and there had always been several Roman soldiers looking down, watching over the courtyard. Rumor had it that there was a secret entrance from the fortress directly into the courtyard itself, to be used only to crush insurrection. The council guard formally turned me over to the Roman guard at the entrance to the fortress, although the council guard accompanied us inside.

I had never been inside the Antonia fortress, and was surprised that within the walls was a substantial courtyard with three stone buildings: a large structure that looked like an administrative building, one that looked like a pagan temple, and one that looked like an armory and barracks. This last one also turned out to hold the living quarters of Pilate. It was the middle of the night, and they awoke Pilate to judge me. They seemed impatient to have me tried before the Passover, since that was a likely time for a revolt. And I too wanted it done before the Passover. I waited several minutes in the courtyard.

A man who was clearly Pilate appeared on a balcony, in full armor despite the early hour. For someone who spent all his time as an administrator, he carried the weight with surprising ease. "Ah, the Jewish magus is brought to me," he called out, with what sounded like a practiced sarcasm. His choice of words annoyed me more than he probably realized.

One of the priests shouted back up to Pilate. "We found this man called Jesus perverting the nation, forbidding to give tribute to Caesar, and saying that he himself is the anointed King of the Jews."

"So, you are the 'King of the Jews'?" Pilate called down.

"It is as you say," I replied.

"That is a rather unambiguous confession. I'm surprised. Please come up," he said to me, as if I were a guest rather than a prisoner. He gestured to the guards to bring me to his chambers. Noting his friendly tone, they loosened their grips and led me, almost politely, into the building. The council guard remained in the courtyard, presumably because they had cleansed themselves for the Passover and didn't want to defile themselves by entering the home of a Roman.

I walked up a series of stone stairs, arranged in a spiral, illuminated by oil lamps every few feet. I had assumed that the walls of the fortress were just a skeleton for a wooden interior, but I was wrong; the building was a warren of complex passageways constructed from blocks larger by two than those we had used in the aqueduct, yet making extensive use of arches. We went up, then up, and then further up; I could scarcely believe how tall the fortress felt from within, and yet this was one of the smaller buildings.

I must not show too much curiosity, I thought. I must be as a man who is going to his death. I pulled my gaze away from the walls and concentrated my vision narrowly on the steps in front.

Finally we stopped climbing and walked through a series of narrow passageways connected by large doors secured with iron locks. The halls finally widened, and I entered a large room decorated with armor and weapons. At one end was a large doorway, its great carved oak door partly obscuring a brightly-lit room. Standing there was Pilate.

"Untie the man," Pilate ordered. One of the guards pulled out a large knife and slashed my bonds. "Wait here," Pilate directed the guards, as he took my arm and led me inside. He was shorter than I had imagined, lean but muscular, with the tanned skin of a man who spent much of his time outdoors. He seemed to be making a point of the fact that he didn't fear me.

"I've heard much about you and I've looked forward to meeting you," he said in a friendly tone. "I'm glad that the council stayed below. They're too pure today to enter my home." I looked around at the cold stone blocks, the narrow windows, and the massive oak furniture that made up what he called "home."

Pilate sat on a large plain wood chair and examined me from a distance of ten feet. "Yes, I'm glad they chose not to come in," he said. "I prefer to talk to you privately. You are an interesting man, Jesus of Nazareth. Or should I say Jesus of Bethlehem? And you are king of the Jews! You don't look like a king, do you?" Pilate's smirk seemed to melt into an almost sympathetic smile. "But that doesn't mean much, does it? It wouldn't be hard to make you look like a king, would it? Some expensive clothing, a little bit of purple dye. . . . For that matter, it wouldn't be hard to make Herod look like a slave." He was quiet for a few moments, and then he laughed. I assumed that he was imagining Herod in slave's clothing.

"You know, don't you, that Herod believes *he* is the Messiah? No reaction? I guess you did know." I was suddenly uncomfortable with the realization that Pilate was reading my reactions with such assurance. "Once he's proclaimed king, do you know what I think Herod would like most of all? To be proclaimed a god! Ha! That got a rise out of you. You shouldn't be so surprised; after all, Herod isn't Jewish. Augustus has been proclaimed a god, now that he's dead. Tiberius is preparing the votes to be proclaimed a god himself when he dies. It's not such a special thing anymore. The Pharaohs were living gods, weren't they? When you die, perhaps your followers will declare *you* a god! Oh, that's right, you Jews allow only one god. So that could never happen, could it?" He looked at me with a knowing smile.

"You Jews deserve better than Herod," he sighed. "You know, I like the Jews. I was told that you would be a bunch of wild fanatics, impossible to govern. Do you know what they say in Rome? Governing Jews is like herding cats! Well, the Romans are right. But it's not your fanatical independence that I like. What I like is that you're a smart people. You're thinkers—that's really your strength. You could be a truly great people some day. Except ... except for your weakness. And do you know what your weakness is?" He looked at me hard, as if he were expecting an answer, but I wasn't about to interrupt his monologue. "Your weakness is that you are thinkers! Ha! Your weakness is the same as your strength! Isn't that ironic?"

Pilate stood up and began pacing the room, looking at me occasion-ally with his penetrating eyes. "Do you know what else I admire most about you?" he asked. "I admire your god. You've invented a truly admirable god! A bit violent, perhaps, and vengeful, but he cares more about you than about himself. That's truly a wonderful idea. He's much better than our Roman gods, even better than our whole collection. We fear our gods, and we solicit their aid, but we don't really care about them, and they don't give a damn about us, except for a little sex now and then. Most of the time we just wish they would leave us alone. Yes, you have a good god. He makes you into a tough people. Of course, your architecture is worthless, and you have no crafts or art that any Roman or Greek would ever bother to look at twice. Your practice of baby mutilation, that rite you call circumcision, is utterly barbaric. Besides your god, which I suspect we'll some day add to our Roman collection, your only other contributions to civilization are your epic poem, that long thing you call your 'scripture,' and your invention of a day of rest. Now I'm not sounding sarcastic, am I? Yes, I guess I am. Forgive me, I meant my compliments sincerely.

"Yet there is something I actively dislike about you Jews, Jesus of Nazareth, something that I detest. It's your stubborn belief in your own superiority. Despite all the evidence to the contrary, you persist in think-ing that you are a special group, a chosen people. What I hate most is the way you treat us as unclean. Like that council, waiting outside, avoiding my home and its ritual dirt!" Pilate glanced towards his window and sighed. "I could never have a Jew as a friend, because a Jew would never have me as a friend. And yet here I am, Procurator of Judea."

I felt sad for this lonely man, Pontius Pilate, who I hoped would con-demn me to death. Perhaps, after everything, he would be a man to keep in Jerusalem, someone to work with. He could help provide civil order. He might even be a potential convert. If, that is, we forego the need for circumcision.

"But I hear that you are different, Jesus of Galilee. You enter the homes of the gentiles, such as mine. Oh, I know, you didn't have much choice this time, but you would have come anyway, wouldn't you? Perhaps I should have invited you sooner. Now tell me, why are you here?" I remained silent. "Why did you allow yourself to be captured?"

Those words sent a chill over my flesh. Did he suspect our plan? If so, then he might not act as expected. I tried not to react. Was he watching my pupils? The thought of losing control was frightening.

"You're doing well at angering the Sanhedrin," Pilate continued. "Is that what you wanted? I angered them recently. It wasn't really so hard to do. I introduced a Roman religious symbol, a lituus, on the coinage. It infuriated them, just as I had hoped. Jews may be great thinkers, but when they're angry they go crazy. And it's easy to keep them angry—oh, so easy! Against the Samaritans, we Romans could win by using horror, but it doesn't work with Jews. Every Jew is a Zealot at heart, willing to commit suicide rather than be defeated. It's futile to try to win them over by force, so we must outsmart them, trick them. If they don't know what we're doing, we can turn them to our purposes. We can crush them with their cooperation." As Pilate said these words, he seemed to be crushing an imaginary Jew with his fist; it was the only sign I saw that night of what might be a deeper, hidden cruelty in the man. "But I don't have to explain trickery to you, do I? You've been a master at it."

I was becoming more and more uncomfortable with the way this was going. Condemn, me, I thought. Condemn me and send me to be crucified. Please.

"How is your old childhood friend Lazarus?" he asked. Even most of my apostles didn't know that Lazarus came from Nazareth—how did Pilate know? "I assume he's feeling well. Your skills at medicine are quite impressive. But why are you trying to overthrow me? Why did you allow yourself to be arrested?" he asked once more, and again there was no doubt in his tone. Pilate's eyes were riveted to mine. He reminded me of Simon trying to read my mind. "Have you come here to commit suicide?" How was I reacting? Could he read my face? Could he read my absence of expression? Pilate looked at me silently for a long time, while I stood there uncomfortably. "Oh, forgive me. I didn't mean to have you stand. Here, let me get you a seat." He went behind a curtain, brought out a chair padded in purple cloth and decorated with gold leaf. A chair fit for a king? He gestured for me to sit, and I did. He sat down on a bare oak bench.

I looked into the eyes of Pontius Pilate, admiring their clarity and intelligence. But why does this man, who fears no one, still sit ten feet from me? Is there something else I see in his eyes? Beneath his arrogance and eloquence, is he also afraid?

"I see it now," he suddenly said. "I was wrong. You think of me as a potential ally! You don't want to get rid of us Romans at all. All you want is to be king of the Jews. You want to be a Herod for Judea. Why had I never realized that before? Not a bad plan. But why then did you allow yourself to get caught?"

Suddenly he said, "You know that Herod Antipas is in Jerusalem, don't you?" My heart thumped. I had not known. This was another surprise—what were the implications for our plan? "Jesus of Galilee, perhaps you should be tried by Herod of Galilee. How would you like that? He's your competitor for the kingship. Which of you two should I recommend to Caesar? I'm not being facetious! At least not completely. You might actually make a better king. But that's not much of a compliment, is it? Would you like to meet Herod? I could send you to him. He normally doesn't like being awakened at this hour, but I know he'd like to meet you. I think he would always be grateful to me for such a favor. I'll do it!" Did Pilate see me wince? "And perhaps he'll know what I am to do with you. It's only courteous that I give him the opportunity."

I was opposed to any delay, anything that might put my trial after the Passover, but I didn't know how to respond. Pilate suddenly stood up, came close to me, took me gently by the shoulder, and guided me off my chair, and walked with his arm around me to the outside, as if I had been a close friend. "This man is from Herod's domain," Pilate said to two soldiers who had been waiting outside his room. "So take this man to him. Tell him that Pontius Pilate seeks his advice, that I ask him, 'What should the Procurator of Judea do with Jesus of Nazareth?'" Pilate disappeared back into his chamber.

The soldiers retied my hands behind my back, and then took me back down to the courtyard. With the council members following along, I was led back through the dark and nearly empty streets of Jerusalem to the Citadel of Herod, a large stone complex that had been built by Herod the Great, a half mile away. One soldier guarded me outside, while the other talked to a servant. I was worried about the waste of time. The servant disappeared into the building, and we waited. Yet another delay. After about a half-hour, we were all led into the building.

Although the outside of the Citadel was massive, like the fortress of Antonia, the inside was quite different. It reeked of comfort and luxury, with fountains and gardens everywhere, large hallways filled with padded furniture. The entire structure appeared to be heated, uncomfortably so. At the end of one hallway stood a group of soldiers. In their midst, on a velvet couch, was a short, pudgy man with pale, oiled skin. He was wrapped in an embroidered green robe decorated with a pattern of pomegranates, looking something like a giant frog. I couldn't get that image out of my mind.

"Jesus of Nazareth!" he said. I guessed that he had been drinking wine, had fallen into a deep sleep, and had been awakened for this surprise visit. "You don't look very powerful now. What's the matter? Why do you submit to this?"

"He has claimed the kingship of the Jews," one of the priests said.

"Shut up!" Herod said rudely. "I've wanted to meet this man Jesus for a long time. Bring him closer." The soldiers, sensing Herod's contempt, were rougher now. Herod stood up, walked around me, played a little with my smock, and closely examined my neck. It suddenly occurred to me that he was checking it for signs that my head had been sliced off, to see if I truly was the Baptist reincarnated. He seemed dissatisfied, and frowning, he went back to his couch.

He looked back at me, and demanded, "Remove those manacles from your hands." One of the soldiers moved behind me as if to untie me, and Herod exploded in rage. "You idiot! I don't mean you! I'll have you beaten! Get out of here. I'm talking the Nazarene. You, Jesus, remove your manacles. Do a miracle. I want to see a miracle. Come on, I'm waiting."

I just stood there watching this unpleasant man trying to behave as he thought a king should behave. Rabbi Shuwal!–yes, that is who he reminded me of. Shuwal was thin, almost gaunt, and this man was fat, with a pasty skin, yet Shuwal was whom I thought of. The spirit of Shuwal in the body of a frog.

"Take that smirk off your face!" he shouted at me, although I was only a few feet in front of him. "So, you are the great preacher? I've had spies reporting to me all about you. I bet you wonder who they are! Well, I won't give away any of my secrets, but I know all about your religion. You think you're so smart. I can summarize the whole of your so-called revelations in one sentence. Want to hear it? Love your enemy, but not his wife!" Herod could hardly contain his glee at his own wit. He laughed loudly, and a moment later looked around. Immediately one of the soldiers also laughed. Herod seemed satisfied. He continued, "I've heard nothing in the last year except of your wondrous miracles. You command the storms, produce bread from the skies, and direct evil demons to enter pigs. Untie your ropes! I command you! Don't just stand there."

Anything I said would draw out this ordeal. He looked so pathetic, this man who thought he was the Messiah, so out of control of the world around him.

Then it occurred to me that he might be thinking those identical words about me.

A pan of dirty water hit me in the face. As the pan clanked to the floor, Herod laughed, and the soldiers joined in. I looked to the priests and elders, and they seemed embarrassed. Herod had thrown the pan at me. It must have been by his couch, although I hadn't noticed it before.

"This man isn't John the Baptist," Herod announced. "He's an impostor. My spies have lied to me. King of the Jews! Ha! He doesn't know what it means to be a king. Here, put this royal scarf on him." He picked up a piece of clothing that had been lying on the floor and flung it onto my shoulder. A soldier came over and adjusted it, and Herod smiled. "Now he probably thinks that is all it takes. It is more than that, Nazareth! Unless you are born to it, you'll never understand."

Herod turned to the soldiers. "Take him back to Pilate. Thank him for the courtesy, but tell him that I did not find this man interesting, not at all."

Back through the barren morning streets of Jerusalem, back to the fortress of Antonia, back up the spiral stones to the room of Pilate.

"So, you would say nothing to Herod. I don't blame you. I find it difficult to talk to the man myself. But now I have a problem. I am to pass judgment on you, for the Jews refuse to do so. They say that you're guilty of sedition. My agents have followed your activities for a long time." I wondered what he meant by that. "You preach love of everyone. You consistently avoid violence, except for that little commotion with the money-changers. And that fig tree—why did you poison it? You claim to be a king of the Jews. Yet it is your own people who brought you here. What kind of king is that?"

"My kingdom is not of this world," I said, breaking my long silence. "If it were, I would have soldiers instead of disciples, and they would fight. I wouldn't be delivered for judgment to you. No, my kingdom is not here."

"But you insist that you are a king. Only Caesar can proclaim kings. You seem to wish to die. Is that it, Jesus of Nazareth? But nobody wishes to die by crucifixion, no sane person, that is. Are you mad? You're no Zealot. You're no danger to Rome. Why should I kill a man who is no threat? What shall I do?" This was no longer simple monologue. Pilate seemed genuinely perplexed.

He took me back outside, around a corner and down a broad stairway I hadn't seen before, and out to the court where the members of the Sanhedrin were waiting. The crowd had grown significantly. Where had they all come from, I wondered? He mounted a large stone platform, on which a chair had been placed.

"You've brought me Jesus of Nazareth," Pilate announced, "and accused him of sedition. I am aware of his acts, and I know of his claims. I have heard the charges, and have considered them." Pilate paused, and I looked around at the large crowd. All eyes but mine were looking at Pilate. "I find no fault in this man," he said.

No! He must condemn me! Everything had been arranged. It's all going wrong! If he releases me, the Sanhedrin could still have me stoned!

The crowd was silent, also stunned, I assumed, by the unexpected acquittal.

Pilate continued, "He has done nothing that deserves the death sentence. I will chastise him—a lashing—and then I will release him."

At the very back of the crowd I suddenly noticed Nicodemus looking at me. What was he doing here? He smiled and nodded, as if to reassure me, but I had no idea what he had in mind. Then a man standing next to him shouted out, "Crucify him! Crucify him!" Several people scattered throughout the crowd immediately picked up on it, and erupted in unison, "Crucify him!" It grew into a roar. "Crucify him! Crucify him!" Even the Sanhedrin seemed surprised.

Pilate shouted out, "What evil has he done? Nothing!"

But they wouldn't be calmed. The priests had now joined in the chanting. "Crucify him! Crucify him!"

Pilate looked down at me with a face full of frustration. He turned back to the crowd, and raised his hands to silence them. It took nearly a minute before they responded. "It is traditional that I release one man from arrest at the Passover," Pilate announced. "I choose to release Jesus of Nazareth." Why was Pilate so eager to acquit me? Did he have his own plans?

The same man who had started the shouting, the man who stood next to Nicodemus, now shouted, "Release Barabbas! Crucify Jesus!" His words were quickly picked up, as before. Barabbas was a Zealot sympathizer who had been arrested after the siege of the Tower of Siloam. Pilate looked confused. Barabbas had never been popular. I worried that the ploy of Nicodemus was going to be recognized.

But it wasn't. Pilate gave me one last look of bafflement, and conceded defeat. He knew better than to confront an unruly mob of passionate Jews on a religious issue. One more crucifixion would mean nothing to the history of the world. "I will have no more to do with this affair," he said. "You Jews can fight it out among yourselves." He reached over to a pitcher of water that had been sitting on a table beside his chair, and with an exaggerated motion he dipped his hands in the water, removed them, and as they dripped he rubbed them together. "I wash my hands of this affair." It was a ritual washing, something the Jews would understand.

The hard part, the only uncertain part, was over. We had manipulated Pilate into saying words that the Jews could interpret as a condemnation, and the machinery of the Roman bureaucracy now took over, a machinery that Nicodemus understood, had penetrated, and could control. It had a job to do, to crucify a man who had been sentenced to die, and it didn't care about the details.

But we *had* worried about the details. Only two days earlier Thomas, Nicodemus, and I had planned the crucifixion. We were meeting in the home of Arimathea. I had worked out the critical sleight. "Have you ever seen a Roman soldier nail a man to a cross?" I asked them.

"No," said Thomas, with a shudder.

"More times than I care to remember," said Nicodemus.

"Think carefully, Nicodemus. Have you ever seen a Roman soldier personally hammering in the nails?"

"No, I guess not. They always have a slave do it, or they hire a Cushite."

"Because nailing helpless men through the wrists and ankles is dirty business, even to them. It isn't glorious, like slicing off arms and heads in battle."

"Ah, I see what you mean. If we could arrange for the *right* slaves to do the nailing—*my* slaves!" Nicodemus owned seven Cushites.

"Plain nails aren't used alone," I said, "because they rip out of the flesh too easily. A block of wood is held against the wrist, and the nail is hammered through the wood, the wrist, and into the cross. Likewise for the feet. We'll use short nails that won't reach the flesh. Other hidden nails will hold the blocks to the cross." I had once constructed a similar illusion for Elymas. My mind raced on. "We'll conceal a small container of blood in the wood that the nails will break. Even a little bit of blood looks like a lot when it splatters." I had learned that too from Elymas. "Ropes will support my body."

"We must arrange for a short duration on the cross," Thomas said. "The crucifixion should be timed for Friday, so the body will have to be removed before sundown begins the Sabbath. But how can we keep the Romans from breaking your legs? They always do that. And then there is the lashing that precedes the crucifixion."

"The legs and the lashing can be handled," Nicodemus said. "Leave those to me. All I have to do is convince the right person that breaking the legs might foment more revolution. If the Roman soldiers are ordered not to break the legs, then they won't do so. If there is anything you can depend on absolutely, it's that a Roman soldier will not disobey orders. As for the lashing, I can bribe a soldier to do it lightly, and to use dull wooden barbs in place of metal or bone. It won't be the first time this has been done. My excuse will be that I want you to suffer more on the cross, and you will live longer if you're not beaten hard. That way the soldier will think he's acting in the cause of Rome, while earning a little silver on the side. We can toughen your back with tannin beforehand, and the lashing will hardly hurt."

48. Forsaken

THE HOURS ON THE CROSS WENT SLOWLY, BUT THEY DID PASS.
It is a strange blessing of the crucified that they get to watch themselves be mourned while they are still alive. Although my apostles were in hiding, I was surrounded by disciples, their presence violating the prophecy of Isaiah that the Messiah would die alone —but that was necessary, for the more people who saw me *die,* the more convincing would be my resurrection. I could not speak to comfort them, for part of my plan was to fulfill another prophecy of Isaiah:

> He was oppressed, and he was afflicted,
> yet he opened not his mouth;
> He is brought as a lamb to the slaughter
> and as a sheep before her shearers;
> yet he never said a word.

Sunset was approaching, and it would soon be time for the end. Clouds passed in front of the sun. They reminded me of the smoke that blotted out the sun when Sepphoris was burning. But that smoke was black, and these clouds were white. Please, Lord, let me forget! But no, the horror returned, my memory of the man on the cross, the screaming eyes, the first crucifixion I had witnessed.

I drifted in and out of a dreamlike trance. Here I am, on the cross. Yet it doesn't hurt! Is this my dream again? No, I am truly on the cross. Was that the meaning of the dream, that I would be on the cross to fulfill the destiny of my father? Is it as Simon Magus said? Am I truly invulnerable?

A soldier had been stationed to stand guard next to me, but he had hardly spent a moment either standing or guarding. He seemed to become alert only when another soldier appeared. "It's about time, Longinus!" he said to his approaching relief. Then he hastened away.

Longinus walked up and looked me over in detail. I was tired and uncomfortable, and I again closed my eyes. Suddenly I felt a sharp pain in my ribs. I winced and looked down to see bright red blood on a spear he was holding. I felt a warm trickle down my side.

"So, you still feel pain!" Longinus said with a laugh. "Then it's not yet time for you to die. Enjoy a few more happy hours up there!"

He continued to probe my body with his spear, just enough to draw more blood. Then he poked at my hands and my feet. I could feel my fear growing before I consciously realized what was wrong. Was he suspicious? The spear tip was between my hand and the acacia wood. I tried moving my hands against the sharp blade of the spear head, to cover the hidden nails. He removed his spear and began probing at my feet, at the false structure that supported them. Had I disguised it well enough? Why hadn't I taken more care? I looked down at his helmet, and suddenly he turned his face up right at mine. A bolt of fear shot through my body as I looked into the glassy green eyes of Pantera.

No, he wasn't Pantera. It had been an illusion, brought on by my exhaustion. The green eyes and cruel smile of this soldier only reminded me of Pantera, the man who taught me the meaning of the word 'enemy.'

"You will not survive this stunt, magician of Galilee!" he said with a malevolent smirk, as he withdrew his spear from probing near my feet.

My God! He has discovered the false nails! He will expose the deception for all to see!

No, I realized with growing terror. He is not going to expose me. He is going to *kill* me. I am hanging on the cross, utterly helpless, and soon this brutal man will kill me as everyone watches.

Or he will wound me and let me die slowly. There is nothing I can do. Never had I been so utterly vulnerable and helpless. I see my life, my teachings, everything destroyed in this instant. The image of the crucified man from Sepphoris flashes in front of me again. The screaming eyes . . .

In despair I look towards heaven and cry, "My God, my God, why have you forsaken me?"

I look down at the soldier, at his sadistic expression, the Pantera-like expression in his cruel green eyes. He is enjoying this. He will take pleasure in killing me.

I am lost, disgraced. *He who dies hung from wood is accursed in the eyes of God.* From triumph to disaster, so quickly! I will die and my teachings will be mocked, ignored, and then forgotten. God has chosen a Roman soldier to end my life and obliterate my work. To destroy me.

Then something happens.

I look down at the soldier again, and instead I see a man, Longinus. In the creases and scars of his face, instead of brutality now I see suffering, pain, and wretchedness. I look into his eyes, beyond their cruelty, and I see a man with a soul, a fellow creation of God.

An exhilaration, a glow, embraces me as I feel love for this Roman soldier. Never before, I realize, have I truly loved my bitterest antagonist. This is the fulfillment I missed in Cana, when I was denied confronting Pantera the centurion. And the gnawing beast within is gone. Never before have I so strongly felt the Godliness of my own teachings.

The dread has faded. It is gone, and has been replaced by a sense of peace. I feel a great calm.

I sought to save the world but failed in that pretentious goal. I caused great pain to others, especially to my mother. I abandoned some, such as Judas, who earnestly sought my help. But have I truly failed?

Something deep within me answers *no.*

Or was it a whisper in my ear?

I call, "Longinus!" and the soldier looks up again, surprised at hearing his name. I glance at the blade on his spear and then look into his eyes. I say to him, "I forgive you for what you are about to do."

I feel a sponge against my face. I turn my head to push it away, but the drug takes effect and the world begins to spin. I look up towards heaven and cry, "Father, into your hands I commend my spirit!"

Epilogue

THE PREVIOUS WORDS ARE THOSE OF JESUS OF NAZARETH, recited to me, his brother Jude, called Thomas. He spoke them after he was removed from the cross, as he lay dying in the home of Arimathea. His story has filled forty-eight scrolls. I feel compelled to add now a few words of my own.

In those final hours, as Jesus was hanging on the cross, I grew anxious and frightened. At times I feared that anyone who looked could see through our deception. At other times I found the illusion so convincing that I drifted myself into believing that Jesus was truly nailed to the wood.

Most of the apostles were in hiding, out of fear that they too would be arrested. Pharisees in the crowd spat and jeered. They dared Jesus to release himself and thus prove he was truly the Messiah. A few faithful disciples who gathered at the foot of the cross begged Jesus to do the same, and they cried when he failed to do so. Our poor mother stood bravely by, feeling helpless to ease what she thought was the agony of her son. I stood close to comfort her and I tried to console myself with the thought that she would soon know joy, when Jesus rose from the dead and confirmed her belief in his Messianic mission.

Finally the sunset approached and with it the climax of the plan. But Jesus, rather than feigning a slow death, had become agitated. Something was awry. He called out to me, "My beloved disciple, care for our mother." What did he mean? Why did he say that? Something was desperately wrong, but what? In alarm I rushed to Arimathea, and told him we could wait no longer—we must proceed at once. So Arimathea announced to the crowd that he would comfort the crucified man in the traditional way, by raising a drink of sour wine to his mouth. But in this wine was a strong dose of haoma, enough to end Jesus's consciousness, to weaken his pulse, and to make it appear that he was dead. Jesus breathed the fumes, and in a few seconds he was unconscious.

Alas, we had planned well, but not well enough. No sooner had Jesus swooned from the drug than the guard raised his spear. I gasped in helpless terror as he thrust it deep into Jesus's body. Jesus convulsed, and his warm blood spurted onto the disciples gathered at his feet, to the horror of some witnesses and to the obvious delight of others. Somehow I found the presence of mind to shout out that it was yet another miracle that a dead man could bleed so profusely. I must have harbored a hope that all was not yet lost, that somehow we could save Jesus's life.

But this guard was an expert in killing. He must have known that no one could survive such a wound, for he allowed us to take Jesus down from the cross. Nicodemus and Arimathea carried Jesus to the tomb, through the hidden door we had built to the adjacent chamber, and then out to the home of Arimathea.

Magdalene nursed Jesus back to consciousness, but his liver had been impaled and we knew that he would not live long. Jesus tried to comfort me by using the words of our mother: "This too will pass," but they did not help, not then. Only now am I beginning to see that he may have been right.

It took Jesus three days to complete his dictation, and for me to write it down. Despite my objections he refused all but a few hours of rest during that time. Afterwards he asked that I bring the apostles to him so that with his remaining strength he could expose the deception of the crucifixion to them himself, tell them about this manuscript, and ask them to spread the truth to all people. I counseled against the meeting. I thought he was too weak and that the stress of the meeting would hasten his death, but Jesus believed his death was near and could not be stopped, and he was anxious to meet with them before he died. I finally agreed to the meeting, provided that he sleep first.

I did not tell Jesus that Judas Iscariot committed suicide, by hanging himself from wood. Nor did I tell him that Nicodemus has been arrested— at least that is what his servants told me. I still do not trust that man.

Magdalene searched out each of the apostles, letting them know that Jesus was alive and that he wanted to meet with them soon. But, for fear that they would disturb his rest, and to avoid the danger that the Sanhedrin would learn his location, she did not tell them he was at the home of Arimathea.

The apostles all reacted with disbelief, and they decided to check the tomb. They explained to the guards that they had heard that the body of Jesus had disappeared. The guards were skeptical, but they helped roll back the stone that blocked the entrance. All were astounded to find no body. The apostles were elated, but the guards were frightened—and with good reason. Either the body had been stolen and they would be punished, or a rebel that they had helped execute had risen from the dead. Either alternative was disastrous. They had nothing to gain by searching further, and so they never discovered the secret exit.

Without telling the apostles where Jesus was, I asked them to come to Arimathea's home the next day. Jesus was still asleep in a back room, but he was breathing easier, and the swelling seemed to have reached its limit. After they arrived I asked them to wait while I went outside to buy fish for a meal.

Jesus awoke while I was gone. He was weak, but he heard the apostles in the front room. He managed to stand and walk through the door. As he entered, he gave his traditional greeting: "Peace be with you." They were startled and frightened—they thought they were seeing a ghost. "Look at me!" Jesus said. "It's me! Touch me! A ghost doesn't have flesh and bones!" They came to him, touched him as he requested, and lost their fear.

When I returned, I was surprised to see him standing among them. It was the first time he had moved from the bed since we had brought him to Nicodemus's home.

"He has risen from the dead!" Peter announced joyously.

I looked at Jesus and realized that he too was confused, but suddenly I understood. Peter thought Jesus had died on the cross and had been resurrected. Perhaps above all others, the apostles had embraced the illusion of the crucifixion.

Jesus appeared to weaken, and he sat down on a bench near the door, looking frighteningly pale. Peter and the others fell to their knees. I was afraid that Jesus was about to faint. His breathing was shallow again, and he looked at me plaintively for help.

"No, no, listen," I shouted back at Peter. "It isn't as you think. He hasn't risen from the dead! Look!" I went to Jesus and opened his robe. The blood-soaked bandage had come loose from his spear wound. Surrounding it was the massive infection, blue and black swollen flesh crusted with dried blood. No resurrected Messiah would have a gaping wound! "See for yourself, Peter!" Jesus is human.

But Peter stared at me as if I were insane. He didn't seem to understand, or want to understand. I opened Jesus's robe further to let in light, and I accidentally touched the wound. Jesus winced in pain. "Oh, my Lord," I said to Jesus, "please forgive me!"

Jesus slowly opened his eyes and put his hand over his wound. "Thomas, now that they see, they finally know the truth. When I was on the cross and did not come down, I could tell that some of my disciples lost their faith. But those whose faith is not dependent on miracles are the most blessed of all." He turned to the other apostles. "I can't stay with you much longer. I shall soon join my father in heaven. You must continue my ministry, but without me. You will be helped by the holy spirit."

Then Jesus turned to me and said, "Thomas, do you have anything here to eat?"

Magdalene had said that it would be a good sign if he showed hunger, and my spirits were suddenly buoyed. I gave him some of the smoked fish I had just purchased. Jesus ate some but then looked even weaker, as if he could not hold it. He asked the apostles to leave, and they did.

Only later did I discover that the apostles misunderstood what had happened. The ploy of my skepticism had been used so often that they had interpreted my actions as yet another instance of "doubting." They thought that Jesus had risen from the dead, removed himself from the tomb, and miraculously appeared first to Magdalene and then to them. They believed that I had not seen him until after they had. And, they thought, I had continued in my disbelief up to the moment that I had touched his wound myself.

Jesus was exhausted by the meeting. He desperately wanted to talk to our mother, but he died shortly afterwards, without ever meeting with her or the other apostles again.

❖ ❖ ❖

As I write this, Jesus has been dead for nearly two weeks. Nicodemus, Arimathea, and I prepared his body, and we buried him as he requested, in a simple grave with no coffin, as befit a poor carpenter.

Before he died he seemed to have found a new spiritual strength, a new peace. Nonetheless, he insisted to the end that he was a sinner. Perhaps he was, and perhaps to be a sinner is the essence of being human. But I know that the fault for his sins is primarily my own. It was my own love of magic that impelled him to use it when it was unnecessary. My lack of faith undercut his. My warnings about Nicodemus were unsure and inadequate. And finally, I bear the guilt of letting Jesus proceed with the crucifixion, indeed of helping him plan it.

Jesus instructed me to show these scrolls to his apostles, and then to all Jews and gentiles. "In truth lies our greatest hope," he said. "Teach them that the only miracles of God are those that we see every day, the ordinary ones, whose true mystery lies in the fact that such wondrous things are considered ordinary. Teach them to find God not in temples and sacrifices, but in their own souls, and in the souls of others. Teach them to worship the Lord not with rules and rituals, but in spirit and in truth."

His last instructions are unambiguous, but they still fill me with confusion and uncertainty. The events following Jesus's death have been as extraordinary as those that preceded it. There is no doubt in Peter's mind about the resurrection—he witnessed it himself. He thinks Jesus has now ascended to heaven. And yet he and the other apostles continue to report sightings of Jesus, in the oddest ways. They meet a stranger whom they later decide must have been Jesus, even though they didn't recognize him at the time. It is very peculiar. I suspect that some of their sightings, particularly the most miraculous ones, are hallucinations brought on by lack of sleep or by overindulgence in haoma. I only hope that whatever supply of this drug Peter has will soon run out. I fear that he believes haoma helps bring the "Holy Spirit," and that he is giving it to others. As our father Joseph said, people love to be fooled, and they are more easily fooled by themselves than by others.

I have always liked Peter, despite his failings. What he lacks in intelligence and learning, he makes up for with his great energy, spirit, courage, and confidence. I certainly covet his self-confidence! And no one outdoes Peter as an eloquent teacher of Jesus's revelations. Peter is determined to spread the revelations. He calls the cross not a symbol of shame, but a symbol of the love that Jesus held for all people. "He has shown us that we all can defeat death!" Peter says. "Death is retribution for sin, but Jesus was without sin. He died for *our* sins, and his resurrection shows that in his infinite love, all our sins are forgiven! He is our savior!"

Savior—that word is now Peter's favorite. We rarely used it when Jesus was alive, and yet it is growing in use among the apostles.

Would it help if I were to convince Peter that Jesus was a sinner? Would Peter believe the story told in this manuscript?

Peter alone among the apostles seems to be confident that he knows exactly what should be done next. James and John vouch for everything Peter says and for all his plans. I don't fully understand the influence he exerts on them.

Will Peter succeed in carrying on the ministry of Jesus? He might, provided he can control his love of haoma. He acts as if he is possessed, not by a devil but by the Holy Spirit that Jesus said would come. Peter's enthusiasm is so great that it even spreads to me. He envisions a "Second Coming" when Jesus will return, and he believes it to be near at hand. There are times that I discover myself practically believing that the resurrection actually did happen. Jesus was right in his prediction that this event would bring about a transformation of his disciples, but he died without realizing that he had indeed been resurrected, at least as far as they were concerned.

Magdalene likewise seems to be possessed of a holy spirit. To my wonderment, she seems to have been strengthened rather than crushed by Jesus's death. And Peter, in his own indomitable way, is spurring her on. A typical incident occurred a few days ago. Peter was bursting with energy. He asked all the apostles to gather, to share stories of the resurrected Jesus. I told Magdalene that we were gathering in the home of Arimathea, and to Peter's evident dismay she appeared. Peter asked who would like to speak about Jesus, and Magdalene was the first to step forward.

"Magdalene," Peter said, "we know that our savior loved you more than the rest of women." He was trying to be polite, but she seemed annoyed. I think she took Peter's meaning to be that she ranked high only with regard to women, not men. "Tell us," Peter continued, "the words of the savior that you remember but that we may not have heard."

"Jesus appeared to me last night," Magdalene calmly replied. Her words caused a great stir among the apostles. Peter's jaw was hanging so wide open that a bird could have built a nest inside. "He appeared in a dream," she continued. "He spoke to me of sins, of the temptations of Satan, of darkness and death. He spoke of anger and hatred, but also of foolishness and benightedness."

Magdalene continued with an eloquence and power that I never knew she possessed. Much of what she said came from the words of Jesus, for I recognized them, but she also spoke of salvation, and the wickedness of ignorance and folly. Peter glowered at her, as if she were addressing him directly, and perhaps she was. Finally she concluded, "Jesus told me to tell all his disciples that women are not to be excluded, for they too can be prophets. 'Tell them,' he instructed me, 'that revelations come to all through prayer. Beware of forming a new priesthood, for those who proclaim themselves specially anointed may instead be false prophets.'"

Peter could take no more. Turning to the other apostles and speaking loudly to interrupt her, he said, "I don't know what you others think, but I don't believe that our savior said these things. He appointed twelve apostles, and he saw fit that they all be men. If he truly said the words she claims, would he have said them to her alone? Would he not have appeared to us too? Did he prefer her to us, to those he appointed as his emissaries?"

Magdalene cried out, "Peter, what do you accuse me of? Do you think I could invent these thoughts myself? Do you think I would lie about our savior?" Then she wept, as if Peter had just abused her physically. And her adoption of Peter's favorite word *savior* seemed to throw him off balance.

Matthew saved the day. "Peter," he said, "you've always been so ill-tempered! Now you come against a woman as if you were no better than the Pharisees! Jesus loved her more than he loved any of us. We all know that. If he found her worthy, who are you to reject her? Be ashamed, Peter! Heal yourself, and preach the good news our savior brought, rather than spending your effort attacking others."

Needless to say, Matthew's words did not put an end to the dispute between the two. Magdalene has told me that she feels we must make the apostles understand the truth, that Jesus did not die on the cross but survived a few days, and that the only true resurrection is that of his spirit. But I don't give her much hope. I already tried to explain to John what really happened, but he just laughed. "Forever doubting, Thomas!" he scoffed, "even when you witnessed it yourself!"

But in this manuscript I have the whole story. At times it seems clear that I have no choice but to honor the request of Jesus and let the apostles know that he has written his "confession." But then I fear that revealing the truth may not accomplish what Jesus intended. Would it convince Peter? He can't even read. Magdalene says Peter would accuse me of writing this account myself to discredit the miracles. And would the apostles really understand? Would they be able to admit that they were deceived?

Regardless of the dispute between Peter and Magdalene, it appears that Jesus has a large flock of followers capable of preaching his revelations. When I see the enthusiasm of the apostles, I feel tempted to destroy the manuscript. Whether Jesus was the prophesied Son of Man or just the son of a man, I believe his word was truly the word of God. He was a prophet, the greatest of all the prophets. His sins were human, but in his revelations lie hope for the salvation of all mankind. Jesus is dead, but perhaps the holy spirit of Jesus can live on.

Did Jesus teach by using deceit? Maybe. But if the teachings of Jesus survive his death, it will not be because of his deceptions, but despite them. It will be because the revelations of Jesus are so clear, so obvious to any who will simply open their hearts and spirits, that the behavior of

Jesus—yes, even the *sins* and deceptions of Jesus—are irrelevant.

❖ ❖ ❖

As Jesus lay dying, I asked him one last question. "I know you always thought of Joseph as your spiritual father. But did you ever deduce your true father?"

Jesus smiled at me. "Do you think the question is important, Thomas? It no longer is to me. Soon I shall be joining my father in heaven."

"But Jesus, remember when you thought Simon was your father? You rejected the idea only because you thought Nazareth your birthplace. But then Mother told you that you *were* born in Bethlehem! So Simon *is* your father!" I announced proudly.

"No, Thomas, I thought of that, but I knew he couldn't be, for another reason. I have the wrong eyes. Simon has blue eyes, Mother's are black, but mine are brown. So I can't be his son."

"How do you know that?"

"The magi learned it breeding cats. They said the same rules work for humans."

"Certainly Simon knew the rule. He would have noticed your brown eyes when he looked in the manger at the child he believed was his son."

"All babies have blue eyes, Thomas. Simon came too soon after my birth to tell."

As Jesus said this, he seemed frail and vulnerable. I could clearly see our mother in him. His breathing became shallow. Only then did I realize how little life he had left.

We sat quietly together as his life slowly expired. I thought of his teachings, of his message of love, hope, forgiveness, and his vision of the world as a miraculous creation of God, abounding with wonders that most people ignore. I thought about the hatred and despair that infected the world, and how all could change if only the word of Jesus reached every person's heart. I looked at Jesus, my brother, this man who was more than a man, this frail yet powerful prophet.

And a surprising thought suddenly came to me.

"Can you be truly certain that your real father was not God?" I asked.

Jesus slowly turned to look at me. He was silent. These were his last few moments of life, and he was to speak no further words. His eyes expressed bewilderment, unlike anything I had ever seen in him. It was obvious that the idea had never occurred to him. Never before had Jesus looked so human, and yet so divine.

About the Author

Richard A. Muller is Professor of Physics and University Distinguished Teacher at the University of California at Berkeley. His research spans elementary particle physics to cosmology. He has received numerous awards, including a MacArthur Prize Fellowship (the "Genius Award"), the Texas Instruments Founders' Prize, and the National Science Foundation Alan T. Waterman Award, for his work in cosmology (measurements of radiation from the Big Bang), optics, and nuclear physics (invention of AMS, the most sensitive known method for radiocarbon dating). He has been deeply involved in issues of national security in his twenty seven years as a Jason advisor to the U.S. Government. He has written articles for *Scientific American* and the *McGraw-Hill Encyclopedia of Science and Technology.* He has published over 100 scientific papers, two nonfiction books (*Nemesis,* and *The Three Big Bangs,* the latter with co-author Phil Dauber), and is presently writing a technical book (with Gordon MacDonald) on the astronomical origins of climate change.

Muller was raised in the south Bronx as a Catholic, but did not read the Bible until he attended Columbia University. He believes that his background in physics, combined with expertise in magic and illusion, gives him unique insight into the history of Jesus. Although he does not believe that Jesus is God, he taught his children that Jesus was "the greatest man who ever lived." Muller's goal was to make his novel both historically accurate and consonant with the events described in the New Testament—although without the supernatural interpretation of the miracles. When the two accounts conflicted, he admits, he chose to follow the Biblical account. Thus, his story includes events considered historically unlikely, such as the nativity in Bethlehem and the visit of the three Magi to the infant Jesus. Muller says his goal was to tell the story of Jesus in such a way that his explanations of the miracles in the New Testament would be not only plausible, but compelling.